W9-BNT-923

TIA'S STORY

A NOVEL

Tia's STORY

JUDY BAER
BEST-SELLING AUTHOR

TYNDALE HOUSE PUBLISHERS, INC., WHEATON, ILLINOIS

Visit Tyndale's exciting Web site at www.tyndale.com

Copyright © 2001 by Judy Baer. All rights reserved.

Photographs copyright © 2001 by Mike Hudson. All rights reserved.

Scripture quotations are taken from the *Holy Bible,* New Living Translation, copyright © 1996. Used by permission of Tyndale House Publishers, Inc., Wheaton, Illinois 60189. All rights reserved.

Designed by Jenny Swanson

Edited by Lorie Popp

This novel is a work of fiction. Names, characters, places, and incidents are either the product of the author's imagination or are used fictitiously. Any resemblance to actual events, locales, organizations, or persons, living or dead, is entirely coincidental and beyond the intent of either the author or publisher.

Library of Congress Cataloging-in-Publication Data

Baer, Judy.
  Tia's story / Judy Baer.
    p. cm.
  ISBN 0-8423-1924-7
1. Businesswomen—Fiction. 2. Abused women—Services for—Fiction. 3. Volunteer workers
in social service—Fiction.   I. Title.
PS3552.A33 T53 2001
813'.54—dc21   2001003162

Printed in the United States of America

07   06   05   04   03   02   01
 9   8   7   6   5   4   3   2   1

For the One who gives me the ability to write.

With all my heart I will praise you. . . . I will give glory to your
name forever.   Psalm 86:12

ACKNOWLEDGMENTS

Thanks to Jacob and to Aubrey for being just the right size for an ultrasound when my character Jenny was supposed to have hers. What a privilege (and great research!) to be a part of that— astoundingly, you are both even more lovable now that you're born! And to Kaitlyn, the latest addition to our world of huggable babies.

Gratitude to my daughters, Adrienne and Jennifer, for being the amazing people that you are—I want to be just like you when I grow up.

And, of course, thanks to my mother, who is the youngest, bravest eighty-something I know. I hope I'm so "with it" when I'm your age!

Appreciation to my neighbor and "prayer buddy," Linda—just because.

Don't store up treasures here on earth, where they can be eaten
by moths and get rusty, and where thieves break in and steal.
Store your treasures in heaven, where they will never become moth-eaten
or rusty and where they will be safe from thieves. Wherever your
treasure is, there your heart and thoughts will also be. No one can
serve two masters. For you will hate one and love the other,
or be devoted to one and despise the other.
You cannot serve both God and money.

Matthew 6:19-21, 24

One girl is more use than twenty boys.

—*Peter Pan* (the boy who could fly), J. M. Barrie

Tia Warden, her rosy cheeks scrubbed to a polish and her damp black hair curling in tendrils around her forehead, imperiously thrust out a dainty high-arched foot as the scent of her mother's bath powder hung in the air around her. "You missed my big toe!"

Libby Morrison, diligently applying nail polish to one of Jenny Owens's little toes, sighed and wiped her bangs out of her eyes. "Just a minute. I'm almost done with Jenny. Then I'll finish you."

Tia stared at her small pink feet. "I don't see why Mom won't let us use anything but this boring clear polish. She has Scarlet Haze in her bathroom. We could have used that!"

"She said nine-year-olds don't need red polish on their toes," Libby reported faithfully. "And that we were just 'playing' and this was 'good enough.' Quit wiggling, Jenny."

"I want Tia to do my hair next," Jenny said. "Can you put it in a ponytail?"

"It keeps jumping out." Tia eyed Jenny's springy blonde curls.
"How can we play beauty shop if you won't do my hair?"

"I specialize in straight hair," Tia announced haughtily.

"You can't do that! You're just a kid," Jenny responded.

"Am not! I'm a *person!*"

"A *kid* person."

Tia arched her neck indignantly. "I'm going to be someone special when I grow up."

"You're special now," Jenny soothed between puffs on her fingernails to dry them.

"I'll be important. And rich. Then I can buy my own red nail polish, have a business of my own, and order people around."

"You do that already," Libby muttered.

"Maybe I'll own a beauty shop." Tia curled kittenlike in her lime green beanbag until she looked like a single pea in a pod.

"And nobody with curly hair will come to you," Jenny pointed out logically.

"Maybe you could be a teacher. They *always* order kids around," Libby suggested.

"Or a recess monitor," Jenny added helpfully.

"Or you could join the army. My dad says *everybody* gets ordered around there."

"I'll have a store and sell something." Tia flung herself out of the beanbag and dragged the card table they used for puzzles into the middle of her room. Next she pawed through her closet and came out with an array of well-loved, ragtag toys, which she placed meticulously on the table in a straight row.

She spread her hands in a grand gesture. "This is my store. What would you like to buy?"

"I don't have any money," Jenny said.

"*Pretend,* silly!"

"Then I want to buy that." Jenny pointed to a stuffed rabbit covered with real rabbit fur. The fur was patchy and worn away in spots because Tia slept with it nearly every night.

"You don't want that old rabbit!" Tia told her. "I'll give you this practically new doll instead. And this necklace. It's on sale."

"If you didn't want to sell the rabbit, why did you put it on the table?"

Tia grabbed the stuffed rabbit and tossed it back into the closet. "You're right. When I have my own store, I'll get one for me *and* one to sell."

"You can't do that!"

"No? You just come to my store and see!" Warming to her idea, Tia added, "For practice, we can have a lemonade stand tomorrow. My sister Sheila is staying at Granny's until Sunday, so Mom will let us. She only gets upset when we're both making messes at the same time. Libby, does your mom have any extra cookies we could sell?"

"I don't think so!" Libby looked shocked at the suggestion.

"Then we'll get store-bought ones and sell them two for a dime. That will pay for the cookies and probably lemons and sugar, too. Anything we make after that will be ours!"

Tia jumped to find a notepad and pencil. "We'll make a list of what we need. And find a big box to use as our store. Jenny, you can make our signs. I wonder where my black crayons are. . . ."

"We won't make any money if we have to divide it three ways," Jenny complained.

"Then we'll have a rummage sale, too!"

"What would we sell?" Libby asked.

"Old toys we don't like anymore, coloring books we don't use, and doll clothes that don't fit any of our dolls. Maybe our moms have stuff we could sell, too. We'd make a *bunch* of money then!"

"Bedtime, girls." Mrs. Warden stood in the doorway, an amused smile on her face. "The beauty shop and store have to close for the night."

"Mommmm . . ." Tia strung the word out with a whine. "Libby and Jenny are here!"

The other girls scurried to restore the room to its former order while Tia looked pleadingly at her mother.

"No, Tia. It's time to go to bed."

Sighing theatrically, Tia pulled the table back to the corner. This was a special occasion. Libby, who often got homesick, rarely stayed overnight. Tia's mother could have bent the rules just this once.

When they'd crawled into bed—Tia and Jenny in the bunk beds and Libby in a cozy nest of blankets and sleeping bag on the floor—Mrs. Warden picked up the book she and Tia were reading together, *Peter Pan*. "Do you remember where we were?"

Tia popped from under her covers. "Peter Pan is a little boy who refuses to grow up. His family is a bunch of other little boys who don't want to grow up either. They call themselves the 'lost boys,' have silly adventures, and act like—" Tia wrinkled her nose—"boys."

Mrs. Warden opened the book. "We'll start here so you girls can hear for yourselves." She began to read.

> *"Where do you live most of the time?" Wendy asked.*
>
> *"With the lost boys," Peter said.*
>
> *"Who are they?"*
>
> *"They're the children who fell out of their baby carriages when the nurses weren't paying attention. . . . But we're sort of lonely. There are no girls to keep us company. Girls are much too clever to fall out of their baby carriages. . . ."*

When the reading was done and prayers and kisses were given all around, Mrs. Warden shut off the overhead light and gently closed the door.

Libby's small voice ventured from the darkness. "We are kinda like that, aren't we?"

"What do you mean?"

"*We* are our own family. I know we have parents and all, but if

we didn't, the three of us would take care of each other—
wouldn't we?"

"Of course! And if I had my store, I'd buy you food and clothes
and everything!" Tia offered generously.

"You would?" Libby sounded relieved.

"Sure." Tia flipped onto her back, and the bunk beds trembled.
"Don't worry, Libby, we've got lots of families."

"What do you mean?"

"We talked about it in Sunday school, remember? We have our
moms and dads and the family we were born to, we have each
other, and we're part of God's family, too. That's the biggest
family of all."

"Hmmmm," Libby purred contentedly. "That's nice."

"Nice," Jenny echoed.

Tia stared for a moment into the blackness, imagining a huge
family with millions of brothers and sisters, a family run by God.
Her eyes popped wide open in the darkness and she smiled.
That made Jesus her *big brother!*

Then she closed her eyes to sleep.

CHAPTER ONE

Rose-breasted grosbeak: A courting male will pull back his head,
spread his wings and tail, dance about, and serenade a female.
The female sings a shorter song to communicate with her mate.

—*Birds: An Explore Your World Handbook*, Discovery Books and David Bird

Tia Warden wandered through the eye-popping displays, which
all vied for her attention, and berated herself for not arriving at
the wholesale market earlier. She realized that she'd better pick
up her pace or they'd be tossing her out and turning the lights
off behind her. All the transportation buses had already returned
out-of-town retailers to their hotels, and the distributors looked
as though they'd had a long day.

Still, when she saw the glorious display of kaleidoscopes, tiny
stained-glass lamps, and trinket boxes, she had to stop. The glittering samples were displayed in folds of jewel-toned velvets. Tia
felt as though she'd discovered a cache of emeralds and rubies
while sifting ordinary sand. She picked up a kaleidoscope and
put it to her eye. As she moved it, changing shapes and glittering
colors transfixed her.

"May I help you?"

"These are so incredibly gorgeous . . ." She looked up and

paused before finishing the comment in her mind. *And so are you.*

Dressed in an impeccably cut charcoal gray suit, the man behind the display was every bit as elegant and unique as the kaleidoscope in her hand—sort of Cary Grant, Robert Redford, Brad Pitt, and Harrison Ford rolled into one. His shirt, a blue so pale as to be almost gray, was the same color as his eyes. His dark hair was such a contrast to those pale, intelligent eyes and that cleft in his chin. . . . Tia could hardly tear her eyes away.

Then she realized he was staring at her. "Sorry. These are amazing."

"I think so, too. My sister, Amber, is the artist. Each is one of a kind. We run our company—Beacons—together."

"Can't say I've heard of it before."

"This is our first time at the Minneapolis market. Until now, we haven't been able to keep up with demand long enough to consider searching out more business."

"I see." Tia was torn between the display and the salesman.

"We began Beacons three years ago, and it's taken off like a prairie fire. Would you like to see some of our other designs?" He reached under the table and pulled out a sample box.

"Oh, I'll take one of these." She pointed to a jewelry box. "My customers will be crazy about this. And these . . . and this . . . oh, this should sell well . . . and . . . ."

As he wrote up her order, Tia studied him covertly. She had an unusually visceral reaction to this man, something she hadn't felt in a long time. A handsome face rarely turned her head. Maybe she was just tired, she reasoned.

"Are the others in your family so artistic?" she asked.

"It's just me and Amber. No other siblings. Although many years ago my mother painted and sold watercolors."

"And now?"

"Not anymore. She and my father are gone."

"Oh, I'm so sorry. . . ." Tia kicked herself for being untactful.

She must have a path worn on her tongue from having her foot in her mouth so often.

He looked up and chuckled. "Not dead. Just gone. They're in Portugal, retired to the country where my father grew up. I think Mother has given up art for a spot under an umbrella near the sea."

Ice broken, Tia pummeled him with questions about designs and workmanship until he handed her a copy of the order.

"My name is Brandon Ainsley, by the way."

"And you already know my name."

"And your credit card number."

"Two of the most important things about me." Tia thrust out her hand. "I'm glad we met, Mr. Ainsley. Your products will be a wonderful addition to my store."

She turned to walk away, but his voice stopped her. "Ms. Warden?"

Tia turned around.

"Yours was my largest order today. I'd like to thank you for your business. Would you care to join me for dinner?"

Tia thought quickly. She *was* hungry. And he *was* definitely charming. But her father's old adage rolled through her mind: *Never mix business and pleasure. Never mix business and pleasure.*

"Please don't feel pressured to say yes. But Amber and I both try to show our appreciation to our customers."

She hardly mixed anything with business these days—except more business. "Maybe just a sandwich . . ."

He handed her a business card with the name of Tia's favorite restaurant written on the back. "I'll be there in thirty minutes. I hope you'll join me." Then he began to dismantle the display, allowing Tia to escape unpressured.

. . . .

Tia drove around the parking lot of the restaurant three times before pulling into a space. Then she sat in the car, tapping a fingernail against the steering wheel. This was not like her, she reasoned. She was never impulsive about her social life anymore. If it wasn't penciled into her organizer—or involved her best friends Libby Reynolds or Jenny Adams—it simply didn't happen.

That thought made up her mind for her. Tia got out of the car and walked inside.

Brandon was waiting for her. He had chosen a cozy booth, and there was already a large shrimp cocktail as its centerpiece and two bottles of mineral water chilling on ice in a champagne bucket.

"Nice," Tia murmured as she slipped into the bench across from him. Discreetly she kicked off her shoes and tucked her legs beneath her, glad that no one could see her making herself so at home. "Usually when I'm at the market I have dinner alone. This is a treat."

"Does that bother you?" Brandon asked. "Dining alone?"

"Not a bit. I'm accustomed to it as I do a fair bit of traveling. I'm glad that, for once, I'm only a few miles from home. That's why I appreciate the Minneapolis market shows so much."

"Since you aren't alone tonight, would you like me to order for you?"

How gallant, Tia thought. Tonight she would allow someone to pamper her. "Please."

When the waiter had taken their order and retreated, Brandon leaned back and studied her. "I wasn't sure you'd come."

"I wasn't either, but I'm glad I did. I'm curious to know more about your background and that of Beacons. You are certainly on the road to success."

"I hope you're right. For Amber's sake as well as my own. I had been working in Europe when Amber sent me samples of her work. I was stunned. I had no idea she was so talented. She wanted to know if I could tell her anything about marketing the pieces. She had no idea how enormous her potential was. So, because I was getting a bit homesick for the United States and particularly the Midwest, I came home. And the rest, as they say, is history."

Tia watched Brandon as he spoke. There was a gracefulness to the way he moved his hands and a slight inflection in his speech—picked up somewhere in Europe, perhaps. She was utterly charmed.

Awash in the rosy glow of the evening, Tia felt as if everything were perfect—the lilies on the table, the individual saltcellars, the string quartet in the background—and the company. For these few moments it was as if she and Brandon were alone in the universe.

When they parted outside the restaurant, Brandon shook her hand solemnly. "I'll stop by a few days after you receive your shipment to see that everything is all right."

Tia couldn't think of a more splendid idea and drove home in a haze of pleasure.

CHAPTER TWO

The smallest bird egg comes from the vervain hummingbird.
It is 0.1 inch long; the bird's nest is smaller than a dime in diameter.

—*Birds: An Explore Your World Handbook,* Discover Books and David Bird

"It's party time!"

Jenny Adams and Libby Morrison burst through the door of Tia's gift shop, Tia's Attic, wearing pointed hats and wide, silly grins. Jenny waved a red-and-white pom-pom in one hand and held a little flag that said "Congratulations" in the other. Libby struggled with a dozen willful helium balloons in bright colors and almost got stuck in the doorway before popping through the entry like a cork from a bottle.

"One, two, three!" Jenny shouted.

"Ta-rah-rah-boom-de-ay, ta-rah-rah-boom-de-ay," the two women cried out, cheerleader fashion. "Tia's the queen today! Ta-rah-rah-boom-de-ay!"

Then Jenny shook the pom-pom, leaped into the air, and came down in the splits. A ripping sound echoed through the room. Libby burst into hysterical laughter, and Tia pounded her fist on her desk. "More! More!"

"I'm certainly not the cheerleader I used to be," Jenny mumbled from the floor.

"What do you two think you're doing?" Tia, in her tailored black suit and highly polished pumps, was a vivid contrast to the two brightly dressed neighborhood clowns.

"First, I'm going to put on the spare pair of jeans I brought just in case you-know-what happened." Jenny scrambled to her feet. "Then we're going to celebrate the opening of Ribbons & Rainbows. It's not every day our friend opens a new store *and* is named entrepreneur of the week."

"It's not as if I haven't worked in a gift shop long enough. It's how I paid my way through college. I should know something about the business by now."

"You were more than working—you were learning. How else would you have dared to buy a store and open Tia's Attic here the day after you graduated?" Jenny observed.

"And Ribbons & Rainbows!" Libby added. "You have both sides of the Minnesota River covered now." She referred to Tia's second, even larger, store located in another Minneapolis suburb.

Tia said nothing. To some extent what her friends said was true. If yesterday's grand opening was any indication, she had another thriving store on her hands already. She still couldn't believe how fast the last six months had gone.

"Where do you want to eat? Kassims, GenTillies, or The Depot?" Libby asked.

"Aren't they a little pricey?"

"Then we'll go to that pizza place with the rock band and water slide."

"How about Kassims?" If these two clowns were going to drag her out to eat, it might as well be somewhere that the food was served on china rather than on paper plates.

. . . .

A tuxedoed waiter refilled their iced-tea goblets, discreetly slid the bill onto the table, and backed away. Libby distributed the mints that had arrived with the black folder, picked up her iced tea, and tipped it in Tia's direction. "To you, Tia, for your bravery, business savvy, and brand-new store."

"Bravo!" Jenny seconded.

"Stores open all the time in the Twin Cities," Tia murmured modestly.

"Not *your* store," Jenny corrected. "Who would have imagined that that little girl who kept crossing her eyes to see if they would stick could be such a successful businesswoman?"

"Have you forgotten all she put us through, Jen?" Libby said. "I recall going door-to-door selling homemade *mud pies* because Tia thought it was a good idea."

"One of my less successful entrepreneurial ventures." Tia's dark eyes sparkled. "But you do have to admit that the day we sold your mother's cookies was a big success."

"Until she came home and found the cookie jar empty."

"Supply and demand. Sometimes it tilts out of balance. One must take risks to make a business grow."

Libby's expression grew sly. "Like Brandon Ainsley, you mean?"

Tia put her hands to her head in mock dismay. "When are you going to give this a rest? How many times have I told you that he's a business investor and associate, *not* a romantic interest? May I remind you that I'm not desperate to meet men. Unmarried does not mean unhappy, you know."

"Of course not. But we've seen the look you get when he's around . . . ," Jenny said.

"That's indigestion!" Tia protested. "Or my shoes hurt."

"Not those expressions." Libby clasped her hands and put them to her cheeks as she stared dreamily toward the ceiling. "These."

"You were so smitten with him that I'll bet you don't even remember what happened the first time you introduced us."

"I do so. You both made absolute fools of yourselves falling over each other to get a closer look at him."

"I tripped," Libby corrected her. "And he was very sweet about helping me up."

"Jenny would have walked right over you if he hadn't," Tia reminded them.

"I wasn't that eager to look him over. I just wanted to ask him a few questions."

"I'm surprised you didn't handcuff him to a chair, turn bright lights on him, and give him the third degree!"

Jenny smiled sweetly. "He *did* get the third degree."

"I had to smuggle him out the back door while you two were occupied in front," Tia teased.

"Maybe we should have him over sometime to finish our questioning," Libby suggested to Jenny. "Without Tia, of course."

Tia shook her head helplessly. They were incorrigible, of course, and had only her best interests at heart. But Brandon had been surprised by all the interest he seemed to be generating in her two friends. He didn't realize, naturally, that Jenny and Libby had been Tia's protectors—and vice versa—for longer than any of them now cared to admit or that she was part of a package, a like-me-like-my-friends deal.

"And I don't make faces when he's around!" Tia protested.

"Oh yes you do," Jenny said calmly.

"A twitch in my eye or a tic. Wearing stress on my face, that's all."

"I'm not talking about that. I'm talking about the radiant expressions you've been wearing ever since Brandon came on the scene," Jenny clarified. "He's the reason you've been forgetting to eat dessert lately."

"And why you've been so absentminded," Libby added.

For a moment, Tia—cool, collected, groomed to perfection, not a black hair out of place—blushed the color of the strawberries on her cheesecake.

. . . .

That conversation with her friends had stimulated something in Tia that she wasn't sure she liked. She wished her mother and father were home, as she would have loved their "take" on Brandon. Both were astute judges of character these days—knowledge that had been hard-won and for which they'd had to pay dearly.

Her parents had been working with people in grief-and-loss support groups ever since Tia's high school graduation and departure to college. Not only had they seen the darkest and lowest moments of people's lives but also the triumphant ones when they finally took those first steps beyond grief and chose to live again. But only because her parents had walked in similar footsteps could they be the effective counselors they were today.

She could go hours now, even entire days, without consciously dwelling on her twin sister Sheila's demise. But at the time of the car accident, high school–aged Tia hadn't been able to free herself from the despair and anger for even a few moments.

She'd blamed herself sometimes, wondering if there had been *anything* she could have said or done to divert her sister from the reckless path she'd chosen. Since childhood, Sheila had been what their mother called "cut of a different cloth." That wasn't to say that Tia wasn't just as headstrong, willful, and full of her own ideas, but she had, ultimately, always obeyed her parents. Sheila, on the other hand, had not.

It was deceptive, Tia mused, because Sheila had been the "innocent"-looking twin. It was that occasional odd quirk of fraternal twins that made them look as if they weren't even related. No one could believe that they had been born within fifteen minutes of each other.

When Tia committed some childish misdemeanor, it had been immediately apparent on her face. But Sheila—with her chubby features, blue eyes, and blonde hair—could hide any number of naughty escapades behind that innocent facade of hers. It had been Sheila who'd given the dog a haircut with their father's electric razor and Tia who'd been punished because she looked guilty about the fiasco. Tia couldn't help but smile at some of the memories.

Her sister had gotten Tia into many a mess—and left her there. Sheila had not been known for rescuing her hapless sister when Tia was taking the blame for one of Sheila's "good" ideas gone awry—the trapping and keeping of field mice in their parents' basement, for example. The mice had quickly multiplied and chewed their way out of the cardboard box in which Sheila had housed them. By the time their father found the multiple nests of the newest generations of mice, he'd had to hire an exterminator to deal with the situation.

Then there had been Sheila's grand idea to sneak out after bedtime and crawl onto the roof to look at the stars. Sheila had managed to fight her way back to the ground on the trellis, leaving Tia on the roof, howling at the top of her lungs for someone to rescue her. It hadn't taken a genius to figure out who would be punished.

Still, Sheila had been a grand sister, always up for fun and adventure. She had been daring and imaginative, reckless and lighthearted. Life had never been boring when they were teenagers, Tia recalled. Much of the strength and derring-do she had now were a result of growing up with Sheila.

Unfortunately, Sheila's common sense always took second place to her desire for fun. While Tia had remained close to Jenny and Libby, Sheila had chosen to run with a wilder, more "interesting" crowd. That choice had ultimately led to her death in a car crash with a boy her parents had forbidden her to see.

Tia recalled the night Sheila had died.

"Don't tell Mom, but I've got a date," Sheila had whispered to Tia after dinner.

"But you're grounded!"

Sheila had rolled her eyes. "I'm always grounded for one thing or another. We're just going to meet for an ice cream cone at Loopy's, and I'll come right home."

"I'm going to tell Mom." Tia had hated being Sheila's conscience, but sometimes she'd wondered if her sister had one at all. Sheila had often scared Tia with her disregard for rules and regulations. Tia hadn't even realized that she was a bit of an insurgent herself until after she'd lost her sister because, in comparison, Sheila had always stood out as the family rebel.

"Don't you dare. There's no use getting her all excited over nothing. I'll be back before you know it."

She hadn't heard Sheila leave the house, but as soon as Tia realized her sister had made good on her word and told their parents, it was already too late. Sheila and her date had been drag racing and challenged someone to play chicken. They'd both been killed instantly.

The aftermath of the accident was devastating. Tia's mother suffered a nervous breakdown, and her grieving father nearly lost his business. It wasn't until they began reaching out to others in similar situations that they were able to pull their lives back together.

Now, as founders of support groups and knowledgeable, compassionate public speakers, their lives had new meaning. It meant that they traveled several months a year, but the rewards of their own healing and spiritual growth far outweighed the problems of their nomadic lives.

Tia wiped away a tear and picked up her Rolodex. She thumbed through the alphabetical addresses until she came to Robin Cooper.

Robin was a Christian counselor who had been recommended to Tia several years earlier. Together they'd worked through the complicated maze of guilt and sadness surrounding Sheila's accident. Through Robin, Tia had tasted firsthand the powerful impact of God's healing. She'd come to understand that she was not to blame for her sister's choices, and since God had already forgiven her any sin of omission, she should surely forgive herself.

It had been a freeing, growing time in Tia's life, and she and Robin had stayed in touch ever since, for what Tia had come to call her "tune-ups." When she wanted a clear, Christian head to give her an honest, unbiased response to a situation or dilemma, she still called Robin. Robin's distance from Tia's personal life and her clear understanding of Scripture always seemed to help Tia chase away the fog of indecision in her life.

Tia picked up the phone and called to make an appointment.

. . . .

"How are you? It's been a while since I've seen you." Robin's gentle, placid features welcomed Tia into her office.

"That means things were going well," Tia responded. She sat down in the large, comfy chair across from Robin's. This office looked more like a cozy personal study than a professional counselor's office.

"Were?" Robin lifted an eyebrow. "But before we get started— coffee? Herbal tea? Chai?"

"Sure. Surprise me."

Robin disappeared for a moment and returned with two large mugs of milky white tea.

"Mmmm." Tia inhaled the aroma wafting from the cup, more relaxed already. "I love this stuff. I should offer chai for my customers."

"How are things at the store? I've followed your expansion. Sounds like business is fabulous."

"Maybe. I don't know. I guess that's why I'm here."

"What's troubling you?"

"Actually, it isn't the store—I don't think. So far things have gone like clockwork. I've been thinking about my sister a lot lately." Tia hesitated. "And I've met a man."

"Aha. Want to talk about it?" Robin's calm voice invited sharing confidences.

"I've been missing my parents. They have a packed schedule and won't be home for three months. I wish my dad were here to give me some advice, and that made me think of what they're doing and why they're gone. My dad is very business savvy, and I would love to sit down over coffee and pick his mind."

"Can you call them?"

"Sure, but they already have enough to handle. I don't want them to worry about me."

"So tell me about this new man," Robin encouraged. "You've dodged the marriage bullet a number of times, Tia. He must be very special."

"He's my new business partner, the reason I was able to open the second store this soon. He's intelligent, handsome, savvy, smooth . . ."

"Too smooth?"

Tia looked startled. "No, well, maybe . . . I've never thought about it. He's pretty gorgeous—sort of like a hero in a romantic novel or a three-hankie movie. I usually don't even notice another person's looks but with Brandon . . . wow."

"Then what's the problem?"

"That's the problem! I don't have one!" Tia almost laughed. "Maybe the time I've spent thinking—instead of *doing*—is bringing me down. You know me; I prefer action to reaction."

"And that's what makes you so strong," Robin said. Then her eyes narrowed. "Perhaps things are happening too fast—the man, the store, the financial commitment. Even when things are going well, sometimes we have a tendency to wonder when things are going to turn bad, when the other shoe will drop."

"This has turned my life upside down. I eat, sleep, and live my work these days. There's room for very little else."

"For long leisurely baths with scented candles burning?"

"Ha! Two-minute showers with the news blaring on the television."

"For an evening in bed reading a wonderful book?"

"Bedtime is set apart for studying catalogs and planning new merchandise."

"For a massage or a manicure?"

"I get pounded enough by distributors and their sales representatives, thank you. And given half a chance, I'd probably chew my own nails off."

"Leisure time to learn to really know this new man?"

"Between business meetings we sometimes have coffee."

"And your spiritual life?"

For the first time Tia really looked dismayed. "Lately it can be summed up with the radio in my car set on a Christian station and prayers on the run."

Robin didn't speak.

Tia leaned back in her chair and gave an embarrassed grin. "No wonder I've been feeling out of sync!" She glared at Robin in mock challenge. "Are you going to charge me for this session? I hope not, since I answered all my own questions!"

. . . .

At lunch the next Saturday, a picnic-style affair in the back of the bakery that Jenny owned, Jenny and Libby raved to Tia about the reception Ribbons & Rainbows had received in the area.

"You were in the business *and* arts and entertainment sections of the paper!" Libby waved a filled tortilla until the insides began to spill out. "And I heard the radio broadcast from the store. It was great."

"Thank you, thank you very much," Tia mumbled Elvis-style. She was having a hard time paying attention to her friends' giddy babbling with her head pounding and a knot in the pit of her stomach. She got up and made herself a cup of fresh tea. Perhaps it would relax the marching band rehearsing in her belly.

"And since it's such a great day, what's wrong with you?" Jenny asked pointedly, her cornflower blue eyes fixed on her friend.

"Me? Nothing. It's a wonderful day," Tia said glibly, annoyed by her own transparency.

"Don't try to fool me, Tia. I've known you too long. You're so preoccupied that you didn't even eat your tortilla wrap."

"That's hardly an indication of unhappiness!"

"Maybe not in other people, but it is in you."

"There's so much to think about . . . so much to do . . . ," Tia finally admitted with a sigh. "My mind won't quit whirling. I feel like a juggler with too many balls in the air, waiting for one to fall and knock me on the head."

"Isn't that why you took on a partner?" Jenny asked.

"Brandon is primarily an investor," Tia corrected. "I'm still the one responsible."

"You said he'd be helping any way he could, including ordering and advertising," Libby reminded her.

"Yes, but . . . ." Tia averted her eyes.

"But what? You never equivocate," Libby said suspiciously. "Something is going on here."

Tia scowled the same daggered look that had graced her elfin features when, as a small child, she was caught red-handed at unacceptable mischief. "Brandon is not an *equal* partner, if that's what you mean. *I'm* still the boss!"

Even though I sound like I'm ten years old.

Libby sat back, crossed her tanned arms over her chest, and stared at Tia. "Of course you are." Libby's steady, concerned gaze broke through the barriers Tia had been so meticulously constructing around her emotions.

"No, I'm not!" Tia wadded up her napkin and pressed it to her lips. A single tear leaked from the corner of one eye, slid across her perfectly made-up cheek, and dripped off the corner of her delicate jaw.

"Spill it, Tia," Jenny demanded.

Tia wiped away another tear with the back of her hand and smeared a glob of mascara down her cheek. "Hormones maybe or my guilt working overtime."

"Why would you feel guilty?" Libby puzzled.

"I'm afraid that I've moved too quickly on these new stores," she admitted softly. "It's a *huge* financial investment. Ribbons & Rainbows has already quadrupled my workload, and yesterday we purchased property for a third store."

"Are you afraid you can't pull in enough sales?" Jenny asked.

"No. Business is good. I'm just second-guessing myself, wondering if I've moved too hastily. I've dreamed of these stores for so long, but . . ."

Jenny and Libby exchanged glances, eyebrows raised.

". . . but sometimes I wonder if I should have refused to expand until I could have financed the entire investment on my own. It would have taken four or five more years, of course. . . ."

"Does this have anything to do with Brandon Ainsley?" Libby asked.

Tia had been uncharacteristically closemouthed about the handsome entrepreneur, although in recent weeks she'd been feeling exceptionally happy despite her hectic schedule.

"You took him on very quickly, Tia." Jenny leaned back in her chair. "We had no idea you were so close to building the third store. . . . Land already? Wow."

"When Brandon appeared on the scene, I was sure God was sending me a sign, an answer to a prayer I didn't even know I'd asked." She looked at them pleadingly, hoping they'd understand. "Brandon is an incredible man. Smart, talented, witty . . ."

"And hunky, too. Love those broad shoulders and that perfect smile," Jenny observed dryly. "But I doubt that's what this is all about."

"This isn't making a lot of sense to me," Libby commented. "I haven't heard anything worth tears yet."

Tia took a deep breath and blurted, "I'm not sure that what I'm doing is God's will."

Jenny and Libby appeared equally bewildered. If Tia hadn't felt so miserable, they might have laughed out loud.

"I didn't *pray* about taking on a partner or expanding the business." Tia's voice was small and ashamed. "God and I haven't had many in-depth discussions since Brandon came along." Her words faded to a whisper. "I've been a little busy."

"Uh-oh," Jenny muttered.

Tia lifted her chin defiantly. "Everything felt right, and you both know how easy it is to take things for granted when life is running smoothly. Until the last few days, I was *positive* I'd made the right decision."

"What changed your mind?" Libby inquired.

"Intuition? My subconscious working overtime? I don't know. All I can say is that suddenly I'm looking at things from a new angle."

She should have known better than to make such huge decisions on intuition and feelings alone, without consulting her normal heavenly business adviser, Tia thought with a pang. *Why* hadn't she let him be Lord of her life in this area before now? Her new insight felt like a sudden, uncomfortable wake-up call from God, and she had no idea where this was leading.

"That's like trusting feelings in your relationship with God," Libby murmured. "Some days he feels close; other days it seems as if he's not there at all."

"I know, I know. Feelings change but facts don't—and God is *fact*. Don't think for a moment that I haven't mentally knocked myself around for going off on my own without consulting him." Tia stood up and started pacing between two baker's racks.

"When I'm with Brandon, I get so involved with his enthusiasm and his ideas that the rest of my life pales in comparison.

He's got such great ideas for growing these stores. We're talking serious money here. And there are catalogs and on-line sales to consider. We complement each other in every way. It's as if he somehow . . . completes . . . me."

"Really." Libby's eyebrow arched so high it nearly disappeared beneath her side-swept hair.

"When I hear myself say that, it sounds self-centered and faithless. Frankly, I'm not sure where God's will starts and my own ends anymore."

"Only God can complete us," Jenny said.

"I know that. I *know* it. I've just never met a man like Brandon before. We can laugh together, share our dreams, discuss the stores' great potential. . . . "

"Is he a Christian?" Libby wanted to know.

"He says he is."

"The proof is in the pudding, Tia. Do his actions say so?" Jenny was blunt.

"Please don't start talking about being unequally yoked," Tia said. "It's not as if I'm marrying him or anything!"

"One never knows," Libby said quietly. "Romances spring out of the craziest places. I should know."

"I'm beginning to see why you've been avoiding us the past few weeks," Jenny said softly.

"You both know that Brandon didn't exactly arrive on the scene at an opportune time," Tia pointed out pragmatically. "My business requires every moment I can give it. I almost didn't take his call the day after we met because I couldn't afford to have a man on my mind or in my life."

"But he's still here," Libby offered. "What happened?"

"First he blew me out of the water by saying he thought we should become business partners."

"And Ribbons & Rainbows was the result," Libby said impatiently. "Go on, go on."

"Initially I told him that I was doing just fine on my own,

thanks. But he persisted; you know the story. He wanted to be a part of my future, to help make my dreams a reality. He insisted that with his financial backing we could have two more stores up and running in no time."

"It would be a shock, I suppose. Libby and I were certainly surprised."

"It was the craziest thing I'd ever heard," Tia confessed. "But at the time it seemed so easy. I believed God had thrown an unde-served blessing my way. I'd already maximized every bit of space in my current building and offered to buy the coffee shop next door if the owner ever wanted to sell. Then suddenly, out of the blue, the chance to expand fell into my lap."

Tia rubbed her temples. "You know me. Competitive, impul-sive, and crazy about my work. He hit me at a weak moment, I guess. You guys have moved ahead with your lives with husbands, families. Here was my opportunity to do something big to fill my life. I wanted it so badly I could *taste* it. I told myself that Brandon was a gift from above. That this *had* to be right."

"Was he surprised that you agreed so easily?" Jenny wondered. This was the first time that Tia had shared these details.

"Not at all. He seemed to *expect* it. He embraced the plan with more enthusiasm than I had imagined possible. It was the equiv-alent of being swept off my feet."

"Didn't that creep you out, just a little?" Libby questioned.

"It put me on guard. But after I'd done the research on him and his company and insisted on final say about creative deci-sions and concerns as to which direction the stores should take, he agreed immediately. He said that since upcoming seasons, color ways, and trends were always on my mind anyway, we should rely on that experience."

"And?" Libby said eagerly, behaving as if she were watching television. "Get to the good stuff."

When had her life become a soap opera? Tia wondered.

"He said he wouldn't have it any other way." Those words had been music to her ears. "He has a great deal of advertising experience, and I'm happy to turn that part of the business over to him. I've always wanted to do more aggressive ad campaigns but just never had the time or money."

"But with more stores, you can't afford not to," Jenny concluded.

"So far he's been the perfect partner," Tia admitted. "I'm ashamed to say that I'm the one having second thoughts. He wants this as much as I do. I don't want to disappoint him. I suppose that's why I haven't been very forthcoming with you two either."

Exactly how much of this *was* good business sense and how much was her selfish longing to fulfill a dream? Tia wondered. She wasn't sure. Or had this become an excuse to spend more time with Brandon?

"It did happen rather quickly. I can see why you might still be adjusting," Jenny said. "Do you trust him?"

"He has excellent credentials. I've seen his sister's business flourish under his control. The bank says he has the funds."

"Then what's your problem, Tia? I haven't heard one yet that's a cause for tears," Libby said.

"So much has happened so quickly that I haven't had time to think it all through yet." Tia hesitated. "And as I said, I haven't really prayed about it either. Robin pointed out to me that I jumped into this feetfirst without thoroughly talking to anyone about it—you, my family, *or* God. I've been very—" Tia searched for a word to express how she felt—"greedy."

"It's never too late to start praying," Libby advised. "And so far Brandon has been a good business partner. *You're* the one coming apart at the seams. Give the man time to prove himself before you decide he's been a mistake."

"You think so?" Tia desperately wanted their words to be true. In spite of her misgivings about her hasty actions, something about Brandon drew her to him like metal shavings to a magnet.

"What other choice do you have?" Libby asked matter-of-factly.

"You're right, of course. It's a good thing God is willing to meet people wherever they are." Tia spoke more to herself than to the others. "I'll admit I acted impulsively and without much heavenly guidance, but I can ask God to take over from here. If I made a tactical error partnering with Brandon, it will become obvious soon enough."

Then she brightened. "On the other hand, it might be the wisest spur-of-the-moment decision I've ever made." Tia's eyes finally took on their familiar sparkle. "My trouble is that I'd rather be a leader than a follower. Only the lead sled dog gets a decent view!"

"You are absolutely right," Libby said when she'd finally stopped laughing. "If it was a mistake, you'll deal with it. Like Matthew said, 'Don't worry about tomorrow, for tomorrow will bring its own worries. Today's trouble is enough for today.' "

Jenny put her hand on Tia's shoulder. "We're all guilty of not going to God first at one time or another. Fortunately *he* hasn't gone anywhere."

I stand at the door and knock.

Tia recalled the artist's rendering of that passage—Jesus, hand raised, knocking on a door that showed no handle on the outside. He was always there, patiently waiting, but the doorknob was on her side, and it was she who had to open the door and let him in.

CHAPTER THREE

*The wood duck has an interesting start to life. The first task of a hatchling
is to scale the inside of its tree-cavity nest, then fling itself some
thirty to sixty-five feet to the water or ground below.*

—Birds: An Explore Your World Handbook, Discovery Books and David Bird

"Jenny, do you have any string beans in your cupboard?" Tia
asked over her speakerphone.

"It's eight o'clock in the morning—not exactly prime time for
eating string beans."

"Would you do me a huge favor and donate a few cans? You
can bring them to Tia's Attic—by noon, if possible. That's when
they'll be by to pick them up."

"What are you talking about, Tia?"

"Green bean casserole, of course. I collected plenty of mush-
room soup and some dried onion rings but not a single can of
beans. If you donate beans, they can make nice casseroles."

"Tia, I have no idea what you are babbling about. Casseroles?
String beans? And who, exactly, are 'they'? "

"Did I forget to tell you about my new project for the food
pantry?"

"Obviously."

"I was serving meals at the mission a couple Sundays ago when I overheard that the food pantry was almost depleted. I had no idea how many families depended on the pantry at the end of the month when paychecks run out, so I offered to sponsor a promotion through my stores. Anyone who donates groceries to the food pantry gets a discount on their next purchase. I've already collected a huge amount of food—just no green beans. A case from you would help a lot."

"Tia, when did you find time to set this up?"

"I made flyers and did some radio advertising. Several people who'd planned to make big purchases brought in food—tons of it—so they could get the discount. The mission is ecstatic."

"You have a heart of gold, my friend. But if anyone *doesn't* have time to take on another project, it's you."

"Food is something no family can go without." Tia dismissed Jenny's concern. Prone to bluster about the tough business decisions she made for the store, Tia rarely acknowledged that her heart was marshmallow soft. She tried diligently *not* to reveal her philanthropic side. "I've decided to do this for a month out of every year from now on. Gotta go. Don't forget those beans!"

....

Tia was bobbing up and down behind cases of cereal, toilet paper, and dog food when Jenny arrived.

"Isn't this great?" Tia squeezed herself between the boxes to pop out in front of Jenny. "It's much more than I expected."

"I guess so—but dog food?"

"That's the best part! I've learned that many families with pets have to give them up because they don't have the resources to feed them. It's awful enough to be hungry—but to be hungry *and* have to give up your pet as well? That's appalling!

"So I'm collecting pet food, too. The mission has agreed to start a little pet food pantry if I'll keep it stocked. What are a few bags of dog or cat food? I can make that donation every month myself."

"Spot, Puddles, and Inky salute you." Jenny referred to her dog and Libby's pair.

"It's for the kids, Jenny. I see how much animals mean to them. They get pure love and devotion from those pets. And, astounding as it is, rumor has it that some people actually like cats! Even if I'm personally not crazy about the species, I don't want that taken away from anyone."

"For someone who squeals every time you get hair from a stray dog or horse on you, you certainly are generous."

"Maybe I like animals better than you think I do."

"*Nothing* surprises me about you anymore, Tia."

Jenny turned to the boxes she'd dragged in. "Green beans, three cases of them. A case each of tomato, chicken noodle, and vegetable soup. And ten pounds of chocolate chips. I hope that will do for now."

"Perfect. Help me put them where they belong." Tia shuffled backward, dragging one of the cases to the corner of the room. "I want to get this done before I go to the Battered Women's Crisis Center to get some new resource material. I've volunteered to take a regular shift on the hot line rather than just a few hours here and there."

"When are you going to do that?"

"In my spare time. I'm doing an 11:00 P.M. to 7:00 A.M. shift once a week."

"I use my 'spare' time between eleven and seven for sleeping," Jenny commented dryly.

Tia rocked onto her heels and looked thoughtful. "There is so much *need* out there, Jen. It hurts my heart. I've been selfish about reaching my own career goals even to the point of trying to tune God out. This thing with Brandon and the stores proved it. There's a lesson in here somewhere, and I need to find it. It's time I woke up and gave back from the blessings I've received."

"Is there money available for charity when you're investing so much into the stores?"

"Not really, but I don't need new shoes or a new brand of perfume every month either. And I've been clipping coupons!"

"I was wrong," Jenny marveled. "I didn't believe you could surprise me anymore, but you have. Coupons? You?"

"I never realized how much money I was wasting."

"Just what is it you think you can do with all this effort, Tia?"

"Feed a family, save a child's pet, or help one woman find her way out of an abusive situation. I'd consider any one of those a major success." Tia sank onto a nearby box. "It's the crisis center that's tearing my heart out. Those women have been robbed of the simplest things in life. Even their ability to laugh has been stolen from them!"

"Perhaps that's something you could give back to them," Jenny suggested softly.

"How?" Tia felt small and worried, dwarfed by cases of food and store inventory. "I feel so . . . inadequate!"

"You love life. You see the funny or the ridiculous in things no matter what your circumstances. That's a God-given gift, as far as I'm concerned. Laughter is one of his greatest inventions. Maybe you could find a way to provide those women with some joy."

"And how am I supposed to do that?"

"I have no idea. That's your job."

"Thanks a bunch. There's no way to buy laughter or hope from a supplier—" Tia paused—"or is there?"

Now it was Jenny's turn to be puzzled.

"It's really not that hard," Tia muttered to herself. "It's an attitude, after all. An 'attitude of gratitude.' With God's help we all have the ability to change our attitudes."

" 'A cheerful heart is good medicine, but a broken spirit saps a person's strength,' " Jenny quoted. "Proverbs."

"Exactly!" Tia beamed. "I could be a purveyor of cheer!"

"Sounds like a role perfect for you," Jenny observed. "You've cheered me more than once. Besides, you can get more delight out of a cup of good coffee or a fresh chocolate chip cookie than others get out of a new car."

"I'll talk to Helen Anderson. She runs the crisis center. But I already know that birdhouses are the first step," Tia said with a particularly Tia-like mental leapfrogging jump.

Jenny looked blankly at Tia.

"Birdhouses outside the windows of the center will remind the residents that life does go on. There's nothing more fragile than tiny birds on toothpick legs, yet they survive. If they can fly— literally—then certainly the women can do it figuratively. Birds are a great metaphor for life. 'Look at the ravens. They don't need to plant or harvest or put food in barns because God feeds them.' "

"That's a little obscure, Tia. Are you sure when someone is hurting she'd make that connection?"

"It doesn't matter. Birdhouses are only the first step. Shopping is the second."

"These women won't have resources to shop!"

"They don't need to buy anything. Haven't you ever gone into a store to try on the weirdest dress you can find? A style straight out of America's Worst Dressed?"

"Can't say that I have."

"Well, you should! It's a hoot."

"You do have odd ways of entertaining yourself, Tia."

"I also enjoy trying on outrageous hats and painting my toenails the color of jelly beans."

"I had no idea . . ."

"Life is *fun,* Jen, if you let it be. We can choose whether to laugh or cry at the twists and turns it takes. I'd almost forgotten that myself. I can't 'fix' these women's lives, but maybe I can show them that humor and beauty still exist despite their situations."

"If anyone can do it, it's you. You are the only woman I know who still occasionally carries her lunch to work in a Wonder Woman lunch box."

Jenny paused for a moment before venturing into uncharted waters between her and her friend by dredging up a name from the past. "Tia, are you thinking about Jason? Is he somehow a part of what's inspiring you now?"

Jason. Tia hadn't thought of him in years. Or had she, in some deep and silent corner of her mind? Why else would she feel such passion toward abused women now? "Maybe I am."

"He affected you deeply, didn't he?"

"He was my first love. I thought he was the most wonderful guy in the world—quarterback, honor roll, handsome . . ." Her voice became a whisper. "He *was* wonderful, except for his temper."

"But you didn't allow him to push you around. You put a stop to it."

"It also nearly killed me to tell him to get lost."

"He slapped you, Tia!"

More than once.

The first time it had happened, she hadn't even believed it herself. It was a freaky anomaly, an accident, anything but intentional. The second time it terrified her. The third time she'd told him to never come back.

"Even though I didn't have anything more to do with him, it took a long time for my fantasy to die," Tia admitted. "In my teenage mind, I'd thought we'd be together forever, bathed in some romantic fog, living happily ever after." She gave a humorless laugh. "Ironic, isn't it? At the time, I couldn't understand why I had to go through such pain and disappointment, and now, here I am, hatching ways to reach other battered women."

"Not ironic at all. God wants us to use our experiences to make life better for others. It's a miracle, really, that he can use something ugly that happened when you were a senior in high school to inspire you to help others now."

"So you think this is more than a passing whim?"

"We never know what God wants us to do or be unless we ask him."

A smile spread slowly across Tia's face. "I like it. I like the idea of people healing with laughter. Laughter is a visible manifestation of inward joy. That's what Birdhouse Ministries is going to be all about."

"What?"

"Birdhouse Ministries. You just helped me to make up my mind. If I get the go-ahead from upstairs—" Tia motioned heavenward—"I'm going to start a ministry for battered women. Nothing fancy, nothing earthshaking—just something to bring a little laughter and God's love into difficult lives. We could really *soar* with an idea like this, *fly* high, help women to *feather* new nests . . ."

"You're being very punny, er, funny."

Tia grabbed Jenny and they spun together around the room, dodging boxes and laughing. When they'd exhausted the space and their own energy, Tia collapsed onto a stool and wiped a tear of laughter from her eye. "Jenny, if God wants to use me, I'm all his. And if he can do that, he can do anything he knows is right—including making this business relationship with Brandon work. I'm going to give the energy I've spent stewing over the stores to Birdhouse Ministries instead. I'm not going to be a *chicken* anymore. I can glide like an eagle *wren* I tell my story."

They were still slinging puns when the crew from the mission came to pick up the boxes.

. . . .

Tia's business decisions were still the topic of conversation at Libby and her husband, Reese's, home at week's end.

"What is another store going to do for you except give you more work and less time for yourself? Especially if you plan to get so involved with the women's shelter?" Mike, Jenny's husband, asked. "I've known you a long time, Tia," he continued, referring to their years of elementary and high school together. "And you've always jumped in over your head. You still haven't learned, have you?"

"You know he's right, Tia," Jenny said softly. "You're so busy that we hardly ever see you."

"*I'm* so busy? Mike's landscape business is, pardon the expression, growing like a weed. You both attend your son's horse shows every weekend." Tia was talking about Luke, Mike's son from a previous relationship and now Jenny's stepson, who spent a lot of time at the stable with his horse, Sunshine. "You're the ones who don't have time for *me!*"

"That's not what Jenny meant—"

Tia wouldn't let Libby finish. "Lib, you and these two hunky wheelchair cowboys of yours are at the ranch every spare moment." Reach Out Ranch was the hippotherapy facility where Libby had first met her adopted son, Robert. She and Reese had even married there, with dozens of equine witnesses as well as friends and family.

"Don't you see? You guys *are* my family! Since my sister was killed, you know that my parents have traveled all over the country speaking out about teenage drinkers and drunk drivers. It's what gives them purpose in life, but it also means that they are gone long periods at a time and that I can't exactly 'drop in' for a heart-to-heart anytime I want. Now that you have families of your own, I refuse to tag along to every event like a pitiful old-maid auntie! I need my own life. That's where the stores and my other projects come in. Sure, I'll be busy, but isn't that better than having me at your homes all the time, unwelcome and underfoot?"

Reese choked on his last bite of spaghetti. "Tia, quit making yourself sound like an unwelcome mat! We *like* having you underfoot."

Tia smiled and stirred her tea. "You are all wonderful. But I do need more to occupy me now that both Jenny and Libby are engulfed in matrimonial bliss."

"Matrimonial bliss, I like it." Libby patted Reese's arm as he rested it on the arm of his wheelchair. A former policeman, Reese had lost the use of his legs when a stray bullet nicked his spine. Now he rode his horse with a specially configured saddle and once again worked on the police force at a desk job.

"Bliss," Mike repeated the word. "Doesn't that rhyme with kiss?"

"This is *exactly* what I mean! I can't watch all this kissy-face, mushy stuff!" Tia complained. "A girl's got to get away from it somehow!"

"Do you want to play with *us*, Aunt Tia?" Robert offered as he and Luke entered the room. Robert's glasses were askew, and he had bright orange sticky notes attached to his wheelchair from some game he and Luke had invented.

Tia cradled his cheeks in her palms and gave him an affectionate smack on the forehead. "No, darling, but thanks for asking."

"We need to get away from them sometimes, too," Luke explained. "Hugging and kissing and giggling—" he shuddered—"yuck."

When the laughter subsided and the boys had once again disappeared—this time to play with the three dogs waiting patiently for them on the deck—the conversation grew serious once again.

"Tia, you've never indicated that you were unhappy or lonely." Libby sounded dismayed.

"It never occurred to me that you were feeling sad or out of place because we're both married now," Jenny added.

"I'm not unhappy, lonely, or out of place because I'm single! I simply mean that I need a life apart from yours. I'm delighted that my dearest friends in the world are happily married. I'm happy for you . . . and I'm happy for *me*."

An impish expression flitted across her delicate features. "This 'always a bridesmaid, never a bride' thing rather suits me. You both chose bridesmaid ensembles that I can wear again; it's a great excuse for a manicure and pedicure, and the food is always fantastic."

"You're *sure* you don't feel left out?"

"Or like a third wheel?"

"Darlings, I'm *positive*. I'm also certain that I can't wait around for you to entertain me." Tia spread her hands wide to punctuate her explanation. "So quit feeling sorry for me and *find me some dessert!*"

Libby disappeared into the kitchen, and Jenny and Tia followed to help with the coffee. Before picking up the fresh apple pie on the counter, Libby gave Tia a big hug. "Brandon is treating you all right, isn't he?"

"Like a princess. Anything troublesome is all in my mind. It's totally my own fault that I keep going back to the fact that I teamed up with Brandon so impulsively. It's so unlike me."

"Remember the time you decided it would be fun to jump on the bus from the shopping center and ended up across town?" Libby reminded her.

"Or wondered just how olives would taste with ice cream?" Jenny added.

"Never mind. I get it. I'm congenitally impulsive. I should be accustomed to myself by now. I need to get a grip." She picked up a tray. "Now let's get coffee to that pair in the dining room."

"Once again you get my vote for Pie Queen, Libby," Mike said.

"You should know," Jenny said mildly. "You had two pieces of each kind."

"Small pieces. Very small ones." Mike shrugged. "Besides, Reese ate more."

"I had to," Reese said unrepentantly. "I didn't want to hurt Libby's feelings."

"Don't blame me for all that moaning and groaning you'll do later because you ate too much." Libby picked up the coffeepot to dispense refills. When she got to Reese, she smiled and added, "And an antacid for you?"

"Very funny." Reese slipped an arm around her waist.

"We should sit in the living room," Libby suggested. "We hardly use it anymore."

"That's because you live in the barn at Reach Out Ranch," Tia retorted as they all moved to the living room.

"Well, these chairs are much better than the old stools in the barn." Libby dropped onto a tufted armless chair, and Reese rolled his wheelchair to her side so they could hold hands.

"How's the therapy going?" Mike asked Reese. "Any more feeling in your legs?"

"I'm not going to be an Olympic athlete, but it's still possible that someday I could get around with a walker or a couple canes."

"God is good," Libby murmured gratefully.

"Robert looks great, too. Gaining weight, I see," Mike said.

"His former foster mother says she's never seen anything like it," Libby said proudly. "She insists he's been growing an inch and ten pounds a month since he came to live with us. She's exaggerating, but . . ."

"Now he's got the harebrained idea that he's going to turn Inky and Puddles into the wheelchair equivalent of sled dogs," Reese commented. "I wonder how many crashes that will involve before he gives up."

"Or gets it right," Tia added.

A comfortable silence settled on the room. These were people who had laughed and cried together, who loved one another. Words were an unnecessary luxury among them.

Tia, stretching catlike, glanced at Jenny. "You haven't said much tonight, Jenny. Do you have something to add to this incredibly stimulating evening?"

Jenny glanced shyly at Mike before answering. "Well, maybe I have one little piece of news to share."

"So share it."

"Mike and I are going to have a baby."

CHAPTER FOUR

*Each summer in the willows and alders across North America, the female
yellow warbler builds her nest and lays her eggs. The nest is occasionally
visited by the female cowbird who adds her own egg. The yellow warbler
may respond by defiantly building a new nest floor over the eggs and laying
new ones. The cowbird, undeterred, may revisit and add another egg.
This can go on with neither bird relenting. On one documented
occasion, a yellow warbler was finally left in peace
with a six-layer nest.*

—Birds: An Explore Your World Handbook,
Discovery Books and David Bird

There was a moment of utter silence, then shrieking so loud that
crystal rattled in the china cabinet. Tia's chair tipped backward
and clattered to the floor as she lunged for Jenny. Libby eagerly
fell on top of them, and the threesome began screaming, crying,
and jumping up and down just as they had as little girls when
something wonderful happened. But this was the most marvelous occurrence of all.

"We're having a baby!" Tia crowed and gave Mike a big kiss on
the forehead.

"Did you hear that, Reese?" Libby gasped. "We're having a
baby!"

Reese winked at Mike. "I'll bet you didn't know this was a
group effort."

"No, but I figured that once the news was out I'd never get any peace and quiet." Mike tipped his head toward his wife and her two beaming friends. "If the nighttime feedings don't get me, the unsolicited advice will."

"Now, Mike." Tia, who'd been oblivious to the men's conversation, turned to him. "I've got baby books at the store. There's one with all the words and music for lullabies you can sing. And I have a tape of simple sentences in several foreign languages. You can play it next to Jenny's tummy so the baby becomes acquainted with other languages right in the womb."

She tapped her foot indignantly when the two men laughed out loud. "Having a baby is a very serious thing, you know."

Mike, suppressing a smile, nodded. "May I point out that I'm the only one in this group who has actually *had* an infant? Remember my son, Luke?"

Tia nodded benevolently. "He's a wonderful boy. But you won't have to do it all alone this time." She turned back to Jenny and Libby to admire Jenny's still-flat stomach.

Mike rolled his eyes and whispered to Reese, *"That's* what I'm afraid of!"

When the men excused themselves and went outside into the yard, the women didn't even notice.

"We'll have a baby shower for you, Jen. Do you want it before or after the baby is born?" Tia was already mentally addressing invitations. "Before is nice because you'll have some things ready—"

"But if we do it *after,* then we'll know if we're buying for a boy or a girl," Libby rejoined.

"Which room will be the nursery?" Tia asked.

"If you're going to paint, be sure to let Mike do it. Paint fumes aren't good for you," Libby, always the cautious one, warned.

"I'm only eleven weeks pregnant! I'm hardly used to the idea myself and you want me to pick nursery colors and a shower date?"

"A fall baby," Tia calculated. "Oh, honey, I'm so happy for you!"

Libby wiped the tears from her cheeks and threw her arms around her friend. "Me, too!"

"Wow," Tia murmured. "Our first baby."

"Auntie Tia and Auntie Libby." Jenny tried the names on for size. "Sounds good."

Tia, ever practical, said, "I want to buy the baby its first Bible. Something you can read at night together."

Since they had already danced, screamed, and jumped around, Tia flopped onto the davenport. "How do your guys feel about the baby, Jen?"

Jenny and Libby took the wing-back chairs across from Tia.

"Mike is ecstatic, of course. He's a wonderful father."

"And Luke?" Libby asked.

"Very happy. Although I do think he's considering how it will affect his life. He's been king of the hill for some time now. He may have a few jealous moments, but otherwise he'll be fine."

"What about Spot?" Tia asked about Jenny's almost-human canine.

"There's the rub," Jenny replied. "Spot firmly believes *he* is the baby of our family. It's going to be a rude awakening for him."

Tia, smiling so widely her face nearly cracked in half, slipped off the couch and moved to kneel in front of Jenny's chair. "I am so delighted for you that I could burst. My prayer for years was that you would find true happiness and now . . ."

Jenny reached out to touch Tia's cheek. "And I pray the same for you."

"God is good," Tia said gently. "I'll just have to wait and see what's in store for me."

....

It was late by the time Tia left Mike and Jenny's house, but she didn't feel like going home. The excitement of Jenny's news had her pumped, and it was going to take more than a few minutes to unwind. She turned her car toward Tia's Attic.

Tia made it a practice to leave lamps lit throughout the store at night to make it appear cozy and inviting to people passing by. The incandescent glow of these lamps made it possible for Tia, a cup of freshly brewed tea in hand, to find her way to the center of the store to a hand-painted rocker with a chair pad of bright red needlepointed poppies and white daisies. She sat down, kicked off her shoes, put her feet on a delicate footstool, and covered herself with the cozy chenille throw that had been draped over the arm of the chair. As large as it was, the store was still a cocoon of tranquility. A fountain splashed in a far corner, and Tia could hear the strains of classical music that she'd fed into the CD player.

To her mind, the store was perfect, all she'd ever dreamed it could be. What's more, she had a lovely home in which to live, enough money to buy whatever she wanted, friends whom she loved as much as she loved her own family. Even the pain of her sister Sheila's long-ago fatal car crash ached less with each passing year, as the wonderful memories of their childhood returned to comfort her.

Why, then, did she feel such a restless stirring in her spirit?

Tia jumped as someone called her name from the back of the store. The voice was familiar. "Dorothy, is that you?"

Jenny's former sister-in-law appeared out of the shadows. "I saw your car and figured you were working late. You *have* to start locking the back door!"

"I forgot. I won't do it again. Sit down?" Tia gestured toward a twin rocker on the other side of a small table.

"For a minute."

"Tea? I can nuke some in the microwave."

"No. Too much caffeine for me this time of night." Dorothy lived alone in the large family home on Maple Street in which she and her brother Lee—Jenny's first husband who'd died from an aneurysm—had grown up. Also single, Dorothy often stopped by at night when Tia's car was parked by the store. Tia was never surprised to see Dorothy or their friend Ellen, who also helped out at Jenny's bakery, for a midnight visit.

She studied Tia. "Is anything wrong? You're here awfully late."

"Nothing is wrong. I've had some great news. Jenny—"

"The baby? She called me tonight."

"Isn't it exciting?"

A shadow of sadness briefly curtained Dorothy's eyes. "I love Mike, but I do wonder how it might have been if it were my brother and Jenny having a child."

"Maybe you shouldn't go there. . . ."

"I know. And there is no guarantee that the codependency and dysfunction that marked my family wouldn't have trickled into Jenny's family through Lee."

"You have to forgive yourself for not telling Jenny that Lee was a compulsive gambler."

"I have. And I know God has. It's my human weakness that tempts me to revisit that part of my life. It's like saying I don't trust God's forgiveness when I keep going back there in my mind."

"Don't be so hard on yourself," Tia said matter-of-factly. "There is one reason to revisit that time—to learn from it. *Then* let it go and don't look back."

Dorothy smiled. "Ever-practical Tia. You are so right. We were never allowed to show weakness or to mention our problems outside the family. My father wanted to control us, to design the appearance we gave to the world, and he managed pretty well. Lee and I, on the other hand . . ."

"If you've already looked back, what have you learned?" Tia rocked gently in her chair.

"To let it all hang out. To be honest. To tell it like it is. To not pretend everything is fine when it's not. To ask for help and accept it when it comes. To show vulnerability and allow others to show theirs as well."

"Then something good *has* come of your heartache."

Dorothy laughed. "You could put a happy spin on a root canal, Tia."

"I wouldn't go so far as to say that."

"Jenny deserves the happiness she has now. My brother caused her a lot of pain."

"And a lot of joy," Tia pointed out. "There were many good times before there were bad."

"Thank you for that. You have all been so compassionate about my brother's gambling problem. If he'd lived . . ." Dorothy shivered. "But I didn't come to talk about that. I came to talk about *you*. How do you feel about Jenny and Mike expecting a little one?"

"Pleased, happy, excited, a little scared . . ." Tia looked into her teacup and didn't speak for a moment. "I'm really the odd woman out in our little trio now. That's why I came here tonight. I needed to think in the place that most reflects what I've done with my life so far." She paused and stared into the dimness of the room as if looking into the past. "As children, the three of us would sit in our tree house and speculate about our futures. None of our guesses turned out exactly as we predicted."

"And they were . . . ?"

"An astronaut, a nurse, and a teacher. Another time it was a deep-sea diver, a waitress, and an Avon lady. Then there was the time we—"

"I get it," Dorothy said with a laugh. "And let me guess who was going to be the astronaut and the deep-sea diver."

"That was me, all right. Miss Adventure—or as my mother simply called me—'Misadventure.' "

"You've always marched to your own drummer."

Tia grinned. "Sometimes I've marched to an entirely different *band*."

"Then why are you so pensive tonight? You're a survivor, Tia. No matter how life changes, you'll thrive. As you've said to me many times, 'With God on my side, how can I fail?' "

Tia took a deep breath. "Libby is married to Reese and they have adopted a son. With both Reese and Robert confined to wheelchairs and her parents in retirement at Fraiser Towers, she's very busy. That, plus her work with the hippotherapy program at Reach Out Ranch, keeps her going all day long. Jenny has the bakery and catering service, Mike, Luke, and now a baby on the way. And me? I have two stores."

"And another coming soon."

Tia sighed. "Let's just say all the bugs aren't quite worked out yet." She pulled the knitted throw a little closer to her body. "Maybe I'm feeling a little sorry for myself."

"You? If you wanted to marry and have a family, there are dozens of men out there ready to say 'I do.' "

"I have turned down a few." Tia's eyes twinkled. "It takes a really good husband to be better than none at all." Her mobile features ran the gamut of emotions before settling on a bright smile. "I admit, I've been moping—and now it's time to quit.

"*My* job is to be the one-and-only me. Jenny and Libby can have all the babies they want—I'm not ready for that. But I will be an A1 aunt and godmother. And I'll be able to spoil the baby rotten and then give it back to its mother. It's a win-win situation for me."

Tia's smile turned into a suspicious scowl. "I'll bet you anything Libby tries to give that baby a pony. I wonder what I could do to top that. Disneyland maybe . . ." She straightened her trim frame and sat cross-legged in the chair, thinking furiously.

Dorothy laughed out loud. "You don't stay down long, do you, Tia?"

"Not if I can help it. I'm very blessed and should be giving continual thanks to God. Shame on me when I forget, even for a moment."

"So now what?"

Tia grew thoughtful. When she spoke, her voice was soft. "I need to quit treading water and get on with my life, too."

"How will you do that?"

"You're just full of questions tonight, aren't you, Dorothy?"

"Sorry."

"It's fine. You're forcing me to verbalize thoughts that have been accumulating in my head. I enjoy my work running the gift shops. Gift-giving is a demonstration of friendship, a way to spread love and affection. What's more, it's an opportunity to tuck tapes or bookmarks with Scripture into my customers' bags and to reflect God's light into the corners of their lives. But I've begun to realize that it's not enough. "

"Sounds like plenty to me."

"Wait until I tell you about Birdhouse Ministries!" Tia leaned forward, her face animated, her eyes sparkling. As Dorothy sat in rapt attention, Tia told her about her vision for reaching out to women through laughter. And she told her about Jason.

"I had no idea," Dorothy said, stunned. "We were all in school together, but nothing was ever said."

"Who was going to say anything? Certainly not Jason. And I was walking around feeling guilty that I was somehow responsible for his actions. If only I hadn't opened my mouth. If only I'd paid more attention to him. If only, if only."

"None of that was your fault. Jason needed to take responsibility for his actions."

"I know that now," Tia stated. "But at the time I was young and hurt. I didn't know why someone who said he loved me would do something like that."

She looked at Dorothy with passion blazing in her dark eyes. "I know how these abused women feel and think. I've been there. The only difference is that I escaped sooner than most. There were no wedding vows, promises, or children between us. Imagine if Jason and I had married! How difficult would it have been to walk away then?"

Tia sipped her tea and stared into the blackness at the outer fringes of the store. "That experience changed me, Dorothy, even though I'd almost blocked it from my mind until recently. It's as though those memories returned now for a reason. I feel driven to use that experience to help someone else."

"Then go for it!"

"I have and I am, Dorothy. Birdhouse Ministries has moved to the top of my list. I have the stores I've wanted. Now is the time to move forward in another area." Tia grew momentarily wistful. "I guess you'd say these stores are my offspring, and now they'll have to share my time with the new 'baby.' "

"And you have some lovely 'babies,' " Dorothy said. She got up and gave Tia a peck on the cheek. "Don't stay here too late. I'll lock the door behind me."

"That's okay; I'll let you out."

The two women walked to the back entry and said good night. After Dorothy was gone, Tia went into her office and turned on the computer. She opened the files that held her bookkeeping and inventory records and studied them intently.

After fifteen minutes, Tia sighed. From the figures she'd seen tonight, she had one very good "offspring," an errant one, and a third on the way. What was she going to do about those troublesome children of hers?

Tia put her head in her hands and prayed. Though she had faith that God was there with her, it felt as if her words ricocheted off the ceiling and swirled around her, adding to the confusion already in her heart.

．．

"What do we have planned for today?" Brandon sat at Tia's kitchen table drinking espresso and watching her put away her breakfast dishes.

"I had planned to work," Tia said pointedly. She hadn't expected him to either drop in or ask her to spend the day with him. She'd thought he'd want a break from her after the grueling workdays they'd been putting in together. "Other than that, my mind is a blank slate."

"Surely there's *something* you've been wanting to do that you haven't gotten around to yet."

"You'd help me clean my house and empty the garbage? How sweet of you!" Tia grinned and handed him a bagel.

Before he could respond, the telephone rang. Tia reached for the receiver. "Hello?"

"Auntie Tia?" a small voice quivered across the line.

"Robert?" She could hear his distress. "What's up, buddy?"

"Could you help me?"

"First you'd better tell me what's wrong." Life with Libby was usually as placid as a lake on a still day, so hearing her child upset was more than a surprise to Tia.

"I kinda forgot something, and now Dad says I have to be 'sponsible for my actions." Robert sounded miserable.

"What did you forget?"

A big sigh came across the line. "I have a project at school that's due Monday morning, and I need a grown-up to help me do it. I forgot about it until this morning, and now Mom and Dad are both busy!"

"Hmmm. So you forgot about your homework until it's too late, and now your dad says you'll have to go to school and tell your teacher what happened?"

"She's gonna be really mad at me—and the project is practically half my grade!" Robert's voice pitched upward, and Tia thought he was about to cry.

He soldiered on, though, to the end of the story. "I was supposed to go bird-watching, find ten birds that live around here, and write a report on them. I have to do it today, but

Dad has people coming to buy some horses, and he's not going to be home. Mom would have helped me, but she'd promised to spend the day with Grandma and Grandpa. She's going to take them somewhere to visit a friend. I'm gonna flunk science!"

Tia could practically see tears running down the little boy's face. "Do you want me to take you bird-watching so you can write your report?"

"Would you?" His voice perked up. "Dad says it's my 'sponsibility to get it done on my own or face the teacher. Some of my friends are going together to the park, but . . ." His voice trailed away.

Tia's heart went out to him. A little boy in a wheelchair couldn't keep up. She remembered a time once before, when Robert had gone off looking for birds and nearly drowned. That memory made her decision for her. "I'll be at your house in twenty minutes, okay?"

"Really? Aunt Tia, you're totally awesome!"

When she turned away from the phone, Tia wore a smile. "Well, Brandon, I just found something I want to do today."

It was a test. Tia hadn't said so, but it was definitely a test.

She watched Brandon's face closely for even the slightest flicker of doubt or hesitation at the idea of spending his Saturday with a small boy in a wheelchair. He passed with flying colors.

"I used to do some bird-watching myself when I was a kid," he confessed, surprising her. Somehow she'd thought he'd been the boy more interested in athletics and competitions than such a solo activity.

"I wouldn't have guessed," she admitted.

"No? I suppose it started with my fascination for the wild turkeys that populated the place where I grew up. They were huge and rather frightening-looking to a young kid, but once I saw one fly I was hooked."

"I didn't know they could fly."

"I devoured—pardon the Thanksgiving pun—everything I could learn about them. They can fly, all right. The fastest ever recorded flew over fifty miles an hour and went about a mile."

She could see the enthusiasm for the subject in his expression. "Amazing. All I know about turkeys revolves around the holidays—not the best time for them."

"Wild turkeys almost died out, but they've been reintroduced by farmers and ornithologists."

"Then you're just the man to come with us. Have you got binoculars?"

"In my trunk."

Robert was waiting in the front yard when they arrived. He wore a brimmed hat pulled down over his eyes, sunglasses, and a long-sleeved shirt. With child-sized binoculars hanging around his neck, he looked like a little Albert Schweitzer.

"Let me guess. The child is also wearing SPF 50 sunscreen, right?" Tia asked.

Libby paused from her job loading freshly baked bread and a bundle of flowers into her trunk. "You'll watch him, won't you? Make sure he doesn't get too warm or too cold? He's got a sweater—"

"Libby! Don't worry! We'll feed and water him, make sure he takes his vitamins, and cut his hair if necessary! I know how to take care of Robert."

Libby looked embarrassed. "I just feel so badly that I'd made these plans. I wanted to help him. Fine mother I am."

"But he took ''sponsibility' and called another adult who wasn't quite so busy today. I think you should be proud of him. And I'll bet he'll never forget an assignment again."

Libby glanced at Brandon, who was waiting in the car. "What's the deal with him?"

"He wanted to do something fun today. Robert called just in time."

"You can't be dragging my son on your date! Maybe I can get one of the high school girls down the street—"

"Nonsense. I want to spend time with Robert, and Brandon actually likes birds. We'll have a great time." And without waiting for any more protest from Libby, she pushed Robert's chair to the car and helped the boy into the backseat. Robert's grin was so wide that Tia could see all the way to his molars in her rearview mirror.

"Where should we go first?" Brandon asked.

Robert dug several sheets of paper and three books out of his backpack. "My teacher made a list of good places to look. She said we'd see a few things around the lakes, but if we wanted to find different birds, we should go to something bigger."

"Then I know just the place. We'll go to Carver Park. We'll be there in twenty minutes."

Tia covertly studied Brandon as he drove. He'd surprised her. She hadn't even expected him to be *willing* to go birding—but to be knowledgeable too!

She felt a growing tenderness within her as she listened to her two "men" discuss hummingbirds.

"Why are they named hummingbirds?" Robert wanted to know. "They don't hum!"

"But their wings do," Brandon said. "When they fly, their wings flap so fast that they make a humming sound that you can actually hear."

"Wow." Robert pushed his glasses onto his nose and flipped through his book looking for a photo.

"Smartie," Tia whispered to Brandon. "You're going to make me look bad."

As Brandon grinned his face relaxed, his guard lowered, and the protective armor of blasé sophistication disappeared. "You can let me have a little fun, can't you? I haven't done this for— too long."

"I just don't see how we can avoid fun today," Tia assured him.

By late morning Tia was exceedingly grateful that Brandon was along to answer Robert's unending stream of questions: "Do birds ever get tired of flying? How many feathers does a bird have? Do all birds take baths? Mom has a birdbath in the back-yard. Do you have a birdbath?"

Tia glanced at Brandon. "I challenge you to answer every one of those questions," she said.

"Let's stop here and get some lunch and I'll try."

"Really?" Robert's head popped up. "You *know?*"

When they were settled at a table on the patio of the restaurant and the waiter had brought a pitcher of lemonade to the table, Brandon began to respond to the drilling he'd been given.

"I think birds get tired, yes. Everything needs rest, but tired of flying? I doubt it. Do you have a picture of an albatross in that book of yours? They go out to sea for weeks—even months—on end. The wind and air currents keep them aloft."

"What do they eat?"

"They drop to the water to hunt, eat, and even to rest on the sea. The only time they come to dry land is to breed."

"Cool. How many feathers do they have?"

Tia was about to tell Robert his questions were getting a little out of hand when Brandon surprised her again—by answering him. "I'm not sure about an albatross, but I do know it depends on the bird. Anywhere from under a hundred to several thou-sand. A bird's feathers usually weigh a couple times its body weight."

Just then a bright orange-and-black bird landed in a nearby tree. Brandon pointed at the saucy creature, and Robert pushed off on his chair to get a closer look.

"You totally amaze me!" Tia marveled when Robert was out of earshot. "I had no idea you were such a . . . a—birdbrain!"

He grinned, and Tia admired the flash of his easy white smile. She liked this new side of Brandon.

"My sister and I were rather bird-obsessed when we were kids. Even now she takes a lot of her inspiration from the colors of birds and the shapes of their feathers."

"Now that you say it, I do see it in her work."

"One year she complained that the birds weren't a good inspiration anymore because they seemed so pale. It was as if the color had gone out of them."

Tia noticed that gradually he'd shifted his chair closer to hers. She chose not to move away. "What happened?"

"If redbirds' diets are lacking in carotene, they become pale. It's the same thing that makes carrots orange. That's why sometimes a pink flamingo in a zoo will look very pale or almost white from an imbalanced diet."

Brandon was just full of surprises today. The breeze on the deck ruffled Tia's hair and the sun warmed her body. Robert was engrossed in his birds, and Brandon chose not to speak. She felt more relaxed than she'd felt in a long time. "This is nice," she murmured.

"So are you."

Tia opened one heavy-lidded eye. "You're not so bad yourself."

After lunch, Brandon took them north to another bird-watchers' dream. Elm Creek Park was alive with native birds. As they sat on the ground beneath an old oak, Robert stationed himself at the edge of a stand of trees and stared intently at a woodpecker *rat-a-tat-tatting* on a tree.

"Robert should be able to finish his quota here," Brandon said. "Maybe he'll even have time to get his report started. I can give him a few tips on interesting bird facts to throw in to impress his teacher. That's not cheating, is it?"

Tia smiled lazily. "I don't think so. I've never seen a child work so hard as he has today to get his notes just right. It was a stroke of genius for you to pick up a disposable camera at the gas station. Now he can even document his report with pictures."

She could have gone to sleep there in the shade of the old tree but for one nagging question in her mind. "Do you think they ever get headaches?" she murmured.

"Who?"

"Woodpeckers. Listen to the jackhammer sound of that little guy Robert is watching."

"Nature prepared them for banging their heads against a wall. They've got shocks."

"*God* prepared them to bang their heads against walls, telephone poles, or buildings," Tia corrected. "But what do you mean 'shocks'?"

"Fluid around the brain—lining the skull—actually. That absorbs the shock so he doesn't beat his little woodpecker brains out."

"Amazing. God didn't miss a step when he created things, did he?"

"Hmmm." Brandon took Tia's hand and covered it with his own. Tia sagged closer to him until her head rested on his shoulder. Her eyes drifted shut, and she felt him shift so that her head rested in the hollow of his shoulder. That was the last she knew until Robert practically pumped his wheelchair across her toes.

"You were almost asleep." Brandon yawned, none too awake himself.

She sat up and rubbed her eyes. "That felt so wonderful."

"Auntie Tia, look how many birds I already have on my list. My teacher is going to be really surprised. I even saw a bird eating upside down!"

"Probably a chickadee," Brandon concluded. "Let me take a look at your list."

"And I saw a bird rolling in the dirt. He went like this." Robert raised his arms shoulder high and began flapping them. "Why'd he do that?"

"He was taking a bath. Maybe it was a sparrow. They do that."

"You can't take a bath in *dirt*," Robert scoffed.

"You can if you're a bird. Chickens and turkeys do it. So do ostriches."

Robert and Tia both giggled at the image of the huge bird flopping around in the dirt.

"It shakes out the parasites living in the feathers."

"I wonder if it feels like talcum powder does after a bath," Tia mused. "That dries up the last bits of moisture on your skin. Do birds get wet under their feathers?"

Brandon nodded as he held out his hand for Robert's list, read it, and scrambled to his feet. "Let's go over to that picnic area so we have a table to work at. You've got your birding books. We can make a stab at that report, too." He turned back. "Tia, are you coming?"

"Not yet. I haven't gotten my full quota of vitamin D. I'll lay here in the sun."

She rolled herself from the shade into the sun, watched Brandon and Robert make their way across the clearing, and marveled. Who would have thought that a little boy and some birds were the key to unlocking Brandon's sophisticated shell?

"Never judge a book by its cover," Tia murmured before she closed her eyes and dozed off to sleep.

It was almost dusk by the time the threesome found their way back to Libby and Reese's house. Libby was outside, pacing across the front porch. Reese was there, too, glancing at his watch and then at the street.

"There you are!" Libby raced toward them as Tia put Robert's backpack in his lap. "I was getting worried."

"We had a great time, Mom. I've almost got my report done, and I saw woodpeckers, chickadees, a Baltimore oriole—he's named for a real Lord Baltimore 'cause the bird was the same colors as Lord Baltimore's coat of arms—and wrens, sparrows, and this cool one called a grackle. Brandon says it's a 'rude' bird, but he looked cool anyway. . . ."

"Maybe you'd better stop and take a breath," Tia advised.

"I have to go inside and look at the encyclopedia," Robert announced. "Thanks, Auntie Tia. Thanks, Brandon." From his chair, he reached out, grabbed Brandon's leg, and gave it a squeeze. Brandon ruffled his hair as Tia kissed Robert's cheek.

"Go for it. You'll have a great report," Brandon said, chuckling.

"Maybe I'll get an A! Or an A plus!" Robert rolled himself up the ramp and into the house.

"It looks like you had a successful day," Reese commented.

"For all of us. It was fun. Brandon is practically an ornithologist."

"Hardly." Still there was a big smile on Brandon's features.

"Can you come in?" Libby asked. "Fresh coconut cake on the table."

"I would love to but I am so tired my brain is about to shut off entirely. Rain check?"

"Sure." Libby hugged Tia and then, impulsively, Brandon. "Thanks for helping us out. Sounds like you were a great success."

"He's a good kid," Brandon said almost shyly. "Thanks for sharing him."

They were quiet as Brandon pulled up to Tia's front door.

"Thanks again," Tia said. "It was a great day."

"Thank *you*." He put the tip of his finger to his lips and then to hers.

She stared after him as he drove away, befuddled and bemused at the day's amazing transformation in Brandon and in her feelings for him.

"Brain overload," she warned herself as she dropped everything at the bottom of the stairs and made a beeline for bed. "I'll have to see how things look in the morning."

. . . .

"What's up?" Tia walked across Libby's front lawn to join her friend, who was staring at a sleek, aerodynamic contraption on the sidewalk.

"Reese's new rig."

"Dad is going to *race*," Robert said proudly. He pointed a finger. "In that!"

"It looks like an overgrown mechanical mosquito."

"It's a racing chair. I'm gonna get one when I'm older. Dad said so. But I have to lift weights first to get stronger."

"We're taking it over to the running track at the school," Libby explained. "Want to come with us?"

"Why not? I've never seen a racing mosquito work."

She helped Libby slide the light chair into the van while Reese and Robert used the lifts to get in. Libby sat in back with Robert, and Tia scooted onto the bucket seat in front beside Reese. "What's all this about?"

When Reese smiled, the lines around his eyes crinkled pleasantly. "A new challenge, I suppose."

"You mean you don't have enough already? A wheelchair, a job, a horse ranch, a new wife and son? Volunteering at Reach Out Ranch? What are you, a glutton for punishment?"

"It would be good for Robert to have a sport. I thought I'd try racing first and see if it would work for him."

"And?"

"So far, so good. Robert still needs more upper-body strength. Power in the arms and shoulders is essential to rolling the chair.

I've found a trainer who works with wheelchair athletes. We've planned out a five-day-a-week training program. I'll alternate track practice with weights. Then I'll teach Robert."

Tia glanced back at the small boy in the wheelchair. His eyes were shining and his face glowed with eager anticipation. He'd come a long way from that lonely little boy in foster care whom she'd first met.

"Here we are." Reese pulled up to the empty track.

When the "mosquito" had been deposited on the ground, Reese transferred himself into the seat. Libby helped him get his feet into place and do the necessary strap adjustments.

"Why racing?" Tia asked. "Why not wheelchair basketball?"

"Robert is small for his age. It might be hard for him to get the ball to the hoop, and quad rugby is probably too rough. With road racing Robert can compete against himself until he's ready to compete with others."

"I never realized there were so many options for disabled people."

"We didn't either until we started looking." Libby looked at her husband with pride as he pulled on heavy black mitts and adjusted them by tugging at the straps with his teeth.

"Why the mittens?" Tia inquired.

"The mitts are for punching the rims. Watch."

Reese maneuvered onto the track, leaned forward until his chin almost touched his knees, and moved the chair forward by batting the inner rims of the tires with his hands. The chair advanced with amazing speed. Robert positioned his chair so he could watch his dad race.

"Cool." Tia flexed her arms. "Doesn't he get sore?"

Libby laughed. "I had to ice his forearms the first couple times he tried it. But you know Reese; once he decides to do something, there's no talking him out of it."

Her men occupied, Libby dropped onto the grass and patted the ground, inviting Tia to join her. "Tell me how you are. We haven't talked much lately." She looked slyly from the corners of her eyes. "Brandon takes up a lot of your time."

"He's actually *making* time for me. If I had to do what he's doing with the other store, I'd spend every waking moment driving between the two shops."

"Of course."

Tia didn't want to turn all schoolgirl giggly or admit what still seemed strange, even to her. Many days she could think of nothing *but* Brandon and longed for the clearheadedness that always threatened to vanish whenever he inhabited her mind.

"Sometimes I have this uneasiness . . ."

"About Brandon?"

"About *me*. Brandon and I have a wonderful time working together. He's smart, witty, charming. When we're hatching ideas for the stores and discussing strategies, I feel like I'm flying. But when I'm alone and begin to consider the magnitude of what I'm doing . . ."

Tia's voice was soft and slow. "It's weird, Libby. Even after I admitted to you how much I've needed God's guidance, how my intention has always been to bring it all to him, Brandon still rarely makes it into my prayers. I . . . I can't explain it, but something is holding me back.

"It's as if I've already made up my mind about what I want concerning Brandon and the stores, and I don't want God to interfere and change my plans. I get an empty spot in my heart when I try to pray about Brandon and the business."

"Tia, if this man and those stores are God's will, everything will work out for the best." Libby's sweet face filled with concern. "But you'd better start talking to God—*especially* about those things."

"I will. I'm trying. I'm just too stubborn and independent. I keep taking charge when I should turn it over to God. And I will . . . I *will*."

Libby, apparently reading something in her friend's expression that had never been there before, asked, "Tia, are you falling in love?"

CHAPTER FIVE

Killdeer: At its nest, the killdeer is famous for its dramatic "broken wing" display: Dragging its wings along the ground as if injured, it detracts predators away from its eggs or young.

—*Birds: An Explore Your World Handbook,* Discovery Books and David Bird

"Good morning!" Tia sang as she entered the back door of the shop.

Wendy Magnusson, whose turn it had been to open the shop that morning, looked up and smiled. "Aren't you chipper this morning?"

"How can I help it? The sun is shining, the sky is a dazzling blue, and the birds outside are a veritable orchestra of sound." Tia tossed her purse onto her desk, slipped her sweater over the back of a chair, and headed for the coffeepot.

Mug in hand, she joined Wendy at the counter. "Birds are practically the noisiest creatures I know."

"In big numbers, they certainly are. One bird alone you can walk by unnoticed, but a flock . . ."

"Just like women," Tia said with a grin. "We may not be able to move mountains on our own, but when we work together— wow!"

"Speaking of moving mountains," Wendy said, "we have a big shipment coming in today. Do you want me on the floor or in back unpacking?"

Tia glanced at the schedule. "On the floor. Dorothy said she'd come by and help me unpack so you and Margot could work out front. She says it's like having Christmas in July, opening all those boxes."

"It's obvious she doesn't have to stock shelves," Wendy observed.

"I know. And I'm not going to ask her to do that or I'd never see her again."

"You have lovely friends," Wendy commented. "Libby, Jenny, Ellen, Dorothy—I can't think of a nicer group."

"A nicer *gift*," Tia corrected. "I think people who come into our lives can be the best presents of all."

Wendy considered the comment. "You're right. Sometimes you know you need something in your life, a friend, and then, there she is."

"God must be a great chess player," Tia said.

"What do you mean?"

"Just think how he organizes people to come into and out of our lives for a purpose—millions of us humans at one time. I get messed up trying to coordinate a couple of rooks and a knight or two."

"As usual, Tia, your thoughts are miles ahead of mine. But I suppose that's why you're the boss and I'm the employee. Which reminds me, I'd better get back to the floor. There will be customers soon."

Tia did what she did every day upon arrival at the store—made sure the tea tray for customers was tidy, coffee and hot cider were brewing, cookies were plentiful. Then she walked through the displays, tucking the corner of a quilt in here, straightening a picture there, rearranging an errant silk rose in its vase. The bell at the back door rang, and she knew her reinforcement had arrived.

"I hope I won't be seen today." Dorothy wiped her hair from her eyes. "I could have dressed up, but jeans are so much more comfortable for this type of work."

Tia rolled up her sleeves. "Very sensible. Now let the fun begin!"

The front door chimed dozens of times as they worked, signaling that customers were entering or leaving the store.

Finally, Dorothy sat back on her haunches and commented, "Sounds like business is good. Can the two out front handle it? If you need to go out, I'll just keep working." She fingered the big stuffed animal in her hand. "I could do this all day. You order such beautiful things for the store."

Tia poked at the belly of the soft, furry bear in Dorothy's hand. "That's Mr. Mom you're holding."

"Odd name for a toy."

"It's got a little recorder inside that plays the sounds of a beating heart, just like a baby hears for nine months in the womb. It's supposed to be soothing to the baby when Mom can't hold him. Maybe I'll give one to Jenny."

"I'd be my own best customer here," Dorothy admitted. "I'd want one of everything."

Tia's easy laughter chimed throughout the room. "You need a much bigger house then—a warehouse, maybe."

"Tia!" a voice hissed.

She looked up and saw Wendy in the doorway beckoning her. "Shoplifter. Aisle 6, by the wall. I saw him slide something into his jacket. I've already pushed the alarm button. Someone should be here soon."

"I'll step out and see what's going on." From the cash register, Tia could see a thatch of fine blond hair and a pimply forehead over the shelves. The boy was bobbing, ducking surreptitiously from display to display. He couldn't be a very experienced robber, Tia thought, because he was very bad at it.

Moments later she saw a police car pass the store window. The young man—who didn't appear to be more than fifteen, though

Tia didn't trust her accuracy at guessing a teenager's age—was moving toward the door. He was now walking slowly, picking up items and setting them down again as if to say, "See? I've put everything back in its place."

Even at his slow gait, he was nearing the front door too rapidly. She tried to swallow the sick feeling rising from her stomach as she watched. He was wearing an old denim jacket and a faded T-shirt with a hole in the front. Though she had no idea what was in style for teens this week, she had a hunch that his outfit was long past trendy. If he hadn't been in the act of stealing from her, she would have felt sorry for him.

He turned his back to the window to glance at a display of wood carvings and duck decoys for one last show of innocence before he left the building. As he did so, two police officers came through the front door.

The boy rotated away from the ducks and right into the police officer behind him. Startled, he let go of the bottom of his jacket and a music box—one of Tia's loveliest—fell from under his shirt and shattered on the floor.

"Wha . . . how'd that happen? I must have brushed it off. . . ." He looked desperately at the display in front of him. It housed nothing even remotely like a music box.

"Who's the witness?" one officer asked.

"Me," Wendy said faintly.

"Then we'll need your statement, and there's a paper for you to sign." He inclined his head toward his partner. "You can speak with him."

As Wendy trailed miserably after the officer, Tia could imagine what was going through her mind. A shoplifter was one thing, but this boy looked as though his first priority should have been food. His hair was greasy in the way of teens who suffered from acne and looked as though it had been cut with a paring knife. A dull knife. His cheeks were hollow and his teeth would have benefited from braces. He was a pitiful sight.

Drugs? Tia wondered. *Or malnutrition.*

"I'm s-sorry, lady," the boy stammered, and Tia was surprised at the pleasant quality of his voice. "I didn't want to steal from you, but I wanted my girlfriend to have a birthday present."

"Doesn't mean you can steal one, buddy," the policeman growled. "Now give me your parents' phone number, and we'll have them come down and pick you up. If they can't or aren't home, they can get you at the juvenile unit later."

Tia stared incredulously at the young man as he blanched as pale as the paint on the wall behind him. For the first time she'd actually seen how the cliché "pale as a sheet" had originated.

"They aren't home. You can just drop me off—"

"No can do. Do you have a work number for—"

"No!"

Tia was dumbfounded. It occurred to her that this man-child was not nearly as afraid of the police or the juvenile unit as he was of his parents. "Officer, could I ask this young man something?"

"Sure, go ahead." The man appeared impatient and almost bored, as though he'd seen and done this a hundred times before.

"Your parents really do need to know this," Tia said mildly, wondering what had gotten into her. She felt *compelled* to speak to this boy.

"Trevor." He filled in the blank Tia had left for him. "But my dad will kill me if he finds out, or—"

"Or what?"

"Or he'll be really mad at my mom. He'll beat on me and then he'll blame her for not watching me better."

"So your parents don't discuss these things?"

Trevor looked at her with an expression that said it all. *Duh, lady. Of course they don't.*

"Officer, if I don't press charges, will he need to go to the juvenile unit?"

"He's got to be somewhere."

"My mom works at Valley Elementary. She's a cook."

"Could you take him there? To his mother, I mean."

Trevor stared at Tia with suspicion and relief, confirming Tia's hunch. It wasn't his mother he was worried about. It was his father. She'd noticed a fading bruise on his collarbone as he struggled around in the too-big shirt under his jacket. Tia realized that this boy might be in for more of a punishment than either she or the law could mete out.

"I won't press charges if Trevor agrees to work off the price of the music box doing anything I ask of him. And I want his *mother* to call me—from work. If that doesn't happen . . ." She shrugged her shoulders as if to say all would be hopeless.

"I can do it, lady. I could sweep floors or . . ."

"Will you have his mother call me as soon as you deliver Trevor to her?"

The officer nodded, signaled to his partner, and ushered the mightily relieved Trevor to the door.

"Are they taking him to jail?" Wendy asked as she and Tia stood in the doorway watching the patrol car pull away.

"I'm not pressing charges." Tia reached for a broom and began to sweep up the remains of the music box.

"Why not? Bad enough that he stole at all but choosing this particular music box . . ." Wendy looked mournfully at the floor.

"He's going to work off the price of the box—any way I decide."

Wendy shook her head glumly. "Then he's going to be working for a long time. Did he realize that imported music box cost nearly five hundred dollars?"

Tia smiled grimly. "No, I don't believe he did—but he will by the time I'm through with him."

Tia barely had time to go to the back room and tell Dorothy what had been going on while she'd had her head buried in a huge box of gift books before the phone in her office rang.

Since that was the number she'd given the officers, she was

sure that Trevor's mother would be on the other end of the line. "Tia Warden here."

"Ms. Warden. I'm Mariah West, Trevor's mother. I'm so sorry. I don't know what got into that child. He's a good boy, never done a thing like this before. And you letting him work off the price of what he stole instead of making his dad pick him up, why . . ." The relief in her voice was palpable.

"I didn't say it would be easy, Mrs. West. But I'd rather make him think than simply put a blotch on his record. Could you meet me someplace on Saturday morning so he can get started?"

"Sure. Saturday's good 'cause I don't have to work."

"Fine. I'll meet you there at 8:00 A.M. sharp." And Tia gave her the directions to Reach Out Ranch.

"Are you *nuts?*" Dorothy barked after Tia hung up.

"I've never been more sane. Why?"

"A kid steals a five-hundred-dollar music box and your punishment is to take him to Reach Out Ranch? If that's punishment for a crime, more kids would steal!"

"Not necessarily." Tia told Dorothy about the bruise on his collarbone and the blatant fear in his eyes.

"I think he needs to learn a lesson, but if there is any chance that means his getting beaten up—and after talking to his mother, I think it does—then I'll choose my own form of punishment. That's taking responsibility for his actions and working off his debt. I imagine Rollie, the ranch's director, could use help mucking out stables, cleaning tack, or filling water tanks."

"It's your decision, Tia, but I don't get it."

"Think about Christ on the cross, flanked on both sides by criminals. He didn't judge. He showed pure love. When he could have been thinking about himself, he was forgiving others instead. If he could do that, the least I can do is this."

"You are sweet, Tia. Sweet but misguided. I've never thought of you as naïve, but this . . ."

"Maybe. But I'm following an instinct here. I think this boy needs to see Christ in other people. I doubt anyone has shown him that before. I can only try."

"Suit yourself." Dorothy sighed. "I just hope it doesn't get out that this is a great shop to rob."

"Are you sure you know what you're doing?" Reese inquired when Tia asked him to drive with her to the ranch.

"No, but I'm trying to step out in faith here, and I could use a little support—and a policeman's eye. If this isn't going to work out, I want to know right away and not subject Rollie to any hardship. Your guess will be better than mine as to whether or not this kid will be a problem."

"I might as well say yes now and do it. You'll just keep hounding me until I agree anyway."

"A sensible man," Tia said sweetly into the receiver. "See you in the morning."

Trevor and his mother were already at the ranch when Tia and Reese arrived. Trevor and his mom had driven an old beater of a car that looked like it should have given up the ghost years ago. But they were both shined and polished to a gleam. Trevor had scrubbed his face until it was bright pink, and their simple clothes were clean and neatly ironed. Mariah West looked about as worried as a human being could manage, and Trevor looked even worse.

Rollie, whom Tia had warned about her scheme, was trying to make conversation with the terrified duo.

"Looks promising already," Reese commented. "They showed up and the mother looks like she cares. That's more than some."

"Here goes." Tia breathed and opened the van door.

Mrs. West had been crying. Trevor's eyes were red-rimmed,

too, but he was struggling to show no signs of weakness. He could not, however, keep his hands from shaking.

Tia introduced herself, hiding the swell of emotion that overcame her as she looked at the frightened pair. "You've been talking to Rollie, I see."

"Yes. This sounds like a wonderful place, but we were wondering . . ."

"Why I asked you here?" Tia looked at Trevor. "You stole a very expensive music box from the store."

"I'll replace it. I can work hard."

"Good. Because that box cost almost five hundred dollars." Both Wests blanched.

"But I didn't think you'd learn much of a lesson if the police took you to the juvenile unit—other than, perhaps, to be more careful next time you stole something. What's more, you'd have a black mark on your record. I'd rather you know what it feels like to earn five hundred dollars. Rollie will keep track of your hours. You can quit once you've paid your debt—if you want to."

"*If* I want to?"

"Reach Out Ranch is rather 'catching.' You might be surprised." Tia gave Trevor an enigmatic smile. "And there are some great role models out here. You might learn a thing or two from them." Then Tia introduced Reese and asked him to take Trevor on a tour. Rollie followed to delineate the boy's new duties.

"I don't know why you're doing this, miss, but we do appreciate . . ."

"I think Trevor might have been punished more severely than even the crime warranted if he'd had to go to court."

"How'd you know—?" Mrs. West caught herself and grew silent.

"He'll be fine here as long as he obeys the rules. It's important that he understand that the clients who come here deserve the utmost respect and kindness."

"Oh, he's a kind boy." His mother sighed. "Not always wise, but he is kind."

"Good. And you might let him know that Reese will be here to check up on him—and that he's a detective with the police force."

"So the police *are* involved?" Mrs. West's eyes grew large.

"No. He's doing it as a favor to me because he's married to one of my best friends. I didn't want to subject Rollie or the kids to any trouble."

"Oh, Trevor won't be trouble. He's so grateful that his dad doesn't know. . . ." She stopped and bit her lip. "That he didn't have to go with the police . . ."

"I know." Tia put a hand on the woman's wrist. "I'm going to give you my card. It has my phone numbers on it. I want you to call me anytime you have a question—" she paused before adding—"about *anything.*"

They exchanged a look that Tia sensed held several layers of meaning for Mrs. West. She would just have to wait and see what those meanings were.

It was nearly two hours before Reese and Trevor returned. Mariah West was grooming one of the mares, and she was looking relaxed and happy. A little color had returned to her cheeks as she'd run her hands over the placid animal.

Trevor, too, looked different. The tension had gone from his features and his eyes were animated. "Mom, you can't believe how cool it is here! Rollie said I could learn to ride if I did a good job with my work. Could I start work tomorrow?"

Mrs. West looked at Tia as if she'd performed a miracle on her son.

Tia smiled serenely at her. *Just wait,* Tia thought, *you ain't seen nothin' yet!*

"He seems like an okay kid," Reese told Tia as they returned to the city. "He said it was the first—and last—time he'd stolen anything. Usually I don't believe that, but this time it might be true.

"And you were right not to press charges. He told me his dad would beat him silly if that happened. I think this Mr. West bears watching. Rollie's going to tell me if the kid ever shows up with visible bruises."

"I hope this works, Reese. I just had to try. For some reason, this pimply, criminally inclined adolescent just pulled at my heartstrings." She looked out the window at the passing scenery. "I'd recently told Wendy that I believe God sends just the right people into my life just when I need them most. Maybe Trevor robbed *my* store for a reason."

Reese didn't even appear startled by that conclusion. They both firmly believed that his wife, Libby, had been God's messenger to him. If God could send a beautiful Christian woman to a bitter, crippled cop, then why not send independent, passionate Tia to this troubled child and his fearful mother?

Tia fingered the strap of her purse. "I've begun to see something pretty profound, Reese. For years I lived my life thinking it was all about *me*. This time, with Trevor, it's not about me—it's about *him*. If I'm God's tool, so be it. I'm grateful to be chosen."

Reese was quiet for a long time before speaking. "I know now why Libby and Jenny love you so much, Tia."

Tia felt tears spring to her eyes—tears of gratitude—and they made the rest of the trip in silence.

....

Tia heard the shop door open but waited for Wendy to greet the customer. She was too engrossed in wallpaper books and paint swatches to be interrupted. Until, that is, a disembodied hand holding two theater tickets appeared in front of her face.

She turned around to find Brandon grinning like a Cheshire cat. "I can't believe I got these! Ninth row, center seats. Opening night. *No one* in town has these."

"Then how did you get them?"

"A buddy of mine swapped with me for use of my Vikings tickets one Sunday in the fall."

"I'll bet his wife or girlfriend loved that switch," Tia commented dryly.

"Girlfriend—and they just separated—the play was her idea in the first place, so he was happy about the trade."

"I didn't know you were such a theater buff." Tia pushed away the books and massaged her tense neck with her fingers. "Who's your lucky theater partner?"

Brandon gave her a strange look. "Well, I thought . . . you."

"I'm pretty busy for the next couple weeks. I'm planning to redo all the displays in this store." She tapped her bright pink fingernail on the wallpaper book. "I'm going to make and paper a few fake walls for dividers. Libby agreed to help me in the evenings."

It was obvious he hadn't expected any reluctance on her part, Tia observed, but when someone said "Jump" to her, she rarely asked "How high?" Her other friends all knew her better than that.

"It's for next Friday. I'd thought we could have dinner first, but if you need to be at work until just before the performance, I guess I could pick you up here." He sounded hopeful.

"I can do that. And if I get most of what I've planned accomplished, then dinner would be great, too." She smiled at him before pulling the wallpaper book toward her again, a blatant hint that she was ready to go back to work.

Brandon studied her with a frown on his chiseled features. "You aren't like any other woman I've ever met, Tia. I didn't know there were any quite as independent as you are."

She dimpled as she smiled. "Why, thank you, Brandon. That's the nicest thing you've ever said to me."

Before he could respond, she went on. "We had some excitement here the other day. A shoplifter."

"I hope you called the police." His eyes flashed. "I have no time for those creeps."

"We did call the police, but I didn't press charges."

"What? Are you trying to encourage that kind of behavior? Pretty soon every petty thief in town will know this store is an easy mark."

"Oh, he's not going unpunished," Tia assured him. Then she explained her idea to have him work off the price of the music box at Reach Out Ranch.

"Are you nuts?" Brandon looked like a human storm cloud. "As if that will have any effect on him! Kids like that need to be taught a lesson."

"I am trying to teach him a lesson. I'm trying to teach him that there is another side to life, a more loving and forgiving side, if only he will make the choice to follow it. I'd like this kid to see people who strive to mirror Christ in their lives. He's not likely to get that if I file a complaint."

"No, but he'll get what he deserves." Brandon sounded angry.

"Thank God we all don't get what we deserve. Instead, because of Christ, we receive eternal life instead of eternal punishment."

"It's not the same thing," he protested.

"No? But it is a little sample of grace. If this boy can see grace and realize that there's much more where that came from, he may become hungry for more of it."

Brandon shook his head in dismay. "You have some very convoluted thinking, Tia. And you're—what are the words from that song?—a 'cockeyed optimist.' "

"I am an optimist, Brandon. If God is for me, who can be against me?"

"I give up, Tia. Do what you want. Just don't cry to me when that kid disappoints you." He touched her cheek with his finger. "Friday night, okay?"

She looked at him sadly, wishing he could understand her point of view. "Okay. Friday."

. . . .

She'd never expected such a production over a dress. "I can wear something I already have for the theater. After all, we're going to be sitting in the dark." Tia and Brandon had spent most of the afternoon in downtown Minneapolis in search of a dress that would suit her at a theatrical opening.

"You don't need to be looking on sale racks, Tia. Here, try this on." Brandon thrust a skimpy evening dress at her. "That other stuff is garbage."

"No, it's not. The dress you've got in your hands might go on sale next week. Will that make it junk?"

"Picked over and rejected, that's what's on sale racks. Let's go up to the designer floor. You deserve better than this."

Tia grabbed his hand and put it to her cheek. "That's very sweet of you to say, but I don't deserve better. I actually feel ashamed even looking for a new dress. There are women at the center who have their entire lives packed in a duffel bag. I should be giving things away, not buying them."

Brandon put his arm around her shoulder and kissed the top of her head. "I know, sweetie, I know. But I'm talking about *you*. The way I feel about you makes me want to dress you in diamonds and swathe you in riches. Since I can't do that, humor me, will you?"

"Did you listen at all to the sermon at church yesterday?" Tia chided.

"Hmmm. Sure."

"Then what was it about?"

"Caught." He grinned. "Guilty as charged. I guess I had other things on my mind."

"I was afraid of that." Tia had noticed him squirming in the pew. She'd attributed it to the difference between their church traditions. Now she feared it had been boredom.

"So now, I suppose you'll tell me what I missed?"

"Gladly." Tia hung the dress back on the rack and pulled him toward the exit. "It was a reminder not to let anything but God become the primary object of your love. The Scripture was from First Timothy: 'We didn't bring anything with us when we came into the world, and we certainly cannot carry anything with us when we die. So if we have enough food and clothing, let us be content. But people who long to be rich fall into temptation and are trapped by many foolish and harmful desires that plunge them into ruin and destruction. For the love of money is at the root of all kinds of evil. And some people, craving money, have wandered from the faith and pierced themselves with many sorrows.' Nothing should be so important it gets between us and God—money, possessions, anything."

"I don't . . ."

"It was a wake-up call for me," Tia continued. "Especially that part about straying from God. We don't always turn our backs on God. Sometimes we just unwittingly drift farther and farther away. It happens so gradually that by the time we realize what's happened we're nearly lost."

"And therefore I can't buy you a new dress? I didn't hear a thing in there about sales racks or new dresses."

He was being particularly obtuse, and Tia's first instinct was to point out his irreverence, but instead she smiled sweetly and patted his cheek. "Actually, there's no way in the world I'd let you buy me clothing anyway. I'm too independent—remember? And since I want to buy a dress only off the sales rack, we'll compromise and I'll find something in my closet from my more wasteful days."

Brandon took her hands and looked into her eyes. "You are a handful, Tia Warden. But I love a challenge."

. . . .

Tia always enjoyed the theater as much for the fashions on the attendees as on the stars. There were stately looking women in elegant black, others in flowing draperies of jackets and wide-legged pants, and the amazing cornucopia of fashion worn by the younger theatergoers.

"Look at that hairdo," Tia whispered to Brandon as she took the ice-cream cup he offered her. They were milling about in the halls, seeing and being seen, eating sweet things in tiny portions, and waiting for the lights to dim, calling them to return to their seats for the end of the play.

"That's not a hairdo; that's a cactus," Brandon scoffed.

The girl in question had short brown hair sectioned off all over her head into stubby little tails. It looked like it might prick you if you touched her head.

"My grandmother sometimes did something similar to her hair with bobby pins," Tia rejoined mildly. "She didn't go out in public that way, of course."

"How about that?" Brandon moved his eyes in the direction he wanted her to look. There was a tall, slender, young woman leaning against the wall. She was wearing a bright orange print dress, thick-soled black shoes, and burgundy lipstick. Her head was shaved all but the very top of her head, which sprouted pure white hair that fell like water from a fountain across her skull.

Tia giggled. "She looks like she designed her hair after a Halloween pumpkin. The only place she left hair was on her lid. Do you think it lifts off to light a candle inside?"

"Why do people do these things to themselves?" Brandon marveled.

"For fun or attention, I suppose. And some just care very much about being trendy. Rather sad, isn't it?"

"Pitiful. I wonder how long that hair will take to grow out. My dad used to shave my head in the spring, and I'd barely have hair for school the following fall. He said he did it so I'd be cool in the heat. I think he just didn't want to bother trying to pin me down and give me a haircut every month."

Tia smiled. She didn't have many images in her mind of

Brandon as a child. As far as she knew, he might have been born wearing a designer suit, tie, and wing tips.

"I wasn't exactly thinking of it being sad in that way. I mean that I think it is very tragic that people work so hard to call attention to themselves. They must not feel very good inside or they wouldn't feel they had to try so hard to be noticed."

Brandon eyed Tia's black hair slicked back dramatically into a cap that fitted smoothly around her face. "It's difficult not to notice you in a crowd, Tia."

She grinned. "I do think color and drama are fun. Maybe some people feel the same way about nose rings. I just have to remember whom I'm representing when I'm tempted to get a tattoo."

"You relate absolutely everything to your relationship with God, don't you?" he observed.

"I *try* to do that. When God is Lord of your life, he's in your closet and your kitchen as well as your church."

Brandon gave her one of those looks he so often did—a look tinged with puzzlement, amusement, and just a hint of suspicion. But before Tia could question him, the lights began to dim and brighten and dim, their signal that the play was ready to begin again.

. . . .

The topic of Brandon seemed to crop up every time Tia and her friends were together. She knew she couldn't avoid the question much longer. She'd been reading it for days in her friends' eyes.

"He's smooth, isn't he? Brandon, I mean." Jenny poured lemonade over thick lemon slices into large glasses as Tia and Libby picked at the cake crumbs on their plates. "And good-looking, too. I like his dark hair."

"Aren't you the pregnant married lady? Should you be noticing these things?" Libby teased gently.

"I'm expecting a baby. Nothing has happened to my eyes!" Jenny retorted. "Anyway, I'm looking for Tia. She doesn't have time to look at potential partners for herself."

Tia practically reared out of her chair. "Wait a minute!" It went against her grain to even think of how badly she was ignoring that don't-mix-business-and-pleasure thing her father advised.

"Oh, don't get your nose in a twist," Jenny teased. "I was just looking for a reaction and I got it."

"He's my *business* partner," Tia clarified for what seemed the umpteenth time, although even she seemed to forget that on a regular basis.

"But if he weren't?" Libby persisted.

Tia took a sip of lemonade. "*If* he weren't my business partner, and *if* I liked the tall, dark, and handsome type, and *if* I were interested in dating right now instead of doing the sensible thing and tending to my business . . . I *might* be interested. But he *is* my business associate, and I'm *not* interested in any romantic entanglements. So there."

"The lady doth protest too much, methinks," Jenny commented.

"And *me*thinks you doth worry too much about my love life. And you doth interfere a lot, too!"

"And we're all slaughtering Shakespeare," Jenny said. "Now back to Brandon—"

"Cease and desist!" Tia yelped.

"I'd like to know more about him, that's all. When we're together all we hear from you two is business. Tell us a little bit about him. What's his family like? Where did he go to college? Was he an athlete in high school?" Jenny asked.

"I don't know."

"Tia . . ." A warning gong sounded in Libby's voice.

"I know plenty, thank you very much. His financial backing is making it possible for me to open new stores. That's good enough for me."

But was it really? She'd never left God so far out of an equation before. Brandon talks the talk . . .

Yes, but does he walk the walk?

. . . .

"Ready to go to lunch?"

"I can't, Brandon. I'm up to my ears in work. By the way, I noticed that you ordered china from a new company without consulting me. In the future I wish you would—"

Ignoring her words, he took her hand and pulled her from the chair. "I have reservations at Carlos and Company. We've got to hurry. Come on. I hear the soft-shell chicken tacos are amazing."

Relenting, Tia allowed herself to be led out the door and into the car.

The luncheon rush was over and the dining room was quiet. Tia could hear the soothing sound of water moving over stones from a fountain in the center of the room. "It's great, Brandon."

"I thought you'd like it."

"You know a great deal about my tastes. Maybe I should be learning about yours."

"What would you like to know?"

There was so very little, really, that she did know about him besides the obvious professional concerns. Jenny and Libby were right. It was astounding how many business decisions she'd entrusted to this man she really didn't even know.

"Your favorite color, beverage, movie, make or model of car, pet . . . anything!"

"Scarlet red, iced tea, *Gone With the Wind,* BMWs, and hunting dogs."

"I had no idea you were a hunter." She paused. "Would you shoot Bambi?"

Brandon, apparently seeing the wary look in Tia's eyes, hurried on. "And I like home cooking, freshly ironed shirts, and everything Italian with lots of garlic." He smiled hopefully. "Is that better?"

Tia didn't want to admit that ironing and home cooking were on her priority list right below scrubbing toilet bowls. Wasn't that what laundry services and take-out restaurants were invented for? Besides, Libby and Jenny, the ultimate cooks, usually provided her with plenty of great meals. And there was no way she was going to get into the garlic thing.

It was becoming more and more clear that her father's old assertion about not mixing business with pleasure was correct. Yet, because of Brandon, her business had become exceedingly pleasurable.

Shifting the conversation from the personal to the professional, she said, "Tell me how things are going at Ribbons & Rainbows. Tia's Attic has been so busy, and I've had so little time to spend there since the grand opening that you've had to shoulder most of the responsibility. Get me up to speed on what's happening at the store."

"It's good," he said vaguely.

"What were the best-sellers at the open house? Candles and wreaths—or those gift baskets you suggested?"

"You were right—as usual. We need to reorder candles and wreaths." Brandon's eyes didn't meet hers, making it apparent that his suggestion for the open house had not been nearly so successful.

Tia was pleased to see the food arrive. She waited until Brandon had been served his burrito before bowing her head to pray. "Dear Father, thank you for this food and this day. Bless Brandon and me as we make our way in this new partnership. May everything we do be to your glory. Amen."

When she looked up, Brandon, fork and knife in hand, was staring at her. A ruddy blush crept up the side of his neck and spilled onto his cheeks. "Do you have to do that where everyone can see you?"

"Does it embarrass you?"

"A little. I'm not used to . . . you know."

"Being grateful to our heavenly Father?"

"Not that. It's just that I'm not a very . . . public . . . Christian. My parents never did that sort of thing."

"That doesn't mean you can't start." This was too important a moment to slip by unused. "Perhaps I'm guilty of assuming things about you because of what you've said in the past. You do have a personal relationship with Christ . . . ?"

"Of course!" He sounded indignant. "I know how important that is to you."

"It's not that it's important to me, Brandon. I know where I stand in the heavenly scheme of things. It's important to *you*."

"Just because I don't talk about something doesn't mean I don't believe it."

"No, I suppose not. But once you get enthusiastic about Christ, he tends to bubble out into conversations. He's a hard one to keep in the background of one's life." *Every time I've tried, you're there, Lord, prodding at my soul. Thanks for not giving up on me!*

Brandon's response was interrupted by the waiter as he refilled their water glasses.

Later, when they left Carlos and Company and Brandon threw his arm across her shoulders, it seemed so easy and natural that Tia was reluctant to edge from his embrace. And when he excused himself, saying he was late for another appointment, Tia found herself feeling surprisingly bereft.

"Don't mix business and pleasure," Tia repeated for the umpteenth time as she entered her shop. With Brandon, that was very hard to do, but if she was worried about mixing business and pleasure, shouldn't she be even more reluctant about a relationship with a lukewarm Christian? Or was that unfair to Brandon? He *said* his faith was real. Who was she to doubt him?

....

"I can't quite reach. Find me a taller stool, will you?" Tia, swathed in layers of chiffon meant for the display she was working on, requested. She balanced precariously on tiptoe while her store clerk clenched her hands to her chest.

"You're going to break your neck," Wendy pointed out. "Come down and let me find a ladder."

"I think I took it home to do some stenciling on my bathroom ceiling." Tia wobbled on her perch.

"Then let me go out and buy one. It's cheaper than paying a hospital bill."

"Party pooper," Tia grumbled, but she did release a few yards of fabric that snaked to the floor in a puddle.

"What on earth are you doing?" Libby demanded from the front door of the store as she entered. "A swan dive off that old stool into a candle display?"

"I'm trying to get this arrangement done by noon, but if everyone keeps fussing and worrying, I'll be here all day." Tia worked her way down to her knees and off her unsteady roost.

"You've got enough fabric here to swathe the entire store," Libby commented.

"I have a vision of a very lush, extravagant backdrop here, and this sheer fabric was on sale for a buck a yard. I couldn't resist." Tia backed up to study the rods suspended from the ceiling at a ninety-degree angle eight feet from the floor.

"Here. I borrowed this ladder from the coffee shop next door," Wendy announced as she carried it to where Tia stood.

"Great. Now Libby can help me finish this, and you can unpack those deliveries in the back."

"Did I come to work?" Libby asked mildly.

"You did now. I want to give the store a totally new look so I'm reorganizing, moving things around, and putting out new merchandise. I don't want my customers bored."

"No one is ever bored around you."

"Good. And I want to keep it that way." Tia wound a few yards of fabric around her shoulders and hiked her way up the ladder. "Hand me rubber bands when I ask, okay?"

Methodically, she wound the voluminous fabric around the poles and draped it to the floor. Then she attached a second yardage in a contrasting color with rubber bands, fluffing it every so often into lush fabric roses. Returning to the floor, Tia bunched the excess fabric into great poufs and secured them with more rubber bands. She turned the unfinished ends under and arranged casual-looking puddles of fabric on the floor. With an unerring eye, she moved into place a Victorian claw-foot table and an oversized wing chair.

After placing mounds of jewel-toned mohair throws, several lamps, a pair of dainty lace gloves, and a stack of made-to-look-like-a-stack-of-old-books video holders in the tableau, she stood back and surveyed her new creation.

"I think we can merchandise this a little more, don't you? Libby, grab a ceramic lap cat and that sweet needlepoint footstool while I wrestle one of those big Great Dane figurines over here."

By the time Tia was done, the illusionary corner looked like a cozy slice of old England, a spot just waiting for its owner to relax with a pipe and worn leather slippers.

"How do you *do* that?" Libby marveled. "You worked magic with a bunch of cheap fabric and whatever was around the store."

"Would you like to have a look like this in the library of your home?" Tia asked.

"If I had a library, sure."

"Maybe I could tempt you to create one. At the end of the family room? Or in that little unused space at the top of the stairs?"

"This would look nice there. . . . Wait a minute! Are you trying to sell me something?"

"*Now* you've got the picture."

"Well, you're good at it," Libby said with grudging admiration. "You almost got me to pull out my wallet, and I'm practically immune to your charms."

"I love this business," Tia said with a grin. "Always a challenge. I'm going to design an Arabian nights room for all those brass candlesticks. Want to help?"

By late afternoon, they had also built the illusion of a bed out of bamboo to make a tropical retreat and turned a hutch into a minikitchen filled with ceramic bowls, flowers, and a dozen kinds of dishes.

"I'm quitting now," Libby said as she wiped a bead of sweat from her forehead. "Why don't you look tired? You haven't got a hair out of place!"

"Industrial-strength hair spray and a list of ideas longer than my arm to try." Tia stepped back to admire their work. "I'd buy something here, wouldn't you?"

"Without a doubt. Can we rest now?"

Tia called to the clerk behind the counter. "Wendy, I'm going to take Libby next door for tea. When I get back you can leave."

Wendy waved them out the door.

In the street, Tia threw back her head and took a deep breath of fresh air. "Isn't it a beautiful day?"

Libby looked at her fondly. "There's nothing that energizes you quite like your work, is there?"

"It's my form of mental gymnastics. Some people do crossword puzzles to keep their minds agile. I hang backdrops and make store displays." Tia opened the door to the small shop next door.

As they entered, Tia was greeted by several regulars and a waitress who brought them a plate of fresh scones, clotted cream, and a container of strawberry jam. When Tia had doled out their tea, she kicked off her shoes, curled her feet beneath her in the booth, and breathed a sigh. "This feels so good."

"Why don't you make yourself at home?" Libby teased. "Relax a little."

"When we go back to the store, you can help me stencil a design on a couple old doors I found at the flea market. They'll make a great backdrop for that shipment of country-style gifts and ornaments. . . ."

"Sorry. I've retired for the day. At least I'm *tired.* And you should be, too. How about coming over for some firehouse-hot chili and corn bread tonight?"

Tia's attention was drawn away from Libby by the woman who now stood in the doorway of the coffee shop. The face was familiar. "That's Trevor's mom."

"Really?"

Tia raised her hand and waved. "Mrs. West, would you like to join us?"

Libby raised one questioning eyebrow at Tia's friendly gesture but said nothing.

"Ms. Warden . . . I was just in your store, and the girl told me you'd come here. I wanted to talk to you. . . ."

"Sit down and join us. There are far too many scones for the two of us to eat. We'll get an extra cup for tea."

"I don't mean to be a bother."

"You aren't. I'd like to hear how Trevor is doing at Reach Out Ranch. Oh, by the way, this is my friend Libby. Her husband is Reese, the one who's been supervising Trevor."

Mariah West grabbed Libby's hand and clutched it tightly. "Your husband is a wonderful man. He's been so good to Trevor." She turned back to Tia. "I just wanted to tell you that I don't know what's come over that boy, but those hours at the ranch mean more to him than anything has in a very long time. I suppose Reese and Rollie were just being kind when they told him he could learn to ride, but Trevor's got his heart set on it."

She took a deep breath and continued. "I thought maybe there would be a way that I could work out there, too, or maybe at your shop, if you'd have someone like me, so that I could afford to pay for some riding lessons for Trevor. . . ." Her voice trailed away, her speech given.

"You don't have to pay Reese to help your son," Libby told her. "One of his biggest joys is seeing someone enjoy the horses. I'm sure he'd give him some tips while he and Trevor are both at the ranch."

"Oh, we couldn't accept that! After what Trevor did in Tia's Attic, I wouldn't blame you if you never wanted to see either of us again after he's paid off the music box." Mrs. West looked caught between shame and hope.

"I spoke with Rollie the other day," Tia said. "He indicated that Trevor was working out just fine. Maybe instead of more punishment, Trevor might thrive with a reward for his willing attitude."

Mariah West looked at Tia as if she were someone very foreign. "People don't usually think that way, Ms. Warden. Nobody rewards behavior like Trevor's."

"Not the stealing. He needs to pay the price for that," Tia assured the woman. "But he's been trying very hard. If the consequence for bad behavior is punishment, shouldn't the consequence for improved behavior be something more pleas-ant?"

The woman wore an expression so confused that Tia wanted to smile. "I've never met anyone like you before."

Tia patted her hand. "I've been told that, haven't I, Libby?"

"More than once."

Mariah didn't meet Tia's gaze when she spoke. "Me and Trevor aren't used to all this niceness."

Tia studied the woman and saw the tired circles beneath her eyes and the strain in her expression. Her clothes were cheap and simple but clean. Her nails were chewed to the quick.

No, I suppose you aren't. Tia had a hunch that Mariah's life and the people in it had been the antithesis of kind. To Mrs.

West she said, "Then humor me. It's fun to be nice once in a while."

Tears welled in the woman's eyes. One slid down her cheek and landed on the back of her hand as she clutched her cloth purse.

They were nearly the same age, Tia realized. Mrs. West had probably been no more than fifteen or sixteen when she'd given birth to her son. But she'd lived decades more in the same lifetime.

"Libby and I will talk to Reese. One of us can give you a call and tell you which day would be good for a riding lesson."

"Oh no! You can't do that!"

"But you just asked—," Tia started.

"You can't call, I mean. Trevor's daddy doesn't know anything about his stealing the music box or your letting him work it off. If he did . . ." A silent shudder ran through the woman's body. "You just can't call, that's all."

"Okay, fine," Tia backtracked quickly. "Then why don't you stop at the store in a couple days, and I'll have an answer for you. And now you'd better have a scone."

After Mrs. West had left and Tia and Libby had returned to the store, Tia gave Wendy the rest of the day off.

Libby dropped onto a stool behind the counter, put her elbows on it, and cupped her chin in her hands. "Now what was that all about with Mrs. West?"

Tia scowled. "There's something nasty going on in that home," she predicted. "And I haven't a clue as to what to do about it."

"You seem to be doing it," Libby observed. "Compassion goes a long way toward building trust."

"The woman has a constant deer-in-the-headlights expression in her eyes. What would make her look like that?"

"Mr. West, probably," Libby said frankly.

"I can't even figure out why that kid picked my place to rob," Tia sighed. "By rights, I should have had him taken to the juvenile unit, but I just couldn't. Something inside me rebelled at the whole idea."

"Then it's a good thing you listened to your insides, Tia. I'm not sure that woman or her son could have stood any other consequences."

CHAPTER SIX

The most famous starling is probably the one that belonged to the great composer Wolfgang Amadeus Mozart. Mozart bought the bird on May 27, 1784, in a pet shop. As the story goes, the composer was charmed by the bird's ability to imitate parts of his piano Concerto No. 17 in G Major. No one knows how the bird managed to learn it, but it may have heard Mozart whistle or hum the score, as was his habit, on a previous visit to the pet shop.

—*The Secret Lives of Birds*, Pierre Gingras

"Wake up, sleepyhead!" Libby's cheerful voice sang across the phone line.

Tia crossed her eyes and groaned. "Even the birds aren't up yet. Take two pillows, go back to sleep, and call me in the morning."

The phone rang again seconds later.

"Don't hang up on me this time," Libby pleaded breathlessly. "Wait until you hear what I've planned!"

"If it doesn't involve closed eyes, nightgowns, and sweet dreams, I don't want to hear it."

"I've got a very special day planned for the three of us at Reach Out Ranch. Something exciting. There is a guest coming to teach us . . . well, you'll just have to wait and see."

"Libby, I love you. I'd do anything for you. You are my dear, dear friend. That said, the answer is still no."

"You'll do *anything* for me? Then get out of bed right now. Jenny and I will pick you up in forty-five minutes. We'll bring coffee and bagels. You shower. Then we'll talk."

"But . . ." Tia scraped the hair out of her eyes and stretched like a kitten. There was no use calling Libby back. She had caller ID and wouldn't answer. Libby would rather arrive on the door-step and spirit her away, bedcovers and all.

Tia tested the cool floor with her big toe before putting her whole foot down, all the while muttering owlishly about her friends. She looked longingly at her tub, wishing for a bubble bath, then groaned and turned the shower on high.

A watery pounding and a clean pair of bib overalls later, Tia was ready. She sat on the front step with her elbows on her knees, her chin in her hands, allowing her hair to dry as she waited for her friends. She'd nearly dozed off by the time they arrived.

"Oh no you don't! You can't fall asleep out here. What do you think you are, a cat in the sun?" Libby greeted her cheerfully.

"Sounds good to me. I'll find a nice sunbeam to curl up in."

Libby grabbed Tia's arm before she could escape. "You're going to love this. Besides, don't we always say we need more 'ladies only' days? Well, I've planned one."

"And we have to enjoy it whether we like it or not, right?"

Libby grinned unsympathetically. "Get in the car. Jenny's got breakfast ready."

The inside of the vehicle smelled like a coffee shop. From the front seat Jenny poured a Colombian brew from a thermos into a plastic mug. She handed the cup to Tia in the backseat and asked, "Plain, onion, or wheat?"

"I'm feeling very plain this morning, thanks." Tia took the bagel Jenny held out.

"Regular cream cheese or pineapple flavored?"

"Pineapple. Why'd you bring onion bagels, anyway? Does anyone ever eat them for breakfast?"

"They were fresh." Jenny handed over a little plastic knife and a napkin.

"Aren't you supposed to have morning sickness or something?" Tia inhaled a whiff of coffee and felt her eyes becoming unglued. She opened them a crack at the streaming sunlight.

"I feel fantastic," Jenny said cheerfully. "Even my fingernails are healthier than usual."

Tia moaned.

"Feeling better?" Libby asked after Tia's second cup of coffee. They were nearing the therapy ranch.

"Good as I can at this time of day."

"You like getting up early!" Libby pointed out.

"On workdays, yes."

"Well, this is a play day and you'll like this even better." Libby hummed as she drove.

Jenny turned back to Tia. "Libby won't tell me what we're doing at the ranch. She just says we'll have a wonderful time."

"That's scary. Isn't Libby's idea of a wonderful time cooking and sewing?" Despite her facade of grumpiness, Tia was getting into the party spirit.

"Here we are!" Libby parked and jumped out. The director of the ranch was waiting for her. "Hi, Rollie."

"Hi, yourself. This is a great idea you had, Lib. We've got a full class, and our guest lecturer is very pleased. You'd better hurry. She's almost ready to begin."

"Begin *what?*" Tia asked suspiciously. All she could see were horses tied to hitching posts. Not her idea of a way to start the day. For Trevor it was fine, but not for her. Hadn't this been her idea of punishment?

"You'll see. It's fun and rewarding, too."

"Uh-oh," Jenny commented. "Libby's going to make us do something rewarding."

"I'm outta here." Tia made for the car, but Libby caught her by one of the seat pockets of her overalls and pulled her along to join the rest of the class.

"This is your horse," Libby said to Tia, pointing to a non-descript brown mare with an oddly shaped head and the most liquid brown eyes Tia had ever seen.

"She isn't wearing a saddle. Too bad. Time to leave."

Libby grabbed for Tia's back pocket again to introduce Tia to her horse. "We aren't going to ride them, silly."

"Then what do you expect us to do? Discuss current events?"

"We're going to massage them." Libby burst out laughing at the expression on Tia's face. "We have one of the country's finest equine massage therapists here to give a class on equissage. Once you learn how, you'll be able to come to the ranch and massage horses anytime you want."

"Oh yeah. That's something that's been missing in my life," Tia muttered.

"I think it sounds fun," Jenny said. "I've read about this in magazines."

Outnumbered—and without a key to Libby's car to escape—Tia relented. She patted the mare's back. "Nice horsey. Nice horsey. Do you feel better now?" Then she looked hopefully at Libby. "She says she's doing fine. Can we go?"

But before she got an answer, a trim, brisk woman in a bright cotton shirt and snug denim jeans strode out of the barn. She turned a high-wattage smile on the group. "Welcome to equine massage therapy, sports medicine for horses. My name is Jeannie Dokter."

Tia opened her mouth to protest, but Libby smiled benignly and put her finger to her lips. "Just listen," she whispered.

"Equissage isn't a substitute for veterinary medicine," the small woman continued. "Rather, it's a preventative measure. By breaking up the tight knots that restrict muscle extension, massage can prevent the muscle pulls and tears in horses that occur during training or competition. Not only does massage increase circulation, relieve tension, and increase range of motion—"

"I could use a massage myself," Tia whispered a bit too loudly.

Jeannie looked in her direction. "I can manage that, too—later. After our equine friends."

The sun was warm, and a light breeze kept flies away from the barn as they worked to learn such methods as compression, cross-fiber friction, and percussion on their large clients. The warm smell of horse—a combination of sweet hay, dust, and distinctive creature scent—the horse's glossy coat, and the unfailing patience of the animal somehow beguiled Tia into laying her cheek against the horse's neck and closing her eyes.

Tia could feel the mare's flesh shiver beneath her skin as a fly landed on the horse's flank, and she could smell the dusky warm scent of hide and fragrant hay. The mare, China Doll, relaxed and, unperturbed, gave a contented sigh and licked her lips, signaling that all was right in her world. It was an experience that Tia had never dreamed she could enjoy. But she did.

"I see you're getting into this." The instructor was smiling at Tia when she opened her eyes.

"Amazing, since I'm really not a horse person. At least I didn't think I was." She scratched China Doll's ears. "Not until you came along, pretty girl."

"There are instructors who can teach you the full spectrum of massage techniques," Jeannie said. "Today is just an introduction; I'm not covering the physiology of muscles, but if you'd like to learn more . . ."

Tia was about to tell her that Libby was the one to talk to when China Doll began to nuzzle the top of Tia's head. Tia reached up and brushed the velvet softness above the horse's upper lip. A contented little nicker tickled Tia's ear.

"Maybe," she found herself saying, "if Libby were to do it,

I might come along." *I can check on Trevor at the same time. I wonder how much of that music box he's worked off so far.*

"Good. Rollie would like several volunteers to learn massage for the benefit of the horses. He feels that such fine servants of the clients here deserve a little extra pampering themselves. I'll tell him to sign you up."

Just then the subject of their conversation walked up behind China Doll to join them.

"Why do you keep your hand on her like that?" Tia asked as Rollie rounded the horse with his hand on the animal's rump.

"To let her know where I am. Never walk behind a horse you don't know and even with the ones that are familiar, keep talking and touching. You've got to let them know you're there or they might startle. Those hind legs are powerful. You don't want them kicking out."

"But she's so sweet!" The horse nuzzled Tia's hair again.

"Humph," Rollie mumbled. "You can't let her lose her manners either."

"What manners?"

"The ones that give you some personal space. It might feel good to have a horse cozy up to you, but if another horse comes along and startles her, she's going to jump out of the way—whether you're standing next to her or not."

"I can't believe she'd . . . uh—"

Just then a bumblebee landed on China Doll's nose. With a shake of her head to rid herself of the pest, China Doll managed to step sideways and force Tia to dive to the ground in a cloud of dust.

"What happened?" An embarrassed blush crept to the roots of Tia's hair.

"I guess she forgot her manners," Rollie said dryly as he extended a hand to help her up.

Tia dusted her hands across her rear, raising another cloud of dust. "That's unusual. I'm usually such a stable person. Get it? *Stable* person."

Rollie shook his head. "If you're going to be spending time out here, you've got a lot to learn. You need to take lessons with that boy you brought out."

"How's he doing so far?"

Rollie frowned. "He's trying. But I never saw a youngster so uneducated about animals, nature, or anything else. It's as if he grew up in a barrel."

"That's odd. His mother seems concerned about his education."

"Yeah . . . about that." Rollie scratched his head. "Is everything okay in that home of his?"

"Far as I know. Of course, kids who get into trouble often have problems at home. Why?"

"Just something he said."

Rollie didn't seem inclined to divulge more, but Tia was not about to let him get by with that. "What do you mean?"

"Oh, we were talking about driving a buggy and how some of the more disabled kids who can't sit on a horse can still be in a buggy. Anyway, Trevor asked who 'beat the horse to make it go.' "

"Beat a horse?" Tia knew that concept was not welcome here.

"He said his dad talked about beating horses and dogs . . . and kids when they were bad."

"Let me know if he ever comes here with a bruise, will you, Rollie?" Tia asked calmly, even though her heart was thumping. "Never hurts to be safe."

It wasn't until hours later, on the way back to her town house, that Tia fully realized what she had done.

"I actually volunteered to massage horses!" She sat in the backseat, a shell-shocked expression on her features. "Me."

Libby smiled serenely at her in the rearview mirror. "Told you so."

Tia slouched against the seat back. "I've been under a lot of stress lately. It was something about the combination of sun, fresh air, and an animal that smelled like sweet grass. . . . I flipped out for a few seconds."

"Actually, I think for once you flipped *in*. You were the old Tia, the one we know and love. You can't continue to live like you have been—work, work, and more work. You've got to have other outlets—like horses," Libby said.

"I have you guys."

"We can't make up for an obsession with your business," Jenny commented. "Things have tilted out of balance, haven't they?"

"Kind of." Tia couldn't argue. "Other than you, even my social life is work related." The hours she and Brandon spent together were growing more and more important to her.

"You haven't been at church much lately," Jenny observed. "Is that out of balance, too?"

"You know how to hit where it hurts, don't you?"

"Just reminding you where your real strength lies."

Maybe both Brandon and I have been mouthing the right words without putting our hearts behind them. The thought left Tia aching.

. . . .

Tia was surprised to find Brandon at the store when she arrived. He was dressed in casual clothing—dark trousers; a dark teal, short-sleeved silk shirt; and hand-laced leather moccasins. Brandon in casual dress was more dapper than another man in a suit.

"You're here ear—" Tia gasped as he circled her waist with his arm and planted an enthusiastic and delicious kiss on her lips "—early." Her nostrils were filled with the woodsy—and expensive—scent of him, and her lips burned with a sweet fire.

"I had to show this to someone. My sister is traveling, and the only other one I know who would understand is you." He pulled out a folder of pages filled with numbers. "Look at the sales figures for Beacons for the past six months. It's going through the roof!"

Business? *That* was what was exciting him?

"Don't you see, Tia? If my sister's little company is doing this well, there's no telling what I—and you—can do with your stores. This is exciting news!"

"Wonderful." She glanced at the pages. "Looks great."

"I see fantastic things in store for us, Tia. This is just one small signal that the gift business is booming. I think we can double my money within the year."

We *can double* his *money. What about doubling* our *money? And why am I being such an adolescent?* Still, that *we* comment had sounded very nice.

Tia hustled inside without showing him her face. She felt as if she'd awakened on the other side of the glass mirror in Wonderland and the white rabbit was really a dark-haired man with pale blue eyes. A mutter of frustration slipped from her lips.

"Hmmm?"

"Oh, nothing—just a brain burp." White rabbits, indeed. What she needed was a serious dose of common sense.

"You look odd." Brandon peered into her face, his pale eyes puzzled and concerned.

She felt odd, too, but she wasn't about to admit it. "I got up early. I'm not a morning person."

"Then let's go out for coffee. I've got some great ideas that I want to share with you."

"Can we swing through here on the way?" Brandon pulled into a huge commercial lot filled with boats as big as semitrailers.

Or maybe they were called "yachts" when they'd grown this large, Tia mused.

"Look at that baby." Brandon pointed to a cabin cruiser of enormous proportions. "One like that is going to be mine some- day."

"Why?"

He glanced over at her in surprise. "Why not?"

"Because you could feed—no, *buy*—a small country for the cost of that thing."

"I could take it through the Great Lakes . . ."

"You could build another women's crisis shelter. Or add a wing to the one I work at now."

"What an experience that would be—the water, the winds . . ."

"You'd feel wonderful about yourself and think of all the good you'd do." Tia knew she was talking to a blank wall as Brandon's full attention was riveted elsewhere, but she spoke anyway. It must be a guy thing, she thought. It was certainly not something that interested her.

There had been a subtle shift in her thinking over the past few months. "Things" held less appeal than ever before. And people meant more. To her, this boat was a symbol of the ultimate "thing"—one more item to care for, store, clean, paint, polish, or fix—a burden.

Thankfully it didn't take Brandon long to shift his attention to the business at hand after they'd left the lot.

He was still talking advertising budgets and expansion possibilities when breakfast was over. "I found an excellent furniture designer. I'd like to add a few smaller pieces to our lines. His leather is incredible. Maybe a contemporary sling chair or two and an ottoman . . ."

"I researched furniture early on and decided it wasn't for me, Brandon. I—"

"Nothing big. Just a few floor models to let our customers know that we can do catalog orders."

"I don't want to hire another interior decorator."

"We don't need that. Here's my idea. . . ."

When Tia got back to the store and Brandon had departed, her head was still swimming. She wasn't even sure what he'd talked her into!

. . . .

When in doubt, have a party.

Tia's cooking skills, dubious by Jenny's or Libby's standards, consisted of making the rounds—delis, grocery stores, take-out joints—where, over the years, she had found the best non-homemade fried chicken, baked beans, potato salad, and cheesecake. That and a package of decorative paper plates plus invitations to her friends' families, Brandon, Dorothy, and Ellen, a friend from church, were a party waiting to happen.

"Do you have pickles?" Libby asked as she entered Tia's pristine black-and-white kitchen. "And chips?"

"Of course. Don't you trust me?"

"Tia, I'd trust you with my life—just not in the kitchen."

"Who's coming? The entire navy?"

"Do you think I have too much food?" Tia studied the over-flowing table.

"Not for three dozen people."

"It's just us. I invited Dorothy, Ellen, and Brandon, but Ellen called earlier to say she got company, so—"

"So we finally get to spend some real time with Brandon Ainsley! It's about time, don't you think, Libby?" Jenny finished slicing pickles into a bowl and washed her hands in the sink. "We usually get to interrogate the men in your life much sooner than this. Every time we've met, you've whisked him away the first chance you get."

"Not man," Tia warned. "Business partner."

"Is that what *you* think when you're together?" Libby asked.

"Sure, he's bright, articulate, charming . . . and cute in a *GQ* sort of way, but . . ." Tia knew immediately that she'd erred. Her two friends were all over her like wrapping paper on Christmas presents.

Libby leaned against the counter, crossed her arms over her

chest, and studied her friend. "Is this your way of admitting that this might be something more after all?"

Tia looked down at the black-and-white floor. "Is there some chemistry between us that makes me want to spend more and more time with him? Definitely. Is there a voice screaming in my head telling me to back off and remember this is a business arrangement? You bet."

There. It was out.

Libby put her arms around Tia and whispered, "Oh, honey, I hope this works out for you—however God has it planned."

"Me, too, kiddo," Jenny added.

Tia's heart was thumping hard in her chest. Saying she cared about Brandon made her feel vulnerable and at risk. She was accustomed to independence, to being the captain of her own ship. Admitting what she felt for Brandon frightened—and thrilled—her.

Just then Luke skidded into the kitchen, holding a pair of old shoes with something round and metallic glued to the bottoms. "Hey, Tia, what's this? Weird."

"Give me those!" Tia lunged for the shoes, but Jenny whisked them out of her son's hands and handed them to Libby.

"I want to know, too." Libby stared at the odd contraptions. "What *are* these things?"

"None of your business." A blush crept up Tia's neck and spilled onto her cheeks. "Give them to me, and pretend you never saw them."

"These are shoes, Tia, not contraband. But why are bottle caps glued to the heels and toes?" Libby said.

"Something I won't admit even to you—so give them back. And, Jenny, tell your son to quit looking in my closet!"

"They were on the dining-room floor by your stereo, honest! I didn't go into your closet."

"Sorry, Luke, I didn't mean to snap at you. I was just trying to keep this my own little secret, but now I suppose I'll *have* to show you." Tia reluctantly kicked off her shoes and slipped the others on. "Luke, start the CD that's in the player."

Strains of "Boogie-Woogie Bugle Boy from Company B" filled the air. Tia did an embarrassed little shuffle to demonstrate her strange invention.

"You're tap-dancing!" Libby blurted.

As the music picked up its pace, so did Tia, until she was giving a vigorous, toe-tapping performance. After a few final step-shuffle-steps, Tia, winded, stopped to lean against the counter. "Okay, so now you know."

"Cool!" Luke crowed. "I like how it sounds!"

Jenny and Libby were speechless as they stared at the homemade tap shoes Tia kicked off with a clatter. "I needed a little exercise, all right?" Tia explained defensively. "I can't stand those boring tapes or classes, so I thought I'd invent my own exercises. I started aerobic dancing, but that was dull, too—"

"So you made tap shoes so you could make noise while you were exercising," Libby concluded.

"You want to try them?" Tia held out the shoes. "I've lost half an inch on each thigh. I'm going to buy real tap shoes soon because they've got to be easier to maneuver in than these things. Be careful that you don't fall."

"Half an inch? On each thigh? Why didn't you say so? Give them to me!" Libby lunged for the shoes.

Moments later Mike walked into the kitchen and cheerfully inquired, "What's going on?" Then he looked at Jenny and Libby, each wearing one shoe and pawing the floor like crazed Rockettes, and his expression grew wary. "Never mind. I don't want to know."

"Getting hungry?" Libby asked and gave a little heel-toe tap with her bottle-cap-shod foot.

Mike slowly backed out of the kitchen. "Whatever you guys are cooking in here, Reese and I don't want any."

Luke followed his father, saying, "I'll tell you what they were doing, Dad. Tia made these cool shoes . . ."

Dorothy had arrived and all the food was on the table when the telephone rang. Tia hurried to answer it. When she returned, her face showed her disappointment.

"Trouble?" Reese asked.

"That was Brandon. He can't make it. Something about bookwork for the business he has with his sister." Tia wore a game smile. "Too bad for him. This food looks great—even if I did have to buy it myself!"

Her friends, obviously seeing that this was not the time to ask questions, gathered around the table and bowed their heads to pray. "Heavenly Father," Jenny began, "thank you for food and family and friendship. You have made us so rich that words cannot adequately express our gratitude. And you aren't done with us yet, Father. Show each one of us what our path in life should be. Amen."

It was difficult to smile and crack jokes when your gut was doing crunches, Tia discovered. And it was virtually impossible to eat. She didn't buy the bookkeeping thing, Tia thought as she played with her salad. That could be done anytime. Who did he think he was fooling?

After dinner, she caught a glimpse of herself in the mirror over the buffet, shored up her unsteady smile, and straightened her spine. If Brandon wanted to miss a great party, that was his problem. *His* problem. There was no use making it her own.

It wasn't worth mulling over an unanswerable question or moping about something she couldn't control. Her innate resilience kicked in. She was always the first to remind others that it wasn't what happened to you so much as how you responded to it.

Okay, lady, it's time to practice what you preach! By sheer will, she was the ultimate hostess for the rest of the evening.

When the last guest had departed, Tia picked up her goofy homemade tap shoes and tucked them into the closet. She moved into the bathroom, brushed her teeth, and put on her nightgown.

Back in her room she took a photo album from a shelf. On the album she had written Matthew 6:1 in glittery gold ink: *"Take care! Don't do your good deeds publicly, to be admired, because then you will lose the reward from your Father in heaven."*

Curling her feet under her on the bed, Tia opened the book and stared down at the photo before her.

She traced her finger over the outline of the small face in the picture. "Hello, Maria . . . Juan . . ." She went through the photos of the children—her children—one by one. Some of them she had supported financially through her church for years. Others were new. She prayed for each child and for his or her family, for their health, for their relationship with their heavenly Father.

When she was done praying for this secret family of hers—not even Jenny and Libby realized the large number of children to whom she was committed—her mind was at ease again and her heart lighter.

If Brandon Ainsley occasionally disappointed her, she could take it. Her responsibility was to do her best not to disappoint her heavenly Father—in business, through the children she supported, in her attitude.

"Father, what would you have me do?" The whispered question encompassed decisions affecting her lifetime—her business, Birdhouse Ministries, Brandon. Knowing that she had asked the right question of the right person, Tia laid her head on the pillow and promptly fell into a deep, peaceful sleep.

CHAPTER SEVEN

Mallard: In early spring, mallard pairs arrive at their breeding ground at the tail end of an intricate series of courtship rituals. Males splash water off their bills at preferred mates and also engage in tail-shaking. Meanwhile, females attempt to beguile their suitors with flirtatious, over-the-shoulder flicks of the bill.

—*Birds: An Explore Your World Handbook,* Discovery Books and David Bird

"What if he hurts himself?"

"Quit worrying, Libby. Reese is a big boy. He knows what he's doing." Tia popped a grape into her mouth and crossed her feet at the ankles as she draped over Libby's sofa like a boneless cat.

"Easy for you to say. He's not your husband."

"Take it easy, Lib," Jenny chided. "If Reese feels ready to race, then he should race. It's not as if he hasn't been working at it hard enough. His arms must be as thick as Arnold Schwarzenegger's from punching the wheels of that chair."

"He *is* daring and a live-life-on-the-edge kind of guy. I just don't know . . ."

"Think of it this way," Tia said bluntly. "What's the worst that could happen? That he'd end up in a wheelchair?"

Libby threw a pillow at Tia. "I'm looking for sympathy and support. You're no help at all."

"But I'll bet I could be," Tia said. "I ran track in high school. I could be his coach."

"He already has a trainer."

"A morale-building coach then. You obviously don't want to do it," Tia replied.

"I love him so much that the thought of his getting hurt . . ."

"He might be just as hurt if you pack him in cotton batting and don't let him live his life."

Libby looked at Tia and sighed. "You're right. You and Reese are much more alike in personality than he and I are. You understand him, don't you?"

"Sure. It takes one to know one. In this case, it takes one risk taker to know another risk taker." Tia smiled comfortingly. "And that's why we both love you—because you are solid, steady, reliable, and take as few risks as possible. You are the human 'home' we can return to when we're exhausted from running headlong into foolhardy adventures and daring exploits."

"That makes you sound like Rocky and Bullwinkle," Jenny observed.

"I want a squirrel just like the squirrel that married dear old Dad," Tia sang. Until, that is, Libby stuffed an entire bunch of grapes into her mouth.

"Okay, enough about Reese," Tia said, spluttering out the grapes. "What else is new?"

"You haven't said much about your life lately," Libby commented.

"Work, work, work."

Brandon had begun arriving regularly at closing time to invite her to dinner. Sometimes they ordered pizza and spent the evening stocking shelves or dusting. And—Tia felt heat rise in her cheeks—there had been more good-bye kisses than good-bye handshakes at the end of the evenings. All her dreams—for her business, her relationships, her life—were becoming tied up in one man. He held her heart in his hand.

When Tia remained silent, Jenny made her own announcement. "I'm going for an ultrasound on Thursday. Mike has got a big job to bid out of town that day. I was wondering if either of you would like to go with me—"

"Would we? You bet! I'd love to see that little one on film. How exciting! I . . . oh . . ." Libby's face fell. "Robert has an appointment with a specialist on Thursday. We've waited over three months to get in."

"It's okay, Lib. There will be other ultrasounds."

"*I'm* free," Tia pronounced. "That's one thing about being your own boss. You can give yourself a day off—without pay, of course."

"So you'll come?"

"I wouldn't miss it."

. . . .

Tia was as excited as Jenny as they waited in a dimly lit examining room filled with space-age equipment and television monitors. While the technician was applying a goopy gel to Jenny's belly, Tia studied the screens and squirmed in anticipation.

As the technician moved the wand over Jenny's belly, a flickering black-and-white image came on the screen.

"What do you see?" Jenny asked breathlessly.

"Nothing" would have been Tia's answer, but the technician said, "A full bladder—here. Oh! Now it's an empty bladder. And a beating heart . . ."

"Can you tell if it's a boy or a girl?" Jenny asked, her eyes riveted to the screen.

"We can take a look if you want."

Jenny squeezed Tia's hand. "What do you think?"

"Have you discussed this with Mike?"

"Yes. It's fine with him. He says then he won't have to paint the nursery twice." Jenny frowned. "Does this feel like cheating, somehow?"

"Times have changed, Jen. Men have been on the moon. The millennium has come and gone. You can buy computers with a gigabit or more and high-definition televisions that are so realistic you feel as though you can pick the flowers off the screen. Because of technology now you *can* know if you want to."

"When you put it that way—" Jenny's eyes brightened—"I want to know!"

Obligingly the technician continued to search the surface of Jenny's belly for the clues inside. Tia stared at the images fluttering on the screen.

"Uhmmm. Hamburger. Congratulations." The technician grinned.

"We want to know the sex, not the grocery list!" Tia said.

"*Hamburger* is the term we use for a little girl. See?" She put her finger on the screen to point to the pertinent information.

"Did you say a girl?" Jenny whispered.

"A girl!" Tia bounced on the tips of her toes. "We're having a girl! Isn't that great?"

Jenny couldn't answer. She was crying.

Tia marveled as the screen continued to change. A bit of hand, clenching and unclenching, a burp, the outline of a skull, a tiny spine. What a miraculous gift, to be able to look through a mother's belly and see the child inside. And what a wonderful and fearful thing to create! Not a cute toy slightly more complicated than a puppy, not a possession, not an answer to a selfish desire, not a permanently lovable doll to take on parade. Instead, this child would become a willful toddler, a rebellious teenager, and finally, hopefully, a beautiful young person who will one day start a family of her own.

Then a thought occurred to Tia. "If girls are hamburger to you, what are boys?"

"In the vernacular of this lab, they are turtles."

"You mean as in thick and slow?"

The technician laughed. "No, but it's a thought."

As Jenny and the technician conversed softly, Tia's thoughts took their own path. Every infant was one more child for God to love, a timeless soul once born, who would live for all eternity. That baby in Jenny's belly would live out a life on earth and then, if she accepted Christ as her Savior, would live forever with other Christians in the heaven God created just for them. Or if she did not embrace Christ's gift . . . Tia shuddered.

Eternity was overwhelming to think about because it was so vast, so long, so *unending*. Nothing on earth was permanent. Even rock wore away eventually. But in the time it took for drops of water to erode a stone, eternity would have barely begun. The words of the hymn "Amazing Grace" always reminded Tia how long Christians would have to spend with God—and unbelievers apart from him in a place so horrible it was beyond her imagination. "When we've been there ten thousand years, . . . we've no less days to sing God's praise than when we'd first begun."

"Tia? Tia? Did you see it?" Jenny was looking at her eagerly, eyes glowing.

"Awesome, Jen. Totally awesome."

"Yes." Jenny sank back with a madonna-like smile on her features. "It is."

They were silent as they drove to a nearby café for lunch, each wrapped in her own thoughts.

It wasn't until they'd ordered the day's special and iced tea that Tia finally spoke. "I am so honored that you allowed me to come with you today, Jen. I saw a miracle in progress. Thank you."

"If Mike couldn't be with me, then who better than you?"

"Libby missed something really special."

"I wish the three of us could have shared it," Jenny mused. "Like we've shared so many other parts of our lives."

"From the look of it, we'll have more ultrasounds to share. I doubt you'll stop at just one child—and who knows about Libby!"

Jenny's face lit with joy. "Oh, wouldn't it be wonderful? And you . . ."

Tia shook her head. "Don't count on me getting on the bandwagon in that area, Jen. I'm not at the same place in my life. A few little details are missing—like a husband, for one."

"That may change soon," Jenny said hopefully.

"Nine months is a long time to be tied up growing a baby. I'm not sure I could give up junk food and live on—" Tia shuddered—"*vegetables* for that long." Then, with her usual quirky twist, she added, "Of course, maybe we should be grateful. How long does it take for an elephant to grow a baby, anyway? Almost two years. Imagine that! And you're afraid you'll be tired of maternity clothes in six months. And the birth! Baby elephants weigh two hundred and fifty pounds at birth. What kind of a delivery would that be unless, of course, you weighed six tons?"

"You're not helping," Jenny scolded, laughing. "Now I have this image in my mind."

"Don't worry. We already know it's just a little bundle. Did you see the size of those fingers and toes? Miniscule! Now compare that to an elephant's foot!"

. . . .

The next morning Tia was still thinking about the black-and-white slices of X rays that were Jenny's baby. They had made Jenny's child a reality, and it was all Tia could do to keep from opening catalogs and ordering every nursery item in sight.

She'd barely heard her office door open and was startled to see Brandon standing in front of her desk with a pink rose in his hand. "What's this?" Tia asked.

"You are the kind of woman who should be surrounded by fresh flowers every day but—" he surveyed the clutter on her desk—"I decided that this was all you had room for." He put it down between her computer monitor and a stack of catalogs.

"You've got that right." Tia shoved ineffectively at the paper. "No one told me that when I opened a new store the paperwork would turn into the Library of Congress!"

She picked up the rose and brushed the velvety petals beneath her nose. "Ummm . . . you didn't need to do this, Brandon. We're *working* today. We have a lot of business to discuss."

"Maybe the rose is for me to enjoy, too. Did you think of that?"

"Not really . . ."

"But you'll let me bring you an occasional flower without giving me any more trouble."

"Do I have a choice?" Tia asked.

It seemed to Tia that Brandon was genetically unable to take the edge off his charm even while they were working. She was usually pleasantly distracted by him, but today needed to be different. Her list of items to discuss was more critical than usual.

"Brandon, about those orders you placed for the Ribbons & Rainbows grand opening. Our sell-through was terrible on the—"

"Coffee? I brought bagels, too."

"I've already had a cup."

"With walnut-and-honey-flavored cream cheese." He dangled a bag from Jenny's bakery in front of her nose.

"We have to talk about those prepackaged gift baskets. I think we had more left after the sale than before we started!"

"Okay, so they didn't sell as well as I'd thought. It's no big deal, Tia. We'll send them back."

"And pay shipping costs both ways? That's a sure recipe for losing money, Brandon."

"Then chalk it up to my education."

She rubbed the sore spot between her eyes. "It's not that easy. You've got to trust me to make the stocking decisions for the store."

"And you will leave me completely alone with the advertising end of it?"

Touché. She hadn't kept her nose out of his affairs either—checking and rechecking copy, changing ad sizes, and second-guessing his timing.

"I've been running this business alone for a long, long time. . . ."

"Don't try to explain." He put his hand on her sleeve. Tia felt as if the heat of his fingers would sear right through the arm of her suit. "We'll learn together." Then he flashed the conspiratorial, knowing smile that made her mind feel laid bare and vulnerable to his charm.

"Now, about these vouchers . . ."

"We'll bring them with us." He began to gather the piles of paper on her desk.

"Wait! Don't mess that up! Bring them where? It's the middle of the morning!"

"That's why we have to get going. I told them we'd be there by noon."

"Who? What?" Tia found herself being gently but firmly dragged to the car.

"I found the most amazing toy factory only two hours from here. I think we should consider ordering from them. And since you are solely in charge of those decisions now, I want you to see it. I made an appointment with the owner."

"You made an appointment without consulting me?" Tia squawked. Jenny and Libby were the only ones allowed to kidnap her and drag her off to parts unknown. She was about to give him a piece of her mind when something else clicked in. *Toys.* Jenny's baby.

"What kinds of toys?"

"Wooden ones. The old-fashioned kind you see in photos of nurseries of the royal family, that sort of thing. They are works of art, Tia. First class. I even saw a baby's hand-turned drinking mug."

"Who'd give a baby a wooden cup?"

Still, her curiosity was piqued. She loved to buy from local artists and craftspeople, and part of her fun was discovering them. This did have promise.

So, ignoring the independent rebel screaming inside her, Tia tucked her hand into Brandon's and kept pace beside him to the car.

"You were right, Brandon. Those toys are fabulous."

They'd stopped at a small café overlooking a lake after the appointment with the toy maker and sat on the porch, stirring their straws in the cold glasses of freshly made, pulpy lemonade.

"We should place an order. They'll sell like hotcakes."

Tia stirred her lemonade a moment before answering. "I don't agree."

His blue eyes clouded. "What?"

"They're too expensive. I'd love to have some on hand for grandparents who think nothing is too good for their grandchild, but for most people, spending that kind of money on toys would be a hardship. Frankly, those items are more for collectors than for children. I can't carry that much in inventory, and lovely as they are, they won't turn over quickly enough."

Tia hoped she wasn't upsetting him, but she needed to take back the reins in the store. His tastes were simply too rich to be practical. He dismissed tuna for caviar, off-the-rack clothing for designer brands, and inexpensive toys for toy-shaped artwork.

His eyes crinkled in a smile. "Let's not talk business right now." He reached across the table and laid his hand on her arm.

His easy acquiescence surprised and relieved her, but she knew the topic would come up again. When he didn't get the answer he wanted, Brandon changed the subject—for the time being. Tia had never minded being "the boss." But the thin line between business and friendship was infinitely smaller with Brandon, and she was never quite sure when one of them was overstepping the boundary.

"What is there to talk about except business?"

"That's both your problem and your charm, Tia. Sometimes you actually don't seem to know." Brandon pushed away from the table. "Let's go for a walk."

"Here?" She wasn't even sure where she was.

"Why not?"

They strolled out of the café and down the main street of town, past a drugstore, a hardware store, a small park, and an implement dealership with a half-dozen pickup trucks parked outside. At the far end of the street stood a white, steepled church, its doors flung wide. A true Norman Rockwell vision of small-town life.

"Let's go inside." Tia tugged on Brandon's hand, which had somehow slipped around her own.

"That's someone else's church." She felt him balk and pull away.

"It's God's church. He is an all-inclusive God, you know."

"When I was a kid, we weren't allowed in the church unless there was a youth meeting or services going on."

"How sad." Tia tipped her head to look at the spire. "I used to go into the church and sit in the back row just to think."

"You did?"

"And sometimes I came to stare at the stained-glass windows. My favorite in our church was of the martyr Stephen. I was fascinated by the depiction of the angry crowd throwing stones and him just lying there, accepting it and praying for those who condemned him. It seemed both gory and grand to me. And so brave. I knew Stephen had to have had great faith."

Tia walked into the church and made a pleased sound at the

gleaming wood of the finely crafted pews, the simple, respectful altar, and the lovely pipe organ. "I'd like to come to church here someday."

"Why?"

"Because God is here and he is loved."

"How do you know that?"

"Look around." She pointed to the foyer where several booths had been set, each with literature, a sign-up sheet, and photos: "Food Pantry, Singles' Ministries, Day Camp for Kids, Rides for Seniors, Bible Study. This church cares about people. They take care of God's children."

As they left the building, Tia felt Brandon staring at her with a mixture of puzzlement and affection. "What are you thinking?" she asked.

"Isn't it strange?" He paused on the sidewalk to look back at the church. "That you and I met such a different God in our childhoods. The one my grandparents introduced me to was stern, righteous, and judgmental."

"He can be," Tia said simply, "but mostly God is about love."

"Not according to them. I always thought the God they preached about was rather cruel." Then, with a complete and sudden about-face, Brandon smiled. "Don't look so somber, Tia! I was a rotten little boy—curious, mischievous, and with an acute sense of selective hearing. It was probably the only way my parents thought they *could* make me behave."

"But . . ."

"Enough about me." He touched her cheek with the tip of his finger, and Tia felt her skin ignite. "What about us?"

She collected her leapfrogging thoughts from the mental puddle of her brain and stammered, "G-good question. I think we should sit down and really discuss ordering those toys we saw today. I know you wanted to make a tentative verbal commitment for an order, and I just don't think—"

"About *us*, Tia! Not about the store!"

That slam-dunked her right through the hoop and left her dribbling on the sidewalk. "The only 'us' needs to be the store." She knew she didn't sound as if she meant it.

"Not anymore. Not for me."

He took her hand and led her into a small white gazebo in the tiny parklike area near the church. Two geese bobbed on a pond nearby, and a bee hovered over a rosebush. Brandon guided her to a bench inside the gazebo, and Tia had a fleeting vision of herself as Liesl in *The Sound of Music*. Would he break into song next?

"I care very deeply for you, Tia. And it's not just because you're a good businesswoman."

Her silence was so complete that the bee's drone sounded like a 747 circling overhead. The geese scrambled out of the water, shook their feathers, and began foraging for buggy canapés in the grass.

"I . . . I . . ." Tia's eyes opened wide. "I'm *speechless!* And I don't think I've *ever* been that before!"

Brandon's indulgent smile widened. "And that's why I care about you. You are funny, witty, outspoken, bright . . . and," he added with obvious pleasure, "totally off the wall."

"That's a *good* thing?"

Something sad and dark flickered across his features but lasted only a second. "That's the best thing, Tia. I've never met anyone quite like you. I grew up in a work-oriented, critical, beware-of-the-wrath-of-God environment. It made my sister into a perfectionist—there's no other way she could do the kind of detailed work she does unless she was driven by some internal engine that demands such excellence of herself."

"What did it make of you?"

"An overachiever. Single-minded. Obsessive. Cynical. A skeptic."

"Not a very pretty grocery list of attributes."

"I'd never seen another sort of role model that made me doubt that my way was best—until I met you. I know you're keeping me at arm's length, Tia. And you keep saying you can't mix business and pleasure. But I still had to tell you. . . . I think you care about me as much as I care for you. I know you keep trying to rebuff me, but I can't give up. You've become too important to me."

Too important to me. The words continued to ring in Tia's ears long after Brandon had dropped her off at her house. He'd rattled her to the core, she realized, with his profession of affection. That made it seem *real.* And made her feel she needed to take her own stand, to give him a response.

So Tia escaped to the one place that allowed her no time for thoughts of herself.

"You aren't on the schedule for this evening," Helen Anderson greeted her as Tia entered the crisis center in jeans, sweatshirt, and flip-flops.

"I know, but I thought you might be able to use my help anyway. It is Friday night."

Helen rolled her eyes. "We can use you any night, kiddo. The phones have already started ringing. She nodded to a carrel containing a telephone and a notepad. "Help yourself."

Tia had volunteered at the Battered Women's Crisis Center off and on for several years, covering occasional weekends for the safe house director, manning the telephone, fielding calls from hurting, terrified women as they came in.

Libby and Jenny had always said that of the three of them, Tia was best suited for the adrenaline-pumping atmosphere of the hot-line room on a weekend night. While Libby volunteered to bake for fund-raisers and Jenny took regular turns in the church nursery, Tia had to be on the front lines, doing battle with evil in the form of violent husbands spurred on by alcohol, drugs, and frustration with their own lives.

Tia was "mentally tough," Libby claimed, a quality needed for the situations she encountered over the telephone and in the lives of the women who called.

"Why is it that everyone in the world seems to love a weekend except me?" Helen asked wearily. She set a cup of thick dark coffee on the desk by Tia.

"Because *you* keep peeking at the seamy underbelly of a Saturday night. Booze, drugs, anger at the boss, financial problems, fatigue—all the stuff that people manage to control during the week and don't release until Friday night comes around." Tia tapped the tip of her pen on the desk. "And you get to see what angry people do to their spouses, the people they *love*."

"Well, whoever invented the phrase 'Thank goodness it's Friday' didn't work here."

Helen was a woman of indeterminate age, with long brown hair streaked with gray that she wore pulled back with a clip, rubber band, or whatever was on hand. Tonight it was a twist tie from a garbage bag. There were lines in her face and a weariness in her eyes that had nothing to do with age or hours of sleep. She was so good at what she did here at the center because she had lived with a batterer herself. She must have heard or used every excuse as to why a man hit his wife, and she had a succinct response for every one. It all boiled down to the fact that men should *never* hit or injure a woman no matter how tired, frustrated, unemployed, high, or drunk they were.

"I haven't been able to get the idea we tossed around out of my mind," Tia said. "Birdhouse Ministries is burning inside me like—"

"A case of heartburn?" Helen drawled.

"Exactly! It's not comfortable because it could become such a huge project, and yet I still can't get rid of the idea!"

"There's no over-the-counter remedy either." Helen rolled her coffee mug in her palms, then set it down. "It's haunted me as much as it has you. We do all we can for the women here, but you're right—there's little joy in their lives. We have plenty of fear, pain, anger, rage, hurt, confusion—" she looked up— "sounds like a dandy place, doesn't it?"

"It *is* a dandy place! If I could have a room here, or a desk, I'd set up shop, find volunteers, implement the ideas. Can you give me a *nest,* Helen, so I can *hatch* some of my ideas?"

"There's an office the size of a wren house next to mine. Can you work standing up?"

"My best position. Thank you." Tia reached out her arms and threw them around Helen's thin shoulders, and another idea for Birdhouse Ministries popped into her head—a *hugging* ministry. Everyone needed human touch. The women here had been touched in anger. Maybe something as simple as knowing there were people here willing to hold a hand and listen.

"Whenever I'm feeling sorry for myself, it helps to come here," Tia admitted. "It immediately puts my cushy life in perspective."

Helen sipped her coffee and leaned against the carrel. "So what problem brings you here tonight?"

Tia scraped her hands through her dark hair and wished for one of Helen's twist ties for her own use. "I'm not even sure it's a problem. A man with whom I have business dealings wants to get romantically involved."

"Stop the presses! Call the cops! This is serious!" Helen grinned. "I'm counting on you to know a healthy man from an unhealthy one, of course."

"I hope your trust isn't misplaced. I rarely think of a man in terms of a possible relationship. I'm not even sure I know what I want or need. Besides, when I'm around him I can't think straight enough to make any sort of reliable decisions."

"So the independent, self-sufficient Tia has finally met her match." Helen looked amused. Then her expression changed. "Be wise, Tia. We see again and again what a bad choice of a mate can do to a woman."

Just then Tia's phone rang. Helen turned away as Tia was transported into another woman's world of fear and confusion, left to walk through the caller's crises with her.

CHAPTER EIGHT

The most famous duck in the world, Donald, is a Pekin duck—
a white breed of our common mallard. Donald is less portly than many
domesticated ducks but he still can't fly—he apparently limits filming
to summer when he's molting. . . . One of the greatest complications
in Donald's life is due to a natural characteristic of Pekin ducks—
females often lay their eggs in inappropriate places, and overall make
somewhat poor mothers. This explains why Donald so often ends up
taking care of his three nephews, Huey, Dewey and Louie.

—*For the Birds: An Uncommon Guide,* Laura Erickson

"Have you got plans for tonight?" Tia inquired as Jenny and Libby drank tea at Tia's kitchen table.

"Not me. Reese is working out."

"There's a gardening seminar at How Does Your Garden Grow? That means a late night for Mike. He always gets cornered after the meeting, discussing the value of a flowering crab versus an apple tree or the merits of mulch."

"Then you're both free for a ladies' night out? Ladies and boys under twelve, that is."

"Aren't you tired?" Libby asked. "You've been working with Birdhouse Ministries every day this week."

"Not a problem. I'm giving classes on napping. I'm more rested than I've been in ages."

"You're teaching people to *nap?*" Libby blurted incredulously.

"What's more self-indulgent or glorious than a good nap? It's relaxing, nonfattening, and free."

"I don't get it," Jenny said.

"The women I meet at the center couldn't risk sleeping with both eyes closed in their own homes, always waiting for someone to stagger in drunk or high. Once at the shelter they lay awake worrying about what will become of them and their children. Can you think of better candidates for a nap than these women?"

"So why don't they just take one?" Libby asked.

"They have too much work, too much responsibility, or too much fear to relax. They have to give themselves permission to indulge in such luxury. That's where I come in. I give them permission. They sign up for the session, and I teach them how to nap." Tia grinned. "And we have a lot of fun doing it."

"Then teach me," Libby demanded.

"You aren't properly equipped. Everyone who comes to class has to bring a pillow and a blanket. The kitchen provides warm milk and fresh cookies. Helen plays lullabies or classical music through the sound system. We do some stretching and relaxation poses to quiet our minds."

"This sounds ridiculous," Jenny commented skeptically.

"I know. That's part of the idea. These women have been involved in such trouble and trauma that they deserve a few minutes in which to relax and be renewed. Sometimes I read a bedtime story. I started using the book of Revelation, but that was a big mistake. No one wanted me to quit reading. Now I'm reading the state driver's manual. Even I fall asleep."

"I can understand it," Libby said. "We're always busy doing things. We need to take time to just *be*. I doubt many people actually know how to be totally alone with themselves."

"Exactly. I ask them to give God their troubles just long enough for them to sleep in peace. Many of the women tell me that when they wake up, they leave their troubles behind. 'Let

God worry about some of them,' one said, 'I've been doing my own worrying, and look where it got me. Let him do it for a while.' "

"That's awesome," Libby breathed.

"That's when I talk about the verses in Matthew: 'Don't worry about everyday life—whether you have enough food, drink, and clothes. Doesn't life consist of more than food and clothing? Look at the birds. They don't need to plant or harvest or put food in barns because your heavenly Father feeds them. And you are far more valuable to him than they are.' It's amazing, really," Tia said softly, "what kind of spiritual meaning you can fit into a nap."

"I shouldn't have doubted you," Jenny murmured. "A class on napping sounds like a wonderful idea."

"I'm discovering that inspiration from God doesn't always mean I'll be doing great things. Sometimes the inspirations are for very humble things that *feel* inspired."

Birdhouse Ministries had become as satisfying and productive as anything Tia had ever experienced.

If only it extended into the rest of her life. . . .

"We still don't know what you're hatching up for tonight in that convoluted little brain of yours," Libby pointed out.

Tia whipped an ad from the newspaper out of the kangaroo pocket of her sweatshirt. "The circus! Clowns, acrobats, lion tamers, cotton candy, foot-long hot dogs, caramel corn, giant suckers . . ."

"Are we going for junk food or to see the show?"

"Either way, I think it's a great idea," Jenny said. "Luke will love it."

"I don't think Robert has ever *seen* a circus," Libby said. "Just watching him will be fun enough for me." Her eyes narrowed. "But I didn't think you liked animal smells and sawdust, Tia."

"Or dirt floors and sticky seats."

"I'm giving myself the opportunity to change my mind.

Besides, I haven't been to the circus since I was ten. What did I know back then?"

"Everything, according to you," Libby muttered.

Tia chose to ignore that. "Libby, you'll have to drive because of Robert's wheelchair. We can all meet at my place—sixish okay with everyone?"

Plans made, they went their separate ways—Tia to the new catalogs that had arrived in the mail, and Libby and Jenny to break the good news to the boys.

. . . .

"Whazat, Auntie Tia? And that? And what's that over there?" Robert's head was turning back and forth with such speed that Tia figured it would eventually snap off and fly into center ring. As usual, when he got excited, Robert's glasses had worked themselves into a skewed position on his nose, and his eyes were as bright as black pearls.

Tia tied a helium-filled balloon to the arm of his chair and handed him the miniature lion tamer's whip she'd purchased. "Luke, why don't you take Robert for a spin around the big top before the show starts? We'll save your seats."

Luke pushed off so quickly that Robert had to reach for the arms of his chair to keep his balance.

"You're very good at this, Auntie Tia," Libby commented through a mouthful of pink cotton candy.

"Cute kids."

"You used to imply there was very little that was cute about either children or animals," Jenny reminded her mildly. "You thought they were messy, noisy, annoying—"

"I've grown accustomed to them, okay? With a new godchild on the way, I decided it was time I refocused my efforts."

"Whoever thought you'd mellow like this?" Libby teased. "Do I sense that this new relationship with Brandon has made you—dare I say it?—cozy?"

"And cuddly and maternal?" Jenny added.

"There are already plenty of babies in the world without a contribution from me," Tia said. "Did you know that if every person in China walked past you in a single line, the line would never end because the reproduction rate is so high?"

"That's even more interesting than the information about the elephants."

"By the way, Jenny," Tia said, "how's that lovely little Tibby doing?" She and Libby had concocted a combined version of their own names for the baby and had come up with Tibby.

"I am not naming the baby Tibby. Quit calling her that or it might stick after she's born."

"Nothing wrong with that. It's a great name, don't you think, Libby?"

Jenny rubbed her stomach gently. "Actually, we have picked out a name. Lacey. It sounds nice with Luke, don't you think? Luke and Lacey."

"It's a great name," Libby said.

"The only name more perfect would be Tibby," Tia admitted. "But since it's your baby I suppose you get final say. . . ."

"Mike picked out the middle names," Jenny continued. "Our baby will be named Lacey Tia Elizabeth Adams."

Libby gasped and Tia felt tears spring to her eyes.

"Mike wanted to name the baby after both of you because of how important you've been in our lives."

For once, Tia was speechless. When recovered, she stammered, "*Mike* wanted this?"

"It was his suggestion." Jenny dimpled as she smiled.

"What a beautiful, beautiful gift," Tia whispered. "You have a wonderful husband, Jen. He's generous beyond words."

"He was a gift, too, you know. Straight from God. I have no

doubt. God was my dating service, and I didn't even know I'd signed up!"

Just then Robert and Luke returned from their sightseeing tour of the big top. Robert started squealing, and they turned their attention to a small clown who'd attached himself to Robert's wheelchair and was pulling silk scarves from the boy's ears.

The din of the arena faded into the background as Tia stared dreamily at the bright colors and happy faces. Lacey Tia Elizabeth Adams . . . she would order something special from the store and have it engraved with the child's name.

Unfortunately, the thought of the store recalled the heated debate she and Brandon had had recently over changes he wanted to make in Ribbons & Rainbows. If given free rein, he'd be an expensive partner with his big ideas for overlarge inventory and a lavish advertising program. She'd had to make it perfectly clear that there was no money for such extravagance but still felt dreadful about it. Her heart was starting to overrule her head. She'd actually become *shy* about telling Brandon when she didn't agree with his ideas because she didn't want to embarrass or hurt him.

"Can I sit by you, Tia?" Luke snapped her back from her reverie.

She patted the bleacher beside her, glad for the diversion. Tonight she needed escape from the nagging questions and confusion that had been pursuing her. She wanted . . . she wanted . . . she wanted. But what she *needed* was to pray. So she did, in the quiet of her heart.

Thank you, Father, for these wonderful friends and for little Lacey. You have given me so much and now, here I am again, asking for even more. Could you give me guidance? What do you want for me? for my stores? for my relationship with Brandon? I trust your answers. Show me, Lord. Amen.

Tia settled back to watch the ringmaster strut around the ring in his improbable costume and high hat. Circuses were meant to be fun and that was what she was going to have, she thought—even if it killed her.

"I know what you're doing, Tia," Jenny said between handfuls of caramel corn. The lion tamer's act was moving out of the main ring, and clowns were pouring out of a miniature car.

"Wearing a silly hat on my head put there by a clown? Eating my third hot dog? Smelling elephant droppings?"

"You're running away from something."

Libby nodded sagely but did not look very wise with pink cotton candy drooping like a mustache from both sides of her mouth. "Running away," she agreed.

"Fine. Just let me run."

"Ever since Ribbons & Rainbows opened, you've been a bundle of nerves."

Tia ignored them both. It was, of course, impossible to ignore five-hundred-pound canaries for long.

"Has Brandon helped your situation?" Jenny asked.

"Is it difficult to adjust to having a partner after all this time?" Libby sounded curious.

"How do you like his management style?" Jenny persisted.

"Do you think he will be . . . ?" They were playing tag team with their questions.

"Please let me have a break from work," Tia pleaded. "I'm there physically for twelve hours a day and mentally for another six. I don't want to work twenty-four-seven!"

To her relief, the trapeze artists scrambled like monkeys up the rope ladders to their platforms, diverting her friends' attention. Dressed in sparkling bronze-and-gold sequins, they looked like newly minted pennies high above the ground. Even with the safety-net apron and bed below them, they looked utterly vulnerable as they began swinging the trapeze between them.

Tia concentrated on the tiny figures as they took their first tentative swings, as if testing the air between the platforms to see if it would hold them. The audience gasped when the sparkling young woman released her trapeze and reached out her hands to the bronzed man who, knees locked around the bar, stretched his arms toward hers. Clapping erupted as their hands met, and they swung together in midair.

Tia was transfixed as the pair artfully swung from side to side as if dancing on the safety of the ground. She did not realize she was crying until Robert touched her cheek. "Are you hurt, Auntie Tia?"

She snuffled and grinned at him through her tears. "No, honey. It's just so beautiful."

Robert looked at her in bewilderment, apparently unsure why a circus act could make her weep. He put his hand in Tia's and said nothing more.

After they'd returned to Libby's and it had been decided that Luke should spend the night with Robert, the boys disappeared into Robert's room. Libby brewed a large pot of tea and set out a plate of homemade ginger cookies, while Jenny and Tia made nests of quilts and pillows on the couches.

When they were all curled into their favorite spots, the tea poured and cookies served, Libby cleared her throat. "Now what was *that* all about? *Crying* at the *circus?*"

Tia took another cookie and nibbled daintily around its edges before speaking. "It was a metaphorical moment, that's all.

"Those trapeze artists couldn't go on to the next bar or the next catch until they *released the one they were on.* The first bar signified security—the one sure thing holding them up. The second bar represented danger and the unknown—would they catch it and succeed or let it slip through their fingers and fall like a rock? To prevail, they had to *trust*—their partners, the sturdiness of the trapeze, the strength of the net.

"It took an act of faith for them to move on, to finish the act. If they didn't let go, they'd never know whether they were successes or failures. I realized I'm a lot like them—only I haven't been brave enough to let go of the first bar to see if I'll catch the second. I've only just realized that I'm *terrified* I'm going to fail."

"At business or at love?" Jenny inquired gently.

"At both."

"You always said that *God* was your business partner, Tia. If you are feeling unsure and confused right now, it's not coming from God." Libby stirred her tea thoughtfully.

The room grew silent but for the wind curling around the house. "Because decision in accordance with God's will brings peace, not discord." Tia shivered and burrowed deeper into her quilt. "I thought I was asking the right questions of God," she mused, "but I'm realizing that 'Thy will be done' doesn't come into play very often for me. Just '*my* will be done.' "

....

Maybe it was the tortilla chips and extra-hot sauce or the fiery enchilada. Perhaps it was that stupid television show about nightmares and the human mind on the science channel. Then again, it might have been Tia's strange mood as she crawled into bed. Whatever it was, it had resulted in the strangest dream Tia had ever experienced.

She went to the bakery for early morning coffee and to tell her friends about the fantasy. "It was just too weird!" Tia took a sip of coffee and began to unravel a glazed twist doughnut as she spoke. "I usually don't dream, but this one was a doozie."

Jenny worked at her desk and Libby tallied inventory as they listened. "So tell us," Jenny urged.

"I was on an airplane. We took off and sailed straight over the ocean at sunset. It was so incredibly beautiful—like a picture God had painted and signed with his name."

"Sounds promising so far." Jenny appeared amused by Tia's latest perplexity.

"I was *sure* I was wide awake and peering out the window at the sea. The oranges and reds reflected off the water so it seemed almost alive. And then—" Tia frowned—"all of a sudden, I was on a bicycle, riding through a bright green pasture filled with trees and flowers."

"Quick trip," Libby commented. "I always like a short flight."

Tia scowled at her and continued. "But I came upon this fork in the road and didn't know which direction to go."

"Symbolic of big decisions to make, if you ask me," Jenny said. She tapped the tip of her pen against her desk as she spoke.

"So I took the path strewn with feathers."

Libby and Jenny both looked up. *"Feathers?"*

"Beautiful ones in bright colors. And there were birds all around me. Chickens, doves, canaries, peacocks, parrots . . ."

"Then what?"

"Then nothing. That was my dream. Do you think dreams mean anything or was it the spicy Mexican food I ate?"

"I don't know about this one, but dreams meant something in the Bible. Joseph interpreted the dreams of Pharaoh's baker and cupbearer," Libby said.

"That's true. In the Bible God revealed himself in dreams," Jenny added. "It was through a dream that God told the wise men to go back to their homes by another route to avoid Herod. And remember Jacob's ladder in Genesis? God spoke to him through a dream."

"Look at it this way, Tia," Libby continued. "God can do anything. If he wants to talk to us in dreams, he will. He also created our subconscious minds, which are collecting information all the time and tucking it away in those miraculous storage spaces called our brains. When people say they have a hunch about something, what they really have is all that information that they don't even remember taking in. That's why hunches are often correct—they are actually facts your mind has processed into reasonable ideas. Either way, God's at work."

"But it was so weird . . ."

"That you dreamed about being at a crossroad? Everything in your life these days involves a decision—which way to go. What to do. And the bike and the airplane? Probably feeling like you need to get away from the mess!" Libby shook her head. "But the birds and all those feathers? I don't know about that—unless, of course, it had something to do with Birdhouse Ministries."

Tia put her elbows on the table and her chin in her hands. "I think I'll stop trying to figure this out and let God do the sorting for me."

. . . .

"Not again!" Wendy glanced through the back-room door, where she'd been discussing inventory with Tia. "You take care of it this time."

Tia peered over Wendy's shoulder to see Trevor West standing awkwardly by the till. He had a little more color in his cheeks today, Tia observed. And a haircut.

"I don't think he's here to rob us," Tia said mildly.

"You don't know that." Obviously, Wendy still doubted Tia's solution to her shoplifter problem. "He's probably scoping us out for his criminally inclined friends."

"Oh, you of little faith," Tia chided as she stepped from the back so Trevor could see her.

He shifted from one foot to the other and dug his hands so deep into his pockets that it seemed they should have protruded from the hems of his pant legs. Trevor reddened as Tia approached.

"Hello there." Tia leaned against the counter, crossed her arms in front of her, and studied him.

"Hi."

"Can I help you?"

"I told my mom . . . and she said . . . but I didn't think you'd want to hear it, but . . ."

"Clear as mud, Trevor," Tia said with a smile. "Let's go next door and get some iced tea while you get things sorted out."

Too surprised to protest, he trailed after her into the coffee shop. While Tia ordered, he sat on the bench of their booth and squirmed as if his pants were on fire.

When they'd been served, Tia said, "Now what exactly did you come to tell me?"

"Th-thank you."

Tia felt a jolt of surprise. She hadn't expected him to make a trip to Tia's Attic to show his appreciation for anything.

"Mom said you'd like to hear what I told her about Reach Out Ranch."

"And that was . . . ?" Tia smiled inwardly. Once again Reach Out Ranch was working its magic.

"I like it there. It's pretty fun, actually. Even cleaning stalls isn't so bad if you don't think about it too much. And Reese started showing me some stuff about horses. I've been cleaning tack and learning about it at the same time. I'm going to be riding soon."

"You have a good teacher. Reese knows more about horses than most people ever will."

"But I've almost got that music box paid off, Rollie says." He looked dismayed. "And then I won't have any excuse to go back out there."

"And you aren't happy about that?"

"Not really. Neither is my mom. She says I'm easier to live with after I've been out there." He pushed away from the table. "I just wanted you to know that I've learned a lot—lots more than I would have learned if the police had taken me in. It was really dumb of me to steal." He snorted derisively. "My girlfriend broke up with me anyway."

He hung his head and spoke so low that Tia could barely hear him. "And I learned about little kids and handicapped people and that they aren't so scary when you really know them. Most of them are pretty cool. I told Mom that if I ever made it to college, maybe I'd be a physical therapist or something."

Tia's heart was melting all over her insides, but she kept a calm exterior. "Do you have plans for college?"

"I didn't. I hate high school. But if I could work with kids like that . . ." His voice trailed away. "But that's stupid to even think about."

"Why?"

He looked at her with eyes that seemed to ache. "'Cause I messed around in school and would have to take some classes over. 'Cause I'd never earn a scholarship, and I'd never be able to pay for it on my own. It's like my dad says, all I'm good for is sacking groceries or pushing a broom."

"Oh, he does, does he?" Tia felt irritation bleeding through her. "There's nothing wrong with honest work like sacking groceries or pushing a broom, but you don't have to settle for that if you set your goals somewhere else."

"What do you mean?"

"If you don't get an education, you will be limited in your job choices, but there's no reason you can't spruce up your grades and get into college."

"And pay with what?"

Tia's mind whirled. Libby had once mentioned that the ranch was going to hire some part-time help to ease Rollie's load and allow him to do more fund-raising.

It was as if Trevor read her mind. "Rollie has me do a lot of the work he used to do. I mow all the grass—acres of it—and answer the telephone sometimes. He says that he might use me to haul feed and mineral blocks, if he can't do it himself."

"Does that ease his workload?"

"He says it does."

"Do you think there might be a part-time job there for you when you're done working off the music box?"

Tia saw his eyes sparkle for the very first time, and she realized what a good-looking kid he was when he didn't wear that flat, stoic expression.

"I thought that if you told Rollie it would be okay, he might think of hiring me. If he thought you trusted me, then . . . maybe . . ."

"*Can* I trust you?" *No use mincing words,* Tia thought.

Trevor hung his head. "Other than my mom, you're the first person who ever believed I could do something right. I don't want to disappoint either one of you again." He blushed. "I'm really sorry I stole that music box, but—it's weird—I'm glad that I stole it from *you* because you—" he puzzled for a moment—"*taught* me something."

"What was that?" Tia struggled to suppress her hope for his answer.

"You taught me that not everyone is the same. That you don't have to treat people rotten to get what you want out of them." He looked up at her with bitterness in his eyes. "If someone is mean to me, I don't care if I hurt them. I want to hurt them. But you've been better to me than anyone—ever. I never want to do something again that would make you feel bad."

His brow furrowed as if he were trying to settle something in his mind. "I think it has something to do with that Jesus hang-up you have. Mom says Christians want to act like him. Is that what you're doing?"

If she'd dared, Tia would have burst into tears then and there. "Yes, Trevor, I am trying to act like him. I'll never be able to do it right all the time, but I do keep trying. He's a pretty cool guy. Would you like to know him?"

"He's dead. Isn't he?"

"He died and was buried, but after three days he rose from the dead. Now Christ lives with God and in people's hearts."

"I don't get it."

"We're all pretty crummy people, Trevor. We're sinners. That means that no matter how we might try, we'll never be perfect enough for God."

"So what's the use?" He'd quit twiddling his thumbs and was listening intently.

"Because Christ has given us a second chance. We deserve punishment for our sins—"

"Like me and the music box?"

"Exactly. And Jesus Christ—God's Son—offered to take our punishment for us. That's why he died on the cross—to pay for our sins—yours and mine included."

"Why? That's dumb!"

"He loves us. He wanted to save us from what we really deserve, so he died in our place."

"That's pretty tough punishment. I wouldn't do that."

"Do you want to hear something really amazing?"

"I guess."

"If you'd been the only person on the planet, he still would have died—just for you."

"I could see it for a whole bunch of people—maybe—but for just you or me? No way!"

"He loves you that much, Trevor. He died so you could live and not take the punishment you really deserve."

"So let me get this straight." Trevor raked his hair away from his face with his fingers. "We're rotten people but Christ, God's Son, loves us. God wants to lower the boom on us but Christ says, 'No, punish me instead and leave them alone.'" He slapped his palm on the tabletop. "And, wham! God throws the book at his Son and lets us get by with stuff?"

"Pretty close," Tia said with a smile. "God loves us just as much as Christ did. After all, he was willing to sacrifice his only child to die for our sins."

"So what does that have to do with us now?" Trevor sounded interested but skeptical.

"When Christ died, he took the blame and the consequences for our sins."

Trevor looked appalled.

"But after three days, he came back from the dead—that's what we celebrate at Easter—and he rose into heaven to be with God again."

"So he just left us here to shape up after that?"

"No. He sent another part of himself to be with us—his Holy Spirit."

"This is getting spooky."

"Did you feel guilty when you put that music box under your jacket?"

"Big time. I felt lower than gum on the bottom of my shoe."

"What made you feel that way?"

"A guilty conscience, I guess."

"The Holy Spirit works through your conscience, showing you right from wrong, good from evil. He's the voice in your heart and your mind that warns you when you're about to do something bad. He prompts the thoughts you have of doing things right."

"Then how come not everyone has a conscience? My dad—" he stopped.

Tia smoothed over the moment by continuing, "Some people ignore the Holy Spirit so long—we call it 'hardening their hearts'—that they don't even sense him anymore."

"So how, like, do you get this Spirit guy to live in you?"

"It's so easy that it seems hard to some people. It's a gift. You just have to take it."

"But how? I'm guessing God doesn't have a store that stocks these things."

Tia had to smile. He was quick, this boy, and so ready to hear what she had to tell him.

"First you repent—that's admit your sins, say you're sorry for them, and choose not to do them again. Believe that by dying for you Jesus saved you from having to go to hell. Accept him as your Savior and trust that what he promises is true. Then the Holy Spirit can really work in you, leading you and teaching you how to live your life."

"And that's when you start trying to act like Jesus?" His eyes narrowed.

"Yes. But you never act like him because you *have* to. Once you invite him into your life and begin to know what he's done for you, you're just so grateful that you *want* to do it."

"And that's why you did what you did for me?"

"It's what I tried to do, yes."

"And that's it?"

"After that, God does have his own kind of 'stores,' where you can find encouragement and others who believe like you do. They're called churches."

"You mean *that's* what churches are all about? How come I never heard that before?" He sounded indignant, as if someone had been holding out on him.

And maybe we have, Tia thought. Sometimes we make churches too mysterious and intimidating. Here was a kid who really hadn't even figured out exactly what churches were for! If God wants us to accept him as a little child might, it's clear that even the young ones can understand the gift of salvation. Are we guilty of making this seem too complicated? Tia wondered.

"Do you want this for yourself, Trevor?" she asked gently.

"Maybe I'll think about it," he said carefully.

Tia sensed immediately that it was time to stop and to wait for the Holy Spirit to move next. "Just a minute, I've got something for you." She dug into her pocket and pulled out a pamphlet that explained what they'd been talking about and offered a simple prayer of confession and repentance. "Take this home and read it. Really listen to your heart on this one. And if you have any questions or anything you want to talk about, I'm here for you. Okay?"

He looked at her as if she were some strange new species in a cage at the zoo. "How come you do all this for me?"

"I told you—"

"'Cause Jesus wants you to," he said. "I ain't never seen nothing like this before."

Tia laid some dollar bills on the table to pay for their order and stood up. "That's how it is when you hook up with God, Trevor. Always something new. He never lets you quit learning or growing. If you invite him into your life, he wants to be in all of it."

"Isn't that a big pain?" he asked.

"It's a much bigger pleasure." She tilted her head toward the door. "Promise that you'll come back and tell me what you thought about that little book."

"Yeah. Sure, I guess."

"And Trevor . . ."

He turned to look at her.

"I'll be praying for you."

CHAPTER NINE

*The blue jay's feathers are not, in fact, blue. They appear that color
only because of the way light refracts off their inner structure.
Crush a feather underfoot and the illusion is lost.
The raucous bird is a master of illusions.*

—*Birds: An Explore Your World Handbook,* Discovery Books and David Bird

"Speed up! Harder! Harder!" Tia screamed as she did a cheer-leader leap into the air. When Reese crossed the finish line, she punched the stopwatch. "Ten seconds faster than last time."

Reese wiped the sweat out of his eyes and grinned at Tia and his wife. "The guy I *pay* to help me get ready for the race doesn't work me this hard."

"He's probably not as competitive as I am."

"You missed your calling," Libby said. "Coach for Olympic athletes."

"Or the prison guard that oversees hard labor in the quarries," Reese added. "I appreciate your enthusiasm, Tia, but I feel guilty letting you take time away from the store to watch me practice."

"Nonsense. I want you ready for your first big wheelchair race."

Reese eyed her suspiciously. "Why do I sense an ulterior motive here?"

Tia looked innocently at the sky. "You're my friend and I want you to win."

"And?" he prodded.

"Then I want to take pictures of you after you win, blow them up, and put them in the front windows of the stores. Puleese?" She dropped to her knees in front of him. "I think that my stores would be a great place to introduce wheelchair athletes to a bigger audience. It's a great inspiration."

"I don't want to be a poster boy for anything, Tia."

"But you *have* to do it. I've already ordered a whole line of figurines from a new designer I found. He's wheelchair-bound, too, and he does these amazing likenesses of people in chairs dribbling basketballs, shooting bows and arrows, racing . . ."

"Tia!"

"If I promote these as fund-raisers for the group we're going to organize to train young wheelchair athletes—"

"Slow down!" Reese glowered at her. "Did you consider asking me about this first?"

Tia wrinkled her nose. "I knew you'd say no. But once you thought about how much it would benefit kids like Robert . . ."

"You are a project looking for a cause."

She twinkled at him as she heard the softening of his voice. "It is a good idea, isn't it?"

"Yes, but . . ."

"And Robert, for one, would benefit from it."

"Sure, but . . ."

"And lots of other kids?"

"Why are you . . . ?"

"Because it's needed! That's why!" She turned to Libby. "I *told* you he'd go for it in the end."

"You knew about this?" Reese raised an eyebrow at Libby.

"Just today. Otherwise I would have warned you. Hurricane

Tia never shows up on a weather map until the first wind has already hit."

"Don't expect me to do or say anything else for your cause unless you ask me first."

"I wouldn't dream of it. And thanks, Reese. You won't be sorry." Tia was grinning as she and Libby climbed into Libby's car and they headed for Reach Out Ranch.

"Do you think he was upset with me?" Tia asked.

"No one gets upset with you, Tia. Your motives are the best. In your enthusiasm you do tend to make decisions for everyone around you, however."

"Believe it or not, I've been working on that. I'm beginning to realize how annoying it is to be around someone like Brandon, who is always sure he's right." Tia sighed dramatically. "And I'm also beginning to understand why the children of Israel wandered around the desert for forty years. Even in biblical times, men wouldn't ask for directions."

The sun was brighter than usual today. And the clouds whiter. Even the wind had a sweeter sound . . . and Tia wanted to slap herself for being so sappy. Since her talk with Jenny and Libby, Tia had not been able to get Brandon out of her mind.

Sure he was self-assured to the point of cocky, self-possessed to the point of annoying, and assertive to the point of crazy—all things that frustrated her about him. But those were the very reasons she loved him. She'd met her match—someone just as confident, bold, and opinionated as herself.

That backhanded reasoning had given her great encouragement and new resolve. She wasn't going to deny her feelings for Brandon any longer. She was going to let the relationship play out and see where it took them.

Tia sat down on her outside steps and looked up at the sky.

"Dear Lord, I've been micromanaging again and trying to *guess* what this relationship is supposed to be. Sorry. *Thy* will be done, not mine. And make it very clear, Lord, what you want me to see and know about Brandon and how he fits into my life. I love him, Lord, but not as much as I love you."

Be careful what you pray for, Tia was to think later—you might get it.

....

"I am so exhausted my head is spinning," Tia observed as she and Brandon left the conference room. "If I hear one more thing about entrepreneurship or business planning, my head will pop."

"Let's stop in the hotel coffee shop and get something to eat. It's almost seven. You've had a long day."

Yawning, she followed him into the café and scooted into a booth. After she'd ordered a salad and swilled down a cup of strong tea, she felt revived.

"Every time I go to one of these seminars I learn so much." Tia kicked off her shoes beneath the table and relaxed against the seat. She had become much more serene since her decision to release the reins driving this relationship—and happier, too. "I really appreciated the comments on stock and ordering. Being overstocked in the wrong places can be the kiss of death for a business."

Brandon winced as Tia hastened to say, "I'm not necessarily referring to the merchandise you ordered. In general it's a wise idea to be careful."

"I feel badly about that, Tia."

"We can break up those gift packages and sell the items separately. With the bath gels, soaps, and hand and body lotions we should be able to recover most of our expense."

"I had another idea." Brandon shifted slightly in the booth, and his eyes grew intense. "I think we should send them back for a refund."

"We can't do that. It was part of a promotion with that company. We committed to buying a certain number and we have to abide by that."

"Not if the items are damaged."

"Nothing was damaged. They're in perfect shape."

"But *if* something *were* wrong with them . . ."

"Then we'd get credit for the order. But they're fine."

His pale eyes shifted from her face. "I gave one to my sister and she didn't care for it. Something broken, I guess."

"Well, if that's the case, maybe we *can* get some of our money back . . ." She paused, feeling slightly uncomfortable. "Brandon, did you *really* give your sister those items to try?"

"Of course!" His head snapped up and he looked indignant.

"Which scent did she have? There were three types in the gift boxes. Maybe that entire carton was damaged in shipping and we didn't notice it."

"The lilac or peach, I can't remember which."

Tia hesitated. "Brandon, there was no peach or lilac scent. Only lavender, watermelon, and lemon."

"One of those then. How am I supposed to remember?"

"You placed the order."

"And believe me, I've regretted it."

She recognized the defensive tone in his voice and backed off. "I didn't mean to upset you. We shouldn't be having this conversation when we're so tired. I'm not even sure I can stay awake to drive home. Let's start over in the morning."

He gave her one of those delightfully disarming smiles and said, "Good idea. Here, let me get the bill."

They walked out of the coffee shop and past a bank of elevators to a recessed alcove near the door. Brandon was about to help her into her jacket when Tia was struck with a wide yawn.

"You're worn out. Are you going to be okay?"

When Tia hesitated for the briefest of moments, he spoke again. "Maybe we should stay here tonight. Then we can really 'start over in the morning.' "

"Brandon, don't be ridiculous. I'm only a half hour from home. What are you thinking?" Swiftly and clearly, Tia realized exactly what he was considering. "You aren't asking what I think you're asking—are you?"

"It won't hurt anything. We're tired. We're tense. We need time together when we aren't working or scrapping over orders and bills."

"And a night together in this hotel would help all that?"

"It wouldn't hurt." He drew a breath as if to steady his resolve. "Tia, we're adults. You must know how I feel about you. I want to take this relationship a step further and, I think, so do you. Tonight I just want to relax, to hold you in my arms . . ."

Tia remained stiff and silent.

"It's no big deal, Tia. No one needs to know!"

"I'll know."

"And you won't regret it, I promise you that. I can make you—"

"And God will know."

"Oh, for goodness sake, Tia! Isn't that stuff about 'lusting in your heart' the same to God as doing the actual deed?"

" 'Anyone who even looks at a woman with lust in his eye has already committed adultery with her in his heart.' It's in Matthew 5."

"Then, if we're sinning anyway, we might just as well—"

"Don't say it, Brandon, please don't."

"This is my way of showing you how very much I care about you."

Tia turned away but looked back to say, "Your sister never even saw the gift pack you claim she complained about, did she?"

....

Tia cried all night. By 4:00 A.M. she was sobbing so wretchedly that she felt as if she was going to throw up. She fell asleep by the toilet, her forehead resting on the cool, implacable porcelain, her eyes muddy with makeup and tears. She was surrounded by wadded tissues, her face stiff and scratchy from the salty remains of her weeping.

She awoke at seven when her clock radio automatically came on, and music from an oldies station blared into her bedroom. "Breaking Up Is Hard to Do" shattered the quiet. By the time Tia had crawled across the tile to the carpet of her bedroom and fumbled at the clock on her bedside stand, "Tears on My Pillow" was playing. Finally she pulled the plug from the socket when she could not make the intrusive little machine silent.

She made her way back onto the bed, curled into a fetal position, and pulled the downy comforter over her head. Today might be happening, but she wasn't going to be a part of it.

By afternoon she had turned the volume off on the telephone to allow voice mail to pick up, soaked in an overflowing tub of water until it had grown completely cold, made herself tea and toast, vomited, and made more tea. Now Tia was up and ready for battle—with God.

Wearing a pair of flannel pajamas, thick socks, and a misshapen old sweater she'd owned forever, she paced the floor of her bedroom, heart pumping, head pounding, mouth dry. She talked, she shouted, and she screamed—from her feet, on her knees, and facedown on the bed.

"I don't get it, God! I just don't get it! What are you doing to me? What do you want of me? Why did you let Brandon into my life if he was going to hurt me so? I don't understand. *I don't understand!*"

When she tired of screaming at the ceiling, she yelled at the floor. And when she was too tired to pace, she fell to her knees. She grabbed her Bible and was about to toss it to the floor when she felt compelled to lay it on the comforter. It fell open to Psalm 55:16-17:

> But I will call on God,
>> and the Lord will rescue me.
> Morning, noon, and night
>> I plead aloud in my distress,
>> and the Lord hears my voice.

Her sobs slowed incrementally until they dwindled into a whimper. *He will listen to me.* And her recent prayer came back to her like a bolt from the blue. "Make it very clear, Lord," she'd prayed, "what you want me to see and know about Brandon and how he fits into my life."

Be careful what you pray for—you may get it.

If this was God's answer, she didn't like it one bit.

But she hadn't asked to like it—she'd simply asked for an answer. "Thy will be done, not mine," she'd said. She'd asked; he'd answered. Trouble was, he'd said no—to Brandon, to a life for them together, to . . . only God knew what else.

Quickly she turned to Jeremiah 29:11: "For I know the plans I have for you," says the Lord. "They are plans for good and not for disaster, to give you a future and a hope."

Tears streamed from Tia's eyes as she sat on the floor hugging her Bible to her chest. What now? *What now?*

. . . .

The next morning Tia showered, sliced a cucumber, and put the cool rings on her eyes to subdue the puffiness, then made a pot of coffee so strong it could have held up a spoon, and ate two slices of toast thick with butter, sugar, and cinnamon. Then she

applied double her usual makeup—especially around her eyes—
did her nails, and put on her reddest power suit. After pulling
her dark hair into a dramatic upsweep and sliding into her highest pumps, she took her Bible and sat down at the kitchen table.
And she prayed.

"Heavenly Father, you really did a number on me last night. I
hit bottom, bounced around, and ended up under the barrel. I
don't get it. I don't know what's going on, and I don't like it. But
I praise you that you allow me to question, to seek, to rant, and
to rave—and that you are patiently there afterward to pick up
the pieces. Thank you for assuring me that whatever this is, you
will see me through it to a good conclusion.

"Did I *dream* last night? Or did Brandon really turn into a full-
fledged jerk before my eyes? I have to see him today, Lord. Let
me know what to do. Am I supposed to help him through this?
Teach him something? Or just let him go?"

Then Tia laid her head on the table, rested her forehead on the
edge of the Bible, and whimpered, "Oh, help . . ."

. . . .

Brandon, a panic-stricken expression on his face, was already
there when Tia got to the office. He hadn't shaved, and for the
first time ever, Tia saw him in rumpled clothing.

"Tia, I . . ."

"Give me a moment to compose myself, will you?" She
sounded more together than she felt.

"Sure. Of course. Why not?" He backed reluctantly away, looking longingly at her.

"Twenty minutes," Tia said gently, her kind heart already softening to this man who was in such misery. "Then we'll talk."

After closing her door, Tia picked up the mail that had arrived
this morning. She would pull herself together by following her
normal routine. Only then would she face Brandon.

The mail was not good—bills, bills, bank statements, more bills. She ran her letter opener through the top of each envelope, giving them a cursory inspection, then a more thorough one. Soon she was scribbling numbers on a notepad and comparing them to the listings in her bank statement. And when twenty minutes were up, Tia had had a conclusive answer from God.

"Ready?" Tia started when Brandon poked his head through her office door. "It's been forty-five minutes."

"Sorry. I lost track of time," she said.

"I'm the one who should be apologizing, Tia, for everything— for suggesting that we return merchandise under false pretenses, for the other night, for suggesting that we . . . well, you know."

"But you still would have sent things back if you could have gotten away with it," Tia said. It was a comment, not a question.

Brandon was startled. "No, of course not . . . well, I suppose if I tried not to think . . . no, no . . . I don't know."

"And if I'd consented, we *would* have stayed at the hotel."

He squirmed uncomfortably and wouldn't face her. Instead he slunk into the chair across from her.

"Well?"

"Yes." He was ashen now. "You're a beautiful woman. The most lovely person I've met in a long time. You're generous, funny, sweet—"

"Gullible?" Tia sat straight and tall, as though a string suspended from the ceiling were attached to the top of her head. Shoulders squared, voice soft, eyes snapping, she—despite her size—was an intimidating figure.

"Tia, *I love you.* I want to be with you. I *need* to be with you. Ever since that night, I've been rolling this around in my mind, and one thing has become perfectly clear. I want to marry you. Will you give me the honor of becoming my wife?"

All the red power suits and good posture in the world hadn't prepared her for this.

She'd asked the Lord to make what she needed to do obvious to her, and he couldn't have made it much clearer. Although Tia looked at Brandon yearningly, knowing that she loved him, she cleared her throat and said, "No."

Her response jarred Brandon with the force of a physical blow. "No? Just like that? Not 'Let me think about it?' or 'Oh, Brandon, this is all so sudden.' Just no?"

"Just no." Tears scalded the backs of her eyes and throat. Her head was filled with an alarming buzzing sound, and she could feel blood pounding in her ears. With a finality that was physically painful, Tia said, "It's time for you to leave, Brandon. We'll talk tomorrow about the business."

"I ask you to sleep with me, then to *marry* me, and this is the response I get?" His face reddened and the veins in his neck swelled and throbbed. "No, I'm not leaving, Tia. Not until I get an explanation!"

"Don't do this. Not now." A quaking ran through Tia, making her fear that her will might break. "Get out," she almost pleaded. "Please?"

"NO!" His roar could be heard all the way into the showroom.

Resigned and resolved, Tia picked up the bills she'd opened that morning and slid them across to him, along with the paper on which she'd been scribbling.

"Wha . . ." His face turned pale again, and he seemed to age before her eyes. His voice was thick and guttural when he spoke. "Listen, Tia, I can explain."

"Where did the money go that was supposed to pay these invoices? They were to be paid through you. Do you realize how many thousands of dollars this represents? Leaving them unpaid means we'll have huge interest rates, too."

"I'll pay the interest. I promise. Nothing will come out of your pocket. I thought I could get the cash back into the account before these bills arrived. I never dreamed . . ." Brandon ran his hand across the lower half of his stubbly face in agitation. "I've got the money right here." He pulled a check out of his pocket and thrust it at her. "See?"

It was a check from Beacons for a sizeable amount of money.

"I was going to put it in the store account today. I would have had those checks paid and in the mail on time, but it took me longer to pull it together than I'd thought."

"Pull what together?" Tia didn't recognize the strangled voice speaking as her own. Her world was crumbling around her and she had no footing.

"My sister, Amber, is a magnificent artist, but she's no money manager. She ordered a ridiculous amount of very expensive glass, some new tools, and several furniture items for the studio. I don't know where she thought she was going to get the cash. I *had* to get it paid off, Tia, but very few of my assets are liquid, and it took some time to get the money. I thought that if I paid Amber's bills first, by the time ours were due I'd have it replaced. Unfortunately it took longer than I expected to free my money.

"But I have it now." He poked at the check lying on her desk. "With interest. Will you forgive me?"

Tia looked at him and smiled gently. "I forgive you."

"Thank heavens."

"Exactly. Thank God, to be more accurate. I couldn't forgive you if I didn't know how much he's forgiven me."

"Then we'll consider it a clean slate. This will never happen again, I promise."

"You are very right about that. It will never happen again because our business connection will be dissolved," she continued calmly.

"But you just said . . . you told me you forgave me!"

"And I do. But that doesn't mean we can continue to have a relationship. You're not the man I thought you were, Brandon. Much of this fiasco is my own fault. I *wanted* you to be the right one. I wanted to have more stores. I wanted you to love me, and maybe I even wanted to marry you someday. But in my greed, I neglected to ask what *God* wanted for me."

He started to protest when she raised a hand to stop him. "God desires more for us than we can dream of for ourselves." She smiled wryly. "I guess I just forgot to remember that for a while."

"This isn't necessary. We can make this work."

Do not be mismatched with unbelievers. . . . What fellowship is there between light and darkness?

She shook her head sadly. "It could never work. When I marry, *if* I marry, it has to be to someone whose faith is strong."

"Are you saying that you don't think I believe in God?" He scowled.

"Not at all. I think you *do* believe in God—you believe he exists, somewhere, somehow. But I don't think you believe he's relevant to your life. You believe in him, but you don't personally *know* him, in such a way that you would ask him into your life to direct it." She smiled sadly. "God doesn't condone stealing money."

"I *borrowed* it!"

"Borrow then. He doesn't encourage any behavior that's not forthright and honest. Nor does he approve of cheating manufacturing companies or of unmarried sex."

"You make it sound as if that's illegal!"

"In God's eyes it is."

Brandon's shoulders sagged and he groaned in frustration. "I don't get it, Tia. If you care about me . . ."

She felt so sad that tears welled in her eyes, not for herself but for the man across from her. He had so much to offer, so much grace, charm, and wit. He was brilliant and clueless all at the same time.

Seeing that he was getting nowhere, Brandon stood up. "I'm not going to let go that easy, Tia, but we'll talk later."

She nodded. "Next week."

He opened his mouth to speak and then snapped it shut again, obviously seeing that she would not be swayed.

After he'd left, Tia dropped her head into her hands and let the tears fall onto the stack of unpaid bills. "Father," she whispered, "I asked that your will be done, not mine, and everything in my life turned on a dime. Was I praying the wrong prayer all this time? Were you humoring me by giving me what I asked for and allowing me to limp along blindly? I never knew what powerful words *Thy will be done* could be."

She wiped away her tears. "And if you had to make such a slam-bang show to let me know that this isn't what you've intended for me, then please show me what you *do* have planned—soon!"

Then Tia mopped at her face with a tissue, reapplied her makeup, and went to the sales floor. Anyone coming close to her would have heard her muttering under her breath, "God will provide. God *will* provide."

CHAPTER TEN

*The common grackle's notoriously bad behavior includes
stealing insects and earthworms from robins and occasionally
killing adult house sparrows and the eggs
and nestlings of various birds.*

—*Birds: An Explore Your World Handbook,* Discovery Books and David Bird

"Have you heard from Tia this morning?" Jenny asked.

"Not since last week. She said she wouldn't miss this race for anything. And now she's not here," Libby explained.

The race participants were already lining up.

"That's odd." Jenny reached for her cell phone. "I'll give her a call."

She hung up after ten rings and tried the store number. Covering the mouthpiece, she whispered to Libby, "They don't know where she is either."

"She said she'd be here for Reese's first race. Tia told me she was taking the day off," Libby said, puzzled. "And she promised to bring the camera so she could shoot photos."

"I don't get it. She was so enthusiastic about this."

"Do you think something is wrong? Could she be sick or . . ."

"Maybe she just overslept. She and Brandon attended a seminar recently at one of the hotels on the Bloomington strip. Tia has been running on empty the last few weeks."

Just then the announcer's voice came over the loudspeaker, and Luke and Robert arrived to demand their front-row seats.

The seat they saved for Tia remained unoccupied.

It was a giddy group that gathered at Reese's van after the race. A large trophy lay in his lap as he maneuvered his chair behind the wheel.

"My dad won!" Robert told every passerby. "He's the champion!"

"Do you think he's proud?" Mike whispered to Jenny. "Or are those buttons popping on his shirt for no good reason?"

Jenny smiled wanly. "What a wonderful role model Reese is for that child. Robert will grow up believing he can do anything, wheelchair or not."

Mike put his arm around her shoulders. "What's wrong, sweetheart? You've been acting odd all morning."

"It's Tia."

"Yeah, I missed her. Where was she—up and running around somewhere?"

"She didn't come, Mike."

His eyes narrowed. "Are you sure?"

"I tried to call, but her cell phone is off, and she's not at the store. I would have gone to look for her, but I didn't feel I could leave until Reese had raced. Libby and I have been frantic."

"Take our car now. Reese and I will buy the boys a pizza. Give us a call when you find her. I'll leave my cell on."

Jenny nodded and stood on tiptoe to give him a kiss. "You're the best."

She held up the keys to Libby. Libby glanced at Reese, who nodded. She followed Jenny to the car. They didn't speak until they were out of the parking lot.

"Where do you think she is?" Jenny asked.

"I have no clue. It never occurred to me that Tia wouldn't be at the race."

Jenny's jaw tightened as she accelerated the car. "Take my phone and call Ellen and Dorothy to see if they've heard from her. Then we'll swing by and ring Tia's doorbell."

Two hours later, worried and exhausted, Jenny and Libby returned for a second time to Tia's and parked in the driveway.

"I don't get it. This isn't like Tia. She hates disappointing anyone. She's worked so hard to help Reese win that it would have to be something very urgent to keep her from the race." Jenny's features clouded. "Do you think she's had an accident?"

Libby jumped out of the car and walked to the garage. When she couldn't stand tall enough on tiptoe to peek in the line of decorative windows across the top of the garage door, she dragged a big clay pot filled with impatiens onto the driveway and scrambled onto that, squashing flowers as she did so.

She gave a little gasp and jumped down. "Jenny, her car is here!"

"You mean we've been driving around like maniacs, and she may never have left the house? We should have looked in the garage rather than ringing the bell last time we were here."

"Do you think we should call 911?"

"I don't know. Let me think . . ."

Just then Tia opened the front door.

"Where have you been?" Jenny and Libby demanded in unison. "We were worried sick!"

Tia looked pale but composed. "Come inside."

Libby hauled the flowerpot back into place as Tia ushered Jenny through the door.

Tia's usually immaculate home looked as though a tornado had hit. There were clothes everywhere—sweats, tennis shoes, jackets, and discarded dress clothes strewn about.

"Sorry for the mess. I've had some things on my mind."

"We were worried sick about you. When you didn't come to the race, we ran all over town looking for you. We even went to Fraiser Towers to see if you'd visited Libby's parents. Didn't you hear your phone ring?"

Tia's face fell. "The race? It was today?"

"You forgot? After all you and Reese have been through? Every-one wondered what happened to his number-one cheerleader," Libby said.

"I am so sorry." Tears, which were so near the surface anyway, sprang to her eyes.

"You don't have to cry, Tia." Libby put a consoling arm around her friend. "Reese won and we're just sorry you missed it. Let me make coffee."

"What came up so quickly that you couldn't at least let one of us know you wouldn't be at the race?" Jenny demanded after Libby left the room. "That you couldn't give Reese a call and wish him good luck? You know how important this was to both of them."

Tia's jaw and lower lip trembled, and misery radiated from her. "I'm *sorry!* Okay?"

When Libby returned with a tray of cups and a bag of fat-free, sugar-free, taste-free cookies she'd found in Tia's cupboard, Jenny and Tia were sitting on the couch hugging one another.

"The race this afternoon never entered my mind. I didn't look at my calendar last night so I had no idea . . . and I had people to talk to. I needed advice. . . ."

"Maybe you'd better start at the beginning," Libby said bluntly. "It's all about Brandon, isn't it?"

And indeed it was. With her friends encouraging her, bit by bit the story poured out in as much chronological order as Tia could muster.

"It's over," Tia finally concluded, "the business relationship and the personal one. *Finis,* done and gone, the end, amen."

Libby and Jenny appeared thunderstruck. Tears ran down Libby's cheeks. "But there must be something to salvage . . ."

"Would you work with a man who 'borrowed' your money to pay his own bills, was willing to lie about damaged stock, and asked you to do something he knew contradicted your values?"

"When you put it that way . . ."

"But if you break up the business," Jenny said, "think how much you'll lose."

"I know." Tia's words caught in her throat. She couldn't think of the stores without thinking of Brandon or vice versa. "It was his investment that allowed me to expand. I'll just have to pull back again. That's all there is to it."

"Sell the land?" Libby said, shocked.

"I've already talked to a realtor. Brandon will have to be involved, but I'd like it on the market as soon as possible. There's no way to keep the land, but I can move inventory here to the main store and have a big sale and see how many of the bills that will pay." She winced. "There's been a lot of outlay."

Tia shrunk into the corner of the couch and put her head in her hands. "I feel like such a fool and I did it to myself! I wanted to run my own life—great job I did, huh?"

"Tia, it's not like that . . . ," Jenny began.

"Yes, it is. The only times I ever prayed about this expansion or about Brandon, for that matter, were when I gave God a shopping list of what *I* wanted! And he let me limp along, allowing me my way, waiting for me to see the light. When I did, it was strobes, megawatts, luminescence, volcanic eruptions . . ."

"What do you mean?" Libby looked confused.

"It happened when I changed my prayer. When I finally saw where this thing was taking me, I quit praying for what *I* wanted and started praying for what God wanted for me."

"So now we're on to God's plan B?" Jenny inquired gently.

"I'm counting on it. Everything else has been stripped away—my romance, my business expansion, my pride." Tia ran her fingers through her hair again. It was beginning to look like she'd combed it with an eggbeater. "Can you imagine what people will be saying? Entrepreneur of the Week one week, Biggest Blunder of the Month the next. I'm going to have bankers and realtors breathing down my neck."

Tia scrubbed at her eyes. "I've failed them all. I'm an embarrassment to myself and to others."

"That simply isn't true. Everyone has setbacks. You just had yours faster and more publicly than most. 'Quick turnaround'—isn't that what you'd call it? You're just being true to form. Remember what we used to call you? Drama Queen. Everything has always been a production with you—I guess that even means mistakes," Libby said.

"Well, here I am again, hanging everything out to dry so the whole world can see it."

"Maybe this is the beginning of the blessing," Libby said tentatively.

Tia frowned. This didn't feel like a blessing.

"You always say we should expect the blessing, find it in whatever happens, anticipate the positive," Libby reminded her.

"I must have said that on a better day," Tia growled, but a wisp of a smile curled one side of her lips. "What *is* the blessing in this? You tell me."

"If you'd gotten in any deeper with Brandon," Libby pointed out, "it would have been even more devastating. You didn't build the third store or marry him!"

"True . . . ," Tia murmured doubtfully.

"We're always tempted to forge ahead without consulting God," Jenny mulled. "When we choose sin, God often allows us to see the results. Maybe sometimes we need to be readied for the blessing."

Tia shuddered. "I've seen all I want and been prepared plenty for the results, thank you very much."

"Brandon didn't love you the right way, Tia. Just as I doubt you loved him like you should have."

"What do you mean, Libby?"

"Even though Reese is in a wheelchair and when I met him I was very lonely, we loved each other more than we *needed* each other. I was getting by and so was he. We're much better together than we are apart, but I'm only with him because I love him. I don't expect any more of him than to love me in return."

"And you think our attraction to each other was because of what we could do together businesswise? Surely it couldn't have been just that!"

"Of course not. If you'd asked him, he would have denied it vehemently—and honestly. But somewhere, deep down . . ."

"I know, I know. The blessing is that I got out while the getting was good." Tia snuffled. "That's a pragmatic blessing if there ever was one."

Jenny took Tia's hand. "Remember when Lee died and how devastated I was? I had convinced myself that life would never improve, that I would be permanently lodged in despair. And you told me it would pass, that God would carry me through."

"Are you telling me to follow my own advice?" It was becoming painfully clear that sometimes God allowed the things people depended upon—houses, money, friends, hobbies, habits—to fall away. It was a hard but effective reminder that he is the only source of goodness, and nothing else can take his place.

"Something like that. And remember, Libby and I are here for you no matter what. You can't shake us. Granted, we aren't heavyweights in the problem-solving department, but we'll try any way we can."

"*You* are a blessing," Tia observed. As tears rolled down her cheeks, she made no move to blot them. She touched Jenny's cheek, then reached for Libby's hand. "The hands of God in human form."

....

Tia couldn't face going to work the next day. It reminded her of everything that had gone wrong in her life in the past months. The huge inventory she'd been so excited about when Ribbons & Rainbows opened had "overdue payment" plastered all over it now. As soon as her employees knew of the changes that were coming, they'd be walking around with faces as long as beagles' ears, and clients would come in asking about the status of the stores.

She stopped at Tia's Attic only long enough to haul several wooden birdhouses to her car, make herself a double mocha, and pick up the mail. Then, dressed in jeans and a sweatshirt and wearing a baseball cap with her dark hair sprouting out the opening in the back, Tia headed out to spread a little joy she didn't quite feel.

"What makes you think you can afford to donate more bird-houses?" Helen Anderson demanded when Tia arrived at the women's crisis center.

"I've got twice as many as I need—literally. I ordered for both stores and now . . . well, let's just say I might have to sell Ribbons & Rainbows."

"That will leave you with only the store you started with."

Tia shrugged, not really wanting to dwell on the subject.

"It's a little like a divorce, isn't it? Dividing what you worked for together . . ."

"*Destroying* might be a better word to use," Tia said with a sigh. "But enough about that. Help me carry some of these things, will you?"

Helen helped her put the houses in the main office. Then she placed her hands on her hips and studied Tia. "Now what?"

"Now I go outside and hang a couple birdhouses and pray that God does something with them."

Helen snorted. "That doesn't sound like a good business plan."

"No? At least the partner I've got now is honest, reliable, faithful, steady as a rock."

"Omnipotent, omnipresent . . ."

"Sounds like a good deal to me." Tia pushed the cap to the back of her head, picked up birdhouses and some wire, and went outside.

"Okay, God. I'm all yours. If it's birdhouses you want, it's birdhouses you'll get. I don't know how you're going to use them. All I know is that I'm going to hang them."

The trees outside the center looked as though they'd been waiting for birdhouses to arrive. The branches were at just the right height and Tia, using her stepladder, hung one. As she was struggling to put up a second, someone cleared a throat behind her.

"Hello there," Tia said as she turned, set the birdhouse down, and greeted the young woman pleasantly. She had brown hair that fell raggedly to her shoulders, indicating it hadn't been professionally cut in a very long time. Her eyes were the color of strong black tea, with flecks of amber near the irises. She was lovely despite the smudgy circles beneath her eyes and the faded cotton dress she wore. The woman folded her hands over her huge pregnant belly and gazed at Tia as if she were seeing an exotic new bird in the branches.

"Hello." The voice was so soft and tentative that Tia wasn't sure if she'd actually heard the word or lip-read it.

"I'm Tia. What's your name?"

"Anna."

"Are you staying here or just visiting someone?" Tia asked tactfully.

"Staying. Till my baby is born, I hope." Anna's eyes darkened and the gold flecks seemed to disappear. "Can't go home or he'd kill us both."

"And that would be . . . ?"

"My fiancé."

Anna seemed reluctant to expand on her answer, so Tia picked up the birdhouse she'd set down. "Where is your room?"

Anna pointed to the window in front of which Tia was working.

"Do you like this birdhouse?"

Anna looked at the others still lying on the ground. "I like that one better."

She pointed to a birdhouse made to look like a barn. It was bright red and trimmed in white. The roof was green, and a cow and a pig were glued to the base. Tia wasn't sure a self-respecting bird would enter one of these things, but for the moment they were what she had to offer.

"Would you like me to hang this here for you?"

"Why?" Anna looked puzzled.

"So that when you look out the window, you will see something cheerful and whimsical. And, hopefully, something that will remind you of birds."

"I don't think on birds much," Anna admitted.

Willingly, Tia explained the idea about the birdhouses and that she wanted to offer the people at the center a little hope, a little laughter, and Jesus.

"I don't think on Jesus much either." Anna scuffed at the ground, and Tia saw that she was wearing tennis shoes with soles that were peeling away. "I figure that if he were real, he'd be here helping me."

"Maybe he sent me to do that."

Now where did that *come from?* Tia wondered. The words had fallen out of her mouth before her brain had even clicked on. She'd had no intention of involving herself personally with this bedraggled-looking girl but there it was, her offer to do just that.

Tia squinted and looked suspiciously at the sky. *Talk about putting words in someone's mouth!*

"You mean it? Jesus sent you to help me?"

The idea again occurred to Tia, and perhaps it was true. She was a set of God's hands here on earth, and he had just presented her with a new challenge. Six months ago she would have given the girl some money and the name and number of a friend who worked in social services. But things had changed now. It was time for Tia to give of herself.

"If you'll help me hang the rest of these, we can go to the store and get bird feed. Maybe we could have a bite of lunch on the way back."

Anna looked as if Tia had asked her to go on a jaunt to the moon. "L-l-lunch?"

"Sure. Your choice. Mexican, Chinese, Italian, or good old burgers and fries."

"I can't remember the last time I had lunch in a restaurant." The gold flecks were back, her eyes sparkling. Then they dimmed as Anna brushed her hands over her dress and belly. "But I don't want to go looking like this. If I'd dared, I would have taken time to get some clothes, but I had to leave while he was asleep and I didn't want to wake him."

Tia winced inwardly but put on her most encouraging smile. "That's easy. We'll stop somewhere and pick up a couple new dresses for you."

"I ain't got no money." Anna looked as if the brightly wrapped packages under the Christmas tree were just out of reach.

"No? Well, I have some and since I volunteer here, I know that sometimes Helen Anderson can find funds for an occasional emergency. We could go to a discount or outlet store or even a consignment shop. What do you say?"

"Why are you doing this for me?" Anna's expression was both longing and suspicious.

"Because I believe God wants me to."

Tia had never dreamed consignment-store shopping could be such fun. Because Anna was so shy, it was Tia who tried on the first outfit—a retro lounge suit in orange and green. She pirouetted in front of the mirror and twisted herself into a pretzel to get a good look at her backside. "This is comfortable. Do you like it, Anna?"

"You look like my aunt Hildy used to look when I was little—but skinnier."

"Then I'll take it!" Tia eyed the three-dollar price tag. "And now it's your turn."

Three maternity tops, a pair of jeans, and a new dress were in Anna's bag when they left the store. She was glowing. "I can't believe I won't have to wear the same thing every day!" Much to Tia's surprise, Anna suddenly set herself into a spin on the street, and Tia had to jump back to avoid being hit by her whirling shopping bag.

When Anna stopped spinning with delight and was staggering around trying to get her bearings, Tia grabbed her hand and pulled her into an arcade that had a photo booth. "Let's take our picture."

They both squeezed into the small space—not easy with Anna's belly and their purchases—and Tia fed dollar bills into the slot. "I remember when these things were cheap," she grumbled as the first light flashed. "Quick, change your expression; we have three pictures left! Oh, my mouth was open."

She'd pried Anna out of the booth just about the time the little strip of black-and-white photos slithered out of the machine.

Anna let out a chortle of glee. "Look, Tia, your eyes are shut on this one. . . . Your mouth is open here. . . . Oh, you turned your head."

"There's a reason I didn't become a model," Tia muttered, wishing she'd put the shopping bag over her head for the photos.

But Anna grasped the pictures to her chest. "Can I have them?"

"I don't know why you'd want them. I look like a baby sparrow on every one. My mouth's wide open. And you look like a deer caught in headlights."

"I want them so I can remember the best day of my life."

Tia froze. "The best day of your life?"

"Uh-huh. New clothes, eating out, laughing . . ." A blissful smile settled on Anna's face—and went straight to Tia's heart.

Tia had done so little and it had been so easy, yet it was still the "best day" of Anna's life. How many more women could be gifted with a day like this? Tia wanted to find out.

Helen Anderson was waiting for them at the door of the center. "Looks like you two had fun."

"It was so grand!" Anna beamed. "I'm going upstairs to put away my new clothes!" Before going to her room, Anna hugged Tia so hard that she nearly lost her breath.

"New clothes?" Helen eyed Tia with a slight smile.

"One of the little shops near Fiftieth and France that sells slightly used clothing. Best forty bucks I ever spent."

"Aha! We've gotcha!" Helen exclaimed.

Tia stared at Helen. "What?"

"You've got the helping bug. It's a high, isn't it?"

"Big time. And I had a wonderful experience, too." Tia finally understood what motivated Helen to sacrifice so much of her time and herself to this place.

"Unfortunately, now I have a favor to ask of you that won't be so much fun. A hospital social worker called to say a woman has been asking for help. She's been beaten pretty badly around the head and shoulders and wouldn't give the phone number of a family member to call. She agreed to have someone from the center be with her, but I can't find anyone else who can leave right now. I'll come when I can. Would you . . ."

As she negotiated her way to the hospital and through a maze of corridors, Tia began to panic. How could she help someone she couldn't get to? She kept repeating the name Helen had given her—Dianne Gray—which, Tia thought, reminded her very much of John Doe. She finally found someone to point her toward the correct room. "In there."

"There" was an examining room housing a woman about her own age, who slumped as she sat on the examining table while an LPN took notes on a chart.

The nurse looked up when Tia entered. "Are you from the crisis center?"

"I . . . yes . . ."

"Ms. Gray asked that someone be with her when the doctor examines her. She agreed to have someone from the center. The doctor will be in shortly."

The nurse closed the chart and walked out of the room, leaving Tia and Dianne Gray to stare at one another. Now Tia studied the swollen eye and split skin above it. The gash looked deep and angry. It was gaping and obviously needed stitches, as did the woman's cut lip. When Dianne leaned forward and tried to straighten, Tia saw that her arm hung at an odd angle from her body.

"I wasn't sure anyone would come," Dianne said. Moving her lips appeared painful.

"But I did." Tia pulled a chair close to the table and sat down. "And if it hurts to talk, you don't have to. I'll just sit here with you until . . ."

At that moment a doctor entered the room. His coat was crisp and white, and he smelled of antiseptic. He smiled pleasantly at Dianne and then at Tia, as if he'd expected her. After examining Dianne, he said, "Looks like a nasty cut, but it will be fine with a little sewing job. Lip, too. And the break in your arm is clean. We'll cast it; it shouldn't take more than an hour."

And what a long hour it was for Tia. She'd never been on the viewing end of stitches before. With each tidy suture she felt her stomach roll. As the doctor worked, he asked questions—the whens, the hows, the whys of these injuries. And to every inquiry Dianne gave him the same unresponsive grunt.

When the stitching was done and Dianne's face cleaned, Tia began to see the woman Dianne must have been before the damage—naturally pale skin, blonde hair that, once the blood was out, would be spectacular, worried gray eyes, a slightly recessed chin and bow-shaped mouth. She was quite pretty.

While the doctor set the arm, Tia allowed Dianne to hold her hand. With every grimace, Dianne's grip grew tighter. When they were done, Tia looked down and saw Dianne's fingers were blue and practically bloodless.

The doctor pulled off his gloves and placed his hands in his pockets. "The police have already been here. Ms. Gray doesn't care to press charges. But she also refuses to go home. She agreed to let us call a safe house. . . ."

An answered knock on the door revealed Helen standing on the other side. Tia drooped with relief. Helen introduced herself to the doctor, explained the center to which Dianne would be transported, and efficiently carried out the plan.

When Tia returned to the center after attending to store business, she found Helen waiting for her with a cup of tea in her hands. "I recommend extra sugar. It always gives me a boost once the adrenaline rush fades," said Helen.

Tia mutely took the cup and added three heaping teaspoons. "I was never so glad to see anyone in my entire life as you when you walked through that door! I didn't know what I was supposed to say or do next."

"I didn't plan to leave you hanging. I just needed you there until I could find someone to cover for me here."

"I felt so helpless."

"I know. But she's already tucked into bed and sound asleep. She probably hasn't closed her eyes in two days. I hope you'll stop by and talk to her tomorrow. You were her first connection with the center and it might be comforting for her to see you again—if you have time, that is."

How could she *not* have time? "Of course I'll be here. Do you know what happened to her?"

"She's not saying much yet. Fear, probably. At least she'll be able to get her wits about her and decide what she's going to do next."

"Call the police, I hope," Tia said grimly.

"If it were only that easy. We also have to educate her on the criminal justice system, potential court appearances, other helping agencies, counseling, housing, employment—"

"I get the picture."

"We've gotten pretty proficient at it, sad to say. And I really appreciate your stepping in today when I needed you."

"Any way I can."

Helen looked at Tia as if she were x-raying her insides. "I'll remember that. Now you'd better go home. You look like you've been dragged through a knothole in a toothpick."

And that was exactly how she felt. At home, Tia pulled off her clothes and fell into bed like a pine tree at a loggers' convention. As she lay on her back staring at the ceiling, a thought came to her unbidden. It was a verse from 2 Corinthians, one that her favorite Sunday school teacher had insisted her students memorize and repeat at the start of every day.

"You are a letter . . . written not with pen and ink, but with the Spirit of the living God . . . on human hearts."

Though she was too exhausted to move, her eyes grew wide in the darkness. Her? A human letter, guided by the Holy Spirit, to write a message on another's heart? What kind of message was she to write by her words and her example?

Tia rolled to her side, tucked her hands beneath her cheek, and smiled. She and God were going to discuss this heavenly postal service thing ASAP.

CHAPTER ELEVEN

White-crowned sparrows have been studied in wind tunnels
to see how fast they fly—their normal flight is about eleven
and a half miles per hour in still air, and in order
to hold their position relative to the ground in high wind,
they've been clocked at thirty-nine miles per hour.
They've actually managed to fly backwards in order
to hold their position against a tailwind.

—For the Birds: An Uncommon Guide, Laura Erickson

"This is so pitiful," Tia muttered as she sat on her deck, teary-eyed and sipping coffee while eyeing the toasted bagel on the paper plate in front of her. She broke one-half of the bagel into bits and threw pieces to the squirrel watching cautiously from the deck fence.

It had been like this for days—weepiness overpowering her when she least expected it, a gnawing in the pit of her stomach, and sorrow that seemed to fill and destroy every fiber within her. She wondered if anyone had ever died from terminal sadness.

Her problems overwhelmed her when she was alone, without the people who fueled her extroverted self, or when deluged with business proceedings the likes of which she'd never even imagined. Downsizing was a nightmare. Whom to let go? Which departments to close out? Which wholesalers to pay and which to plead with for another month's leniency? What to tell the customers who had become friends and family to her? Worst of all were the people she was afraid she would have to disappoint—the charities she'd offered to help, the wheelchair athletes . . . the list was huge.

For the first time in her life, Tia couldn't see through to the other side of a dilemma. Through the hazy curtain of her current problems, she could see no light shining.

Brandon called so often she'd quit answering the phone and had begun to let her voice service pick up. His first calls had been apologies, expressions of regret, and sorry pleas to make amends. Then he'd begun to justify his behavior and attempt to cajole her into giving their relationship "just one more try." Thwarted there, he had turned to bribery, then anger.

"Who do you think you are—some high-and-mighty, pompous do-gooder? Condemning me for mistakes as though you've never made any!" he'd said the last time they'd spoken together.

"I'm not condemning you. I'm just saying that we can't work together because our values are so very different."

"There, you admit it. You think you're so much better than me. Is that what all that 'faith in God' stuff has done for you—made you holier-than-thou?"

It was blatantly clear that he'd had no idea how her faith worked. It made Tia weep each time she thought of how reckless she'd been and what a sorry sort of person Brandon was right now. She'd had the ultimate reality check—she was so much weaker than she'd thought, and embarrassingly proud.

She groped around the table for her Kleenex box, gave an unladylike honk into the tissue, and reached for the other half of her breakfast. Libby and Jenny had been yipping at her to eat because even her slimmest clothes were beginning to hang on her tiny frame. Tia felt around the plate for her bagel but it was not there. It was, in fact, not even on the table—or under it.

Was she losing her mind too? *Oh, well. I'll probably feel better without it.*

Then a movement on the deck railing caught her eye. The squirrel, who'd greedily gobbled up the bits of bagel Tia had tossed him, had obviously not had enough. He sat on the railing staring at her through beady black eyes, the entire second half of the bagel in his mouth. They locked eyes for a moment. Then the squirrel turned, flicked his tail at Tia, dashed precariously across the railing, and launched himself into a tree.

The weight of the bagel nearly toppled him backward, but by sheer strength of will and sharp nails, he hung on. Tia watched in fascination as the little animal maneuvered his treasure into the crook of the tree.

She stared at him as he sampled his trophy, tiny jaws grinding rapidly. He looked back at her as if to say, "See? I knew I could do it."

A chuckle swelled in her throat, then another and another, until Tia was practically rolling on the deck floor clutching her sides with laughter. "Oh . . . oh . . ." She held one arm close to her aching ribs and hoisted herself to a standing position.

If that silly little squirrel could get that huge hunk of dough up a tree, then she could certainly carry at least as big a load relative to her own size!

"Quit the pity party, Tia! Be like the squirrel. Don't think about the problems, just the solutions!" Then she tilted her head and looked upward with a suspicious eye. "Did you give me that squirrel on purpose, Lord? As a metaphor for my own life?"

. . . .

"Tia? Is that you?" A gruff male voice on the other end of the line made her straighten at her desk.

"Rollie? You sound odd. Is something wrong?"

"I don't know. I've got a funny feeling about something, but maybe it's those breakfast burritos I had this morning. That kid of yours, Trevor, didn't show up today."

That kid of "hers"? She didn't think of Trevor in quite that way, but she supposed it was true. She'd certainly taken him under her wing and he seemed to be thriving.

"Had he promised to come?"

"Yes. And he never misses a day. He loves it out here. A pretty good worker, too. That's why I was so surprised when he called."

"If he called, why are you concerned?"

"I'm not sure. He sounded funny—upset or scared, maybe."

"What could have frightened him?"

"I have no idea. He only said that his mother couldn't bring him out. They only have one car. I heard her in the background, but she didn't sound right either. Maybe they'd had a disagreement, but she's been as anxious for him to be here as Trevor has himself. It doesn't make sense because when they left the other day, they both said they'd see me this morning."

Rollie sounded unsure. "I just feel a little uncomfortable, and I can't put my finger on why. I thought you might want to know."

"How did Trevor's mom sound? Could you hear what she was saying?"

"That was odd, too. She was making little squeaking sounds—like a mouse or a new kitten."

The hackles rose on the back of Tia's neck. "Thanks for calling, Rollie. Maybe I'll drive to their house and make sure she's not sick."

"It might be a good idea. Something just wasn't right about that call." He paused. "And be careful, okay?"

"I intend to be," Tia muttered as she dialed Libby's number. "What's up?" she asked without preamble when her friend answered.

"I've been baking," Libby responded cheerfully. "Reese and Robert went through the house like tornadoes and ate everything in sight. They even emptied the freezer. Robert's in a growing spurt. I don't know what Reese's excuse is—just fun, I guess."

"Could you take a few minutes to go for a ride with me?"

"Sure. If you'll stop at a grocery store so I can get some eggs before we get back. Where are we going?"

"To Mariah West's house. Trevor called Rollie this morning and said he couldn't come out to the ranch."

"Curious. He never misses. He confided to Reese that he was happier at the ranch than anywhere else on earth. And Mariah told Reese that she'd do anything to make sure he got to work on time."

"That's what I thought. Rollie had some sort of vibe about the call, so I want to check it out. That's the most friendless family I've ever met. I want to make sure something isn't really wrong."

"Pick me up," Libby said. "I'll be ready."

"Nice neighborhood," Libby commented as they drove down the street toward Trevor's home. The houses were small, old, and poorly kept. "What does Mr. West do for a living?"

"Trevor has never said. Once I got the idea that he had a bad back and didn't work regularly, but I can't say for sure."

"It certainly looks like he doesn't strain himself around the house," Libby said dryly as they pulled up to the curb.

The house was sided with a gray, old-fashioned, shingle-type siding that had been around since the home was built. The shingles looked as though they'd been haphazardly patched over the years. Still, the windows gleamed crystal clear in the sunlight, and a planter filled with a riot of moss roses sat on the step.

"Aren't there restrictions against things like that?" Libby pointed to the open garage. It was stacked floor to ceiling along the walls with greasy car parts, old jars, and sagging cardboard boxes. In the middle was a junker of a car with most of its innards strewn across the heaved concrete floor. "Looks like a fire hazard with all those greasy rags."

Tia bit her lip. The whole place looked like some sort of accident waiting to happen. She'd known, just looking at Trevor and his mother, that money was a scarce commodity at home, but seeing it firsthand made Tia's heart sink. There was no car in the driveway, which probably meant that Trevor's father had taken it today. Perhaps she and Rollie had succumbed to overactive imaginations, and Trevor's only reason for not going to work today was no transportation.

"They must not have a car today. Guess I pulled the alarm before I even saw smoke. We might as well say hello anyway." Tia walked up the steps and knocked on the door.

It took a long time for anyone to answer, even though Tia could hear footsteps and whispering inside. And when Trevor opened the door, he looked unhappy to see them.

"Hi. Talked to Rollie this morning, and he said you couldn't get a ride to the ranch. If you still want to go, I could take you." As she spoke, Tia's gaze wandered over the boy's shoulder. The house was spotless but threadbare, as though the West family had not purchased anything new in a very long time.

"Thanks, but it's already pretty late. Maybe he'll let me come in another day." Trevor looked like a bird puffing out his feathers to keep warm. He seemed to make himself twice his normal size to block Tia's vision into the house.

Tia had no reason to think Mariah wasn't just fine, but there was something so . . . . "Is your mother okay?"

"It's okay, honey. They can come in."

"But, Mom . . ."

"I don't care if they see me, Trevor."

At her words, the boy shrank out of the doorway.

Mariah West was still in her flannel nightgown. She was barefoot, and her hair was pulled starkly away from her face. An angry bruise spread high on her cheekbone, and a knot the size of a small egg sat at her hairline.

Tia and Libby froze in the doorway.

"Trevor is always trying to protect me," Mariah said quickly. She looked at her son with tenderness. "But he doesn't have to protect me from you."

"What happened, Mariah?" Tia asked.

"Just a stumble on the stairs, that's all. Silly of me. I'm so clumsy sometimes."

"Ah, come on, Ma! He hit you! You might as well say it," Trevor blurted. "He's always hitting you!"

"Trevor! Don't say things like that. It was a stumble . . ."

"Yeah? Because Dad was standing behind you and shoved?"

Tia stepped between mother and son. "Maybe we could talk about it, Mariah. I work with the Women's Crisis Center. We could help you."

"I'm not having a crisis, for goodness sake! Now you ladies are just being silly. Trevor's got your imaginations working overtime. Would you like some coffee? I've got part of a cake left from yesterday. Lemon filling." She looked at them expectantly, as if she always entertained barefoot in her nightgown with a gory black eye and a lump on her forehead.

"No, thank you. Mariah . . ."

"No, Tia. I don't need help."

Tia slipped a card out of her pocket, one she'd grabbed from the top of her desk after Rollie's call. It was Helen Anderson's number at the center. "If you change your mind, will you call me? If you need help immediately, call 911. This is the director at the crisis center, and she will help you in any way she can."

Mariah's giggle was as phony as a television laugh track. "I won't need that! You girls . . ." She shook her head as she showed them to the door. Behind her, Trevor's face was a contorted mask of fear and indecision.

"Do we dare leave her there?" Libby asked breathlessly when they were back in the car. "You didn't believe her, did you?"

"Of course not. But she's a grown woman. If she won't press charges or go for help, there's not much we can do."

"Unless he practically kills her. Why would any woman protect a man who treated her like that?"

"Fear. Of the man. Of what might happen if he left her. Shame. Low self-worth. Besides, he's Trevor's father and her husband. She probably feels she has nowhere else to go."

"Well, I'm telling Reese when I get home. Somebody needs to know about this."

"And I'll talk to Helen. She knows much more about these things than I do. I'll also visit with Trevor. He may be the piece that completes the puzzle."

"Maybe she feels it's being disloyal," Libby mused. "'In sickness and in health, for better and for worse' and all that."

"No one's asking her to walk away from her marriage, Lib. We're asking her to walk toward help—for her, for her son, and even for her husband. If he sees the light and gets counseling, things could turn around. But she needs to be safe until then."

"Wow," Libby breathed. "I've always admired the fact that you've volunteered at the center, but I had no idea . . ."

"People don't want to know what really goes on around them, Lib. It's painful to think about some people's suffering and be helpless to do anything about it."

"Then what keeps you going back?"

"I'm not sure. I feel like I'm being led—no, pushed—in that direction, that's all. And if God has plans for me in this area, I want to stick around to find out what they are." Tia gave a little laugh. "Seems unlikely, doesn't it? A single businesswoman, on a crusade to help other women in bad relationships?"

Libby sat back in her seat and stared out the front window of the car. "Not really. We've all seen God work things out often enough to realize that we can't imagine what God can do or who he'll use. Even our wildest imaginings are restrictive to God."

Tia nodded emphatically. "No doubt about that. There is no putting limitations on him."

"I've done it myself," Libby admitted. "I catch myself saying, 'Surely God wouldn't do this or couldn't do that.' Then I realize God is God. There is no way to box him in or decide what the *right* thing is for him to do. It's a pretty pompous notion, isn't it?"

"And I am so glad I don't have to make every decision by myself," Tia sighed. "I have no idea right now what to do about Trevor and Mariah." She turned her eyes upward. "Help!"

. . . .

"What are you three doing in here?" Libby asked as she and Jenny entered the kitchen. "You're laughing like you're all insane . . . oh, excuse me . . . you *are* insane."

Tia, Luke, and Robert were seated at the kitchen table eating Cheerios with chopsticks. Robert was so delighted by the silliness that his glasses were falling off his nose.

"Where did you get those things? Or do I need to ask?" Libby eyed Tia, whose purse was open on the floor beside her. More chopsticks sprouted out the top of the designer leather bag.

"This is great, Mom!" Luke's Cheerios showered over the side of the table and pelted to the floor. "Can Tia come over for breakfast more often?"

"Next time it will be toast. *Finger* food."

"Party pooper," Tia commented as she got up and followed her friends back into the dining room, where their own brunch waited. "Next we were going to have a burping contest."

"I know why the boys love you," Jenny sighed, "but you make their mothers look dull in comparison."

"Mothers are supposed to be dull. It's their job. Mothers don't get interesting until the kids grow up. Now not having parental interests means I can be as goofy as I want." Tia poured herself some coffee.

"So tell us, have you been looking for bargains on the shopping networks late at night?" Jenny asked.

"Or ordering things from infomercials?" Libby inquired.

". . . while dipping potato chips in fudge?" Jenny continued.

"Watching reruns?"

"Taking too many naps?"

"And writing letters with three colors of ink on alternating lines?" Libby added.

"Actually, I was using two colors and alternating every other word."

"That depressed, huh?" Jenny said sympathetically.

Tia nodded ruefully. "You know me like a book."

"We know how you distract yourself when you're feeling down. You've been trying awfully hard lately, haven't you?" Libby asked.

Tia leaned forward and cradled her forehead in the palms of her hands. "I really thought I could tough this out, but once I got right down to missing Brandon and trying to accept the idea of losing so much of my business . . ."

"We're really proud of you, Tia. You did the right thing and you still are doing it." Jenny patted Tia's hand.

"Tell that to Brandon and his lawyers," Tia muttered.

Libby looked aghast. "What lawyers?"

"The ones who have stepped in to sort out our investment. What could have been fairly simple has now become very difficult."

"Why is Brandon doing this?" Libby moaned.

"Anger, hurt, revenge, blindness—I don't know. He's just showing his true colors." Tia looked over Jenny's shoulder through the window to where the boys were now playing outside with the dogs. "I've been praying for him, though, asking God to step in and provide him with whatever he needs in order to be whole."

Tia grinned weakly. "If I started praying to God for all the things I think Brandon needs, I'd probably pray that his hair and teeth fall out."

"Not very gracious," Jenny said with a smile, "but honest."

"Besides, my prayer list has gotten so long that it's difficult to tend to all of it. There are women at the crisis center who make my heart ache. I can't get them out of my mind. A woman came in yesterday who'd been pregnant but had lost her baby because her husband beat her."

"Oh!" Instinctively, Jenny grabbed for her own expanding belly. "How dreadful."

"I know. She's in so much emotional pain that it's agonizing to watch. But she actually smiled when I showed her the birdhouse that was going outside her window. It's a miniature gingerbread house. I hope it isn't so bright it scares away the birds. She could certainly use a canary right now. Even a wren.

"Today I'm taking Dianne—another woman from the center— out to lunch. Fried chicken in the park. She's very skittish and won't say much about her relationship or how it turned sour, but she did admit she'd married the man more because she was in love with the idea of being married than with the man himself.

"Ironic, isn't it? I wanted a package, too—the business, the man, the happy-ever-after. I should have known that life doesn't come in such tidy gift packs. I feel a real kinship to her, even though we know very little about one another. Dianne, if that's even her real name, had big ideas, too—and the big ones break the hardest."

"Humpty Dumpty Tia sat on a wall, Humpty Dumpty Tia had a great fall. And all the king's horses and all the king's men couldn't put Tia together again," Jenny quoted a rhyme they'd often used in their childhood when someone had taken a spill off her bike or tripped over the jump rope.

Tia smiled gently. "Only God can put Tia together again."

. . . .

"I'd forgotten how pretty it is here!" Dianne, in one of the new outfits Tia had purchased for her at a rummage sale they'd visited, dropped onto a park bench and watched the sky through the moving kaleidoscope of leaves. She drew a deep breath and threw her arms out wide. "Listen to the wind in the trees. It sounds like music! And the fresh-cut grass . . ."

Tia watched Dianne indulgently, feeling like a mother whose child was discovering the world for the very first time. Dianne was still rugged-looking—her face and body all bony angles, dusky smudges of fading bruises, a broken tooth—but her eyes actually looked as though there was a light behind them now, as though the resident was finally home. She had some color in her cheeks, and her hair was pulled into a tidy ponytail. Tia could see that there had been beauty in this woman once—and that there could be again.

"It's as though my senses had been turned off, and they just switched on again!"

They explored several possible picnic spots before settling on one. As Tia spread out the food, Dianne watched. Her appetite was back. She ate steadily for some minutes before speaking. "I'd like a life like this."

"This is your life."

Dianne shook her head. "I mean a life where I had clothes and a place to stay and the freedom to spend time in the park . . . you know, a better life."

"Then do it."

Sadness blanketed Dianne's features. "I don't know how. I dropped out of school to marry. The only jobs I ever held were in fast-food restaurants and as a hotel maid. I can't pay for anything decent to live in on that kind of salary."

"Then perhaps you should consider going back to school."

Dianne looked at Tia skeptically. "I don't think you realize what you're saying. You might as well tell me to go to the moon."

But Tia, with her squirrel and his bagel in mind, was already hatching plans. "It wouldn't have to be a four-year program. Something you could finish more quickly, like computer or secretarial training. I could check into it for you."

"Where would I live? And what would I pay for it with?"

Tia chewed on her lower lip for a moment. "I know Helen has talked about transitional housing. Maybe she could help us—"

"Tia," Dianne's voice was uncommonly firm, *"look* at me!"

And Tia did. What she saw was a woman barely hanging on to hope and to her own physical health. "How much did you weigh when you got married?"

"About thirty pounds more than this."

"When was the last time you had a physical?"

"I can't remember."

"Have you seen a dentist?"

Dianne pointed to her broken tooth. "Does it look like it?"

As usual, Tia's eagerness to help had painted Dianne's picture with glowing pink optimism. But the real picture was much less rosy. "At least let me talk to Helen about transitional housing. And think about learning a trade."

Dianne was looking so skeptical that Tia put her hand on Dianne's arm. "Let me help you."

"How?" Suspicion tinged her question.

"I could mentor you. Help you with the things that feel too overwhelming, drive you to job interviews, find you some medical and dental help, take you to church, gather some furniture when you get a place to stay. . . ."

"You'd do all that for me? Why?"

Pure and lasting religion in the sight of God our Father means that we must care for orphans and widows in their troubles, and refuse to let the world corrupt us. Here was Tia's opportunity to live James 1:27. But she understood Dianne's misgivings. Tia didn't know if she was up to her task either.

Suddenly Tia realized how long they'd been in the park and glanced at her watch. "Uh-oh, gotta go." She scrambled to her feet and quickly gathered their paper plates and napkins. "I've got an appointment with an attorney at two. I'll come to see you tomorrow and we'll talk some more."

"Attorney? More troubles?" Dianne's brow furrowed. Apparently she, too, had heard bits and pieces of Tia's business woes.

"I certainly hope not."

. . . .

But it *was* trouble—and plenty of it.

Tia had finally quit hyperventilating by the time she got to Jenny's bakery, where Jenny was completing her part of a big catering job for that evening. Libby and Dorothy had pitched in, making tiny open-faced sandwiches with designs of watercress, fingernail-thin slices of olive and pimento, pinhead-sized piles of caviar, and dabs of egg salad. Their friend Ellen was filling cream puffs the size of cotton balls with a tuna concoction.

They looked up in welcome when Tia entered, but their smiles didn't last when they saw the expression on her face.

"Conference," Libby whispered.

Jenny put down the pastry tube she'd been wielding and followed her two friends into the office. "What's up?"

Tia pinched her thumb and forefinger over the bridge of her nose. "Migraine time."

"How'd the appointment with the attorney go? Did you get anything figured out?" Jenny demanded.

"Lousy. And I don't like what he figured out." Tia looked up, feeling unnaturally flushed. The veins in her forehead throbbed and her eyes were blurry. "I think I'll have to close *both* stores. Fortunately, I saved for a rainy day. But even so, between the center and what's happened with the stores, I realize I need to change my spending habits."

"But Brandon had nothing to do with your original store!" Libby protested.

"No, but this little adventure is going to cost me. I have bills to pay. We shared the business; we shared the bills. Big ones. The inventory grew to astronomical proportions, thanks to Brandon's enthusiasm. Refurbishing the new facility to get ready for Ribbons & Rainbows was much more expensive than Brandon had revealed to me. What stock can't be returned, we'll have to pay for one way or another. If I sell what I can and scale back to cut current expenses, maybe I can do it."

"Where is Brandon in all of this?" Jenny asked.

"In Canada, selling new products for Beacons."

"And you're here trying to put the best face on this mess?"

"Looks like it."

"Oh, Tia, we are so sorry." Libby flung her arms around Tia for a comforting hug. "Things weren't supposed to turn out this way."

"It's not the way I had it planned, but I still have to believe that something good will come of this."

"It's just not fair!" Libby retorted.

"Life isn't always fair." Tia regarded her friends with affection. Jenny and Libby were rigid with righteous indignation over the situation.

"Why is it our lessons are always so hard?" Libby asked angrily.

"Because we don't learn them the first time?" Tia leaned against the wall and stretched her neck to relieve tension. "From now on, I'm going to learn my lessons early."

Tia turned to her friend. "Jen, you've been quiet. Don't you have anything to add to our profundities?"

Jenny abruptly sat down with an odd expression on her face. "I . . . I can't." The quiver in her voice brought her friends to attention. "Something's not right." She rubbed her hand over the bulge at her waist. "Something with the baby."

"It's too soon!" Tia breathed.

"I know." Jenny looked up at them with tears in her eyes. "Please call Mike. I think I need to see a doctor."

The ensuing flurry took minutes but seemed like hours. They bundled Jenny into Tia's car and went directly to the hospital, where a somber Mike was already waiting. Nurses spirited Jenny away with Mike trailing behind, leaving Tia and Libby wringing their hands in the waiting area.

"She couldn't be in labor . . . could she?" Tia asked.

Libby's face was as white as the sterile wall behind her. "You don't think she'll lose the baby, do you?"

Tia grew very still. The issues of her business and personal life seemed very small and far away right now. The ultrasound pictures of that tiny creature in Jenny's belly loomed large and clear in her mind's eye. A little burp. A beating heart. A thumb groping its way to a tiny mouth. A wave of nausea rose in her gut.

"Let's go somewhere quiet," Tia said. She led the way to a small family waiting room that was empty. She and Libby sat down in chairs across from each other, clutched each other's hands, and prayed.

Later Tia was to realize that she didn't know which prayers were spoken aloud and which ascended silently from her heart. All she did know was that nearly two hours had passed when Mike found them.

Tia and Libby leaped to their feet. "How is she?" Tia asked.

"What did the doctor say?" Libby questioned.

"Is she going to be all right? And the baby?" Tia heard her voice quiver as she spoke.

Mike held up a hand to silence them. "Jenny is staying here tonight."

"Does that mean something is really wrong?" Tia asked, a sick feeling settling in the pit of her stomach.

"She just had an ultrasound, and the doctor believes she has cervical incompetence. The cervix is too weak to hold a pregnancy to term. As the baby grows, the weight becomes too much for the cervix and it can't stay closed. If it is weak enough, gravity may be enough to let even a preemie's weight make it dilate."

"But it's too early!" Libby cried.

"That's why she's staying. They want to observe her for twenty-four hours and screen her for infection. Then they'll perform cerclage. That's stitching the cervix closed until the baby is ready to be born."

"Ewww!" Tia blurted. "That sounds horrible!"

"Will she have to have a cesarean?" Libby asked.

"Not necessarily. The doctor says the procedure can be very effective, and success rates are high. She'll need to have plenty of rest, cut down on her physical activity, and see the doctor every week. They'll keep doing ultrasounds to monitor her progress."

"But the baby . . . ," Tia began.

"If this works, she will be fine."

But if it doesn't . . .

Mike touched Tia's arm. "We'll need both of you now."

"Anything you want. Libby and I are here for you."

Mike raked his fingers through his hair. "She'll spend the entire time she's resting stewing about the bakery and catering service. If I could tell her that it was in good hands . . ."

"I'll take over the management," Libby said. "I do it part-time anyway. I'll just plan to work full-time for as long as Jenny wants me to."

"And I'll do her bookwork," Tia added.

Mike's shoulders sagged in relief. "I was hoping you'd say that. What Jenny needs to concentrate on right now is staying off her feet and growing that baby."

"Well, tell her she's not welcome at the bakery until she's got little Tibby in her arms," Tia said firmly.

CHAPTER TWELVE

*White-breasted nuthatch: Unlike brown creepers and woodpeckers that
forage along bark in the expected heads-up, tails-down orientation,
the gravity-defying white-breasted nuthatch takes on tree trunks
upside down. From this rather original perspective, the bird can
spot those tasty insects that slipped the eye of upright foragers.*

—Birds: An Explore Your World Handbook, Discovery Books and David Bird

"Have you seen her yet?" Tia popped her head into the bakery door, where Libby was packing pastries into shallow boxes.

"I talked to Mike before work, and he said Jenny was still sleeping. I told him we'd be over this evening if she was up to company," Libby answered.

"Did he say how the procedure went?"

"No problems so far. Mike sounded pretty frazzled. I invited Luke and Spot to spend a few days at our house to give them a break. Robert will be ecstatic."

"It's not like a sure thing, though, is it? That they'll save the baby, I mean."

"There is only one sure thing that I can think of in this world, Tia."

Tia dropped onto a stool by the door. "I know. But nothing can happen to Jenny or Tibby. *It just can't.* What a mess."

"Speaking of messes, do you have anything to report?"

"Nothing but another meeting this afternoon. I'll find out *exactly* where I stand and what I'll have to do to resolve this debacle."

"Are you optimistic?"

"One minute I am and the next I'm Chicken Little with the sky falling on me. I honestly have no idea what the final tally will be. Brandon hid huge expenditures from me. I should have been more watchful . . . but I trusted him."

And loved him.

They stared at each other over a pile of cooling cream puff shells.

"Fine pickle we find ourselves in," Libby commented.

It was just like Libby to feel as much a part of someone's crisis as if it were happening personally to her. Tia, Libby, and Jenny had known each other so long that if one suffered, they all suffered. No matter what else went on, Tia felt blessed by such faithful, compassionate friends.

"I think I'll make a pot of soup and take some bread and pastries from the bakery over to Mike and Jenny tonight when I pick up Luke. Want to join us for dinner at Jenny's?"

"Sure. My cupboards are bare." Tia stuck a thumb in her waistband and wiggled the loose fabric. "I could use a little meat on my bones. I'll have my cell phone on if things change and Jenny's not up to it. Meanwhile, I suppose I'd better go meet with all those 'suits' that are waiting for me."

"Are there any 'skirts' in the bunch?" Libby inquired, tongue-in-cheek.

"No. Seems like there should be at least one female lawyer or accountant, doesn't it?" Tia frowned. "Now I feel really disquieted."

And, Tia thought later, she was right to be uncomfortable. Her entire life was about to tumble down around her ears.

. . . .

Unsteadily, Tia left the office building and stared vacantly up the street. She was so rattled that she'd momentarily forgotten where she'd parked her car. The sunlight seared through her shuttered eyelids as she made her way to the parking ramp.

A foreign buzzing in her ears and a spinning in her head plagued her as she sat in her car gripping the wheel and breathing deeply. Fortunately she hadn't lost her poise until after she'd said her bit and stormed out of the meeting. The voices she'd listened to upstairs still echoed in her head.

"There was some very imprudent overstocking at the new store."

"Since most of these items cannot be returned . . ."

"We discovered some other unpaid invoices we were not first aware of."

"It is the advertising program that nailed the lid on the coffin."

"I've seen businesses twice your size with half this budget."

Brandon had managed to undo in a matter of months what it had taken Tia years to develop. It was now apparent that, while he'd nodded and agreed with everything she'd wanted for the stores, he'd given only lip service to her and then followed through in the ways *he'd* thought best.

But what had worked for Beacons had failed miserably at Ribbons & Rainbows. The differences in overhead between the two operations had been vast—a small art studio located in a reasonably priced building in a small town was nothing compared to Tia's expenses. But that evidently hadn't occurred to Brandon.

There was no way to save either of the stores unless she was willing to downsize dramatically and move Tia's Attic out of her current location into a low-traffic strip mall tucked away in one of the suburbs where she could afford the rent.

The whole idea behind her stores was luxury—pampering and pleasing her clients. What she'd created couldn't be duplicated in any space she could afford to rent. Though they hadn't said it in so many words—they hadn't needed to—Tia's stores were now history. All that was left were the going-out-of-business sales.

How was she going to face anyone ever again? So much of who she was had been tied up in those stores. She wasn't even sure who Tia Warden was without them. And they were gone. Everything was gone.

Not even planning where she was going, Tia drove aimlessly until she reached a most unlikely spot—Reach Out Ranch.

"Hullo there." Rollie greeted her as if she were a regular and not one of those who had been vocal concerning her misgivings about the merits of animal therapy. "Are you out here to massage one of the horses? Libby said you enjoyed the class."

She would, Tia thought. Aloud, she said, "I guess so." Guilt nipped at her. At the equissage class she'd agreed to help out— and hadn't shown up since.

"Good. Tillie needs a rubdown. She's been working hard all morning." Rollie thrust a curry comb into her hand and eyed her business suit doubtfully. "Are you going to wear that?"

"Why not?" Tia said numbly. She didn't have anywhere else to wear it now.

"By the way," Rollie added, "I have to thank you for sending Trevor my way. He's a good little worker. I'm really going to miss him when he's worked off whatever he stole from your store. I can't imagine what even drove him to try something stupid like that."

Reminded of the Wests' desperate situation, Tia asked, "Could Trevor continue to work here after he pays off the music box?"

"We can always use more help," Rollie admitted, "but I'm not sure how we can afford to pay him."

"I'll run the idea past Libby. She makes so many quilts to be auctioned off for the ranch that maybe she'll have an idea how to pay Trevor enough to stay on."

"Good thinking," Rollie said and went back to work.

Feeling better, Tia eyed the creature in front of her. She walked up to the little mare muttering, "I'm here. Don't kick me.

Or why not kick me? Everyone else has today." She set comb to hide and began to brush. Tia brushed until her arms ached. Then she found another comb and untangled every hair in Tillie's mane and tail. When that was done, she started practicing the massage techniques she'd learned in class. As she worked, she saw Tillie's eyes close and her head droop. When Tillie licked her lips and gave a sweet little sigh, Tia knew she was doing something right.

And as she kneaded and stroked, Tia mumbled to the nearest willing ear, "How could I have trusted him, Tillie? What was wrong with my brain? I, of all people, should have known better and yet I'm as guilty as he. I trusted my instincts, my experience, and my own judgment so much that I left prayer out of my business loop." Tillie shifted slightly and Tia felt her great muscles ripple into place.

"I was fooled," Tia continued, finding it comforting to vent to this warm, placid creature. "He seemed so good—on the outside at least. I was so sure . . . I had no idea how misguided he was."

She made a disgusted sound, and Tillie opened her eyes. "Just like the Pharisees! He looked good on the outside and was spoiled on the inside." She massaged even harder. "Of course, I'm no better. 'Pride goes before destruction, and haughtiness before a fall.' I should have known. . . ."

Finally, when Tia's arms were too tired to hold up any longer and her black suit was dusty gray and decorated with horsehair, she simply laid her head on Tillie's side and listened to her breathe. It was like taking a tranquilizing drug. As she'd worked on Tillie, her own anger and frustration had slipped into more appropriate proportions. She would have bet her high heels that her blood pressure was lower and her pulse slower than when she'd arrived.

Tillie turned her head and gave Tia a loving, grateful look. And Tia, so appreciative of Tillie's undemanding, soothing company, leaned over and kissed Tillie right on the neck. Immediately realizing what she'd done, Tia stepped back to spit the dust and hair from her mouth. But Tillie was smooth and clean from the grooming and smelled of a beautiful perfume of sweet grass, clean hay, and fresh air blended with the earthy fragrance of horse.

On the drive home, Tia examined her sanity from every angle. Her—kissing a horse? But it made strange sense. Tillie was reality. She wasn't credit or a debit column or a bill for advertising she hadn't even seen. Tillie wasn't an invoice or a credit card receipt; she was a tangible reality totally without artifice—just what Tia needed most right now.

She dropped the suit into a bag for the dry cleaners and hoped they wouldn't cancel her as a customer. Then she put on jeans and a sweatshirt and drove to the center, one place she could always find someone far worse off than herself.

Helen, who was big into bulletin boards, had posted letters from women who had passed through the center while in the process of pulling their lives together. Tia stopped to read the messages—some scrawled on cheap paper, others neatly typed, indicating the writers had probably gotten themselves into school or found a job.

> *My mother was killed by a violent man. I don't want my dad to kill me, too.*

> *What he does to me isn't love.*

> *Why wouldn't anyone listen until it was too late?*

> *Have a good day? Not when you've been raped.*

> *It wasn't my fault.*

In the center of the letters, Helen had created her own message.

Abuse	Health
Bitterness	Open doors
Uselessness	Prayer
Shame	Excitement
Enmity	

THE CHOICE IS YOURS

"You like it?" Helen walked up behind Tia.

"Powerful."

"Good. I want everyone to get the idea."

"It's a real passion with you, isn't it?"

"The fire burns deep; I can say that much." Helen studied Tia. "And I'm beginning to see that fire in you as well."

"I had no idea it was in me, but maybe . . ."

"You could help a lot of women, Tia. You're funny, articulate, intelligent, brave, savvy—a great role model and a marvelous mentor. Every day Dianne is growing a little stronger because of you. You could do it for others, too."

"How? Chipping away at the problems one at a time is overwhelming. For every person I might help, a hundred more hurting women are waiting. I'm willing, if that's where God wants me, but I don't know if I could stand it without burning out."

"Hey, you're looking at a pile of burned ashes. But I'm like a phoenix, rising again, just when I think there's nothing left in me to give. God can restore ashes. He does it for me every day."

Tia hooked her thumbs in the hem of her sweatshirt and stared into space. *Ashes.* That was exactly what was left of her life right now. It would be interesting to see what God made of her personal rubble.

. . . .

"Don't get up!"

"Tia, the doctor said I could be up some of the time," Jenny explained patiently. Since her friends had arrived for dinner, she hadn't even been able to twitch in their presence without getting scolded.

"Fine. You get up when he's here. Stay put while I'm around."

"Ditto for me," Libby said. "We know how to take care of you."

"That's for sure. Can you drink soup through a straw?" Tia asked.

Mike finally came to Jenny's rescue. "She'll be fine at the table. It's standing that causes the most pressure." He scooped her off the couch and carried her to a chair in the dining room, while Libby and Tia followed irately, like crotchety mother hens whose eggs had been disturbed.

"We've been discussing me so much I haven't had a chance to ask about you," Jenny said. "How are you, Tia?"

"Going day by day. Hour by hour. It's harder than I believed possible."

"You loved him. You cherished your business, and you had important dreams. How could it be easy to let go?"

Tia understood the term *brokenhearted* in a new way now. It felt as though there were a crack as wide as the Mississippi in her heart. "I'm trying. I really am."

"She's been painting," Libby revealed. "I saw the easel in her living room."

"Snoop," Tia accused. "I don't paint; I play with color."

"You'd done a whole row of little shops on a street. There were flowers in every window box and a sun half the size of the sky. What was that about?"

"It was fantasy, a sunny life filled with flowers and blue sky—and stores."

"*Was* your fantasy? Are you saying you won't start another business?" Jenny asked.

"Two weeks ago I would have said, 'Yes, definitely, I'll be back in business as soon as possible,' but today I don't know. Maybe what I was doing with my life wasn't important enough or didn't give enough to others. No one came into my store who couldn't already afford to shop. Perhaps it's time I concentrated on those people I wasn't reaching before."

"Like how?" Libby passed Tia a bowl of vegetables.

"I haven't a clue. It's just a recurring thought."

"Are you feeling better about what happened between you and Brandon?" Jenny asked.

"Oh, sure," Tia said sarcastically, "except for the times I sit in my car and shout in frustration at the top of my lungs."

"You really do that?" Jenny asked.

"Actually, I do." Tia flushed. "But I've quit doing it at stoplights. I scared some poor woman and a carload of kids yesterday. I'll pray in the car and scream somewhere that I can't be seen. At least in prayer, only my lips move."

Jenny chuckled and rubbed her belly. "Your faith is still intact anyway."

"Tattered around the edges but still there." Tia put her hand over Jenny's. "And I'm praying for you more than I'm praying for me."

....

The next morning, Tia showered, dressed, and wandered around the house like a lost child. She'd told her staff that she wouldn't be in today. She couldn't go to Jenny's, and Libby was busy at the bakery. Tia wondered if Luke and Robert would be able to come out and play later and then considered that even the dogs Spot, Inky, and Puddles would be better company than she was for herself.

Impulsively, she got into her car and started for the pet shop to buy treats for the mutts for an afternoon in the park. Before she reached the pet shop, she noticed a large Humane Society sign on the side of another building. Without thought or reason, Tia pulled into the parking lot of the animal shelter.

Inside the building, the reception area smelled of powerful antiseptic. Tia's heart began to pound and her palms grew damp.

"May I help you?"

"No . . . well, maybe . . . as long as I'm here . . ."

"Yes?" The receptionist appeared puzzled. "Would you like to look at some dogs?"

"Actually I have dogs." Surely Libby's and Jenny's dogs counted as her own.

"Cats then. Come this way."

Cats? She didn't like cats. At least she never had in the past. Actually, she hated them. Wasn't she the one who'd refused to go to the musical because she couldn't bear the idea of seeing cats dancing and singing for two hours? The only reason she was here was the weird compulsion she had felt.

"You can look as long as you like. If you want to hold any of them, call one of the staff and we'll get it out." The door closed behind the receptionist, leaving Tia in a room that was filled floor to ceiling with cages, each containing a cat.

As if on cue, every cat got up, rubbed its side on the cage, and meowed or purred. Only one huge, shaggy, brown-and-black cat with a white belly and paws stayed where he was, opening one eye to peer at the intruder. Some thrust a paw through the wires as if to say, "I raised my hand, so pick me, pick me!"

Kittens tumbled, felines arched their backs, a few hissed and spit, but most put on their most beguiling expressions. Tia stood in the middle of the room, her arms hanging limply at her sides. What was she *doing* here?

The door opened, and a little girl and her mother entered with a staffer. "I want those kitties!" The child pointed at two half-grown kittens that appeared to be from the same litter.

"Missy, we can only get one kitty."

"But they're sisters, Mom. We can't take them away from each other!" Missy looked as though she were about to cry.

"Honey, I know you've been saving your money ever since Christmas to get a kitty, but you can only get one. Having it spayed and giving it shots are very expensive."

"Er . . ." Tia cleared her throat. Both the mother and daughter seemed to notice her for the first time. "If you didn't have to pay the vet bill for the second kitty, could you get it then?"

"Well, sure. But it's not in the budget right now."

Tia stepped between mother and daughter, her back to the child and whispered, "I'll pay for the second cat if that will help."

"What did she say, Mom?" The child pulled on the bottom of her mother's shirt.

"Ah . . ." Mother considered Tia's offer. "She said she'd pay the expenses for the second cat."

The little girl was all eyes. "You would? Why?"

"Because I want to. I don't like seeing these kittens without homes either. I'll bet they'd play well together—and that you'd be very kind to them."

"Oh yes." The child nodded somberly. "I'd play real gentle and love them a lot."

"We couldn't take this from you. . . ." The mother was obviously torn.

"Look at it this way," Tia began. "I was drawn here for a reason, and I'm not going to leave without giving a donation. I'd be very happy if one more animal got a home as a result of my gift." She turned to the worker. "Can I do that?"

"Of course. I wish more people like you would come here."

"Well, when you put it that way . . ."

The child gave a squeal of joy and ran to the cages. "Help me get my kitties out!"

The staff person turned to Tia. "Would you like to hold one of the cats?"

"Oh no . . . I don't think . . . how about that one?" Tia pointed to the only cat in the place who had looked disinterested in her when she'd entered. She was sure she wouldn't cozy up to that one.

"Melvin? Good choice. He's a great cat but he's pretty aloof." The woman reached into Melvin's cage and hauled him out.

He was bigger than Tia had first realized. His warm, solid body felt like a purring concrete block in her arms. She hoisted him higher to get a better grip on him. Melvin yawned and stayed limp. "This thing is a monster!"

"Melvin is a Maine coon. They are big cats, some weighing fifteen or more pounds."

Tia staggered a little. "I can see that." But the calm warm body in her arms was having some of the same effect that Tillie had had on her the day before. She sat down on the only chair in the room, and Melvin wound himself contentedly into her lap. By the time the mother and little girl had finished the paperwork for their two kittens, Tia's legs were asleep from the corpulent animal's weight. And she'd made a decision.

"I'll take him, too."

The little girl clapped and the staffer grinned broadly. "Great! Wow, three cats with new homes. I love it!"

Lugging Melvin to the car in a huge cardboard box with air holes, Tia wasn't so sure *she* loved it. Melvin had come with a stack of papers, an owner's manual, and several coupons for cat food. She set the carton on the front seat beside her and peeked in one of the top air holes. A big golden eye stared back at her, blinked once, and closed. Melvin, it seemed, had decided to go to sleep.

Grateful that he had not howled like the other two cats when they were placed in their travel carriers, Tia decided to buy Melvin a treat when she stopped for cat food. To her horror, the clerk recommended a realistic-looking, catnip-filled mouse, complete with rabbit fur and a dreadfully authentic-looking tail.

Since she'd already gone insane, Tia reasoned as she wrote the check, what was one more creature in the house, anyway? Besides, she'd already invested in a plastic carrier, an electronic litter box that raked unpleasant deposits into a little holding bin so Tia would never have to touch it, a scratching post, and a window platform so Melvin could have a front seat to the outside world. As an afterthought, she'd also purchased a lint roller and six refills.

"I'm nuts. I'm nuts. I'm nuts," she muttered as she dragged her purchases into the house. Then, cautiously, she opened the carton and welcomed Melvin into her home.

She'd been told that he would likely be frightened at first and run for the nearest hiding place until he became acclimated. Not Melvin. He strolled around the room as if he'd purchased it himself, tested the nap on the rug with his claws, and jumped onto the couch into Tia's favorite spot. Purring, he clawed at her beloved pillow, wrapped himself into a large ball, closed his eyes, and went back to sleep.

Tia sat and stared at him for half an hour, wondering what had possessed her to bring him home—and what had possessed him to look so immediately comfortable. Still, the house didn't seem quite so empty and, when Tia went to bed that night, she hauled the big cat with her and let him sleep on the extra pillow on her bed.

CHAPTER THIRTEEN

It can take up to two hours for a turkey to lay its egg.

—*The Secret Lives of Birds*, Pierre Gingras

With each passing day, Tia became more and more grateful for Melvin's presence in the house. The snowball that had been Brandon's influence on her businesses was now avalanching out of control, and she spent much of every day asking for God's will in how she should approach the mess.

Melvin enjoyed Tia's prayers. Wherever she was, he cozied up beside her, turned on his loudest purr, crossed one paw over the other, and seemed to pray right along with her. It was weird but sweet and strangely comforting.

And God was answering—but not in the way Tia had hoped.

"We've settled on a buyer," Tia told Libby when they met for lunch. "They're taking both stores lock, stock, and barrel."

"You don't want to do that!" Libby was horrified. For days she'd been saying that Tia would find some way out of her predicament without losing everything.

"Of course I don't, but it's the only way to preserve some sanity and some sense of dignity. If I scavenge the stores piece-meal, I won't get much more money and it will break my heart. This way, I can leave the original store just as it is. With the sale, I'll pay off all my debt and start with a clean slate."

"What next?"

"I don't know. I'll have to wait and see. All I can say is that since this decision was finally made, I've found some peace."

Libby stirred her iced tea thoughtfully. "Maybe you're right. Doing it any other way would drag out the torture. At least now you'll go out on your own terms . . . and with a little class."

"Class . . . I remember . . . that was a quality that used to be so important to me."

"To me, class means taking the high road no matter how diffi-cult it may be," Libby said. "And you've definitely got class."

"Whatever. Let's not talk about me anymore. How are you?"

"Fine, I think. The catering business is hopping—as you know from keeping the books. Luke and Spot have virtually moved in with us so as not to disturb Jenny. And Reese and both boys have spent most of their time getting ready for an upcoming race."

"This time I won't miss it," Tia vowed. "I wish Jenny could be there."

"It's scary, isn't it?" Libby said softly. "She's trying so hard to hang on to that baby, to do everything the doctor says, but there are still no guarantees that her efforts will be successful."

"But every week that passes is one more week of growing for the baby."

"True. But she has six weeks to go. Tibby is still very small."

"I feel so helpless. Visiting for fifteen minutes at a time and bringing pizza for the guys doesn't seem like anything."

"You talk to her on the phone."

"True, but I don't want to discuss what's happening with my business any more than necessary. She gets upset."

"You are a tough cookie, Tia. Look at you! You've had your

heart broken, your business destroyed, your dreams crushed, and you're still thinking about others."

"Jenny—and you—are like sisters to me. How could I not be concerned? Besides, you just don't see the teary outbursts. I cry at night when it doesn't interfere with the rest of my life. But God is good. Every time I've thought I'd crack, he's shored me up some way or other. Sometimes in really weird ways, I might add."

"What do you mean?"

The time had come. Tia had to admit the secret she'd been keeping from everyone, even those she loved most. "I think he gave me a cat."

"He gave you a hat?"

"No. A *cat.*"

Libby pounded on the side of her head as if her ears had stopped working. "Did you say cat? As in *meow* and *purr?*"

"Yes, that kind of cat."

"But you don't like cats. You don't like animals at all."

"I've learned to love your dogs. And I've actually massaged a few horses."

"Under duress, maybe. But a cat?"

So Tia told her the story of the shelter, the little girl, and Melvin.

"You named the cat Melvin?"

"He was named at the shelter but it fits. I knew right away that he was a Melvin. At first I thought he might be an Oscar or a Fred, but he's definitely a Melvin."

"Okay," Libby said slowly, "I'm having a hallucination, and I want you to talk me out of it. Then take me to the emergency room for an examination."

"Why don't I just take you to my house and introduce you to Melvin?"

"How long have you had this animal and not said anything?" Libby stared at the extraordinarily large cat as he lay on his back, spread eagle in the sunlight. The soft tufts of white fur on his belly rose and fell with each breath.

"Awhile. He's been my little secret. I knew I'd have a lot of explaining to do once you and Jenny discovered what I'd done. And, of course, Ellen and Dorothy will have a fit . . . so I just didn't say anything. All I know is that I've been sleeping better at night with him by my side."

"So he sleeps in your bed. Does he eat off your plate?" Libby's tone was inching from stunned to sarcastic.

"Actually he prefers not to do much jumping. His weight, I suppose. I feed him in a little dish beside my chair."

"I can't believe it. I just can't believe it."

"He makes me feel safer and not so lonely. I know it's dumb, but it works."

"Of course you feel safe. If someone broke into the house and Melvin decided to attack, he could knock over a linebacker. That cat weighs more than our dogs!"

"His fur makes him look larger than he is. Sort of like that pair of ugly yellow pants I wore last summer. Don't you remember how my thighs—"

"Tia! You are driving me nuts!"

"I'm just discovering what you've known all along. There is something very soothing about a pet. What's that verse in Genesis? 'God made all sorts of wild animals, livestock, and small animals, each able to reproduce more of its own kind. And God saw that it was good.' If God thinks it's good, who am I to argue?"

Just then Melvin gave a gigantic yawn that exposed his pink mouth, sharp white teeth, and probably his tonsils, then rolled to his side. He jumped gracefully to his feet and walked toward Libby, passing by Tia's leg for a stroke on the way.

"Why is he looking at me like that?" Libby asked nervously. "He's got eyes like X rays."

"If I knew what Melvin was thinking, I would have read

Brandon's mind and not gotten into all this trouble in the first place. All I know is that Melvin is on *my* side."

"I hope so." Libby took a step backward as Melvin padded toward her.

When he reached her leg, he let out a rumbling purr akin to the sound of a 747, stuck his tail straight in the air, and wound himself around her leg.

"He likes you!" Tia crowed, pleased.

"And . . . and I like him, too."

Melvin was now doing figure eights through Libby's legs, and a smile was beginning to grace her face. She stepped back and sat down on the couch to pick him up but let out a scream when a tiny furred creature popped out of the crevice between the cushions.

"Mouse! There's a mouse in your couch. Quick, maybe we can catch it!" Then Libby apparently realized the gray, shabby thing wasn't moving. "It's *dead!*"

"It's Melvin's catnip mouse. He likes holding its tail in his teeth and shaking it."

Libby tossed it to the floor and Melvin pounced on it. Though Tia wasn't sure, it seemed the floor shook where Melvin landed.

"It is also the most disgusting thing I've ever seen. Do not show this to Jenny until after the baby is born or she might give birth right here on your floor."

But despite the mouse incident, by the time she said good-bye, Libby was holding Melvin in her arms—she had to use both of them—and rubbing her nose into his fur. "This is some cat, Tia. Of course, it would take a special cat to win *you* over."

"But when I fall, I fall hard." Tia had the sense to look embarrassed. "Next time you come over I'll show you Melvin's photo album."

"Don't tell me he's a photographer, too," Libby retorted.

"I've taken several wonderful pictures of him. I was thinking of sending some in to *Cat Fancy* magazine."

Libby left Tia's house scratching her head in puzzlement—at least Tia hoped it was puzzlement and not fleas.

. . . .

Tia was dreaming she'd had an accident at the shop. A huge box of freight had toppled onto her leg and pinned her helplessly. The more she squirmed and turned, the heavier the box seemed to become. Therefore, she was relieved to be awakened by the sound of her telephone and to realize that it wasn't a box of freight pinning her down, but Melvin, spread over her leg, head on one side, tail on the other. She jerked her leg out from under the snoring mass, and Melvin awoke to give her a dirty look. As she picked up the phone, he hauled himself to the edge of the bed and lay down again as if to indicate it was far too dangerous to sleep close to her tonight.

"Hullo," Tia mumbled, her voice thick with sleep.

"Tia?"

She was immediately fully awake. Tia swung her legs to the side of the bed and looked at the clock—3:00 A.M. "Mariah? Why are you calling? Is something wrong?"

A little sob traveled the line. "Trevor and I are at a phone booth about fifteen blocks from the house. We don't know where to go."

"Your husband . . ."

"We waited until he went to sleep. He'd been drinking . . ."

"I'll come and get you. Give me an address."

"But where will we go?"

"We'll figure that out when I get there."

They were a pathetic sight—Trevor standing guard outside the phone booth while his mother slumped on the seat inside. Both saw Tia immediately as she turned the corner and were waiting at the curb by the time Tia pulled up.

"Please get in so we can get out of here," Tia said.

"I'm so sorry, so sorry," Mariah repeated once inside the car, Mariah in the front, Trevor in the backseat. "I didn't know who to call and then Trevor mentioned you . . ."

"I'm glad you did, and I want you to know you can call me anytime. Are you okay?"

"Yes . . . I think . . ." Mariah looked at Trevor for confirmation.

"What happened?"

Mariah choked back a sob. "He hit Trevor this time. He'd been drinking and didn't like Trevor's music. They got into an argument about the volume and—" her voice quivered with indignation and fury—"he had no right! No right to hit our child!"

"Ma, it's okay . . ."

"No it's not! I can take it, but you shouldn't have to." She turned to Tia. "Trevor's been doing so much better lately because of you and Reach Out Ranch. He's like a new boy and now . . ."

Ironic, Tia thought. What Mariah wouldn't do for herself she would do for her son. Her hands tightened on the wheel.

Just then Mariah noticed that they were no longer driving on pavement. "Where are we going?"

"I called Rollie. He's waiting for us. He said Trevor could stay there for the time being. Is that okay with you, Trevor?"

"Yeah. Rollie's cool." It sounded like he was trying to be brave.

"He said he'd drive you to school and pick you up." Tia grinned at Trevor in the rearview mirror. "I think he might squeeze a few more hours of work out of you, if you don't mind."

Actually, Rollie had said he'd keep the boy too busy to spend much time thinking about what had happened. Fortunately, Tia thought, the ranch was usually populated with people who'd had experience with troubled, disabled, or handicapped children. Between that and the way Trevor loved the horses, she knew it was the best place for him right now.

"Here we are." Tia parked under the yard light.

Rollie was waiting. When Trevor walked up to him, the older man put his arms around the boy and comforted him.

On the drive back into the city, Mariah was silent. When she finally spoke, she said, "Thank you. I won't have to worry about him out there. His father couldn't find him even if he wanted to." She stared out at the passing buildings. "I wish I knew where I could go."

Tia heard the wistfulness in the woman's voice and her heart ached. But when she spoke, her voice was determinedly cheerful. "I've got that figured out too. I've already talked to Helen Anderson at the women's crisis center. They're waiting for you. You'll have your own private room and the opportunity to rest. Whenever you're ready, Helen will talk with you. She's seen or heard just about everything, so I'm sure she can answer any questions you have."

Tia glanced at Mariah from the corner of her eye. "Does your husband know you left?" Tia suddenly realized that she didn't know Mr. West's first name. Mariah never used it. She always spoke of "he."

"He will when he wakes up. I left a note." She wrung her hands as she spoke. "I told him that I wouldn't have him doing any more hitting or swearing and that he'd have to quit drinking before I'd come back. I said that if he got help, then we'd talk."

"Do you think that will make a difference?" Tia asked.

Mariah sagged against the seat. "I don't know. Maybe it's too late. Maybe he won't go to counseling. He calls it 'woman stuff.' But if he did . . ."

"Then . . . ?"

"I still love him, Tia. I remember how he used to be before he got laid off at work and started drinking. He was a real good worker until the alcohol took over. Now he gets fired from every job he tries. It's like my husband left that body and some other sick man took him over." She sighed. "I'd give anything just to have my husband back."

"If he'd agree to get help and work at it, I bet you'd find him again," Tia said gently.

If . . .

"I can't trust him now, but I'd be willing to try if he would. I'm not a believer in divorce, but he can't keep hurting Trevor."

"Or you," Tia added. She put her right hand on Mariah's arm. "We'll find people to help him, if he'll allow himself to be helped. And you, too, Mariah."

"For a long time I thought it was my fault." The woman's voice drifted out of the darkness of the car's interior. "I didn't cook well enough or clean like I should have. I was too lenient with Trevor or too strict. Nothing I did was right."

"But it wasn't you; it was him."

"I'm beginning to see that. What happened to that man I married, Tia?"

Tia was glad to arrive at the center. She didn't have an answer to Mariah's question—other than sin. It polluted everything it touched, including Mariah's marriage.

Helen, who was there to let them in, promptly put Mariah at ease. A little food and a cup of cocoa later, she escorted them to Mariah's room. It was simple but cozy and surprisingly comforting. Tia knew that volunteers worked hard to keep these rooms as welcoming as possible on their shoestring budget.

Mariah almost melted onto the bed and was dozing off from pure exhaustion as Tia and Helen left the room.

Tia explained quickly what had transpired.

Helen nodded. "Tomorrow we have a counselor coming in. If she has a pastor, we'll call him. She'll be okay, Tia. She's safe, warm, and where she can get some help. If the husband wants help, we'll give him some recommendations of counselors and the nearest AA meetings. It's going to take some time, but we'll help her get things worked out."

Tia nodded, too tired to voice all the questions rolling around in her mind. The only thing she could do right now was pray. Which she did—all the way home.

. . . .

"Did I miss anything?" Tia dashed up to Mike as he waited by the track for Reese's latest wheelchair race to begin.

"Not a thing. Libby took the guys to the van to get sodas, and Reese is out there getting ready to line up."

"Good. I haven't been a very good cheerleader for him lately, have I?"

"You've been a good example of keeping your head up in bad circumstances. That's a spirit booster if I've ever heard one."

"It's getting harder, Mike." Tia's shoulders sagged wearily. "We got a closing date for the sale today."

"That's good, isn't it?"

"It still means the stores won't be mine anymore. It's all beginning to feel very permanent."

Mike scuffed his battered tennis shoe on the ground. "I've lost a lot of things I didn't want to let go of over the years. Sometimes it turned out to be a good thing."

"But your business, your partner, and someone you might have married—all at once?"

"No, you've got me there. Still, I've found that once I truly let go, I find a door open somewhere else that is even more interesting. Sometimes our 'stuff' drags us down. Losing things means your load is lighter and you're free to move in new directions."

"Then I'm free as a bird. . . ." Tia gave a weak grin. "Free to spend more time on *Bird*house Ministries." She wiped a tear from her eye. "But sometimes I don't feel strong enough to go on. I'd like to lie down in bed and pull the covers over my head and stay there. I'm exhausted, Mike. I refuse to take calls from Brandon anymore because he makes me so upset. I screen my calls so I don't have to talk to anyone who is not crucial to my life. And, with Brandon gone and Jenny in so much distress of her own, sometimes I'm so lonely I could weep."

Tia looked rueful. "Then I think about your baby and wonder how I could be so selfish as to think of what's going on in my life as having any importance at all!"

"Ease up on yourself, Tia," Mike drawled. "If you don't mind, I'd like to give you some advice I've learned the hard way."

"Please do. Anything you can say that might help."

"It's something I learned both in life and in gardening. All you can do is hoe to the end of the row."

"And that means . . . ?"

He chuckled. "You can't stop in the middle, Tia. You have to get to the end of this. Don't run away or try to hide from it, because it will probably jump up and bite you. Keep slogging away, dealing with one thing at a time, and eventually you will be done with it. You'll come to the end of your row. If you can do that and wrap this mess up, you'll be able to move on, not having to look back.

"It's the same way with Jenny right now. There is nothing she can do but what the doctor orders—and pray. But if she does her best following medical advice, trusts God and prays for his will, and prepares herself for any situation, she'll get to the end of the row, too."

"But you're talking about your baby!"

"I know. But what are our choices, Tia? Nothing will make these problems go away except seeing them through. So we might as well lean on God and do the best we can with them."

His words made sense, harsh but true.

"I'll feel better once I've tied up the loose ends and walked away," Tia admitted. Then she gave a small snort of disgust. "All I have to figure out is what to do with my life and discover if I'm meant to share it with anyone! Easy as pie, right?"

"Not easy, but doable. Besides, what options do you have, other than the choices between bitterness or gratitude and despair or joy?"

Tia considered his words. "How'd you get so smart?"

"We went to the same school, remember? You're smart, too. You just have to start using your smarts now."

Tia reached out and squeezed his hand. "My friend Jenny is a very lucky woman to have a husband like you."

"No, I'm the lucky one. And not only do I have her, I have her friends to keep me in line."

"You're right," Tia said cheerfully. "You *are* lucky to have us. Not many men are so fortunate as to have the wisdom of *three* women. . . . And I'm going to choose gratitude and joy for my life, just like you said." Her expression grew determined. "Even if it kills me!"

"A kamikaze joy seeker. It paints an image in my mind's eye."

They were both laughing when Libby joined them. "The race is going to start any minute! Turn around or you're going to miss it. What have you two been talking about?"

Tia and Mike smiled conspiratorially at each other before turning to the race.

. . . .

Tia glanced at her caller ID before picking up the telephone. It was Helen Anderson's number at the center. "Hi, Helen. What's up?"

"I've got someone here who'd like to speak to you."

Tia heard rustling as Helen transferred the phone. Then a timid but familiar voice came on the line. "Tia? It's me, Anna."

"Hi, stranger. Haven't seen you for a few days!" Tia immediately remembered the young pregnant woman from the center whom she'd befriended.

"I ain't been feelin' so good."

Tia stiffened. "Have you seen a doctor?"

"Yeah. He says it's just my body gettin' ready to have this baby." Anna's voice turned to a whisper. "I don't think I'm ready."

"It's one of those things you can't turn back on now," Tia said gently.

"I'm scared."

Tia's heart went out to the woman. Anna wasn't much more than a child herself, and she'd already lived a lifetime of pain. Why shouldn't she be frightened?

"Is there anything I can do?"

"Would you come to the hospital with me?"

"When you have your baby? Sure."

"Could you meet me down here in a couple hours?"

"But your baby isn't coming now . . . is it?"

"My contractions have started but they're far apart. The doctor said I should make arrangements for a ride 'cause I'd probably need it by this afternoon."

Now she had Tia's full attention. "Sure. Of course. Ahh . . . anything else?"

"I just don't want to be alone."

Anna's voice haunted Tia as she changed clothes and fed and watered Melvin. It was completely unfair that Anna had to go through this ordeal alone. A child's birth should be a happy time, a celebration, not just one more problem in a life full of them.

Anna was sitting on a bench outside the shelter's door when Tia arrived. The only thing robust about her was her belly. Her legs and arms were thin to the point of scrawny, her hair lank and mousy, her skin sallow. She was wearing one of the garments Tia had purchased for her at the consignment store.

"You could have waited inside," Tia chided.

"I wanted some fresh air." Anna lowered herself into the car with great difficulty. "And some sun on my face." Then she winced.

"Contraction?"

"They're coming pretty regular now." Anna massaged the dome of her stomach. "Guess it's a good thing I called you." She paused. "Thanks for coming."

"It's an honor to be asked." Tia patted Anna's hand. "This is a very exciting moment—a brand-new life about to make a debut. Astounding."

"I wish Frankie thought so." Anna stared out the window at the passing buildings. Frankie, Tia knew, was the father of Anna's baby. Helen had kept a close eye on Anna, fearing that he might find her and do her harm because of his uncontrollable temper.

"Do you know where he is?" Tia asked with what she hoped sounded like mildly curious interest.

"Left town. Got in some trouble with the police. Helen checked for me. Doubt he'll ever be back in this state." Anna grimaced and rubbed her belly. "Ow! That was a hard one."

Tia stepped on the gas. "Have you got a plan for after the baby is born?"

"Been takin' child-care classes. Didn't know there was so much to learn. Teacher says I'll be a good mother, though, 'cause I'm gentle and caring."

"Where will you live?"

Still massaging her belly, Anna contemplated the question. "I could live with my grandma, but she's old and little kids make her nervous. My brother said I could stay there, but he's got a bunch of rowdy friends that would probably keep us both awake. Helen's looking for some place for us to stay while I get my feet on the ground."

"I hope you'll choose wisely," Tia advised. "You're carrying a very special gift from God. His own Son came to earth as a child, too. "

"That's what I've been hearing. The chaplain who comes on Sundays was talking about it last week. Also said something about 'teaching your children to choose the right path, and when they are older, they will remain upon it.' What does that mean, anyway?"

Anna was trying to keep her mind off her discomfort, and Tia was more than happy to help her. "What you teach children when they are little is what they'll remember all their life. That's why it's so important that you tell them about God and that Jesus loves them."

"Same stuff you've been telling me, huh?"

"The very same." Tia couldn't help smiling. Anna had a curious, inquiring mind and had obviously soaked up everything Tia had given her to read on faith, salvation, and the Bible.

"That shouldn't be too hard then," Anna concluded serenely.

Tia hadn't expected that calm response. "Oh?"

"Yeah. I was gonna tell you. Me and God had a talk a few days ago. I told him that I was tired of being a sinner. If I'd been looking to him and not to myself, I would never have gotten hooked up with Frankie in the first place. Anyway, I told him I was sorry and that I was gonna change my ways. I asked him to start showing me what he wanted me to do. I've felt lots better since. If he promised to save me, then I believe him. I want my baby to know the same thing. Is that what it means to 'teach the right path'?"

"I couldn't have said it better myself."

Before Tia could say more, Anna gasped. "Oh, Tia, I'm sorry!"

"For what?"

"I think . . . you know . . . well, I'm afraid I just made a big wet mess in your car."

After her water had broken, Anna's contractions speeded up, and Tia was relieved to deliver her to a nurse at the emergency-room door. After she'd parked, Tia went inside and looked for Anna. She found her in a room that looked more like a large bedroom than a delivery room. Anna was panting like a train engine on an uphill climb.

The doctor was already there, nurses swarming around him like bumblebees. "Don't push yet. Just wait until I tell you," he said.

"Tia!" Anna squealed. "It's coming."

Tia dodged a medical cart and went to the far side of Anna's bed. Anna glommed on to her hand and gave it such a squeeze that Tia was sure her hand was broken. "I'm glad we didn't wait any longer to bring you, or this baby would have been delivered by a policeman in the front seat of my car."

Anna groaned. "Can I push now?"

Tia realized that she was gritting her teeth in empathy with her friend. They were both relieved when the doctor gave Anna the go-ahead to push.

Things happened in a blur after that—Anna making unearthly sounds; the doctor's and nurses' soft, soothing words; the bleep of a fetal monitor; and then the indignant, complaining cry of a brand-new little boy.

"David!" Anna gasped. "My own baby David!" She was utterly oblivious to the doctor's finishing ministrations or the nurses moving carts and equipment out of the way. After a quick weigh and measure, some tests and drops in his eyes, David was swaddled in a blue blanket and tucked into Anna's arms.

Tia nearly wept when she saw the very first look between mother and child, a look so tender and so intense that she could almost feel the bond between them solidifying as she watched.

Anna looked up. "My daddy's name was David. I've always loved that name."

Tia nodded, unable to speak.

"And there's that guy in the Bible, too. Christ's relative, right?"

"Exactly right."

"Then it's a really good name." Anna leaned back on the pillow and closed her eyes. "Whew, having a baby wears you out."

"You and David rest. I'll be back in an hour." With a last look at Anna's blissful face, Tia slipped from the room.

When Tia returned, Anna was sitting up in bed drinking a cup of tea.

"I nursed him, Tia! He's so smart—he knew right what to do!"

Tia grinned and flopped into the chair by Anna's bed. "Just like baby anythings—God designed them for just that."

"It's a miracle," Anna concluded. Then she peered at the packages lying at Tia's feet. "Whatcha got there?"

"I went shopping for David."

"You shouldn'ta done that. I don't have money to pay you back!"

"These are gifts. Besides, I went to our favorite store."

"The consignment shop?"

"It was close, and I found a million things you'll need." Tia picked up the first bag and emptied it onto the foot of the bed. A dozen blue sleepers in all sizes, little T-shirts, booties, tiny hats, and denim rompers fell out. In the next bag were crib sheets, a bumper set, and a diaper bag. The third bag was full of rattles, crib toys, and a baby monitor so that Anna could be in one room and still hear little David in another.

By the time they'd examined every single thing and Tia had refolded and stacked it all, the dresser and two chairs in the room were piled high.

"He's already got more clothes than I've had my whole life," Anna marveled.

"About that . . ." Tia picked up the last bag. "Here are some new shirts and a pair of jeans. If you don't fit them now, you should in a couple of weeks when your tummy goes down. Until then, you can wear these jogging suits. Cute, huh?"

"More than cute! They look brand-new."

"I ran into one of my former customers at the store. She was just bringing in piles of her own clothes and some things her grandson had outgrown. She has exquisite taste and a healthy spending allowance. I purchased practically everything she brought in. There's more for you in the car, including a winter coat. And the shop thought it was great—they didn't have to price a thing. They estimated what each might earn and I wrote a check. Cool, huh?"

A shadow passed over Anna's features. "You spent a lot of money, I bet."

Tia put her hands on her hips and looked sternly at her friend.

"My dear, I paid less for everything than I know my customer paid for that coat alone. The only reason I didn't shop at a regular store was that I knew you'd feel guilty. So quit worrying your pretty little head about this. I'm having more fun giving you this than you could possibly have receiving it!

"And now, pictures." Tia pulled a disposable camera out of her purse. "Let's have the nurse bring that baby in here."

As she snapped photo after photo of Anna and David, posed Anna's nurse with the pair, and took close-ups of the beet red, scrunched-up face of the sweetest little boy in the world, Tia thought about Jenny's unborn child.

Tibby would be born into a household with a father, mother, brother, and faithful pet and greeted by a host of family and friends. She would be cared for like a princess and grow up knowing she was truly loved.

This baby deserved that, too. Consignment clothing and pictures from a disposable camera hardly seemed enough, but Tia knew that more would cause Anna discomfort and tempt her to turn the gifts away.

No matter how humble the gifts, there were people happy that David had entered the world, and there was no doubt in Tia's mind that David's mother would love him every bit as much as Jenny would love Tibby. If one could choose between wealth and love, there would be no choice, Tia thought. The only choice was love.

. . . .

Being at the crisis center always made Tia feel better, but this was her best idea so far.

She didn't know what impulse had made her pull into the beauty-supply house but, once inside, Tia couldn't keep herself from grabbing things from the shelves and tossing them into her cart. Pumice stones, nail files, buffers, cuticle cream, polish remover, scented lotions, fragrant soaps, French manicure kits, clippers, one of every color of polish, and plastic soaking tubs filled her shopping cart by the time she was done.

With her strange booty, Tia arrived at the center in time to meet Helen walking in from the parking lot. "Hi there. Could you help me carry this stuff inside?"

"What did you do? Lose your mind at the mall?" Helen picked up two sacks and followed Tia into the building.

"Sort of. On impulse, I stopped at a beauty-supply store and I had this great idea—manicures and pedicures!"

"What a novel idea," Helen commented wryly. "Who'd ever think of that in a store full of nail polish?"

"Don't you see? For the women at the shelter! I'll bet there are a few here who'd really appreciate the pampering."

"And who's going to do that? Or teach anyone how, for that matter? Not to mention who'll pay for this stuff." Helen put the packages on the floor beside her desk.

"I've already thought of that. Birdhouse Ministries will cover this." At this point, Tia pretty much *was* Birdhouse Ministries— administrator, worker, pocketbook—but she was determined to believe that a time would come when this would be more than hers alone.

"Manicures and pedicures are hardly biblical sorts of things," Helen muttered.

"Oh, but they are! The night of the Passover, Jesus washed the disciples' feet. It was the perfect example of his servanthood. I looked it up. Here." Tia thrust her New Testament into Helen's hands. It was open to John 13.

Helen skimmed the verses and then began to read out loud:

> "He now showed the disciples the full extent of his
> love. . . . So he got up from the table, took off his robe,
> wrapped a towel around his waist, and poured water into a
> basin. Then he began to wash the disciples' feet and to wipe

them with the towel he had around him. . . . After washing their feet, he put on his robe again and sat down and asked, 'Do you understand what I was doing? You call me "Teacher" and "Lord," and you are right, because it is true. And since I, the Lord and Teacher, have washed your feet, you ought to wash each other's feet. I have given you an example to follow. Do as I have done to you.' "

Tia explained, "I'll give pedicures—and I'll teach the women to do manicures and pedicures for each other. Just think how it will feel to be so loved and so humbled, both at the same time."

Helen studied Tia with a stare. "You're able to translate more of the Bible into everyday life than almost anyone else I've ever met."

"Read it and do it." Tia tapped a finger on the Testament Helen still held. "It's advice that never gets old or ineffective, that's all."

"Birdhouses, naps, pedicures, manicures . . . what will be next, Tia?"

"I have no idea," Tia admitted. "But if I pray about it and stay attentive for the answer, I'm sure it will come."

"Just so it doesn't involve pillow fights or water balloons," Helen warned. "I do not want to vacuum feathers out of the curtains."

"That hadn't occurred to me, but now that you mention it . . ."

The activity room became Salon Central. Half the group were sitting on chairs with their feet in buckets of water; the other half sat cross-legged on the floor watching Tia demonstrate the art of nail filing.

Tia had Dianne by the foot and was waving a long emery board like a wand. "Remember now, only file one way. Otherwise you'll weaken the nail. I've already shown you how to apply cuticle softener and use the orange sticks. And remember to massage those feet. Think how sore and tired yours are at the end of the day and how you'd like someone to massage your own feet. Use lots of lotion. It's good for softening calluses, and it feels marvelous. Now I'll demonstrate on Dianne."

After a couple of minutes of hysterical laughter, Tia got the women to calm down. "And next time I will not demonstrate on someone with ticklish feet." Dianne was still twitching and giggling despite Tia's glares. Then the women got to work. The soft hum of quiet conversation, soothing background music, and the dimmed lights created a tranquil atmosphere.

"I thought this might be gross," Anna admitted to Tia, "but it's not. It's kind of . . . nice." She was sitting on a small stool, massaging a juniper-scented "revitalizing" cream into the feet of one of the newer residents of the center. The woman, whose name was Ginny, had her eyes closed and an expression of sheer bliss on her features.

"In the Bible, a woman named Mary poured expensive perfume on Jesus' feet and wiped them with her hair," Tia commented.

"I don't think I'd want to go that far," Anna said honestly. She ran her thumbs down the center of Ginny's foot between the ball and little toe. "And I hope it's my turn soon." She studied Tia with those somber, intelligent eyes. "Life around you isn't like anything I expected."

"I don't know what you mean," Tia responded.

"I didn't exactly have the best life, but the people around me all seemed pretty much the same. They went to school, got married, got a job . . . and that was it. Some were richer than others or had more kids or a bigger house, but nobody ever talked much about God or church or anything. And the ones who did, never seemed to have any fun. But everything you do is fun—" Anna paused—"isn't it?"

Tia chuckled. If only Anna knew just how "unfun" her life had been lately! Still, despite her problems, Tia could now begin to see hints of the silver linings in all her clouds.

"I'd say the only difference between me and everyone you speak of is hope."

"What's hope got to do with anything? You can't eat hope or live in it or spend it."

"No. But without it, who feels like eating? or shopping? or doing anything else, for that matter? Hope, to me, is faith that someone is in charge of my life—someone who wants better things for me than I can even imagine for myself."

"God again, huh?"

"Always." Tia offered Anna a hand and helped her to her feet.

Anna smiled at Tia. The connection of friendship between them, Tia thought, seemed as solid and tangible as the floor beneath them.

When Helen peeked into the room, Tia was carrying a pan of water to the sink to refill.

"It got so quiet in here, I thought you'd all gone to sleep," Helen observed.

"Almost. I've never seen so many relaxed faces in this group. Interestingly enough, both the servants and the recipients seem to be getting something out of this."

Tia set down her pan and wiped a stray hair out of her eyes with the back of her hand. "There's something that feels so . . . right . . . to me about this. It's like the last words Jesus says in that passage from John: 'You know these things—now do them! That is the path of blessing.' There is a blessing in serving others. From the outside, that sounds unlikely, but once you try it . . . ."

All sorts of things that had once seemed unlikely were becoming "normal" to her, Tia mused after Helen left. What did it all mean?

. . . .

"Glory, glory, hallelujah, glory, glory halleloooooojah . . ."

Libby pounded on the door with both fists before Tia heard

her over the motor of the vacuum cleaner and her own singing. She went to the door, wiping her hands on her makeshift apron—a dish towel suspended at her waist from a pink leather belt. She wore a macaroni necklace around her neck that Robert had strung for her, and her legs were covered in bright green tights.

"What are you guys doing here?" she greeted Libby, Ellen, and Dorothy, all straight from the bakery after a morning's work.

"We close early on Saturday, remember?" Libby reminded her.

"Don't you have anything more interesting to do than visit me? Surely your lives aren't that dull!"

"There's nothing more interesting than visiting you," Libby assured Tia, pushing past her into the house. "I thought you only vacuumed when your housekeeper was sick."

"She's on sabbatical until I get my finances straightened out. Besides, the rug gets a little messy since, you know . . ." Tia hesitated. Ellen and Dorothy didn't yet know about her new roommate.

"Since Melvin?" Libby finished.

Two sets of ears perked up. "Melvin? Who's that? Tia, are you dating someone new and not telling us?" Ellen demanded.

"Now you've done it. I'm going to have to explain about Melvin all over again!" Tia pulled off her apron and led them into the kitchen. "Mel. Mel! Are you in here?"

"He's here now?" Dorothy swatted at her hair with the palm of her hand. Ellen tucked her shirt deeper into her pants.

"I think he's still in the bedroom. Come on."

Dorothy and Ellen glanced at Libby, who shrugged helplessly. "She lets him in there all the time."

They entered the room and there he was. Melvin was a large, furry presence in the middle of Tia's bed, once again sleeping on his back—back legs splayed, front ones folded over each other on his belly. He was lying with his head thrown back, and something like a snore was emanating from his mouth. The fur on his belly quivered with each breath. The realistic catnip mouse lay next to him like prey captured and forgotten.

Ellen and Dorothy wouldn't have been more surprised if they'd found a hippopotamus in the center of Tia's bed.

"This is yours?" Dorothy croaked.

"You don't like animals—especially cats!" Ellen stared at the monster fur ball.

"He's not a cat really," Tia tried to explain. "He's a gift, actually, from God. And he makes a great foot warmer. He's more of a companion in cat's clothing."

"Do you think she'll come with us willingly to the psych ward?" Dorothy asked.

"She was such a bright young thing, too. So sad to see her crack up," Ellen added.

"Knock it off, you two. Everything else has changed in my life. Why shouldn't I start liking cats?"

"That thing is more like a mountain lion!" Dorothy corrected.

"He's large, but the only time it's a problem is when I carry him up steps."

"Why do you carry him anywhere?" Ellen was slack-jawed with amazement.

Tia flushed. "He doesn't really like to move all that much. So when I have things to do on one of the other levels, I just carry him with me. For company."

The image of tiny Tia wrestling that cat up and down stairs sent all three of her guests into gales of laughter. Melvin opened one eye, stared disapprovingly at the rowdies, and closed it again. Tia turned and went down the stairs into the kitchen to make lunch.

"Okay. You're cooking, cleaning, living with a pet cat, giving away all your power suits and high heels and . . ." Dorothy ticked off Tia's dramatic changes one by one.

". . . sold that dumb art collection I never liked much anyway. I hung some drawings a lady from the shelter gave me," Tia finished.

"Any more transformations we should know about?" Dorothy asked. "Although I can't take many more surprises after seeing that cat."

"Just one. I've decided to be grateful for this huge mess I've been in."

Ellen picked up a baby carrot and popped it into her mouth. "And what made you do that?"

"It was something Mike said that was reiterated by the pastor at church. Pastor told us that God sometimes tests the ones he wants to use. I figure I'm being refined like gold, shaped like pottery, or hammered like fine brass because he has a purpose for me. Therefore, I've decided to take all this trouble as a challenge to prove my worth—and as a compliment that God thinks I'm strong enough to withstand so much testing." Tia flexed the muscles in her arms. "How am I doing so far?"

"Amazingly well, I'd say," Ellen said softly, a look of love and admiration in her eyes. "You've picked yourself up and dusted yourself off, that's for sure."

"God is good. He's shown me some things about myself I wouldn't have believed a year ago." Tia grew thoughtful. "Back then I thought I was doing his will, that he and I were in perfect tune. Now I realize I was wrong, and I've been forced to start over. I've shed my original trappings and I like it!

"I'm smarter than I was a year ago—stronger and lighter. What I lost were actually things I *needed* to shed. I'd allowed the stores and my relationship with Brandon to keep me away from God, not to draw me closer. I'm not so busy now and I spend a lot more time in prayer. I gave up Brandon and gained Melvin— a male who is much easier to understand. I didn't lose the important things like God's love—or my friends."

"And you aren't angry at all?" Dorothy wondered.

"Yes, at first I was angry. But with God's help I've learned that anger holds you back and keeps you from moving on with your life. I wouldn't have chosen to lose my business, but now that it's happened, I believe that God's got something even more special for me to do next. I'm like an onion being peeled away one layer at a time—pretty soon he'll reach my heart." Her eyes danced. "You ladies understand that image, good cooks that you are."

Just then Melvin waddled into the kitchen, disdainfully checked his empty food dish, hunched up his rump, and launched himself into Libby's lap. The frenzy that followed made any more discussion impossible.

. . . .

"How's it going, kiddo?" Tia greeted Jenny as Jenny sat at her kitchen table reading the morning paper. "Pay no attention to me."

Tia dropped an armload of flowers onto the table, opened one of Jenny's cupboards, picked out a large vase, filled it with water, and began to create a floral arrangement. When she was done, she stepped back to study the results. "What do you think?"

"Am I supposed to pay attention to you now?" Jenny asked sweetly. "Because if I am, I'd like to say they are fantastic."

"They are pretty, aren't they?" Then, with as much familiarity in Jenny's kitchen as in her own, Tia took a mug out of the cupboard and filled it with coffee. "Do you have any sweet rolls?"

"Sticky buns under that foil." Jenny folded the newspaper and watched her friend. "And to what do I owe the honor of this visit?"

"I've missed you. This bed-rest order has taken you too far out of my life. It's no fun trying to Do Not Disturb you." Tia sat down across the table from Jenny. "I talked to Mike in the driveway. I'd planned to give him the flowers, but he said to bring them inside since you were sitting up."

"I can't lie around every minute of the day. Doctor said it was fine as long as I don't stand up. This baby is going to be born not having experienced any direction but horizontal." Jenny leaned forward and massaged her lower spine. "Besides, it makes my back ache."

Tia frowned at Jenny's belly. "Are you okay in there, Tibby? Is your mom drinking enough milk? Is she playing those 'Teach Your Baby Languages' tapes to you? Have you learned Japanese yet?"

"This is already the most pampered child on the planet, and she hasn't even been born yet."

"How does it feel? To be a mother, I mean."

Jenny rubbed her stomach thoughtfully. "It's different than I expected it to be. I'm excited, of course, and happy. But I also feel such a huge responsibility."

"To be eating right and taking your vitamins?"

"To take care of myself so that I'm around for Tibby for a long, long time. I never thought much about traveling, driving faster than I should, crossing intersections on yellow lights, or even high cholesterol—and now . . ."

"No more yellow lights?" Tia puzzled.

"Not for the sake of the light, silly—for the baby's safety. I feel more . . . significant now. I love being Luke's stepmom, but now I have a whole new person depending on me. I want to be the one to notice her first tooth and see her first steps. I want to take her to Sunday school and read her Bible stories at bedtime. I want to be the one to teach her colors and her ABCs. It's as if no one else could mother her quite like I could. It makes me feel like wrapping us both in cotton batting and living in a cocoon."

"No one can be exactly like you, Jen. You and Tibby have a bond tighter than any other in the universe. That's not to say someone else couldn't raise her, but you're the one who already knows when she sleeps and when she's restless, when she burps and when she likes to roll around like a bowling ball inside you. It's natural that you feel that way."

"I didn't know my protective maternal instincts could be so strong. Of course, I've experienced them with Luke, but this is different. Now I understand why a mother tiger is such a vivid— and dangerous—image."

"You go, girl!" Tia said with a grin. "Tibby has made you feisty!"

"Enough about me," Jenny said. "How about you?"

"One day at a time, one foot in front of the other. But I'm fine." Tia didn't want to talk about her own life anymore. She was tired of her own problems. She couldn't imagine how sick of them everyone else might be. "I feel like I've turned a corner but haven't seen what's ahead of me yet. But I'm like you, Jen. Feisty. We're both going to be fine."

They sat quietly together in Jenny's kitchen, neither speaking, each lost in her own thoughts about which of life's mysteries might show itself next.

"Have you got a minute?" Helen caught Tia in the hallway of the center.

Tia had just come from a pottery class with Dianne. It had seemed so appropriate at this moment in her life, that she'd signed them both up. "For you, I've got ten. Why?"

"Something just came up that has your name written all over it."

"Do tell."

"A women's group from one of the nearby churches heard about your nap classes."

"Uh-oh."

"They did some research and found out about Birdhouse Ministries. They think it's a great idea and want you to speak to their women's conference about putting fun and joy back into people's lives. And, if you sell Birdhouse Ministries well enough, I think they might be interested in sponsoring a program or two."

"You're kidding! Right? You *are* kidding? This isn't real. No, it's too good to be real." Tia spun on her toes.

Helen handed her a slip of paper. "I accepted for you, of course. The twenty-fifth of next month. Here are the time and details."

Tia studied the sheet intently, as if she could learn to be a public speaker just by reading the page. Then her stomach did a rolling flip-flop, and a sweat broke out on the back of her neck.

"What? Only a month to get ready? Can I use your computer? I'd better get started."

CHAPTER FOURTEEN

The house wren is the plainest of the North American wrens,
but makes up for this in personality and song.

—*Birds: An Explore Your World Handbook,* Discovery Books and David Bird

"You'll have to quit squirming," Libby advised as she hooked the clasp of Tia's gold necklace. "You'd look great if you'd stop acting like a jack-in-the-box."

"I can't hold still. I'm going to throw up."

"Don't you dare. This is a fabulous dress and you can't ruin it." Libby stood back and admired Tia's simple black jersey sheath.

"I don't need to be fashionable to go to a property closing," Tia grumbled. "The only thing I want to look is invisible."

"This is the last step to freedom," Libby pointed out. "You've said it yourself. Once this burden is lifted, you can spend all the time you want with Birdhouse Ministries and the crisis center."

"Fund-raising, bookkeeping, mentoring . . . I just jumped from the frying pan into the fire." She contorted to check her hem in the mirror. "Can you see my slip? Do I have a run in my hose?"

Libby laughed out loud. "You'll be the best-dressed invisible person at the title company."

A horn honked outside the window. "There's my realtor," Tia muttered. "Here I go."

They were early. While Howard Fletcher went to check on available conference rooms, Tia paced nervously in a small waiting room. She was staring out the window when she heard the door latch click behind her. She turned to speak to Howard. "If we have time, I'd like to visit a bit more with the new owner." She felt a punch of surprise in the pit of her stomach. "Oh, Brandon, it's you."

He was as cool and impeccable as always. He'd lost ten or fifteen pounds, which had chiseled his features. Tia felt her insurgent heart lurch.

Traitor. Don't do this to me. But her heart didn't listen. Even now, after all the trouble, anger, and resentment, she still felt drawn to him like a meteor to the sun.

"Hello, Tia. You're looking great. Thin, but great."

"Hello, yourself."

He took a step toward her and then hesitated, careful not to intrude on her personal space. Hands clasped behind his back, he looked every bit as handsome as she'd remembered—and more. "I hear you've started something new," he began. "Some sort of chicken-coop thing . . ."

Tia had to smile. "Birdhouses, not chicken coops. I've been doing some fund-raising and organizing volunteers. We've had a heartwarming response."

"No one could resist you, Tia." There was a new and unfamiliar expression in his eyes. This was Brandon and yet it wasn't.

"Are you all right?" she asked. "You seem . . . different . . . somehow."

"About time, huh?" He fixed his gaze over her shoulder and out the window. It dawned on Tia that she'd heard regret in his tone.

"Listen, Brandon—" she moved closer until she could have

reached out and stroked the lapel of his jacket—"this thing with the stores is over. I've put it behind me. I want you to know that."

"Over? You lost your business because I was so cocky that I thought I knew your business better than you did. I was a dishonest scoundrel and I hate myself for it. It's all I've thought of these past weeks, and I'm sorry about those things I said to you in anger. I had no right."

"I've said it before and I'll say it again. I forgive you, Brandon, for everything."

"You don't have to forgive me. I messed up your life. You have every right to hate me."

"I don't have time or energy to hate. Besides, I *want* to forgive you. The worst time in my life has led to some of the best times. I love working with the women I meet, I've discovered I'm a great fund-raiser and mentor, I have my first big speech coming up soon, and I don't have to wear panty hose to work."

"How do you do it, Tia?" he marveled. "You're a surprise at every turn."

"Same way as always—by expecting God's blessing no matter how bleak the circumstances. Holding tight to my faith in God and believing he's holding even tighter to me. And sometimes I just fly by the seat of my pants."

She was glad to see him smile. That stiff, pained demeanor was too hard to look at. Brandon Ainsley was a humbled man.

A knock on the door broke the tension as the attorney called them into the conference room. "Time to put your name on the dotted line."

Brandon and Tia looked at each other. When he offered her his arm, she took it and allowed him to escort her to their final business dealing.

When the formalities were done, Tia escaped into the hall to pull herself together. She felt as though she'd just signed adoption papers to give away her firstborn.

While she was leaning against the wall next to the watercooler, Brandon approached. "May I speak to you for a minute?"

"I suppose so, but hasn't it all been said?"

"Not quite. There's one more thing I have to say. I wanted you to know that your behavior through all of this has pried something loose in me. I *wanted* you to hate me. It would have been far easier if you'd taken the bait when I tried to provoke you. I messed up not only my life but yours, and still you've been kinder to me today than I've been to myself."

He thrust his hands into his pockets. "I think I'm going to try to meet your God, Tia. He's obviously not the angry, judgmental one I heard about while I was growing up. If he can allow you to forgive me, then maybe he can help me forgive myself."

Her throat was so filled with emotion that Tia couldn't speak. Just then someone called Brandon's name and he walked away, leaving her alone with her tears.

. . . .

"This is just *too cute!*" Jenny held up a pink-and-white dress with a mile of ruffles around the skirt. The beribboned tail of a helium balloon, one of a dozen bouncing off the ceiling of Tia's living room, floated past her face and she brushed it aside. Then she settled her hand on her round belly and sighed. "You've all given me too much."

Even the light fixtures were dressed in festive pink-and-white netting for Jenny's baby shower. Colorful posters of adorable infants covered the walls, and a rocking chair tied with a huge pink bow sat in the middle of the room, a gift from Tibby's godmothers-to-be.

"You've still got this one to open," Ellen said. She and Dorothy wrestled a flat, rectangular box toward Jenny. "It's from Libby and Tia."

"Not *more*—the rocker, the clothes, the toys . . ."

"Humor us," Libby advised. "We couldn't have had more fun if we'd spent the day shopping for ourselves."

The guests were visiting among themselves, finishing their *pink* cake with *strawberry* frosting and *pink* lemonade, while Jenny opened the final gift. Libby and Tia helped her lift the large framed photo from its box. Tears began to stream down Jenny's cheeks when she saw what it was.

"It's *us!*" She turned the framed print toward the guests. It was an old black-and-white photo of three little girls. It had been enlarged and hand-painted in pastels—a touch of yellow on the curls of a round-cheeked little girl, clear green eyes on a serious-looking child holding a tattered copy of *Black Beauty,* and rosy lips and brown eyes on the face of a tiny girl with black hair and a defiant expression on her features. Behind them was the massive trunk of an old oak tree.

"We thought Tibby might enjoy seeing what her mother looked like as a child," Libby murmured. "And her godmothers, too."

"Jenny, you were the healthiest little Scandinavian child in the world by the look of it," Ellen said with a laugh. "Except for those skinned knees."

"Look at Tia's legs. She looks like a recruit just back from World War III," Jenny said.

"I fell down a lot—whatsit to ya?" Tia growled. "Besides, my mom had an endless supply of Band-Aids. Every afternoon, I'd manage to lose mine and get a whole new batch after my bath."

"And Libby was already interested in horses." Ellen pointed to the book.

"But I didn't know it yet."

Jenny sat back and grinned from ear to ear. "Well, ladies, the nursery is painted—"

"P . . . ink," Tia chimed.

"The furniture—white—is in place, and this picture will be the final touch. Now if she'll just keep growing a bit longer, we'll be ready for our baby."

"*Our* baby," Tia echoed. "The child with baby-sitters already waiting in a holding pattern to take care of her." Tia took one of Jenny's hands while Libby reached for the other. "We can hardly wait."

....

If her knees would stop knocking and her teeth stop chattering, thought Tia, she might be able to hear the annoying nervous rumble in her gut.

The month between Helen's announcement of Tia's invitation to speak and the actual moment had seemed like both years and seconds. During this time—other than the baby shower—Jenny had remained quietly at home, resting and growing a stomach that was beginning to look like the Metrodome. Libby'd done what Libby did best—take charge of Jenny's business and nurture everyone and everything around her.

Several of the women Tia had mentored at the shelter had "graduated" to other locations—apartments, homes of family members or friends, and one to a college dorm room. Tia had spent her free time wondering what kind of fool she'd make of herself in front of this group of three hundred women. She'd made pages of notes, written dozens of speeches, and thrown them all away. Finally she'd turned the whole affair over to the ultimate Speechwriter and asked him to guide her words and ideas.

"Tia?"

She turned to the voice behind her and saw Mariah West, dressed in a lovely new dress. Her hair was cut and styled, and the warm blush of makeup lit her face. She was genuinely beautiful.

"Don't you look nice!" Tia held out her arms for a hug. "I'm so glad you came."

"I wouldn't have missed it for anything. I wanted to show you my support. You've certainly given me yours."

"Any news?" Tia referred to Mariah's husband, who'd left for an alcohol treatment center two weeks before.

"We've got a date for Family Day. Trevor is finally going to see his dad completely sober and have a chance to express himself. Carl needs to hear what his drinking has done to us."

So that was his name. Carl. Tia figured it was a good sign that Mariah was finally using his name instead of calling him the usual generic "he."

"Carl's agreed to go to counseling and AA when he gets out. He knows I'm serious this time, and nasty as he was sometimes, I really do believe he loves us. He's scared, Tia, of losing us, of facing the mess he's made of his life and the hurt he's caused me and my son.

"I've already made up my mind that we're going to have to date after he gets back. He knows he has to show himself as trustworthy before he can come live with us again."

"Sensible idea," Tia said with a smile. "I hope he treats you like a princess. You deserve it."

Mariah brightened. "Trevor even made him promise he'd go to church with us when he got home. I don't know exactly what you told that boy, but something has come over him. He's studying all the time, trying to understand the Bible. He asks me questions until I'm about to faint. I've started going to a Bible study at church, just to keep up.

"Trevor is as happy as a hog in slop about his new responsibilities out at the ranch. Rollie and Reese have been as kind to him as his father should have been. I'm so glad Trevor has good role models now."

"How's the new job?" Tia asked gently. If she thought any more about Trevor and his mother studying the Bible, she might break into tears. Happy ones, but tears nonetheless. And she was going to speak in only a few minutes. Her mascara had to stay in place for that.

"And my cashier job is going really well. It's good to have

another source of income while my job as a cook at Valley Elementary School has stopped for the summer. Maybe I can do both jobs in the fall. Helen is also going to help me find some evening business classes to take. I'm taking computer classes first. Can't get anywhere without that these days."

"And how will you do your homework?"

"Helen says I can volunteer at the center. If I work as receptionist, I can use the computer when I'm not on the phone or greeting people. Plus, then I'll have that job on my resume, too—and a recommendation from Helen."

Mariah reached out and grabbed Tia's hand. "No matter how many times I tell you how much what you've done for me and my family has meant to me, it will never be enough."

"The same is true for me, you know," Tia pointed out. "I never dreamed that helping someone could be so rewarding. That experience has convinced me that it's what I want to do with my life. Thank *you*."

"I have to go," Mariah whispered. "Otherwise we're both going to cry. I'll be praying for you."

Tia watched Mariah slip away and took a deep breath. The moment was almost upon her.

"We're so happy you're here. We've been hearing really good things about Birdhouse Ministries." Inez Halliway, the coordinator of the conference, had designated herself Tia's hostess for the afternoon. She was a small, quick-moving, woman, not unlike a bird herself.

Birdhouses decorated every nook and cranny of the room where Tia was to speak.

Inez apparently noticed Tia's eyes straying across the cacophony of color. "We thought it would be fun to decorate with a birdhouse theme," she whispered as they came in sight of the platform. "You will, of course, be given all we've purchased to use in your ministry."

"I-I can't thank you enough . . . ," Tia stammered. And she couldn't. Her tongue was wrapped around her molars and her mouth so dry she was sure she felt a camel walking across it.

Then they were in front of a seemingly endless sea of people, and Inez was giving a glowing introduction of the day's speaker. "And without further ado, here is Ms. Tia Warden."

And Tia was alone at the podium—she and three hundred of her closest friends.

It's your time, Father. Tell me what you want me to say and then make me say it. Anoint my words. And keep my knees from buckling.

Miraculously, she could see in those faces before her the many women she'd met while at the center—old and young, every race and color, pretty and plain, hopeful and hopeless—and she was no longer talking to a group of strangers, but to a group of people she loved and cared for most. Her legs quit quivering, saliva returned to her mouth, and she no longer needed to support herself with the rostrum. When she opened her mouth to speak, her voice was strong and rich with emotion.

"I am so glad you are here today, even though you are probably as puzzled as I am as to why *I* was given this opportunity to speak to you." She touched the roof of the birdhouse beside her on the podium. "But I believe it all started with one of these and at a very bad time in my own life when God spoke to me of looking for the bright spots in the dark places, of giving praise when things to be thankful for seemed few. . . ." Her notes forgotten, for the next thirty minutes, Tia spoke the words written in her heart.

When she sat down to a thunderous round of applause, Tia realized that she couldn't remember what she'd said. She'd been merely a conduit through which a message was sent. Tears of thankfulness stung Tia's eyes as she sensed that God had indeed used her to get his point across. But she didn't feel "used." She felt blessed, gifted, rewarded, and overwhelmingly grateful.

Inez managed to continue to applaud enthusiastically and still nudge Tia with her elbow. "Look."

The women in the audience were on their feet, clapping and smiling.

Thanks, God. Thank you, thank you, thank you. Let's do this team speaking again someday.

She returned to the podium as the audience quieted. "I'm staying for lunch. I hear they are having a Death by Chocolate buffet, and you couldn't pull me out of here until I've sampled everything. If you have questions or comments, I'd love to speak with you and give you a Birdhouse Ministries brochure. If anyone would like to help with this ministry, there is a simple form to fill out.

"I will contact each and every one of you personally—mostly because I'm my own staff and also because Birdhouse Ministries is very personal for me. You don't have to feel brilliant or special in any way to do powerful work. By being a woman of faith who wants to help others, you fill all my application requirements. Sometimes the best thing you can do is just *be.* Be there to listen when someone needs to talk, be there to hold a hand, wipe a tear, haul a child on your hip, throw a Frisbee, or pick out a different hairstyle for a new friend. We aren't human *doings;* we are human *beings.* If you can *be* there for someone, Birdhouse Ministries is for you."

During the next ninety minutes, Tia barely had time to take a deep breath, let alone eat the chocolate desserts that kept accumulating beside her.

When the last woman had gone, Inez pushed a large white cardboard box toward Tia. "One of every kind of dessert. Once we realized you weren't going to have time to eat, we thought we'd pack a little care package for you to take home."

Tia wiped her hair out of her eyes and leaned back in her chair. "What just happened here? A stampede? An avalanche?"

"You touched a nerve and made them laugh at the same time.

What a lovely way to introduce God's work to others." Inez held out a stack of application forms in one hand and a basket overflowing with unsolicited donations to Birdhouse Ministries in the other. "Looks like you'll be on the phone for a few days, but when you're done, you should have much more help for your projects."

Tia reverently accepted the forms and basket and stared at them in awe. She'd prayed and he'd answered. Just like before, just like always—in his own way and his own time—and now she held the physical proof in her hands.

A swell of assurance swept over her—confidence that she was exactly where she needed to be, doing exactly what she needed to do. The stores no longer were important. She was, in fact, delighted to be rid of them so she could attend immediately to the names of those who were willing to serve. Nor did she feel the nagging loneliness she'd experienced after her separation from Brandon. There was no need to be lonely when there were so many friends waiting to be made and so many women needing to be helped.

Her life had become one of Brandon's beautiful kaleidoscopes, each piece of it having been turned and jiggled and turned again, until it had finally fallen into place in a startlingly lovely mosaic that was bright with color and potential. She knew for certain that she was where God wanted her to be, in step with him, in a harmony so peaceful and lovely that she had no words to express it.

When she got to her car, Tia leaned her forehead on the steering wheel and gave such enthusiastic prayers of thanks that she forgot herself and even honked the horn.

. . . .

"So you don't plan to go back into any sort of business?" Libby asked.

The three friends were at Jenny's, discussing Tia's debut as a public speaker.

"No. Not now. I have other fish to fry."

"I think it's 'fishers of men,' Tia, not 'fryers of fish,' " Jenny commented.

"Whatever. I've learned so much from my experiences of the past few months that my head feels as if it's going to explode."

"You make me feel a little envious," Libby admitted. "All I know is that, for the time being, I'm supposed to continue to do what I'm doing."

"Run my store, care for my child and his dog, keep your own beautiful family happy and healthy," Jenny listed, "be our best friend, volunteer for Reach Out Ranch, and be the best fund-raiser they've ever had since you've been making quilts for them to auction—"

"Okay. I'm doing important things, too. Thanks for reminding me." Libby gave Jenny's shoulders a hug as she lay on the couch.

"And, Jenny! You are doing the most amazing thing of all! Creating life! Growing a baby . . . hatching a human egg . . . sitting on the nest . . ." Tia rejoined. "You have family responsibilites. I'm free—as a *bird!*"

"Hard to believe the world ever got along without us, huh?" Jenny giggled.

Tia recalled their night at the circus. It seemed like eons ago now, but she still remembered the trapeze artist boldly releasing her bar, trusting that her partner would be there in midair to catch her. They'd taught her the lesson that no one could move forward without letting go of the past. And no matter how difficult it is, or how brave one has to be, it has to be done in order to go on.

When Jenny made a small strange sound, Tia's attention quickly turned to her. "Jen? What's wrong?"

"I just had a pain."

"Where?" Libby asked.

"I've been feeling odd for a couple of days and attributing it to the cabbage salad and baked beans Mike cooked . . ."

"Ewww!" Tia wrinkled her nose.

"But this is different." Jenny looked alarmed.

Libby reached for the phone. "I'll call Mike. He'll want to come home and take you to the doctor."

"It's too early for the baby. It's not her due date yet."

"Maybe Tibby takes after her Aunt Tia and is too impatient to wait any longer," Libby said calmly.

"Don't blame me for this!" Tia leaned close to Jenny's belly, shook her finger at it, and said, "You just hang in there, little girl. We're not ready for you yet. If you insist on being born now, you're going to be stuck with Tibby as a nickname, and no self-respecting young lady would want that."

Jenny was halfway between laughter and tears as the pain returned and the antics of the Two Stooges escalated around her. With their help, Jenny dressed in a fresh blouse and applied a slash of lipstick and a brush of blush.

When Mike arrived, however, he didn't stop to admire his wife's good looks. "I talked to the doctor on the phone. He wants me to bring you right to the hospital. He said it's a miracle you have hung in there this long. Like it or not, Jenny, we're probably going to have a baby today."

. . . .

Luke, Robert, and the dogs were not allowed in the family waiting room of the obstetrics ward, so Reese played with them outside.

Tia and Libby behaved like expectant fathers inside the birthing room. It was large but snug, with frilly curtains and table lamps that glowed with soft light.

"So Tibby will be born right here?" Libby asked.

"Yes. They will turn this into a delivery room just before she's born." Mike was the most calm and collected of the lot.

"What's in here? Oh . . ." Tia peered into a closet and saw the carts containing medical equipment. She shut the door quickly. "I like it better like this."

The room was filled with the comfortingly steady sound of the baby's heartbeat emanating from a monitor attached to Jenny. It seemed a cozy place for this new little soul to be born, Tia thought.

"The doctor was in while you two were checking out the cafeteria," Mike said. "Everything is going according to plan. He foresees no problems and expects a natural birth and a baby before midnight."

Or sooner. Jenny gave a lusty moan and started her breathing techniques. The nurse grinned and said, "That was a big one. A few more contractions like that and we'll be ready to deliver this baby."

The contractions came more quickly after that, and Jenny and Mike became so involved in each other that Tia and Libby tiptoed out of the room unnoticed. The nurse winked at them as they left. "I think it's time."

Out in the hallway, the minutes were passing like hours. "Oh, oh, oh . . . ," Tia chanted. "Oh, oh, oh. My turn!"

She pulled at Libby's shoulder to pry her away from the birthing-room door where she'd planted her ear. "It's great! I can hear Mike counting and Jenny breathing. It's so cool."

A cry sounded on the other side of the door. It was lusty, robust, and furious. Tibby Adams had arrived, and she wasn't any too happy about it. Tia and Libby collapsed on each other in tears of joy.

"Oh . . . ," Tia groaned as they waited in the family waiting room.

"Now what?"

"I bought two boxes of chocolate cigars that say 'It's a Girl,' and I forgot them at home."

"Aren't cigars Mike's job?"

"I've got some for him, too. This baby already has a slew of parents—we might as well admit it and just hand out the chocolate."

Then the subject of their conversation entered. "What took so long, Mike?" Tia demanded.

"Cleaning up the baby so she's ready to meet her new family."

"And Jenny?"

"Waiting to see you."

Looking tired and happy, Jenny was now resting quietly, a bundle of pink blankets topped with a small pink warming hat cradled in her arms. "Tibby is just beautiful!" were her first words.

"Tibby?" Tia echoed in surprise.

Jenny smiled foolishly. "Much as I wanted it not to, I'm afraid it's stuck. And she does look like a Tibby—just a little tidbit of a thing. So tiny and delicate . . . and what lungs!"

"She must have inherited that from me," Tia said with a smile as she peered at the tiny face screwing itself up for a big cry.

"This child has the tiniest fingers and toes! And her nose is just a button. The doctor said she was 'all girl.' " Tears filled Jenny's eyes. "I have so much to be grateful for."

Tia pulled a chair close to Jenny's bed and curled into it. "What do you think those little girls in the tree house all those years ago would have said about us now?"

"They would have predicted our futures pretty accurately. Libby would be doing good in every spot she could, I'd be a wife and mommy, and you, Tia, would be involved with something that no one else had ever thought of, like birdhouses."

"I suppose that would have been difficult to predict," Tia agreed. "Although, we did sit in that tree house a lot. It makes sense, really. A little girl who spent her childhood in a tree would be bound to spend life with her head in the clouds and birdhouses as her business."

"Tia, look!" Libby was pointing to a bluebird perched on the window ledge, peering in at them with bright-eyed curiosity. He cocked his head as if to ask what interesting thing was transpiring beyond the pane and why the three friends staring back at him wore such joyful smiles on their faces.

Judy Baer lives in Minnesota and raises quarter horses and buffalo in North Dakota. She is the mother of two grown children, Adrienne and Jennifer.

Judy began writing in 1982 and to date has published more than sixty books. During her career she has been the recipient of numerous awards, including Woman of the Year in 1995 for the North Dakota Professional Communicators' National Federation of Press Women, and the Concordia College Alumni Achievement Award in 1997.

Tia's Story is Judy's third full-length Tyndale House novel. Her other books include *Jenny's Story* and *Libby's Story,* and she was the lead author for the Tyndale anthology of romance novellas entitled *Reunited.*

THE
CRUSHING
DEPTHS

THE
CRUSHING
DEPTHS

DANI PETTREY

BETHANYHOUSE
a division of Baker Publishing Group
Minneapolis, Minnesota

CANCELLED
Rocky River Public Library

© 2020 by Grace & Johnny, Inc.

Published by Bethany House Publishers
11400 Hampshire Avenue South
Bloomington, Minnesota 55438
www.bethanyhouse.com

Bethany House Publishers is a division of
Baker Publishing Group, Grand Rapids, Michigan

Printed in the United States of America

All rights reserved. No part of this publication may be reproduced, stored in a retrieval system, or transmitted in any form or by any means—for example, electronic, photocopy, recording—without the prior written permission of the publisher. The only exception is brief quotations in printed reviews.

Library of Congress Cataloging-in-Publication Data
Names: Pettrey, Dani, author.
Title: The crushing depths / Dani Pettrey.
Description: Minneapolis, Minnesota : Bethany House Publishers, [2020] |
Series: Coastal guardians; 2
Identifiers: LCCN 2019054279 | ISBN 9780764230851 (trade paperback) | ISBN
    9780764233449 (cloth) | ISBN 9781493425075 (ebook)
Subjects: GSAFD: Mystery fiction. | Christian fiction.
Classification: LCC PS3616.E89 C78 2020 | DDC 813/.6—dc23
LC record available at https://lccn.loc.gov/2019054279

This is a work of fiction. Names, characters, incidents, and dialogues are products of the author's imagination and are not to be construed as real. Any resemblance to actual events or persons, living or dead, is entirely coincidental.

Cover design by LOOK Design Studio

Author is represented by Books & Such Literary Management.

20 21 22 23 24 25 26   7 6 5 4 3 2 1

To Dee Henderson
I'm so blessed by your friendship, guidance, and support
over all these years. But I am most grateful for your example
of living a life of devotion to and in relationship with God.
May I walk daily with our Father as you do. Love you, friend!

The silence of the abyss engulfed her.

ONE

Greg Barnes clinked along the grated metal steps, his boot heels rasping with each shuffle as he headed topside for a much-needed breath of smoke.

Thrusting the door open with a resounding creak, he stepped out into the night air. A litany of protestors' chants mimicked the shrill whining of cicadas.

He glanced at his watch. *1930.* Didn't those eco-nuts ever give it a rest?

As if the cursed rig wasn't enough—they had the dang relentless protestors going practically day and night.

Exhaling, he rubbed his thumb along the smooth surface of the tarnished gold lighter in his pocket. His tight muscles seized, making his movements stiff. He shook his head. Those people needed to get a life.

Edging around the far corner of the main separator facility, he pressed his back against the structure's cool outer wall. Generators whirred across from him, finally drowning out the clatter. He scanned his surroundings and exhaled in relief. Finally, alone.

His leg twitched. Just one drag . . . maybe two. It'd been an awful day, and that was the gentleman's way of putting it.

7

With unsteady hands, he pulled the plastic-wrapped pack from his shirt pocket.

It crinkled beneath his hold and the sweet scent of tobacco wafted beneath his nose. He tamped the cigarette in his palm and slid it between his cracked lips. *Just one drag.*

Tugging the lighter from his pocket, he flipped it open, then rolled the pad of his thumb across the ignitor.

A spark flashed and fire roared, hissing over him in a sizzling cascade of torment.

TWO

Rissi Dawson sat at the long table on Dockside's waterfront deck, gaping at Mason Rogers. He turned to look at her, his green eyes illuminated in the bright pole lights lining the wooden structural beams. She averted her eyes as heat rushed up her throat, spreading across her cheeks. He'd caught her staring *again*. Embarrassment drenched her. It'd been three days since his arrival, and she still couldn't wrap her mind around the fact he was actually sitting next to her.

The boy she'd had the biggest crush on as a teen was back in her life. And on her Coast Guard Investigative Service team.

He handed her the basket of hush puppies the restaurant served instead of bread to start everyone off. His hand brushed hers with the movement, and her heart fluttered. "Thanks," she said, keeping her gaze fixed on the red basket as she pulled two balls of fried cornmeal from it. She plopped the still-warm puppies onto the round plate to the right of her Coke. *Get it together, girl!*

The whir of a boat's motor dropping to an idle sounded over the deck's edge. A teen jumped out of the white outboard and onto the pier, tying her up to the cleat. Rissi loved living in a place with a boat drive-thru.

Noah raised his glass of iced tea. "Everyone . . ." The team lifted their glasses in response to their boss's prompting.

9

Noah dipped his chin. "Welcome, Mason. Happy to have you on board."

The team clinked their glasses together, even Caleb, who sat brooding to her left. Observant as he was, there was no chance he missed the way she looked at Mason. In recent months, he'd developed feelings for her, so it wasn't surprising he'd bristled at Mason's arrival—especially after learning she and Mason shared a past, though he didn't know the half of it. Only that they spent time in a children's home together for a handful of months as teens.

The opening riff of "Sweet Home Alabama" emanated from Noah's jean pocket. He hitched up as he extracted his phone. "Rowley," he answered. "Yes?" Standing, he headed down the ramp toward the restaurant's pier.

"Rockfish tacos," the waitress said, placing the plate in front of Rissi. The sweet, tropical scent of the mango slaw swirled in the air.

The waitress handed out plate after plate to each of them, setting Noah's burger at his spot while he continued to pace the pier.

Caleb bit into his Carolina BBQ pork sandwich, the scent of vinegar wafting in the night's gentle breeze.

Finn Walker did the same with his crab cake sandwich. He and Noah, who was from Maryland, had argued for months over which state had the best crab cake. Finn had been convinced it was North Carolina, right up until Noah had crab cakes flown in fresh from Jimmy's Famous Seafood in Baltimore. It took two bites for Finn to concede the win.

"Sorry about that, folks," Noah said, retaking his seat.

"Everything okay?" Emmy Thorton asked. Rissi looked forward to seeing the quirky angel every day at the station.

"Rissi, Mason." Noah lifted his chin in their direction. "I've got an assignment for you."

Her and Mason? They'd worked a case his first day on the

team, but Finn had joined them for most of the investigation. This would be the two of them . . . alone. A mixture of elation and fear sifted through her.

"Great." Mason set down his lemonade.

"We've got a death out on the *Dauntless*."

"The offshore oil platform?" Mason asked, swiping a drop of lemonade from his bottom lip.

Stop staring, girl. So he's jaw-dropping gorgeous. So you share a past. Still, staring is plain rude. Despite not having a mother to teach her, Rissi knew, or at least had come to learn, her manners.

Noah laid his napkin across his lap. "You two need to determine if the death was an accident or if foul play was involved. Helo is leaving from Textra Oil's copter hub in forty-five. I need you both on it."

Mason pushed back from the table. "No problem."

"Great," Noah said. "You'll be joining the head of operations, a commercial diver, and the deceased's replacement on the company copter."

Rissi took one last bite of her taco before setting it down. She dabbed the corner of her lips with a napkin. "They aren't wasting any time in replacing the deceased."

"The deceased's name is Greg Barnes. I talked to the head of operations, Bob Stanton, and he said they needed to replace him ASAP."

"Must be an important position." She reached for her glass and took a final sip.

"You'd think," Noah said. "But Bob said the main reason they need to replace him fast is they've been working with a skeleton crew."

Mason's brows pinched as he stood. "Why?"

"Several guys didn't show up for their three-week rotation transport out," Noah said, popping a fry in his mouth.

"I know why they didn't show up for that copter ride out

there." Tom Murphy leaned toward them from his table situated to their right.

"Why?" Mason asked, moving around to the back of Rissi's chair. He held it out for her as she stood.

She glanced over her shoulder at him and smiled. "Thanks."

He nodded.

Tom, one of Wrightsville's most colorful fishermen, crooked his index finger, drawing them in. "That rig's cursed."

"Cursed?" Caleb chuckled. "You can't be serious?"

Tom waggled his finger. "It's no laughing matter, young man."

"I'm sure it's a good story, Tom," Rissi said. No reason not to be polite. "But I'm afraid we've got to catch a copter ride."

Tom shrugged and turned back to his food. "It's your lives at stake."

"What do you mean?" she asked before they passed his table, unable to stem her curiosity.

"You'll see." He smiled, his right incisor missing. "Henry's curse is real."

"Henry?" Why was she letting herself get sucked into this?

Tom let out a high-pitched chuckle. "Oh, you'll learn all about Henry."

"Shall we?" Mason said, gesturing to the wooden ramp leading down to the gravel parking lot.

Excusing themselves, they moved down the ramp. Mason leaned in. He smelled of the ocean and warm spice. He whispered, "Did that guy seriously just cackle?"

She nodded, strangely curious about the old man's ghost story.

"I thought people only did that on *Scooby-Doo*."

She let out a slip of laughter.

"I wouldn't be laughing," Tom called after them as they rounded the ramp on his side of the deck. "You two be careful out there, you hear? It's a dangerous place to be. Just ask the men on board."

THREE

"Well, that was interesting," Mason said, walking on Rissi's left into the parking lot. Almost as interesting as the fact he was headed for his first assignment alone with Rissi.

"I carpooled with Emmy today," she said, "so I guess you'll be driving."

"No problem."

She glanced around the lot. "Where's your car?"

He lifted his chin at his Triumph Bonneville parked less than three feet away.

She angled her head, her gaze flitting over his motorcycle. "Nice ride."

"Thanks."

"I can give you a ride," Caleb said, sidling down the ramp and stopping less than a foot away. "No need for you to ride on *that*."

Mason dipped his chin. "*That*?"

"On the back of a bike," Caleb said, his broad shoulders square. "It's gotta be more comfortable for Rissi in a car."

Rissi looked up at Caleb, who if Mason gauged right was six-three or possibly six-four. Either way, he towered over her.

"I'll be fine, but thanks," she said with a soft smile. "It makes more sense to head with Mason to the helipad."

The muscle in Caleb's jaw flickered in the restaurant's front floodlight. He shuffled, his boots scattering a few pebbles. "Okay. Be careful."

"Always," she said.

Caleb's gaze shifted to Mason. "Take good care of her."

"Always," Mason said.

Caleb nodded and headed back up the ramp for the restaurant's deck seating.

Mason opened the right saddlebag and pulled out a yellow-and-orange helmet. He handed it to Rissi. "For you."

"Thanks." She flipped her hair over her shoulders and slid the helmet on.

"Let me take a quick look." He stepped closer to inspect the helmet. It needed to fit right. "Just a small adjustment." He pulled the straps taut, his fingers grazing the supple skin along her neck.

"Is it okay?" she asked, blinking up at him.

"Ye—" He cleared his throat. "Yes. You're good."

"Great."

He grabbed his helmet off the gas tank, slid it on, and straddled the bike. Rissi followed suit and adjusted to fit around him. His throat constricted, every nerve ending in his body sparking.

Focus, man. Precious cargo.

"Ever been on a bike?" he asked.

"Definitely. I've ridden with Logan. No one can be as crazy as him. He drives like he's a MotoGP rider."

Mason laughed. "Good description."

"You've already ridden with him?"

"He showed me the best back roads in the area last night. We had a blast."

She chuckled. "I hate to imagine."

Mason turned the ignition, and the bike rumbled beneath them.

Revving the engine, he eased out of the gravel lot. Reaching the pavement, he rolled on the throttle, and the bike flew.

Rissi clasped hold of him, her hands hugging his waist. He took a sharp inhale, praying she didn't feel him quiver beneath her touch.

They crossed the bridge connecting Wrightsville Beach to Wilmington, and he fully twisted the throttle. Wind pressed against his visor. Salt infused the air circulating around them.

Twenty minutes to meet the helicopter. They were cutting it close. Thankfully, his ride with Logan had shown him a good number of shortcuts around town. Ridgely Way, in particular, held some wicked turns and would shave a good five minutes off their drive.

Signaling, he made the turn. "Hang on!" he hollered over his shoulder.

She shifted, securing her arms about his waist, resting her elbows atop his hip bones.

He swallowed. Maybe this wasn't the best idea. He needed to focus on the corkscrew ahead. Praying for focus and pure thoughts, he pressed the left handgrip and shot through it.

Rissi's hold remained firm, but her sweet, unbridled laughter lit up the night.

Now, if he could just shake the weight lodged in his gut— the one telling him they were headed for a completely different kind of danger.

FOUR

A rush of wind whistled through Rissi's hair, fluttering it about her helmet. Her arms snug around Mason, she leaned into the last turn, wishing the ride would never end. This was what being fully alive felt like.

The tarry scent of asphalt on the warm night seeped through her helmet as they pulled into the transport lot. Their time together was about to shift.

Anticipation surged through her.

What were they heading into? And why had Tom's silly curse story spooked her? She didn't spook.

Mason killed the engine, flipped down the side stand, and climbed off the bike. Rissi followed suit.

He removed his helmet, his spiky hair flattened and mussed.

She bit back a smile and removed her own, wondering what her helmet hair looked like.

Her gaze fixed on the helicopter. The floodlights beaming down on the helipad illuminated a man standing in the copter's open bay door. He cupped a hand to his mouth. "Over here." His words sounded more like a whisper than the shout his contorted face suggested. It fell nearly silent under the pulse of the copter's whirring blades.

Mason rested his hand on the small of Rissi's back as they ducked beneath what were essentially razor-sharp machetes spinning overhead.

The man extended his hand.

Rissi gripped hold, and he helped her into the helicopter. Mason climbed in behind her.

A faint holler of "Wait!" reached her ears. Turning, she spotted a man racing across the tarmac. Out of breath, he darted into the front passenger seat, landing with an *oomph*. Clutching his briefcase on his lap, he pulled his door closed. "Let's go."

The pilot turned back. "I'm Max."

"Rissi."

"Mason." He lifted his chin in greeting.

"Can one of you close the bay door, then grab an open seat?"

"Sure." Mason moved for the door and slid it shut. A reverberating shudder rumbled through Rissi's chest.

"Let's get this thing going," the man up front snapped, pushing his glasses against the bridge of his nose.

"As soon as they're buckled in," Max said, flipping switches.

Rissi sat down and slid the black strap across her chest, clicking it into the silver buckle.

Mason sat beside her. As he shifted to adjust his buckle, his muscular thigh brushed hers.

She bit her bottom lip at the warmth of his inadvertent touch. It was so strange seeing him as a grown man. He was the same . . . but different. His shoulders broader, his jaw more chiseled, a dusting of hair on his forearms, and his handspan nearly double hers.

"It's about a half hour ride out to *Dauntless*," Max said, "so sit back and enjoy the lack of view." The moon slid behind wispy clouds, shrouding them in darkness.

Rissi relaxed into her seat and assessed the men riding with them.

"I'm Bob Stanton," the latecomer said from the front seat. "Head of operations for Textra Oil."

"Nice to meet you," she said.

Mason leaned forward and shook the man's hand.

"Chase Calhoun," the man who'd been beckoning them to the copter chimed in. He was tall, with curly blond hair and deep blue eyes. He reminded her of a young Paul Newman.

"What do you do on the platform?" Mason asked Chase.

"I'm an underwater welder. Apparently, they are having some trouble with the risers, so I'm heading back out yet again to inspect them all."

"Risers?" Rissi asked, unfamiliar with oil production platforms.

"The risers are pipes that connect *Dauntless* to the subsea system the drilling rig put in place for them to come in and start production."

"You must hit some pretty good depths," Mason said.

Chase lifted his chin with a smile. "My deepest without a diving bell is just over four hundred feet."

Mason whistled. "That's impressive."

"You dive?" Chase asked.

"Some," Mason said.

"Some?" Rissi shook her head. "He was a master diver with the Guard," she said, having just learned that yesterday, but it fit with the man he'd become. She was learning who he was now, but somehow, she already *knew* him. It was strange how time worked, especially when it came to matters of the heart.

"Nice," Chase said, resting his hands behind his head. "I've heard the training in the Guard can be brutal."

Mason chuckled. "It definitely has its moments."

Chase tilted his head, his eyes narrowing. "I was told two CGIS agents were joining us."

"I'm CGIS now," Mason said.

Chase's smile thinned. "You gave up diving?"

"I specialize in dive investigations."

"Hmm . . . I imagine you see some interesting things on that job."

Mason shook his head on an exhaled whistle. "I could tell you some stories."

"I wouldn't mind hearing them myself," the dark-haired man across from Rissi said. "Joel Waters." He leaned as far forward as his strap would allow and extended his hand. Rissi and Mason each shook it in turn.

"He's the man who's going to fix my problem," Bob said from the front passenger seat.

Joel's jaw tightened. "You can't *fix* a dead man."

Bob shifted to half face them, his clasped knuckles white on the edge of his briefcase. "Mr. Barnes's death was unfortunate, but we have a production platform to run. I need you to determine what happened and ensure we are ready to continue production."

Joel shook his head with an exhale. "Right. Can't let a man's death prevent production, now can we?"

Rissi studied the man. If he was so offended, and it appeared he had every right to be, why agree to come along?

Mr. Stanton slid his glasses off and wiped the lenses with a handkerchief he'd pulled from his tan overcoat. "I don't appreciate the sarcasm, Mr. Waters. I've already said that Mr. Barnes's death was unfortunate, and, believe me, I intend to find out what happened, but . . ." He exhaled, slid his glasses back on, and popped his handkerchief back in his top jacket pocket. "You need to step back and look at the big picture."

He shifted his attention to Rissi and Mason. "In case you didn't know, Joel here is, and Greg was, a safety engineer. I suppose it is rather ironic he died from a lapse in safety." Bob snorted, then cleared his throat. "I'm sorry. Very inappropriate of me." He lifted his hand in apology but continued his hushed laughter under his breath.

Rissi stared at Bob. A man was dead, and he was cracking jokes?

Joel reclined, linking his arms over his chest. "It wasn't a safety overlook by Greg that got him killed. *Dauntless* is cursed, and Henry's wrath is just getting started."

"Ah, come on." Chase swiped his hand through the air. "Don't tell me you believe that nonsense too?"

"You're a fool for not paying heed to Henry's curse," Joel countered.

Not the curse again. "That's the second time we've heard something about a—"

A ferocious roar cut Rissi off. An ear-piercing alarm shrieked, blistering her ears.

"What happ—?" Joel hollered.

The copter pitched into a nosedive.

Rissi lashed forward, but her restraints halted her free fall, knocking the wind from her lungs. She grappled for a breath.

Mason's arm braced across her, trying to shield her. But she didn't think anything could prevent what was coming.

FIVE

"Mayday! Mayday! We're going down," Max called over the headset as he wrestled with the stick between his legs, trying to level the plunging copter. "I can't get her back."

Rissi drew a sharp breath, but her panic eased when Mason lowered his hand to hers, clutching it as they spiraled for the sea.

"Dear God," Bob shrieked.

"I've got you," Mason said, his grip tightening on her hand. "Don't let go."

She nodded, pressure pinning her head back.

Twenty feet.

Ten.

Five.

Metal collided with water.

A bone-jarring jolt thrust Rissi forward, then snapped her back—her head ramming into a metal panel. Pain whirred in her ears, sparks flitting before her eyes.

A wicked crack zigzagged down the side window. She clutched Mason's hand tighter. He was her grounding.

A splintering explosion burst through the cavity.

Mason lunged across her. "Cover your face!"

Water gushed in feverishly, rushing over her ankles and up her knees and torso.

Her throat constricted. *Please, Jesus.*

"Deep breath," Mason said, his voice an anchor of sanity in the cold, dark void.

She jerked in a last gulp of air before swirling water swallowed her whole.

Mason gripped her wrist, tugging her to follow him. Something held her down, pinning her to her seat.

Think. You're trained for the extreme.

Her mind settled.

Weight pressed across her shoulder and thighs—constraining her.

Seat belt.

She fumbled in the dark for the buckle, her chest tight.

Please, Jesus, where is it?

She fixed her right hand around the belt and traced it down to the buckle. Mason's hand was already there, jerking the clasp, but it wouldn't budge.

Stretching her arm and fingers as far down as they would go, she retrieved the knife strapped to her calf.

Mason held by her side.

Sliding the blade between her body and the belt, she jerked outward, and the restraint pressing into her chest released.

Lowering the blade to her waist, she slid it beneath the belt and flinched as a razor-sharp sting lanced her skin. Biting back a grunt of pain, she squirmed her way out of whatever was tangled around her legs.

Mason tugged her in front of him. She swam toward the shattered window, but the black abyss shoved back. A faint light flickered on the control panel. They paused, scanning the copter. The light was so dim she didn't know how they'd see anyone, but they had to try.

A moment later, not seeing anyone, they swam through the jagged window opening. A burning sting pierced down the inside of her shoulder blade as they passed through. Intense pain radiated down her side, but she pressed forward.

Once free of the wreckage, she and Mason swam in the direction she prayed was up.

Bursting through the ocean's surface, she swallowed a gasp of air, coughing and sputtering as it seared her lungs.

"Anyone there?" Bob's pained voice echoed above the thundering sea.

"We're here," Mason called, treading at Rissi's side.

"So am I," Chase said. "Joel's here, too, but he's knocked out."

"Max?" Mason shouted.

No answer from the pilot.

"Max!" Mason hollered.

Something swooshed past Rissi's calf, and she stilled.

There it was again.

Her breath hitched, her gaze shooting to the water.

"What's wrong?" Mason asked, his husky voice deep.

"I don't—" Another swish, this time by her hand. Something coarse and . . . slimy.

Her throat constricted.

What was in the water with them?

SIX

Falling rain spattered Brooke Kesler's cheeks as she raced across the tarmac for the orange MH-65 Dolphin medevac helicopter.

Climbing inside, she hopped into her seat, buckling in as the rotary blades sliced through the air.

Jason and Brad, two of the Coast Guard's best rescue swimmers, aka aviation survival technicians, rushed across the tarmac. The open hangar's floodlights silhouetted their broad shoulders and rescue gear: snorkel, helmet, face mask, harness—everything needed to help them hold to the USCG's motto "So others may live."

"Good team tonight," Harvey, the pilot, said as the men climbed aboard and buckled in.

Brooke agreed. She couldn't have handpicked a better team.

"Kesler? What are you still doing here?" Jason asked, folding a piece of gum into his mouth.

"Busy night. I offered to extend my watch a couple hours."

"Again?" Brad tipped his chin up as a smirk curled on his ridiculously handsome face. "You need to get a man."

Jason shook his head with a chuckle. "Oh, you did not go there."

Brad leaned forward as the copter hovered up in the air. "I'd be glad to help you with that."

"Oh. Do you know a real man?" she shot back in jest.

"Dang." Jason whistled, laughing at Brad as he sat back with a chagrined smile. "You just got burned."

"It's all right," Brad said as they soared out over the ocean, "one of these days, she'll come around to me."

"Don't hold your breath." Brooke chuckled. Brad teased, but he was just messing with her. She didn't take it personally. It was part of the brotherhood.

"That's right, princess." Jason laughed, elbowing Brad in the ribs. "Man, next time you come to a battle of wits, you might want to come armed."

"Is that right?" Brad pinched Jason's shoulder.

Jason shrugged him off, jabbing him in the shoulder.

Brooke just shook her head at boys being boys and stared out at the thrashing sea below as the gravity of their mission fastened back in her mind.

"What do we have?" Jason asked Harvey.

"A Textra Oil company copter went down four minutes ago. The pilot called in a Mayday. Radio silence within seconds."

"How far out?" Brad asked.

"Twenty-two miles. They were en route to *Dauntless*."

Rain pinged off the copter's windshield—slow at first then increasing in intensity.

"All right, folks," Jerry, head of Air Station, Wilmington's air traffic control, cut into the comm, "we've got a manifest. Pilot Max Schaffer and five passengers. Oh no . . ."

Brooke stiffened. "What's wrong?"

"There are two CGIS agents on board."

Brooke lurched forward. "Who?"

"Agents Dawson and Rogers."

She squeezed her eyes shut. *Not Rissi* . . . She didn't recognize the other name, but she'd heard they had a new agent. Must be him. They had to reach them in time.

"Jesus, please . . ." was all Rissi could mutter. Something slithered along her back, circling around the front of her. Her salt-burned throat constricted as another one slipped between her legs.

There were two of them?

The dim moonlight finally peeking out from the mottled clouds gave her enough light to see movement gliding around them . . . everywhere.

Another squirmed through her treading legs, something hard scraping her shin.

How many of them were there, and—she swallowed, pain scraping down her raw throat—what were they?

Rain pounded in the churning sea—causing rings to ripple out amidst the movement just beneath the surface.

"Just stay as still as you can," Mason said, barely treading beside her. Instead, he looked as if he were sitting on a chair that didn't exist.

"What is *that*?" Bob hollered.

Rissi squinted in the direction of his voice and made out his flailing figure about fifteen yards to their twelve.

"Stop acting like a pansy," Chase said to their six. Rissi glanced over her shoulder. Chase lay in a reclined back float, Joel positioned unconscious across his chest.

"Is Joel okay?" she called.

"He's breathing, but it's labored."

"Coast Guard rescue should be here soon," she said, reassuring herself as much as Chase.

"They're taking their time about it," Chase grunted.

It'd been less than a handful of minutes. They'd be there soon. She held on to that. She could tread water as long as she needed to, but not knowing what was surrounding her was terrifying.

"Whoa!" Bob squealed.

"That's not going to help. You're just going to stir them up," Chase said.

"Them?" she asked.

"Stingrays," Mason said a second before Chase did.

Of course. Migration season.

"They are harmless . . . most of the time," Mason said.

"It's the 'most of' part I'm concerned about," Bob clipped out. "I saw what happened to Steve Irwin."

Horribly sad. But, man, he'd been an inspiration to Rissi. Steve Irwin was a man who lived life to the fullest, pursuing the passion of his soul—his family and wildlife conservation.

Noah draped his arm over the back of his seat at Dockside. It was getting late, but he was enjoying the comradery of his teammates—well, those present. Caleb's tense jaw when Noah had assigned the *Dauntless* investigation to Rissi and Mason spoke volumes, but Caleb had to get used to Mason being part of the team. And pairing the two made the most sense. Rissi was a stellar profiler who could read nonverbal clues in a way he'd never seen. And Mason had come highly recommended. Noah wanted to see what he could do. He liked how the man carried himself, though Mason's superior in Kodiak said that while he'd never worked with a braver man, Mason's penchant for pushing his limits when another's life was at stake caused him to hold his breath more than a time or two.

Noah's phone vibrated as "Sweet Home Alabama" played. He shifted, once again pulling it from his jeans.

He glanced at the number. Air traffic control. The hairs on the nape of his neck pricked. "Rowley."

"It's Brooke Kesler, Coast Guard medic." The patch-through was crackly—her voice only clear in spurts.

27

"Hi, Brooke." Noah pinched the bridge of his nose, painfully awaiting her next words. *Please don't let this be going where I think it is.*

"The copter Rissi and Agent Rogers were on went down into the ocean. We're six minutes out. I knew you'd want to know."

His stomach plummeted. "Thanks for calling. Can you keep me posted?"

"Will do. And . . . I'm sorry."

The call dropped. He looked up to find the team staring at him.

"What's wrong?" Emmy asked, eyes wide.

Noah exhaled, his muscles tightening as adrenaline shot through his veins. These were the moments he wished he wasn't the one in charge. "The copter Ris and Mason were on went down."

Caleb's face paled. "When? Where?"

"Coast Guard rescue is en route. Brooke Kesler's the medic aboard. She said she'll keep us posted."

SEVEN

A bright light flashed across Rissi's face. Instinctively turning her head, she blinked back the spots.

"Finally!" Chase rumbled.

Exhaling the pent-up tension riddling her body, Rissi stared back in the light's direction. She looked up to see the Coast Guard's helicopter but found only the starless black sky and silence overhead.

The hum of a boat's motor reached her ears as an outboard raft bounded toward them, smacking up and down along the ocean's choppy surface.

A second light flicked on, spreading its beam over the black surface, fully illuminating the gliding movement surrounding them.

Stingrays, as Mason had said.

Relief it wasn't a bed of eels or a shark filled her. Then the reality that numerous stingrays with barbed venomous stingers were circling her kicked the anxiety back in.

The lights grew bigger and brighter until they glared in her eyes. She lifted her hand.

"They won't hurt you," a man in the raft said as it idled beside them. Tall with curly strawberry-blond hair and a smattering of whiskers on his chin, he bent with outstretched hand. "Let's get you out of that water."

29

Hands gripped her underneath her armpits, and she was heaved upward. Mason planted his hands on her hips and lifted as the man pulled. Her back arched over the rounded raft edge, and with a wince at the pain streaking through her right side, she tumbled onto a damp, rubber surface.

She stared up at a second man kneeling over her. Dark, straight hair, intense eyes, and a handful of years younger than the first man. "I'm Nate," he said. "And this"—he pointed at the man who'd pulled her in—"is Trevor."

"Rissi," she said. "Thank you." Air seared her lungs as she waited for Mason to climb into the raft after her. What was taking him so long? He treaded water off the outboard's port side. How could he tread so easily, looking like he was barely moving?

"Hand me one of your floodlights," Mason said to Nate.

"Okay." Nate handed it over.

Mason swept the light across the churning sea. He spun in a three-sixty. Then a second time . . . slower. "Come on . . . come on!"

Rissi bounced her leg.

Why wouldn't he get in the raft?

"Max must be trapped in the copter." Mason inhaled and exhaled a few rapid full breaths.

Rissi tensed. "Wh . . . what are you thinking?" He wasn't seriously about to . . . ?

"Going down to look for him."

"He's not in the copter!" Chase yelled. "He was thrown out the side window upon impact. I tried to grab him, but it all happened so fast. He's not in there, dude."

Mason swam away from the raft, moving out of Rissi's reach.

"He's down there somewhere." Mason took another round of quick inhales and exhales. "I've at least got to try."

Rissi's chest burned. *Don't do it.*

Mason dove under the water, the soles of his shoes the last thing she saw before he disappeared beneath the surface.

Chase shook his head at Rissi. "That guy is crazy!"

Rissi swallowed. During their time together as teens, he'd always looked out for others. Even if it was to his detriment. She loved that about him, but it unnerved her all the same.

Please bring him back to me. Warm tears tumbled down her cold cheeks. *And, as impossible as it seems, let him find Max.*

Trevor's beams landed on Chase with Joel, still unconscious, wedged against his chest, and then over Bob, his eyes wide, arms still flapping.

He maneuvered the raft to idle beside Chase and Joel.

Trevor and Nate pulled both men in and then moved for Bob.

Chase lay in the raft taking deep breaths as Trevor stopped the raft beside Bob, who was finally holding still.

Once in the raft, Bob released a large sigh—one quickly drowned out by the approaching thwack of copter blades.

The Coast Guard helicopter hovered above them, and the side door slid open. A woman stood gripping the hold bar. Rissi narrowed her eyes. It was too far and too dark to tell for sure, but the woman's build and long, dark hair definitely looked like Brooke Kesler's.

Relief swept over Rissi until she looked over the side of the raft and could no longer see Mason's floodlight. How deep had he gone?

Caleb paced the office, where they'd all decided to hang out after leaving Dockside. No one wanted to be out of the loop when the call came in that Rissi and Mason were safe. There was no other option. He couldn't fathom the possibility that—

He cut that line of thinking off.

He sniffed, shaking off the suffocating fear strangling him.

"What's taking so long?" He needed to do something—*anything*—to help.

"Sweet Home Alabama" sounded, and Noah jumped to answer his phone. "Rowley."

Finally. Caleb held his breath, watching Noah's expression for any sign that the call was positive. It *had* to be positive. She had to be safe. And Mason too. While he wasn't a fan of the obvious bond the two shared, he wouldn't want anything bad to happen to Mason. He was part of the team.

Noah turned his back to them. "Yes," he said. "And?" His shoulders dipped a fraction of an inch. "Okay. Thanks for calling. Please keep us updated."

Hanging up, Noah turned to face them. Caleb was the only one besides him standing. The rest of the team sat on the couches facing the case board. Finn's girlfriend and Noah's sister, Gabby Rowley had joined them after hearing the news. She and Rissi had become very tight since Gabby's arrival back in town.

"Noah!" Gabby blurted. "Speak."

Caleb inhaled. Only the boss's sister could get away with that, but he was thankful she was pressing. Anticipation thwacked in his chest, strumming in his ears.

Noah strode over to the sofas, taking an at-ease stance in front of them. "Coast Guard rescue has arrived on site."

"Thank you, Jesus," Emmy said.

"Thank you, Coast Guard rescue," Logan added. Surely, he wasn't choosing this moment to counter their faith in Christ with his stout unbelief.

Emmy glared at him.

"I'm just saying I'm thankful Coast Guard rescue is there. I swear," Logan said. "Now is not the time to point out the flaws in your belief system."

Caleb couldn't take it anymore. "Is Rissi okay?" He shook his head and added, "And Mason?"

"Brooke saw Rissi safe in a civilian raft when they arrived."

"And Mason?" Finn repeated, scooting to the edge of the couch.

Noah swiped his nose. "He wasn't in the raft. We don't know more than that. Brooke radioed in as soon as they arrived, knowing we'd be worried. We should know more in the coming minutes."

Caleb exhaled. *Please let it be good news for all involved.*

Two rescue swimmers jumped from the copter, smacking into the water. A rising plume sloshed across the raft in their wake, soaking Rissi anew.

They swam for the raft.

"Everyone okay?" Jason asked. "Ris? Man, I was worried."

"I'm okay," she said.

"You're not injured?" Brad asked.

"I'm all right, but we're missing two. One who didn't surface after the crash—the pilot, Max—and CGIS Agent Mason Rogers, who went down to try and find him."

"I'd say that's crazy, but that's Mason," Jason said as he climbed into the raft and knelt beside the still-unconscious Joel Waters.

Rissi's brow pinched. "You know Mason?"

Jason nodded as he felt for Joel's pulse. "I served with him in Kodiak before I got transferred here." Jason sat back on his heels. "Ok, we've got a pulse. He's breathing, but it's raspy. We better get him in the copter, let Brooke start treating him."

So it was Brooke in the copter. Joel was in good hands.

"Not to distract you," Rissi said, "but Mason's been down there more than two minutes." Her knee bounced. Where was he?

Brad circled his finger, communicating with Brooke. Soon the basket lowered, swaying over the thrashing ocean waves. "Mason swam with us the last two mornings at 0500 for an hour of rigorous training," Brad said. "He's a strong swimmer.

Knows what he's doing." He looked over at Jason. "I'll make a sweep for him while you get Joel and this one"—he gestured at Bob Staton's gashed leg—"loaded up."

"Roger that," Jason said.

As Brad was about to jump off the raft's starboard side, water sloshed behind Rissi. She turned to find Mason sucking in air. *Thank you, Jesus.* Adrenaline released, burning through her cold limbs.

"Dude. That had to be at least three minutes," Chase said. "You've got serious free-diving skills."

"Any sign of the pilot?" Jason asked.

"Afraid not." Mason shook his head as he heaved himself up into the raft.

"So the stories Jason tells about you are true?" Brad said.

Mason arched his brows as he settled beside Rissi. "Dare I ask what stories you've been telling?"

"Just some of our Kodiak tales," Jason said, moving quickly on. "There's a cutter en route, but we'll take these two in the basket." Jason lifted Joel's lids and shone a pencil-thin light in his eyes. "Brad, you want to take this guy?"

"Sure."

"Careful on the way to the basket. We don't know what he's damaged."

"Roger that."

Brad jumped out of the raft and hovered at its side as the basket swayed just above the ocean's surface—the waves bubbling through the openings with each rise.

Jason lifted Joel, moved him to the edge of the raft, and arched him over the side. Brad wrapped him in a choke hold and swam backward toward the basket as Jason prepared Bob Stanton for the exchange. "The cutter should be here for the rest of you within fifteen minutes."

"We're running supplies and a change of volunteers out to the *Freedom*," Trevor said, thumbing over his shoulder at a forty-foot vessel now fully in sight. A row of concerned people lined the starboard side. "They can come on our transport boat while they wait for the cutter. It'll be warmer and more comfortable than the raft."

Chase's water-beaded face pinched. "You're with the *Freedom?*"

"Yes."

"Great." He lolled his head back. "We're with the environmental nuts."

"We're scientists," Trevor snapped.

"We're a marine research vessel," Nate clipped out.

"Who've been hassling *Dauntless* ever since it arrived on site."

"Wait," Trevor said, swiping rain droplets from his glasses. "You're with *Dauntless?*"

"Dang right I am."

"Great." Trevor pushed his still-moisture-speckled glasses up his broad nose. "We just saved our enemy."

"Whoa. 'Enemy'?" Rissi said. "I think that's too strong a word."

"Please," Chase scoffed. "They've been protesting into all hours of the night, trying to disrupt the rig's work, inciting trouble . . ."

"*We've* been inciting?" Trevor's pitch rose. "That's rich." He turned to Rissi while pointing at Chase. "*They've* done the inciting."

Chase's shoulders tensed. "Don't try and feed me that load of—"

"That's enough!" Jason said. "We need to get these men to medical assistance. You two can argue all you want once we're out of here."

"Right. Sorry." Chase held up his hand in apology.

"I apologize as well," Trevor said. "And we need to be on our way to the *Freedom* to . . . continue our research."

Chase coughed. "To continue to badger *Dauntless*, you mean."

Jason arched a brow as he offloaded Bob Stanton to Brad,

and both sullen men dropped the argument. Once Brad had the injured man strapped in, Brooke pulled the basket into the copter bay.

"Is the *Freedom* anchored near *Dauntless*?" Rissi asked.

"Yes," Trevor answered hesitantly.

"Could you give us a lift to *Dauntless*?" Rissi asked.

Trevor's chin dipped. "You're with *Dauntless* too?"

"Mason and I are with CGIS. There's been a fatal event aboard *Dauntless*, and we're headed there to investigate."

Trevor looked at Nate. "A fatal event?"

Nate exhaled. "I'm sorry to hear that, but sadly I'm not surprised."

"A man's dead," Chase said. "Show some respect."

"Respect for that plague on the environment? You've got to be kidding."

"No. Respect for a man's life lost."

"Denouncing the platform that killed him is not disrespectful. If anything, it's the opposite," Nate countered.

"Enough," Mason said, glancing at the water, his jaw tight. "More than one man has died tonight. This is not the time to be in each other's faces."

Trevor and Chase shut up, but neither apologized this time.

Nate rubbed his eyes and looked toward the transport boat. "No need to bring the cutter all the way out here. We can take you to *Dauntless*."

"Are you sure?" Jason asked. At Nate's nod, he turned to Rissi and Mason. "You should at least let us check you for injuries before we head out."

"I'm fine," Rissi and Mason said in unison.

Jason shook his head. "Of course you are."

"I'm fine too," Chase added. "Karl, the rig medic, can check us all out if needed."

Jason exhaled after a moment. "We'll call the cutter off if you're sure you're okay?"

Rissi opened her mouth to speak, but Jason cut her off with his palm held up.

"Never mind." He shook his head, whistling on an exhale. "I already know the answer."

He might find her and Mason exasperating, but she really was fine—only a minor cut where she'd nicked herself while loosening the seat belt, and a slight one on her shoulder from exiting the sinking craft.

She shifted gingerly . . . and a tender side. She could easily bandage the cuts. Worst-case scenario, she had a bruised rib. Undertaking the investigation as quickly as possible, before the elements affected the evidence, was their first priority.

EIGHT

The wind shear of the blades as the helicopter flew away blanketed the water into long, spread-out sheets of white.

The small rescue raft smacked against the choppy water, spraying gushes of saltwater over the bow, before they idled up to the forty-foot transport vessel's dive platform.

A woman in her thirties with curly brown hair pulled back in a loose, low ponytail bent to greet them. "You poor things," she said, reaching her hand out to Rissi.

Rissi clasped hold. The woman's hand was slender and cold.

Mason rested his hand on Rissi's back to steady her, and she winced. Maybe she had hurt her back more than she realized. She stepped onto the metal dive platform, and Mason followed.

"I'm Gwyneth," she said as Chase, Trevor, and Nate boarded the boat. "Let's get you all warmed up."

A few minutes later, with a cozy blanket draped over her shoulders, Rissi took the speckled, camping-style mug of tea Gwyneth offered.

"Thank you." Wrapping her hands around it, she let the warmth spread through her trembling limbs.

She looked over at Mason, and her eyes widened at the cuts across the tops of his hands. "What happened?"

He looked at them and shrugged. "Just from the crash."

From when he'd shielded her during the windshield explosion.

"It's nothing," he said.

She looked to Gwyneth. "Do you have a first-aid kit on board?"

"Of course." Gwyneth turned her attention to the lanky lady entering the ship's narrow galley. "Sarah, could you grab the first-aid kit for them?"

Sarah nodded, her blond braid slipping over her shoulder.

"Really, I'm fine," Mason said.

She ignored him. "Thank you," she said, taking the kit from Sarah.

"You're welcome to use the lower cabin."

"Thanks," Rissi said, clutching the first-aid kit.

"Down the stairs at the end of the hall," Gwyneth said. "It'll give you more space and privacy. We should reach the *Freedom* . . . and the *Dauntless*"—she named the rig with obvious disdain—"in a half hour or so."

"Thanks." Rissi got to her feet and waited for Mason to join her. He had to know when she made up her mind . . .

He exhaled a long sigh but stood.

She climbed down the steps and strode to the door at the end of the passageway. Sliding open the wooden accordion-like door, she stepped in and felt for the light switch, finding it on the third swipe.

The room had two desks built into the ship's walls, two chairs, and two laptops. Charts of stingray migration routes were pinned to a corkboard over the port-side desk.

"That could have come in handy a little while ago," she said.

"No joke."

She pulled out one of the chairs. "Take a seat."

"I'd argue, but—"

"It'd be useless." She smiled as she slid the other chair over to face him.

She pulled the supplies she needed from the first-aid kit—antibiotic cream, alcohol swaps, and Band-Aids.

"Okay, if you take care of my hands now, you don't argue about seeing the medic aboard *Dauntless*. Deal?"

She pulled out the first alcohol swab. "Let's just focus on you for now."

She started with his left hand. It'd grown since she was a teen—his handspan wide, his fingers long. She wanted to linger there, but she had a job to do.

"This might sting," she said of the alcohol wipe.

"I'm good," he said.

Of course he was. After the beatings he'd taken at Hank's hand in their hell-house of a children's home, a sting must feel like the flutter of a butterfly's wing.

She ran the square white cloth over his cuts with care, looking to be sure no small shards of glass remained. As minute as the pain might be for him, she instinctually bent and blew across his hand to lessen the sting and—

He cleared his throat.

She looked up. His green eyes were heady. "You okay?"

"Fine," he said, his voice tight.

She moved on to the antibiotic cream and finished with the Band-Aids. "There," she said, putting the leftovers back into the kit.

"Thanks," he said.

"This was quite a change."

He tilted his head. "What do you mean?"

"Me taking care of you instead of the other way around."

His face softened, his gaze locked on her, the air between them heavy. "You took—"

"Knock, knock," Sarah said from the open doorway. "Everything okay in here?"

"Yep," Mason said, not taking his eyes off Rissi.

"Gwyneth made you each a fresh cup of tea. Come drink it while it's hot. It'll warm you up."

Despite the still-wet clothes, cold was the last thing Rissi felt.

As they entered the galley, Gwyneth turned to them. "I radioed *Dauntless* to let them know we have three of theirs."

40

"*They* aren't *ours*," Chase said, his frown deepening along with the creases at the edges of his eyes. He cast his gaze at Rissi and Mason. "They're outsiders."

Mason cocked his head. "Now, that makes it sound like you don't want us aboard?"

Chase lifted his cup of coffee. "Infer what you will."

NINE

"What do you mean she's not coming back?" Caleb struggled to keep his voice even.

"You know Ris," Finn said. "She's fiercely independent."

Gabby bumped her hip against Finn's. "You say that like it's a bad thing."

Finn smiled and kissed the tip of her nose. "Not a bad thing at all, but it does bring risk and danger into the picture."

"So you're saying I'm risky?" Gabby smirked.

Finn intertwined his fingers through hers. "That's one word for it."

She cocked her head. "Dare I ask what the other word for it is?"

"Come on!" Caleb grunted. He was all for their happiness. Really, he was. But he had no patience for Finn and Gabby's lovey-dovey stuff tonight.

He stalked to Noah's desk. "Do you think it's smart for them to head to the *Dauntless* without being properly checked by a medic?" Noah was the station and regional supervisor. He had the authority to order them back.

"Like Finn said, Rissi is independent and strong willed. If she feels she's okay to continue with the investigation, and Mason with her, I'll trust their decision on that count."

Mason *with* her. The words bit hard. He'd seen how Rissi looked at Mason, and how he looked back.

Caleb exhaled. He had two choices. Audibly tell her how he felt and hope for a miracle. Or silently suffer as he backed off and watched the two of them grow closer. He should have told her months back, when his feelings for her shifted from friendship to—dare he say it—love. He hadn't wanted to make things at work uncomfortable, but with Rissi being a master profiler, she had to know about his feelings for her. He had to man up and have the conversation he'd been putting off. It was time. Unfortunately, he already knew the outcome.

"Trevor tells me a man died on *Dauntless*. What happened?" Gwyneth fiddled with a honey stick in her hand. She'd offered Rissi one for her tea, and it tasted splendid.

"I'm afraid we can't discuss an open investigation," Rissi said.

Gwyneth continued twirling the honey stick between her long, polished fingers.

Rissi focused on the woman's perfectly painted yellow nails. Gwyneth was not at all what she'd expected for an environmental protestor. Not that environmental protestors couldn't be stylish, but the protestors she'd met tended more toward the natural side. None had worn neon-yellow polish.

"Still, if it were clearly an accident, you wouldn't be out here," Gwyneth said, her gaze locking on Rissi.

Rissi chose to remain silent.

Gwyneth shifted. "I'm sorry to hear someone lost their life, but it was merely a matter of time."

Rissi tilted her head. "Why is that?"

"Because not only are those oil production platforms a plague on the environment, they are one of the most dangerous places to work in the world."

Trevor had used the same term, Rissi noted. Sounded like they had their dogma down pat.

43

Gwyneth rested her forearms on the table. "Big oil companies like Textra only care about making money. They couldn't care less about human lives."

Rissi took a sip of tea, mulling over Gwyneth's words but more importantly her body language and facial cues.

She was antagonistic, spirited, and quite intelligent. Or at least that's the vibe she gave off, whether she realized it or not.

"*You* people are the ones who couldn't care less about our lives," Chase said, as if trying to get a rise out of Gwyneth. "You care more about animals than humans, and your concern is solely for them."

Rissi took another sip of tea. The warm liquid coated her parched throat as she waited to see how this conversation would play out.

Mason sat back, lifted his coffee cup, and draped his arm across the counter behind their bench. His arm rested just above Rissi's shoulders. Near enough she could feel him, but too far away for a full-on touch. How she longed for the latter.

Focus, girl! You're not a smitten teen anymore. You're a strong, sensible woman. So what if Mason's arrival had resurrected those feelings? Who was she kidding? Her feelings for him had never gone away. How that was possible after all their years apart, she had no idea, but it was true.

"Animals are innocent." Gwyneth's pitch rose. "Unlike most men."

Chase leaned against the counter and shook his head with a snort. "So now I'm guilty. Wow. You *really* are something. All the guys on the platform talk about your beauty, but they don't know what a—"

"Let's keep it clean," Mason said, cutting Chase off. "There are ladies present."

Chase's jaw shifted, and he looked to Rissi. "Lady. I'll agree with this one," he said in Rissi's direction, then shifted his gaze to Gwyneth. "That one is a shark."

TEN

Never having been on an offshore oil production platform, Rissi hadn't been sure what to expect. The *Dauntless* was the first platform off the Eastern Seaboard, and she'd seen all the controversy on the news when it was launched. But none of that coverage had prepared her for the complexity and size of the structure towering over the top deck and up into the night sky. It was as if they'd built a manufacturing plant on top of a tanker.

A man stood on a loading platform, awaiting their arrival. As Trevor idled the raft up to the metal pier, he came more clearly into view. Five-foot-nine, maybe ten, she'd guess. One hundred and seventy-five pounds. Bald with—she waited until Trevor's floodlight swept over his face—blue eyes. Craggy features accentuated his rugged vibe.

He lifted his oil-covered, calloused hand to wave.

"Seriously?" Trevor snorted. "That guy maligns us daily, but now he's greeting us?"

"He's not greeting us," Nate said, inclining his head toward Rissi, Mason, and Chase. "He's greeting them."

"Glad to see you three," the man said. "Sounds like you've had a hellacious evening." He extended his hand to Rissi.

"That's putting it mildly," Chase said, bypassing Rissi's turn and trudging onto the pier.

"Ladies first," the man said, his voice directed far more at

Chase than to her, but Chase just turned around and stood at the back of the hydraulic platform, irritation lancing his brow.

Ed offered his hand and she took hold. "Thanks," she said, stepping onto the bobbing metal platform—water sloshing across the edges.

Mason braced his hand on her lower back for support, and a whimper escaped her traitorous lips.

"You okay?" His whisper brushed her ear.

Her back ached, felt bruised.

She loathed bruises. They were a sign of weakness. "I'm fine."

"Uh-huh," Mason said, his scrutinizing gaze fixed on her. He knew better. Always had when she was hurt.

"Ed Scott," the man greeting them said, and Rissi shifted her attention to him.

"Agent Rissi Dawson with CGIS." She shook his hand.

"Glad you're okay."

"That makes two of us," Mason said. His heartfelt gaze swept over Rissi before he turned his attention to Ed and extended his hand. "Mason Rogers."

"Mason, good to meet you."

The outboard motor hummed, and Rissi shifted her attention back to Trevor and Nate as they idled away.

"I can't thank you enough for coming to our rescue," she called.

"*You* and *Mason* are welcome," Trevor called back.

"Really?" Ed said, his hands propped on the brown leather belt resting at the top of his hips. "You're still taking jabs tonight," he hollered. "We have two men in the hospital and a missing pilot."

"And one dead on your platform," Trevor shouted back. "Who's to blame for that?"

Ed swatted the air as Trevor and Nate crossed the hundred-and-fifty-yard gap between the *Freedom* and the *Dauntless* and disappeared around aft, by the dive platform.

He swiped a hand across his bald head. "Don't mind them," he said. "They care more about sea life than men."

"Surely, some care for both," Rissi said. There were two sides to every story.

"Not from what I've observed of those aboard the *Freedom*, but yes, I'm sure that many do care about both. I do," Ed said.

She hadn't expected that response. Not with his antagonism toward those on the *Freedom*.

"Environmental protestors, at least the ones I've encountered, assume because I work for an oil company that I'm a horrible person who couldn't care less about wildlife. Not true. Textra Oil adheres to the strictest federal and state regulations." He shoved his hands into his jean pockets. "I grew up on and in the water. Far more than Trevor ever did."

"The dude can't even swim," Chase muttered.

"He can't?" Rissi asked.

"Nope." Ed shook his head. "The other day a team aboard the *Freedom* was trying to tag one of the stingrays to track their migration. Trevor leaned over too far and fell in. You'd think the world was coming to an end. Gwyneth had to jump in and save him."

"Gwyneth is . . ." Mason began.

"Interesting to say the least," Ed said.

"You seem to know the *Freedom* crew pretty well," Mason said.

"They've been pestering us long enough. There hasn't been a day since I've been on *Dauntless* when they haven't harassed us. Even when we rotate out for our three weeks off, a group of them harass us on land. Gwyneth even showed up at my house one day, trying to 'reason' with me." He shook his head. "She's the one who refuses to listen to reason."

"Harassing you guys on *Dauntless* how, exactly?" Mason asked.

"Besides shouting, waving bloody signs, and tossing stink bombs on board?" Chase asked.

"Yeah," Rissi said, wanting to understand the depth of animosity between the two groups.

"This morning after crew one transported out for their leave," Ed began, "Erik dove down to take a look at one of the risers we were getting a pressure warning on and discovered two of the buoyancy cakes all jacked up. That's when we called Chase in."

"Let me guess," Chase said. "Gwyneth and Nate were diving underneath the platform again?"

"To what purpose?" Mason asked, curiosity dancing in his green eyes, flecks of gray—like tiny storm clouds—dotting them.

"They claim to be protecting stingrays and other sea life our 'monstrosity of a vessel' endangers."

"But you think . . . ?" Mason said, giving him the lead-in.

"All of a sudden one of our risers needs repair? You tell me," Ed said.

"You think they are compromising parts of the rigging?" Rissi asked.

"I wouldn't put it past them or the malfunction that cost Greg his life," Chase said.

Rissi fought to keep her expression neutral. That was some claim.

"Let me get this straight," Mason said. "You're saying you believe Gwyneth or someone on her team is responsible for Greg's death?"

Chase shrugged. "It's a possibility."

Rissi tried to wrap her head around that possibility.

"But I'm afraid we need to put this discussion on hold until you all see Karl," Ed said.

"Karl?" Rissi asked. "The medic Chase mentioned?"

"Yep." Ed nodded.

"Thanks, but I assure you, I'm fine," she said, ignoring the pain in her lower right side.

Ed chuckled. "Your boss said you'd say that."

Her brows perked. "You talked to Noah?"

"He radioed as soon as he heard you were bypassing transport back to the ER."

Great.

"I gave him my word you'd head to the medical bay as soon as you arrived. If you don't go, I'm supposed to kick you off the vessel."

She studied Ed's deadpan expression. The man wasn't kidding.

"We'll go," Mason said, barely brushing her right side as he placed his hand on her lower back.

She winced, biting the inside of her cheek to stall her grunt of pain. "Mason, I'm fine."

He dipped his chin, his brows rising. He wasn't buying it.

"Fine." She exhaled. "Let's get it over with."

"Great." Ed turned to Chase. "You do the honors."

"About time," Chase said, lowering the power switch. "I could have just taken the ladder on the port side."

"The platform is safer," Ed said.

"Ladders and stairs are just as effective to get off the platform." He cranked the handle and the lift rose.

"Hang on," Ed said as the platform jerked and rose.

Rissi gripped the railing, as did Mason. Chase just linked his arms across his chest. Talk about antagonistic . . .

Reaching the top deck, they found another man awaiting them. Brown semicropped hair, probably an inch or two shorter than Ed, but about the same weight.

"Adam," Ed said, greeting a man Rissi would peg as only a handful of years older than her. "Would you kindly see these three to Karl straightaway?"

"Of course." Adam nodded.

"I'll take a pass," Chase said.

"No," Ed said. "You won't."

"I don't work for you." Chase's voice was cold, like the ocean air swirling around them.

"You're contracted by Textra, not to mention on the company payroll. You're required to abide by company rules."

Chase released a humorless chuckle. "There's a rule for this?"

"If you've been in an accident or injured in any way, you have to be cleared by the medic before you can return to work."

"Whatever." Chase stalked off.

Ed inhaled, then blew it out in a rush. "Ignore Chase. He can be . . ." He shrugged. "There's no need to go into what he can be." He turned to the man still waiting at the platform's edge. "These are CGIS Agents Mason Rogers and Rissi Dawson."

"Adam Jones," he greeted them. "Glad you both made it." He gestured for them to follow him.

"After you," Mason said, moving aside for Rissi to step down the ramp that started where the platform ended.

Mason had always been considerate as a teen in a gritty, rough-around-the-edges sort of way, but now he was a mature, considerate gentleman. She liked it.

He followed her onto the deck.

Enormous structures—white buildings, yellow pipes, and production apparatus—covered the entire top deck. The whir of machinery spun around Rissi.

"You'll need to wear these at all times when on deck," Adam said, pulling white hard hats from a yellow metal cage.

"Got it." She placed the oversized hard hat on, ignoring, or at least attempting to ignore, the slight smile tugging at the corner of Mason's mouth. Either he liked the sight of the hat teetering on her head, or she looked like she felt—a total goofball.

Adam slipped one on himself. "Medic's in the main tower." He pointed toward the aft of the ship and at what had to be at least a six-story-high building with windows on every level.

The top one had an entire row of windows spanning the full, curved front of it.

"That's the bridge." He walked as he talked. "Main control room. Rest of the control rooms are also in the tower, as we call it, along with living quarters, rec center, gym, galley, and a shop for things we might forget to bring from home."

Making their way to the structure, Adam led them through the first door on the left. The tower was white—odd choice for an oil production and storage facility. But other than some scuff marks on the floor, the hall looked surprisingly clean. "Here's where we get suited up and cleaned off," Adam said, pointing at the door on their right. "It keeps the rest of the quarters fairly clean." He indicated the stairs. "Medic's on level three."

Adam headed up the red metal steps. "I was sorry to hear about Max."

Had his voice caught on Max's name? "Did you know Max?" Rissi asked.

"Yeah." Adam paused, looking back. "He's the one who flies—" he inhaled—"flew our crew rotations in and out."

"Rogers. Dawson!" Rissi turned back to see Ed perched on the bottom step, looking up. "I almost forgot. Agent Rowley asked for you to call him as soon as you're cleared by Karl."

"Roger that," Mason said.

Hopefully Karl cleared them. Worst-case scenario, she had a bruised rib. It definitely wasn't broken. She'd endured that intensity of pain before, and this wasn't close.

All she wanted to do was to get on with the investigation. She had zero desire to play guinea pig for the next hour while a stranger examined her—a male stranger. Her stomach flipped. She'd purposely handpicked female doctors, still unable to sit through an exam with a man.

Besides, she knew her own body and what was best for it. And that definitely wasn't a male stranger touching her, let alone poking and prodding with stethoscopes or tongue depressors.

"You all right?" Mason asked below his breath as they followed Adam down the third-floor corridor, passing the galley as they went. "Ris?" he said again, not letting her off the hook.

She was hoping she could get away without answering, but she should have known Mason wouldn't ignore a concern for her. No wonder elation swam through her at the thought of him being back in her life—physically, at least. Mentally and emotionally, he'd been with her all along, dancing through thoughts, memories, and dreams.

Dear Diary,

Today is the first day I'm writing in you. You are a precious gift from Mason.

Every time I write his name, every time I think of him, my insides tumble over. It's the strangest sensation, but one I don't want to go a day without.

I wonder what he thinks of me. If he thinks of me.

He must to have given me this gift. I don't even know how he bought it. It's beautiful, and it has Aslan's crest in bronze on the burgundy cover. He remembered how much I adore the CHRONICLES OF NARNIA. *Maybe we'll read aloud in the crawl space again tonight. If he sneaks in after Hank's asleep.*

I pray he comes to see me. He has every night for the last month. He's the only peace I have here. With him, I feel safe.

"Ris." Mason's hushed whisper grew in intensity, his breath tickling her ear. "You okay?"

"Yeah." She swallowed, shifting her mind back to the present. "I'm fine."

He tilted his head. "I know better."

Great. He still possessed the ability to see right through her. She exhaled. "I don't like male doctors." She pinned her gaze forward. She'd never admitted that to anyone. She swallowed, wondering what he thought of her confession, nervous he'd view her as weak.

Mason offered a gentle smile. "Well, we can't have that, now, can we?"

She narrowed her gaze. Noah had ordered them to the medical bay. During their time at the children's home—also known as Hank's House of Horrors—Mason had viewed Hank's rules and orders as challenges to break. But those rules had come from a sadistic man, not their CGIS boss.

He strode forward with purpose, not saying a word. Didn't he realize . . . ?

"Noah will fly us out of here straightaway if a medic doesn't clear us," she said.

"Good thing I'm a certified paramedic, then," he whispered.

ELEVEN

"Here we go," Adam said, stepping into the medical bay. "Karl." He lifted his chin as a very Scandinavian-looking man stepped out from behind a privacy curtain.

"Hello." He dipped his head in greeting. "I'm with Chase right now. He needs some sutures. Please, have a seat, and I'll be with you as soon as I can."

"Thanks," Mason said. "I'm a certified medic myself. My partner has something going on with her back. I'll examine her since you're busy." If having a male stranger examine her made Rissi uneasy, he'd take care of her. He had many times before—treated her back after Hank had lashed it up. His hands involuntarily curled into fists, his fingernails drilling into his palms. Surely she didn't think of him as a stranger. It might have been a decade, but he prayed she didn't view him that way.

"Okay." Karl nodded, pointing to the white metal cabinet. "You should find anything you might need in there. Just be sure to fill out an inventory form for anything you use, so I can manage my supplies."

"Will do." Mason nodded. "Thank you."

Karl ducked back behind the curtain.

A moment later, Chase grunted. Apparently suture time had begun.

Adam jabbed his thumb over his shoulder. "I'm going to give

y'all some privacy. I'll be back around. Have Karl radio me if you need anything."

"Thanks," Rissi said.

"Shall we?" Mason asked.

"I'm fine," she insisted.

"Uh-huh. Up on the table." He patted the white-paper-covered exam table.

"This really isn't necessary." She inched her way toward the table as slowly as he'd ever seen anyone move.

"It's me or Karl," he whispered.

She exhaled. "You."

"All righty, then." He patted the table, and the thin paper crinkled beneath his hand.

She hopped up, grimacing as she sat.

The paper absorbed moisture from her still-damp clothes. As soon as they were done here, they needed to hit the plat-form store and grab some dry clothes. No way he was having her spend however long their investigation took in cold, wet clothes.

"Okay," he said, riffling through the drawers underneath the exam table.

He found what he was looking for, tugged the gown out, and shut the metal drawer with a clang.

Rissi arched a brow, casting her gaze to the baby blue ma-terial clutched in his hand.

Her brilliant blue eyes narrowed. "What's that for?"

"For you." He handed it to her. "I'm going to need you to remove your shirt, so I can see what you did to your back. I see blood on your top." He wasn't surprised the others had missed it. The blood blended into the dark green shirt. But he hadn't overlooked it. "I'll step out and pull the privacy curtain closed. Put the gown on, opening in the back."

"Is this really—"

"Necessary? Yes," he said before she could argue further.

"Mason . . . I . . ."

"It's okay," he said softly, knowing her concern. "I've seen your back before."

Her embarrassment was palpable. But there was nothing to be embarrassed about. If anything, it was physical evidence of her bravery and strength.

She bit her bottom lip, and her eyes filled with . . . ? He couldn't place it, but suddenly he felt the room fading. It was just the two of them again in the hidden crawl space she'd found behind the closet in her room at the children's home. They'd spent so much time there.

His heart hadn't stopped thwacking since the crash. The terror at the thought of losing her again after just finding her had choked the breath from his lungs.

He caught her gaze. She was anxious. "I promise it'll be quick," he said. "I'm just worried you might have injured something internally. I at least want to check your back and your lungs."

Her jaw shifted, which meant she was deliberating.

He waited for her answer, praying she'd say yes. She needed to be examined and have any injuries tended to.

"All right," she relented.

"I just want to make sure you're safe."

"I know."

He tugged the privacy curtain, the rings clinking along the track as he pulled it closed.

So many memories and emotions tracked through him.

Rustling sounded behind him as he took a protective stance in parade rest—his active-duty training embedded in him, for the better. He'd been an angry teen. Angry at God for taking his family away. Angry at his aunt and uncle for opting to put him into the system rather than raise him as his parents' will had stipulated. Angry that good people, beautiful people—inside and out—like Rissi got abused by men like Hank Willis.

Thankfully, the Coast Guard had given him direction and purpose and rules he wanted to follow because they were the right thing to do. He still carried hurt over the loss of his parents. He didn't think that would ever fully go away, but the anger had simmered. Maybe he was finally in a place where he could be the man Rissi deserved him to be.

Paper crinkled beneath her movement.

She grunted behind the curtain. He'd seen evidence of some sort of wound on her upper back and a tenderness on her lower-right back. Those injuries needed to be addressed.

His hands clenched into fists. *Her back.*

Memories of trying to help heal the belt lashes Hank had laid across her back that summer day raced through his mind. It had been the worst damage Hank had ever wreaked upon sweet Rissi. Her wounds had been raw and sore. Open flesh and streaks of blood.

He squeezed his eyes shut at the memory and swallowed the thickness gripping his throat. Earlier that day, Rissi had confided in one of the women on staff, a woman she thought she could trust. But she couldn't have been more wrong. Hank's fury, once unleashed, possessed an ugly, evil power that was rarely quenched. It was a wonder he'd been able to distract Hank at all. Only after he took a swing at Hank did the monster shift his fury to him, letting Rissi escape.

His chest squeezed. Seeing such a precious girl suffer at the hands of evil had left him raw.

"Ready," she said a moment later, her voice more tentative than he'd heard it since his arrival.

TWELVE

Please, Father, direct me to see where Rissi is hurt and guide me in how to best help her.

Mason gripped the edge of the curtain and slipped behind it, looking over his shoulder to make sure Rissi had full privacy coverage in the event Karl and Chase finished up before them.

His gaze tracked over the white tile floor, across a black smudge mark from a boot, and then up the base of the table and finally fixed on Rissi's face.

She blinked, the usual fire in her eyes only half-stirred. Was she nervous about *him*? He'd taken care of her many times before, but it'd been years.

She swung her legs out and back in.

He reached for the blood-pressure cuff. "Am I making you uneasy?" That's the last thing he'd want her to feel around him.

"No." She shook her head.

"May I?" he asked, reaching for her arm.

She nodded, stretching her arm out.

He wrapped the cuff around her upper arm. "That feel all right?"

"Yep." She nodded, her fingers tapping the table as she nibbled her bottom lip.

Why was he making her so nervous? He'd seen her back before, and while tentative, she'd never been nervous in his presence before. She'd trusted him. Had time erased that bond?

He prayed not.

He believed, or *had* believed, that nothing—no amount of time or space—could damage their bond. But what if he was wrong?

A weight sank in his gut.

"I think you have to press that Start button," she said, pointing at the blood-pressure machine cradled in his palm.

"Right. Yeah." *Smooth, Rogers. Real smooth.*

He pressed the button, shaking off his woolgathering—as his mom used to call his introspective daydreams before she was taken from this world. The machine beeped, and air streamed up the navy blue tube, and the cuff started inflating.

For being only six at the time of his parents' deaths, he still thought of his folks often. Of the happy memories he had of them and of the very worst—the crash that took both of their lives and his unborn baby brother's.

Everyone he loved and held dear, or at least everyone who'd actually loved him, was ripped from his life right in front of him. One minute life was good, then a freak flash flood resulted in a watery tomb for all but him. He was rescued. Or at least a part of him was.

The carefree child he'd been died that day, vanished as quickly as the roaring waters had flipped their car into an arroyo while they were on vacation in New Mexico. None of them had seen it coming. In a blink of an eye his family was gone.

The monotone beep signaled Rissi's blood pressure reading was done.

He looked at the panel. "One-forty over eighty-seven. It's higher than I like, but it's been a rough day. Let's get this off of you." He pulled the Velcro apart with a scratchy sucking sound.

He grabbed the pulse oximeter. "May I?" he asked, reaching for her hand.

She nodded. He slipped the reader on her finger, which was still ghost-white and puckered.

"We need to get you warmed up. And in dry clothes."

"Agreed for both of us."

Mason looked around the space.

"What are you looking for?" she asked.

"A blanket for you."

"I'll be fine. My clothes are drying."

He pulled off the finger monitor. "Pulse is sixty-eight. Good. All your vitals look good." He grabbed the stethoscope he'd hung around his neck and said, "I'm just going to take a quick listen."

She took a sharp intake of breath.

Trying to be as respectful as possible, he pressed the stethoscope to her chest, listening to her heartbeat. He moved the stethoscope over a few inches. Everything sounded good.

He straightened. "I'm going to need to listen to your lungs and examine your back."

"Okay." She nodded, her fingers once again drumming on the table, the paper crinkling beneath her delicate touch. Stepping around to the side of the exam table, he slipped the stethoscope through the gaps in the tied-back gown.

Her back flexed.

She was tender, but no sense pointing out the obvious.

"Okay, deep breath." He listened. "Good." He moved the stethoscope over an inch. "One more . . . Good. Everything sounds good."

"So we're done?" She shifted forward.

"Not quite yet." He laid a gentle hand on her uninjured shoulder. "I need to examine your back."

"It's fine," she answered far too fast.

"I'll be quick."

She winced and flinched every time something came in contact with the area. She needed treatment.

"I'm feeling better already."

"The grimace on your face says otherwise. If you'd prefer Karl examine you, I can—"

"No." She grabbed his hand before he even took a step in that direction. "Go ahead."

"You're sure?"

She nodded.

"Here we go." He untied the two knots she'd fashioned with the gown's strings. The fabric slipped forward.

Rissi clutched the gown to her chest, fastening it in place. She wore a purple sports bra, but he could work around that. A seeping gash near her right shoulder blade was deep enough to need stitches.

His gaze dropped from her shoulders to the center of her back, and his breath lodged in his throat.

Scars. So many of them.

He remembered bandaging some of those scars when the wounds had been raw. But a cluster he hadn't seen before comprised the center of her back. Heat burned through his limbs. His jaw clenched. What had Hank done to her after he'd aged out?

His muscles taut, he balled his hands at his sides.

"Does it . . . look okay?" she asked.

That's why she was anxious about him examining her. She didn't want him seeing those scars.

"Yeah, you've got a gash worthy of stitches near your right shoulder blade"—he surveyed her lower back—"and some nasty bruising along the right side of your rib cage."

"Great."

"On the plus side," he said, hoping to bring some levity to her, "it'll match your sports bra."

She chuckled a little, and the sweet sound, however guarded it might be, resonated in his soul.

But the pleasure rapidly faded as he focused on the bruises. He needed to press on the area, to see if any ribs were broken. "Okay. I'm going to apply some pressure, but I'll go as gently and as quickly as I can," he said, rubbing his hands together to warm them up. This was going to hurt. She didn't need an added jolt of cold. "You ready?"

She clutched the edge of the exam table. "Go for it."

He positioned himself at her nine. "All right, here we go." He slid his right hand along the right side of her rib cage and his left hand along her back, pressing from top to bottom in rapid fashion.

She remained remarkably still until he hit the third rib from the bottom.

She stiffened on a jagged inhale.

"Got it," he said. "Hang in there for me." The words left his mouth just as they had all the times he'd bandaged the wounds Hank had inflicted on her.

Justice reigned the day that evil man died, though a heart attack seemed too good for him. He should have stood trial for his crimes against kids rather than dying quickly in his cell while awaiting it. But Mason took solace in the fact that, while Hank didn't face men in judgment, he certainly had to face God for what he'd done.

"You're doing great. Just a few more minutes. I've got you."

"This is starting to sound eerily familiar." Her words were light, but the emotion behind them hung thick in the air.

They'd spent so much time like this after Hank's tirades. But they weren't in the crawl space anymore. They were free, and Rissi was an even stronger woman. He was still in awe of her.

"Almost done," he said, feeling awful that he hadn't thought about how his tending her might resurrect memories, but it had in them both. "I've got to press harder on this rib, to be sure it's not fractured or splintered. I'll go as quick as I can. Take a few breaths in and out of your mouth. It'll be over soon."

She braced her hands on either side of the exam table, and he ran his finger along the rib in question. "Here we go." He pushed hard, following the rib down, really hoping he didn't feel a break.

He lifted his hand. "It's not broken."

She let out a pent-up burst of air. "Great. That would have been really inconvenient."

"Inconvenient?" Had she seriously just said that?

"Noah would have insisted I head back to the ER and be treated."

He tilted his head. "And that's a bad thing?"

"It is when we've got an investigation before us."

A smile tickled his lips.

She cocked her head. "What?"

"You know most women don't talk that way, let alone think that way."

Her eyes narrowed playfully. "Mason Rogers, are you suggesting that only men are strong and focused?"

He held his hands up. "Not in the least. I should have said most *people* don't talk that way. They have a sense of self-preservation."

"Seriously?" Her eyelashes did that quick flutter thing.

He still didn't understand *how* she did it, but *when* she did it, he knew he was in the middle of an argument he hadn't even realized he'd walked into. "*You're* talking to me about self-preservation." She released a laugh.

He planted his hand on the edge of the exam table before she could hop off. "Don't try to turn the tables on me, and you most certainly don't need to be getting off this table."

"And why not? You said yourself the rib's not broken." She shimmied to the end of the table, her still-damp jeans chafing against his thumb. He placed his left hand on the other side of her, effectively caging her in.

She dipped her head, her big, beautiful blue eyes staring up at him. "You can't be serious."

"I know you could probably knock out of my hold with little to zero effort, but—"

"Could *probably*?"

He shook his head on a pent-up exhale. "There isn't much we can do with that rib besides your icing it and taking some painkillers, but the cut near your right shoulder blade needs some stitches. The one along your waist just needs bandaging."

She released a belabored huff, the hair framing her face fluttering. "Is all that—"

"Yes," he said, interrupting her before any further argument could be uttered on her part. "It's necessary." He grabbed the supplies from the cabinet, noting them on the inventory sheet, and returned to her. He laid out the supplies on the silver tray-table he rolled to her side.

"Let's start by cleaning out the upper wound and taking care of the stitches."

She nodded, and he got that part over with quickly. She never flinched.

He hesitated as he moved to the smaller cut near her waist and the area around her bruised rib.

"It's okay," she said, placing her hand over his at her side.

He warmed at her touch and proceeded to clean and bandage the smaller wound. He pulled an ice pack for her bruised rib out of a dorm-size fridge and freezer beside the supply cabinet.

"All done, kid," he said, backing away. He'd always called her that at the children's home, but they weren't kids anymore. Actually, neither had been since a very young age. He linked his arms across his chest, studying the gorgeous, strong, and vibrant woman before him. She was as fierce as ever, but now she embraced it, embraced who she was, rather than hiding herself from the world. She was real with her team. She trusted them. And she still trusted *him*.

Relief swept through him. That bond hadn't been broken, and it was one he'd *never* break—no matter what it cost him. Trust was everything where they'd come from.

A knock sounded on the wall inside the medical-bay door. "Agents, you still in here?" It sounded like Adam Jones.

"They're over there," Chase said, his shadow stalking past their privacy curtain.

"Stitches," Adam said to Chase as his tall shadow stepped past. "Good thing you saw Karl."

"It was overkill and a lost hour of sleep," Chase grumbled. "Are those dry clothes?"

"Ed wanted—"

Chase cut Adam off. "Just give me mine."

"He's a peach," Rissi whispered.

Chase's shadow stepped around Adam and stalked out of the door.

"I'll grab your clothes from Adam and give you privacy to get dressed," Mason said.

"Mason," she said just as he grasped the edge of the curtain. "Thanks." Her expression conveyed a depth of thanks for something far beyond a simple tending to. Had she been worried he'd bring up the scars he hadn't seen before? Push her to discuss something she was clearly embarrassed about?

But he'd never push. If she wanted to talk about it, she would, and he'd be there for her.

"No problem," he finally said, realizing he hadn't responded. "I've stitched up many a wound."

Her gaze held him captive. "I remember." The words were soft, quiet, and drenched in memories.

"I'll set your clothes out here on the counter," Adam called. "Just have Karl radio us when you're done here."

Mason's gaze didn't budge, and neither did Rissi's.

"Thanks," they both said, their gazes still locked.

Brooke grabbed the Barnes & Noble package from her front stoop and entered her house, excited about the latest Lee Child book's arrival. She'd been wanting to dig in since it released last month. Though it was late, an hour of reading would be the perfect way to unwind after her hectic watch. But first she needed a hot bubble bath.

She rolled her shoulders, then arched her back, working out the kinks. It'd been a long, rocky day into an even rockier night, and she was ready for some decompression.

She hung her keys on the rack and stilled as she realized she stood in semidarkness. Only the street light shone across her entryway.

Odd.

She'd set the timer on the hook-shaped reading lamp beside her couch, always preferring to come home to a lit house.

Stepping into the living room, she bent to check the timer but found it unplugged.

Her muscles tensed. She definitely hadn't unplugged it. She plugged it back in and clicked the lamp on. Light bathed the space in a soft glow.

She lifted the pile of mail she'd left on the coffee table, needing to pull out the electric bill before she forgot to pay it.

Flipping through the letters, she frowned. They were no longer in alphabetical order.

She looked around her living room and froze as her gaze landed on the oval mirror. A chill raced up her spine.

You hurt me. Now I hurt you.

The words were written in all caps in rose-colored lipstick. Someone had been in her house.

Her chest squeezed. *Are they still here?*

She raced for the door, bolting across the lawn. Her feet squished in the rain-drenched grass that separated her house from Mrs. Peach's. She hated to wake Mrs. Peach at this hour, but her instinct kicked in, and all she could focus on was getting out of the house.

In the rush, she'd left her bag and therefore her keys and

phone in the house. She'd have to use Mrs. Peach's phone to call . . . Who? Gabby and Finn?

Her heart skittered about her chest as she rang the doorbell. Would Mrs. Peach even come to the door in the middle of the night? Shadows danced behind every tree and car lining her street. She took a deep inhale. She was letting fear get to her. She looked back at Mrs. Peach's dark house.

Dare she ring again?

Her heart ticked off the seconds. Fifty seconds later, a light came on and Mrs. Roxy Peach, her favorite neighbor, peered out the oval window glass on her door. "Brooke. Is that you, sweetheart?"

Brooke nodded.

Mrs. Peach flung open the door, and the sprightly sixty-something stood wide-eyed in a blue chenille zip-up bathrobe, fuzzy orange slippers, and pink-foam rollers.

Try as she might to speak, all Brooke could do was stare.

Roxy stepped forward. "What's going on, honey?" Her gaze settled on Brooke, and lines spread out in spiderweb patterns from the corners of Roxy's narrowed brown eyes. "Is something wrong, dear?"

She finally managed the words. "Can I use your phone?"

"Of course." Roxy studied her. "Are you okay?"

"No. Someone was in my house." Perspiration beaded on Brooke's forehead. "Still could be."

THIRTEEN

Mason leaned against the counter, his arms folded across his chest. To get the closest fit possible, Adam had brought them what were basically track pants—black Nike pants with two white stripes down the side. Easier to fit and more comfortable than wet jeans. He was waiting for Rissi to finish so he could make sure she didn't need anything before he swapped places with her to change.

The privacy curtain drew back with a clink of metal, and she stepped out.

He pushed off the counter, his gaze skimming over her, searching for any sign of injury he may have missed in all the commotion.

Clad in an oversized gray T-shirt with *Textra Oil* stitched in bold white letters across it, she stepped toward him. She raked a hand through her still-damp hair, slipping it over her shoulders and twisting it into a loose braid. Her gaze narrowed. "You haven't been examined yet."

"I'm fine."

"Noah insisted. If we don't both comply, he will order us back."

Mason let out a stream of air. "Okay."

"Hop on up." Karl patted the exam table after rolling fresh paper across it.

Mason complied but wasn't happy about an unnecessary exam.

"All right." Karl began with his blood pressure and temperature, and then listened to his lungs. "You took quite an impact. Does anything hurt? Your back, head, or neck? Those are the usual areas we see injuries from that type of jolting impact."

"My neck is tight, but I'm sure it just jerked wrong. I'm fine." Rissi linked her arms across her chest.

"Fine," Mason said, and Karl moved behind him to check.

Placing his hands on Mason's neck, he tipped his head gently forward, and his neck cracked.

He ran his thumbs along Mason's cervical spine. "You've got a misaligned disc. I can put it back in place."

"Go for it," Mason said. The sooner he got this over with, the sooner they could start investigating. And truth be told, his neck smarted.

With his okay, Karl maneuvered his head forward, then back. "Look to your left."

Mason did so.

"There it is. Okay, I'm going to use a form of manual therapy where I do spinal manipulation. It shouldn't hurt at all."

"Okay."

Karl maneuvered Mason's neck just so, and the pain shooting through it ceased.

"Try moving your head now."

Mason followed the pattern Karl instructed, moving his head front to back, then side to side. It moved effortlessly, without pain. "Good job, Karl. I'm impressed."

Karl smiled. "Thank you."

"Now," Rissi said. "Go change. You need to get out of those damp clothes."

"Yes, ma'am," he said, hopping down. Rissi always possessed a defiant will, but now it'd shifted to one of perseverance, with a good dose of stubbornness tossed in. He liked her confidence, loved seeing her happy and without fear always lurking in her beautiful eyes.

Stepping into the other exam area, he changed his clothes, and tucking his damp ones under his arm, pulled back the curtain to find Rissi already talking with Karl. She really didn't waste any time getting on with an investigation. He smiled. They were still very much alike.

"And what's the first thing you remember happening?" she asked.

Karl ran a hand through his wavy blond hair. "The fire alarm blaring."

"Okay," Rissi said. "And then?"

"Then Adam radioed down that there'd been a flash fire on deck and one of our men was badly injured. I hauled my butt topside ASAP."

"Speaking of hauling butts," Adam said from the doorway, looking from Mason to Rissi. "Your boss is on the phone, and he's none too happy."

Rissi gave Mason a clenched smile. "I forgot to call."

"Yeah," Adam said, leaning against the doorframe. "You wanna follow me?"

"I'll go," Mason said. "You keep talking with Karl."

"Not an option." Adam shook his head. "Your boss insisted he speak with *both* of you."

Rissi's shoulders tensed.

Mason paused. The girl had been in a copter crash, had a bruised rib and a gash on her shoulder that had needed stitches. None of that had fazed her. What on earth did that say about their impending call with Noah?

Needing some room to pace without the rest of his team watching him, Caleb opted to head home with Noah's promise that he'd call as soon as he received any updates.

He tried not to think of Rissi and the fact she could have died tonight. Or the fact that he'd regret not telling her how he felt.

He'd waited too long to express his feelings for her, missed his chance—if it had ever existed.

It might be a defeatist attitude, but it was simple reality. He was about facts, and the fact was she cared about him, but not in a romantic way. It'd only been a couple of months since his feelings had shifted from friendship to romantic love. He'd hoped her feelings would shift, too, if he just gave her some time, but he now realized they never would.

His hope, no matter how thin at times, had held out, but it ceased to exist the day Mason Rogers reappeared in her life.

A man she'd never mentioned to him but clearly knew well.

Pressure weighted his chest until taking a breath became laborious.

Whenever Mason walked into a room, Rissi's eyes widened, and a smile Caleb hadn't known she possessed broke out on her face. *He'd* never made her smile like that.

The way she'd looked at Mason said it all. She loved him.

Caleb took a deep breath and released it. He needed to get his head straight. *Focus.* Compartmentalize his thoughts and, most importantly, his feelings.

FOURTEEN

After Mason talked to Noah, he handed the phone to Rissi.

"The medic cleared you too?" Noah asked as commotion swirled around Rissi in the control room.

She looked at Mason and smiled. "Yep. I was checked out by a medic."

Mason smiled back.

"And you were cleared to continue with the investigation?" Noah asked, his tone not wavering in seriousness.

She rocked up on the balls of her feet. "Yes."

"Did he find any injuries?"

"A cut on my shoulder needed stitches, and I have a bruised rib. But, as with all bruised ribs, it'll just need to heal on its own. I have an ice pack and over-the-counter painkillers if I need them, but I'm doing fine."

Noah exhaled. "Okay. Now, tell me the truth."

"All right." He didn't need to stipulate. He knew she wouldn't lie to him. She *never* lied. That was her mother, not her.

"Are you positive you're up to continuing? Because if not—"

"I'm positive."

Noah paused, no doubt rubbing his chin. "All right, you two proceed with the investigation. Call when you've wrapped up, and we'll send a Coast Guard copter to pick you two up and Barnes's body."

The thought of getting back on a copter did not sit well,

but the rational CGIS agent in her recognized the chances of another malfunction were next to zero. "Will do," she said.

They'd be the next link in the chain of custody for transporting Barnes's body back to Medical Examiner Ethan Hadley.

"Caleb headed home about a half hour ago, but I know he's going to want to hear from you. Give him a call on his cell, would you?"

"Of course." Poor Caleb. He must be sick with concern. She should have thought about calling him and Noah from the *Freedom*, but their time aboard had been busy and short.

"Oh, and, Ris," Noah said.

"Yeah?" She leaned against the counter.

"The NTSB is going to want to talk to you when you arrive back on shore."

"Absolutely." She was glad the National Transportation Safety Board was so thorough an investigative agency. She wanted to know why the helicopter had gone down. She was confident it hadn't been Max's fault. Something else had gone wrong. And she wanted to know what.

"They've already had one of their copters fly over the area where you went down. First thing tomorrow, they're diving down to locate the wreckage."

"Okay." She prayed they managed to find Max's body, at least for closure for his family, but the chances of him not being pulled far from the wreckage by the current were little to none.

"Take care. Both of you," Noah said.

"We will." Disconnecting, she dialed Caleb. He answered on the first ring. "Eason."

She slipped a loose strand of hair behind her ear. "Hey."

"Hey, Ris. You actually okay? Not *fine* like you usually say when you're not?"

"I'm okay." And then, after a probing pause on his end, she added, "Really."

"I don't like the situation."

"I know." The only question was which part he objected to more—her health, which of course he cared about, or that she and Mason were paired together thirty-eight miles out to sea?

Speaking of Mason, she looked up to find him . . . observing her. That was probably the best word to describe his level of focus. He was watching her as she had him earlier, only he wasn't gawking as she so embarrassingly had.

"I'll be fine." She caught herself. "I mean, I'm good. I promise." A little bruise never hurt anyone. Compared to some of the wallops she'd taken, this was nothing.

"I'd rather you come in and let a doc at the ER check you out."

"I know, but I've been checked thoroughly."

"How do you know the medic is any good?"

"He did a great job."

A smile tugged at Mason's lips.

"Okay," Caleb said, followed by a momentary pause. "Just promise me you'll be careful."

"I will. I better get started with the investigation. Get some sleep."

"Take care," he said.

"You too. Bye."

"Bye." His tone was reluctant, but he hung up.

She did the same and strode back to Mason's side. "We're good to go," she said to Adam, who stood on Mason's left. "Let's get this investigation underway."

"Where do you want to start?" Adam asked.

"With Ed giving us a tour to review what happened, where, and when."

"I can do that," Ed said from the control panel. "I just have to finish running a systems check and convince the Chemical Safety Board that we're safe to resume with production. Can you give me fifteen?"

"Sure," Mason said. He turned to Rissi. "How about we start with the body?"

"Good idea. That'll give Ed the time he needs."

"I'll come find you in the medical bay when I'm done," Ed said, his hand covering the receiver. "Greg's body is in the auxiliary freezer. It's the closest thing we have to a morgue-type thing."

Out of sight was smart. Between the supposed curse, a co-worker's death, and a downed helicopter, the crew had plenty to freak them out—and a lot to question.

FIFTEEN

Returning to the medical bay, they found Karl at a small desk, if the word *desk* qualified. It was actually just a chunk of Formica countertop attached to the wall.

Karl looked up and swiveled around on the three-legged stool to face them.

"I was just putting my notes in order," he said. "It's been a hectic night."

That was putting it mildly.

"Thanks for taking time to talk with us."

Karl slipped his rimless glasses on top of his wavy hair. Definite Scandinavian ancestry with his light hair and skin and blue eyes—though she'd seen many a Scandinavian with green eyes, brown hair, and narrower nose.

"Happy to be of assistance," he said. "Do you want to pull up a chair?" He dipped his head toward the four muted-rose plastic chairs with silver frames. It reminded Rissi of the chairs in the nurse's office at school, way back before her mom had ditched her.

"Allow me," Mason said, grabbing two chairs and carrying them over.

"Thanks," she said as he set one down for her and then followed suit for himself.

Karl crossed his arms. "What would you like to know?"

"You said the first thing you heard was the fire alarm?" Rissi began.

"Yes."

"What time would you say this happened?"

Ed would give them the time log, but it was always good to ask each individual. You never knew what would come up or what deviations might arise.

"Right about 1930," Karl said.

"What were you doing when it went off?" Mason asked.

"Watching *Jeopardy!* First round. That's how I know what time it was."

"That's helpful," Mason said, jotting it down with the pen and notebook Ed had provided them.

Everything except the clothes on their backs was lost to the sea.

"What did you do when the alarm went off?" Mason asked.

"Followed protocol," Karl said.

Rissi crossed her legs, shifting her weight to her unbruised, though slightly tender, left side. *Man,* that'd been a hard hit, but she'd taken harder. And God had again brought her through— once more in the care of Mason Rogers.

"And the protocol is?" Mason asked.

"We head to the port side," Karl said, "where the lifeboats are kept. But Ed radioed me before I made it out the tower door. He said to bring my kit and hurry."

"Did he say what was wrong?"

Karl swallowed, his Adam's apple bobbing. "He said a man was on fire."

SIXTEEN

"So you grabbed your kit?" Mason said, clearly trying to keep Karl on track.

It was difficult to press eyewitnesses to tragedy, but in their line of work, it was necessary. Rissi understood that, and she knew Mason did too.

"Yes," Karl said, his fair skin now having a slight greenish pallor. "Then I rushed outside."

"And?" Rissi softened her voice.

"I saw men rushing for the port side." He cleared his throat, his hand clutched to his mouth. Then he exhaled. "Ed radioed again, directing me aft, between the separator room and the generators. Garrett and Jayce were already there."

"Garrett and Jayce?" Mason asked.

"They're our damage control team—firefighters, hazardous waste. Basically, anything goes wrong, it's their job to take care of it."

"Okay. That's helpful to know," Mason said. "Please continue."

"Ed was yelling at them to hurry up. Garrett was spraying . . . spraying the fire extinguisher on Greg."

"Were you aware it was Greg at that point?" Mason asked.

Karl shook his head. "No. The fire hadn't been completely doused, and he was covered with white foam from the extinguisher."

"And then what happened?" Mason asked, his voice respectful of the delicacy of the moment.

"Garrett put the fire out on Greg, while Jayce fought the ancillary fire on the outer wall of the separator room. Thankfully, he was able to get it out before any of the oil inside caught fire, or we would have had a major catastrophe."

"And after the fires were out?" Rissi asked.

"I knelt down by Greg. I could tell it was him when I got close up. He was badly burned, third-degree throughout his body. He was trembling and gasping for air. I held the oxygen mask to his face, and it helped his gasping, but within a minute he was gone."

"I'm sorry," she said. "I know losing a colleague is painful."

Karl's hand rested against his lips and nodded.

Rissi looked to Mason, and he nodded in return.

"We're going to need to see the body," Mason said.

"I understand." Karl stood. "We put him in the auxiliary freezer. Thought the body in the exam room, even covered, would be too upsetting for anyone else I needed to tend to tonight."

"Who else did you treat?" she asked.

"Garrett and Jayce. It's protocol to check them after any incident. And then Chase"—he looked to Mason—"and you."

"You don't have to be present while we examine and photograph his body, if you prefer," Rissi said. "However, we will need your medical assessment, as well as details about how the body was moved, who touched it, and so on."

Karl led them through the back of the galley to the auxiliary freezer, pulled the handle, and stood back as the fog swirled around him. Cold air meeting warm.

"You didn't lock the freezer?" Mason asked.

Karl's eyes narrowed. "Why would we need to lock it?" He snorted off a laugh. "Are you worried he might come walking out?"

"No. I was referring to people going in."

Karl shook his head. "Who'd want to go in there? If any-thing, the crew is totally spooked. Most view Greg's death as another part of the curse." He rolled the stretcher, with Greg Barnes's covered body on it, out of the freezer and back into the exam room, leaving the few men they passed standing and staring in their wake.

"Will you close that door?" Karl asked, pointing to the main door leading into the medical bay. "We don't want to subject any of the men to seeing Greg like this when we pull back the sheet."

Mason did so and returned to Rissi's side.

"Brace yourselves." Karl exhaled. "It isn't pretty."

Rissi nodded. Death never was.

Karl unzipped the body bag. The nauseating smell of burnt flesh seeped through the room, hovering thick in the air. Just as Karl had described, Greg Barnes had third-degree burns cover-ing his body. Only scraps of his orange uniform remained on his flayed skin.

Karl looked away.

It was horrible to think of how Greg Barnes must have suf-fered. Examining a severely burned body was difficult, but death itself no longer bothered her. Probably because she'd been ex-posed to it at such a young age. Finding her stepdad after his suicide had been traumatizing.

Mason looked at her, making sure she was okay, which was sweet, but she was fine. "Do you want to do the exam or the photographs?" he asked.

"I'll do the exam," she said, pulling on a pair of blue latex gloves.

Mason did the same and grabbed the digital camera Ed had been kind enough to lend them.

Karl hovered at the edge of the stretcher.

"You don't need to be present," Rissi said. "I know it's got to be difficult with someone you know."

Karl slipped his hands in his pockets. "He had a family, you know. A wife and two kids."

"I'm so sorry for their loss," Mason said, a crease of pain etching his brow.

Mason knew what losing a loved one was like too. Rissi remembered the day in their attic hideaway when he'd finally opened up, let his fastidious guard down. He'd told her part of his story. A part that broke her heart. He'd been in the car when his entire family died in one fell swoop. He, the lone survivor.

How was it that he'd lived through that—and all that came after—and had still become the amazing man standing beside her?

Brooke cupped the mug of tea, trying to still the shaking in her hands.

Roxy had changed from her bathrobe ensemble into a red bedazzled Zumba outfit, with a purple bandana covering her pink-rollered hair.

The doorbell clanged, and Brooke nearly jumped out of her seat.

"Don't worry yourself," Roxy said, popping up like a Jack-in-the-box. "You sit and rest." She swished toward the door, a spring in her step. The woman possessed more energy than Brooke did at half her age. How was that possible in the middle of the night?

"Hi, Mrs. Peach," Gabby said.

"Hello, dear." Roxy's gaze then shifted to Finn. "Well, hello, handsome."

"Mrs. Peach," Finn said with a smile.

"Uh-uh . . ." Roxy inclined her head.

"Roxy," he said.

"Much better, dear," she crooned.

Brooke chuckled under her breath. *Such a flirt.*

Gabby rushed for Brooke, concern blanketing her face. She wrapped her in a tight hug. "I'm so glad you're okay."

"Thanks for coming. I know your flight leaves insanely early, so if you can't stay, I understand."

"We have plenty of time," Finn said. "I'm going to go clear your house, and then I'll come back to get you."

Brooke nodded as he walked out the door.

He seemed concerned but calm. She guessed being a CGIS agent, he encountered stuff like this all the time. She, on the other hand, did not. Her still-shaking limbs were definitive proof.

"I feel like I'm making a bigger deal out of this than it is. . . ." she mumbled.

Gabby brushed the damp hair from Brooke's clammy forehead. "Someone was in your house. He, she, or they left you a threatening message. You are anything but overreacting."

Brooke reached for Gabby's hand. "Thanks."

Fifteen minutes later, Finn returned. "Whoever it was is gone. I've got my kit in the car. Let me grab it, and I'll process your house."

"Won't that take quite a while? I don't want you two missing your flight. I'm sure Finn's mom is excited to meet Gabby."

"We've got time," Finn said.

"Besides, with Finn being in law enforcement, we kind of get the speed pass through." Gabby looked Brooke in the eye. "But that's the last thing you should be worried about."

"Okay. Thanks, Finn." Brooke swallowed and, after thanking Roxy, walked arm in arm with Gabby to her house while Finn popped in his car to grab his CSI kit.

Brooke moved to open the door.

"Hold off on opening the door," Finn called from behind her. "Let me run it for prints."

"I already opened it when I came home. Sorry," Brooke said.

"All good. There are likely multiple prints there, but we might get lucky."

While Finn did his thing on the door, Brooke and Gabby waited on the porch's wicker love seat. The night air was growing chilly, so she was thankful they could wrap up in the knobby throw blanket she'd pulled from the trunk serving as a coffee table or footrest—whichever folks preferred.

When Finn finished, he opened the door with gloved hands and gestured them inside. "Show me anything you think the intruder might have touched."

"All right." She inhaled deeply, then released the stranglehold on her chest. "My timer for this lamp"—she strolled to the reading lamp, now on—"was unplugged, but I plugged it back in." She grimaced. "I'm sorry."

"Stop apologizing. Your reaction was completely normal. We can still pull prints and just rule yours out."

"Okay." She gazed around her living room. The eerie feeling of someone having been in her home lingered. "The stack of mail. And the mirror . . ." She pointed to the rose-colored lipstick message scrolled across it.

"On it," Finn said, moving first for the pile of mail.

Gabby rested her hand on Brooke's back. "Let's make a cup of tea while we wait."

Brooke nodded, rubbing her arms.

"Do you think it might have been Brodie?" Gabby asked as they settled at the kitchen table over a cup of chamomile.

Thoughts of her ex-boyfriend and the rocky way they'd left things a month ago resonated through her mind. Brodie had been furious about the split, and his anger spilling over resulted in a restraining order. Had he just broken it?

Gabby's hand rested lightly on her arm, tugging her from her fears. "You okay?"

"Yeah." She swirled the spoon around in her mug, clanking the sides as she mixed the honey in. "Just frustrated." *With me and yet another example of my poor taste in men.* "I can't believe I dated him as long as I did."

Gabby wrapped her arm around Brooke's shoulders. "You *stopped* dating him. That's what matters."

She nodded and took a sip of her tea.

Brodie had been fabulous at the start, attentive, kind. They both served others through their jobs—she a Coast Guard medic and he a firefighter. But just when she started falling hard for him, he did a one-eighty on her. He grew jealous, controlling, short-tempered. And then . . .

Brooke took another sip, hoping Gabby and her reporter's intuition didn't pick up on the embarrassment and shame brewing inside her. The death knell came when they'd gotten into an argument.

Or rather, he'd started an argument over something inconsequential, and when she didn't kowtow to his point of view, he'd grabbed her upper arms in a viselike grip and shaken her. Releasing her, he'd shoved her back into her kitchen counter and, thankfully, stormed off.

She wasted no time in texting him that things were over, and after he'd spent hours banging on her front door or waiting for her at her car, then verbally threatening her, she'd gotten a restraining order.

She thought about pressing charges for the kitchen incident, but she was so embarrassed, she just wanted him to go away. But it looked like there was no chance of that now.

Gabby waved her hand in front of Brooke's face. "You still with me?"

"Yeah." She took a deep inhale, her chest still tight. "Sorry."

"You never answered my question."

Brooke stared at her.

"Do you think Brodie did this?"

"He definitely could have. I mean, who else could it be?"

SEVENTEEN

The door opened, and Ed popped his head in. "I'm ready whenever you are," he said as they finished their exam. "Sorry for the delay. As you can see, it's been extremely chaotic around here."

"Understood," Mason said. "Thanks for taking the time to help us with our investigation." It was always good to have the boss on board.

"Trust me," Ed said. "I want to know what happened too. These men are my responsibility. A man died on my watch, and I want to know why."

They thanked Karl—who said he would roll Greg Barnes's body back into the auxiliary freezer and lock it up until they transported it back to ME Hadley—and followed Ed into the hall.

As they walked, Ed said, "The first thing we need to do is figure out why the gas sensor didn't go off to warn us gas was leaking."

"Has that ever happened before?" Mason asked.

"Not on my watch. Not until now." Sadness edged Ed's cracking voice. "Tonight, it failed us."

Mason inhaled. "If the sensor didn't go off, how do you know it was a gas leak?"

"Given the delicate nature of our work, we have two damage control guys on board. They make sure we always adhere to fire safety guidelines, and if, heaven forbid, a fire starts, like it did tonight, they are here to fight it."

Karl had mentioned the damage control team and how Garret and Jayce had fought the fire, but it was helpful to hear information from everyone's perspective.

Mason turned his attention back to Ed as he continued. "Corporate started placing damage control teams on each platform and oil rig after a gas explosion on one of our drilling rigs in the Gulf of Mexico when twenty men and two women died."

"I'm sorry to hear that," Rissi said.

One more flight of stairs and Ed pushed open the exterior door. Floodlights illuminated the deck, gleaming bright in the dark night.

"Wow." Rissi shielded her eyes from one angled her way. "You sure keep things bright."

"I thought it would be helpful for our purposes to light her up."

"Thanks," she said, shifting a few feet to the left so the light was no longer beaming in her eyes. "That was thoughtful of you."

"So you were saying about the gas sensor and a leak," Mason said, circling back to Ed's original concern.

"Right," Ed swiped his hand over his bald head. "Jayce and Garrett said a flash fire like that is caused by a flammable liquid or gas. No liquid was near the site, so they believe it was gas. We checked the sensors, and they showed no gas leakage, so Jayce took a reading with one of their portable gauges, and it showed a definite gas leak coming through the exterior vent from the compressor, which we've shut down until we are sure it's safe to run again."

"What caused the gas to ignite?" Rissi asked. All fires needed three components to start. Oxygen, something flammable—in this case, gas—and a source of ignition.

"Greg's bunkmate, Peter, said he saw Greg slip a pack of cigarettes into his shirt pocket before he went to 'get some air.'" Ed shook his head. "I can't believe he lost his life over a smoke."

"We'll need to speak with Peter when we're finished here," Mason said.

"Of course." Ed nodded. "Oh, that reminds me." He pulled a folded piece of paper from his back pocket. "The employee list you asked for. The names on crew one are in the left column. The names on crew two, who are on the rig now, are in the right."

"Thank you," Rissi said, skimming over the list as Mason glanced over her shoulder. Long list meant a long night.

"We'll need addresses and phone numbers as well," she said. "Especially for crew one, as we'll need to interview them back on land."

"Of course," Ed said. "I'll put Adam on it." He radioed his second-in-command and relayed the order.

"Just to confirm. What time was the last crew transport rotation?" Mason asked.

"0600 this morning." He looked at his watch. "Make that yesterday morning."

Rissi mulled over the information. Had the problem started with the departing crew or the arriving one?

Mason looked at Rissi's finger tapping on a name. "Recognize someone?" he asked.

"Lucas Eason?" she said more as a question than a statement.

"Yes," Ed said. "He's one of our mechanics."

Mason shifted. "Eason? As in . . . ?"

She looked up at him. "Caleb's nephew."

⁂

Caleb stood at the water's edge, leaning against the farthest pylon from his house. The bottle's neck perspired in his grip.

He lifted the brown bottle to his lips, the hoppy scent mixing with the stagnant night air.

He took a draught and looked out over the sea. Waves broke

a good thirty yards out, crashing and pummeling the frothy surface.

He pinched the bridge of his nose at the realization she was never going to love him back—not that way.

He took another sip, emptying the bottle as the knowledge permeated his thick outer skin and drilled down to where his fears lay. Setting the empty bottle atop the pylon, he pulled another from the six-pack. He flipped the top off with the bottle opener and took a swig.

EIGHTEEN

"The fire occurred between the separator building and the generators," Ed said, leading them around the piping and buildings to the far end of the vessel.

Rissi's mind still held on Lucas. She had no idea he was working on the *Dauntless*, and neither did Caleb, or he surely would have said something.

Last Rissi heard, Lucas was at the University of North Carolina Wilmington working on a marine biology degree. Why he'd left school to fall back on the trade he'd learned from his last stepdad, a mechanic on oil rigs, she didn't know, but it wasn't surprising. His mom, Caleb's flighty sister, Susie, never stayed in one place long.

It was a shame Lucas hadn't inherited any of his uncle's discipline or fortitude. He was a floater like his mom, drifting from one thing to the next—never finishing anything.

When Caleb learned Lucas wasn't in school, he'd freak. Rissi hated to be the one to tell him.

Ed stopped at the edge of the char marks marring the concrete and running up the outer wall of the separator building. "It was a high-temperature fire," he said.

"Man overboard!" The shout echoed over the whirr of the machines. "Port side, amidships."

Mason followed the holler to find Adam standing on the railed passageway on the top floor of the tower. He was pointing to the port side, his arm waving frantically.

Mason rushed to the port-side rail, followed by Ed and Rissi as a shrill alarm rent the air.

A spotlight flashed across the choppy sea below. Its beam swept over movement in the water. A man's flailing arms.

Mason climbed up the railing, straddling it.

"What are you doing?" Rissi asked, her eyes widening.

"Be right back." He jumped off the side feetfirst.

"Maaasonnn." Her beautiful voice echoed from above.

Air rushed up to meet him until he smacked into the ocean—a column of water enveloping him. Moving with the current, he kicked for the surface. Rising above the churning sea, he did a one-eighty until his eyes locked on the spotlight. He caught a glimmer of a hand a few inches above the waves and swam for it before the man sank entirely.

A splash of water smacked behind Mason as he grabbed the hand slipping beneath the surface. Locking on the man's wrist, he heaved up until the man's head rose above the water.

The man spluttered, seawater spewing from his mouth as he clawed for Mason.

He heard someone swimming toward them but dared not turn, lest the man shove him under in an effort to save himself.

Despite the salty scent of the sea and the fresh air, the heavy odor of strong alcohol oozed from the man's breath.

"Stop!" Mason hollered as the man scrambled to climb up on him in an attempt to find stability, but he was only managing to push Mason under.

Having no choice, Mason jabbed his elbow back hard. A splintering crack resounded, and the man let go. He sputtered, trying to cover his nose as waves washed over him.

Mason took advantage of the man's confusion and moved around him, placing him in a choke hold from behind.

90

"Well done," a burly man said, swimming up to them as yet another man jumped into the water. "I can take him from here."

"Sure," Mason said, letting him swap places.

"Thank goodness you were bold and jumped," the man said. "Jayce was crashed out in his bunk, and I was in the shower. By the time we made it into the water, it might have been too late for Peter."

"Peter . . . as in Greg Barnes's roommate?" Mason asked.

"Yes."

"You must be Garrett. Part of the damage control team," Mason said as a rubber raft rounded the platform for them.

"You got it," Garrett said. "You're CGIS?"

"Yes. Mason Rogers," he said as a second man—just as burly as Garrett but with lighter hair—joined them.

"That was a bold move, dude," he said.

"More instinct, I think." He reacted rather than thought when it came to those situations, and it'd earned him a rep in the Coast Guard. *"Always pushes limits"* his quarterly reports inevitably read. A vein of recklessness still coursed inside. He didn't think that would ever fully dissipate, but the angry-at-the-world pain he carried as a teen had ebbed when he accepted Christ as his Savior.

The raft bobbed beside them.

After Garrett rolled a stunned and cussing Peter into the raft, Mason climbed in and the second swimmer followed.

"You must be Jayce," Mason said.

Jayce took a seat. "One and the same."

Mason shifted as pent-up adrenaline loosened its grip, releasing warmth through his chilled limbs. He didn't believe in curses, but even he had to admit the *Dauntless* seemed to beckon danger.

NINETEEN

Mason stepped onto the dive platform as Garrett and Jayce headed for the medical bay with the very inebriated and disoriented Peter.

Rissi handed Mason a mariner-style blanket and helped him wrap it around his shoulders. "I'd ask if you've got a death wish, but . . ."

"But?" he asked at her dropped sentence.

"Your . . . let's just call it bravery, saved a man's life."

He didn't know about bravery. For him, there wasn't any fear involved, and he'd been told that true bravery meant acting in spite of fear.

"Let's get you another set of dry clothes," Ed said, leading Mason toward the tower.

"And something hot to drink," Rissi added.

Ten minutes later he was outfitted in a new set of Textra Oil sweats. Along with an extra pair of Ed's boots—thankfully close enough in size to work. He joined Rissi and Ed back on the main deck, where a westerly wind howled through the metal corridors that the machinery's placement formed, to continue the conversation they'd begun regarding Greg's death.

"I thought it would be helpful to have Garrett and Jayce join us as they can speak to the fire itself and better detail the event for you. The rest of us just stared in horror as Greg . . ." Ed inhaled and, lowering his head, pinched the bridge of his nose.

"I can't imagine," Rissi said, giving him a graceful cutoff.

Mason couldn't imagine seeing a coworker—seeing anyone for that matter—burning to death. It had to be horrific.

"Garrett and Jayce should be out here shortly," Ed said. "After escorting Peter to the medical bay for Karl to tend to, they went to change out of their wet clothes."

"In the meantime," Mason said, "why don't you walk us through what you saw."

"Sure," Ed said. "I was in the control room. We'd had a seamless crew rotation, minus the two men from crew two who called out."

"Called out because?" Rissi asked.

Ed shook his head with a hearty exhale. "You aren't going to believe me, but Rob and Joey bought into this whole asinine curse nonsense."

"Curse?" Mason said.

"Oh, right," Ed said. "You wouldn't have heard."

"Actually, we heard about it," Rissi said.

Ed arched his brows. "Oh?"

"One of the old fishermen in town was talking about a curse— Henry's curse—but we couldn't stay and listen to the whole story."

"Those old fishermen love to tell tales." Ed clasped the side rail with his right hand, propping his booted foot on the lowest rung. "It's all nonsense, just stupid superstition, but some of the guys have bought into the legend. You put an idea in someone's head, put them out to sea for three weeks, and they'll start seeing signs of the curse in everyday occurrences."

"Everyday occurrences like . . . ?" Rissi asked.

"Like Greg's death. Some of the men are blaming the curse."

"But you don't believe that?"

"Of course not." Ed snorted. "Greg's death was an unfortunate accident."

"You feel confident it was an accident?" Mason asked.

"Absolutely." Ed's brow furrowed. "Don't tell me you two have curse fever too?"

"No," Rissi said. "Absolutely not."

"What we're asking is whether you're confident it was an accident and not foul play?" Mason said.

Ed's forehead bunched. "Foul play?" He shifted his stance. "What are you suggesting?"

"Not suggesting anything," Mason said. "But it's our job to determine if Greg's death was an accident or—"

"Or what?" Ed asked.

"Or if his death was intentional," Mason said.

Ed's craggy blue eyes narrowed. "As in murder? Is that what you're saying?"

"Murder?" Garrett stepped up behind them, now clad in dry clothes.

"Shh," Ed said. "Don't start circulating that nonsense."

"We're not saying there was foul play," Rissi said. "We're saying it's our job to confirm whether or not it was an accident."

"But the alternative to an accident is murder," Jayce said, joining them.

"We don't want to spook the crew," Mason said. Especially if they were already freaked about some curse. But figuring out what happened was their job.

"This is my teammate, CGIS Special Agent Rissi Dawson," Mason said to Jayce and Garrett before they continued.

They greeted her, shaking her hand in turns.

Ed turned to Garrett and Jayce. "Could you guys walk the agents through what happened?"

"Of course," Garrett said, his voice deep.

"Actually, Ed," Mason said, "let's go ahead and finish with what you saw before we move on to Garrett and Jayce."

"Sure," Ed said. "Where was I?"

"You were in the control room."

Ed inhaled and released it in a stream. "Right, I was in the control room. Shift one—7:00 a.m. to 7:00 p.m.—rotated off. They were heading to the galley to eat. Shift two was starting their twelve-hour shift. Everything appeared to be routine. Then all of a sudden the fire alarm goes off. Seconds later, I get a frantic radio call from Adam yelling someone was on fire."

"Did he say who?"

"No. I don't think he knew at that point. He'd come out of the separator building and heard screaming. He rounded the corner and saw—" Ed swallowed. "That's when I called Garrett and Jayce, who were already pulling on gear and rushing out. I raced out after them." He paused, appearing uneasy about continuing.

"And then?" Mason asked, wanting to keep them on a roll. Wanted the information to flow without them pausing to think. That's how he got the most accurate information. When people stopped to think, they often analyzed and prefaced things rather than just saying it straight.

"Then Garrett and Jayce took over," Ed said.

"How'd you put out the fire?"

"With AFFF," Garrett said.

"It's a foam concentrate used for chemical flame inhibition," Jayce explained. "It interrupts the chemical chain reaction and kills the flame. It's the preferred method with gas or liquid fuel."

"How'd you know it was a gas fire?"

"I watched the flames," Jayce said. "You can tell what's feeding the flames by how they move."

"Did you smell gas?" Rissi asked Ed.

"No." He shook his head. "In its raw state, natural gas has no scent. It's why we rely so heavily on the gas sensors to alert us to leaks."

"And it didn't go off?" Rissi asked.

"No," Ed said, slipping his thumbs into the belt loops of his weathered jeans.

"And you said that hasn't happened before. Is that correct?" Mason asked.

"Not on *Dauntless*."

"So Greg would've had no idea there was a leak before he lit that cigarette?"

"With natural gas being odorless, I don't see how he could have," Ed said.

"Poor dude," Jayce said. "He was so nervous about the curse with everything going on, probably figured the smoke would calm him down."

Rissi's eyes narrowed. "What do you mean by '*everything going on*'?"

"A lot has gone wrong since we started," Jayce said. "People getting sick . . ."

"Lack of hot water," Garrett added.

"Parts overheating . . . You name—" Jayce looked at Ed and stopped short.

"It's just . . . uh . . . what I'm . . . uh . . . hearing."

"Thanks, boys," Ed said through thin lips. "I think we're done here."

He looked at Rissi. "Is that right, ma'am?"

"Yes," she said. "Thank you. If we think of any follow-up questions for you two, we'll find you."

Garrett and Jayce nodded and strode away at a fast clip. But not before Mason caught a glimpse of Garrett punching Jayce in the shoulder. Rambling on about the curse in front of the boss probably hadn't been the best idea. No wonder Ed was so frustrated. Things going wrong on a vessel with such a complex operating system certainly didn't mean curses existed. But as Ed said, you put an idea in a man's head, and he'll start seeing it in everything.

"When will you know what failed in the compressor to cause the gas leak?" Mason asked.

"I have my best mechanics tearing it apart to find out, but it'll take at least a full day's work, if not more, to get it completely disassembled and determine which part failed." He shifted his stance. "When Joel is discharged from the hospital, and we get him out here, he will do a full investigation and review. I'll make sure you get a copy of his report."

"Thank you," Rissi said.

"Hang on." Mason's stance widened. "You're saying there were two different equipment failures in one night? The leak and the gas sensor failing?"

Ed shrugged. "Had to be." His gaze narrowed at Mason. "I'm not sure what you're thinking, but no one on my crew would intentionally harm another crew member. We're family. A family of roughnecks, maybe, but a family all the same." He cast his gaze out over the water. "If any foul play was involved— and that's a big *if*—you're looking in the wrong place."

"Oh?" Mason's brows arched.

"If anything was done to intentionally harm someone on this platform, it's them"—Ed pointed at the *Freedom* anchored less than two hundred yards off their starboard side—"you should be looking at."

"The *Freedom* crew?" Mason asked, surprised Ed agreed with Chase's earlier accusation.

"Those dang protestors have been hounding us since we anchored. They were here for the drilling, and now they are harassing us all through production."

"Yeah," Mason said. "No one aboard the *Freedom* seemed happy about your presence."

Monstrosity had been the term they'd used for the *Dauntless*, if he recalled correctly.

"They are like buzzing gnats. They never let up. I'm surprised they're quiet now. They usually work in shifts to keep up the protesting around the clock."

"They know there was a death on board. Maybe their silence is a sign of respect."

Ed snorted. "Sign of respect?" He shook his head with a whistle. "They have zero respect for us."

"The majority of them being marine biologists or other scientists, I'm sure they are worried about the impact *Dauntless* might have on the environment," Rissi said.

"We've already been through this." Ed sighed. "We adhere to the stiffest regulations. They are just mad that we've found oil off the Eastern Seaboard."

"I imagine they think if you're successful, *Dauntless* will be just the start of oil production along the East Coast."

"They can think or worry all they want, they aren't going to stop oil companies. Look at the *Deepwater Horizon* disaster. They had the two corporate rig supervisors, Donald Vidrine and Robert Kaluza, up for manslaughter for the eleven deaths and the charges were dropped. They got off scot-free. Oil companies are out of reach. You can't stop them. You can get fines out of them, but millions are like pennies to them."

"Doesn't sound like you respect the industry you work for very much," Mason said.

"I respect my crew. I was raised with a good work ethic, unlike a lot of folks today, and I love being on the water. I do my job well, and I take pride in it. When a man goes down on my crew, I *will* find out what happened. But if there was foul play, I'm telling you, you're looking at the wrong vessel."

"Okay, let's say *hypothetically* that foul play was involved," Rissi said, "and someone on the *Freedom* was responsible, how would they get on board without anyone seeing them?"

"This platform is huge. We can't be everywhere at once. And we've already caught them diving underneath the vessel."

"Right, the buoyancy cakes," Mason said.

"Exactly. It wouldn't be that hard to use one of the ladders to come up and then back down, disappearing beneath the surface."

It sounded a bit farfetched to Mason, but if foul play was

involved, he understood it was easier for Ed to think it had been an outsider rather than one of his own crew. And he had seen people go to great lengths—even deadly ones—for a cause.

He prayed Greg Barnes's death was a horrible accident, but the chances of two equipment failures in one night, along with a helicopter crash, seemed beyond slim. They were definitely missing something.

TWENTY

An hour and a half and several cups of tea later, Finn finished processing Brooke's house. He leaned against the kitchen doorframe. "I called Noah," he said to Brooke. "I hope you don't mind, but I don't feel right, with us heading across the country, for you to be dealing with this on your own. Noah will be here anytime you need him."

"That's sweet of you, but not necessary."

The doorbell rang.

"That would be him." Finn pushed off the doorframe and headed to the front door. "Hey, man."

Brooke and Gabby stood and walked into the front room.

"Thanks for coming over," Gabby said as her brother, Noah, stepped inside, ducking his six-three stature to pass through Brooke's five-ten entryway. Apparently, the builder and original owner felt that was a tall enough doorway. Brooke liked the quirkiness of it and the many other idiosyncrasies of the house, but it made it interesting for the taller people who visited.

"Yes, thank you." Brooke reached out and shook his hand. His touch was warm and soothing. He always exuded a measure of calm assurance. Their paths had crossed professionally many times, but it was only at the family gathering at Nana Jo's last weekend where she really got a glimpse of him outside of work.

Gabby had been so sweet to invite her to join her family at their mom's home.

Noah dipped his head as he stood at parade rest. "Sorry to be seeing you under these circumstances."

"It was very kind of you to come over so late at night, but I don't want to put you out." Or explain that she had a restraining order on her ex for harassment. Heat flushed her cheeks. It was mortifying.

"You're not putting me out," Noah said. "We only recently left the office after dealing with the helicopter crash. Thanks for your part in the recovery."

"Sure. It's my job, but I was glad I could help."

"And I'm happy to help you while Finn and Gabs are out of town."

"Thanks." She rolled her right foot in, shifting into her comfort stance. Tonight, she needed all the comfort she could get. Someone had been in her home. The eeriness of it still clung to her.

"Noah, I'm going to drop the evidence samples at the station on our way to the airport," Finn said. "I'll text Emmy and explain what I need her to do."

Noah nodded.

A man of few words, at least when he was in work mode. The only time she'd seen him even slightly unrestrained had been while he was horseplaying with his niece and nephew. Talk about melting a girl's heart. A six-three muscular man on the floor having a tea party with his four-year-old niece was absolutely adorable.

"I hope I'm not out of line," Finn said, looking at Brooke with kindness. "But I think there's someone Noah should interview."

She cringed. Here it came. Mortified, she looked up at Noah and cleared her throat. "Finn's talking about my ex."

"Oh?" Noah's voice remained even.

Brooke intertwined her fingers behind her back, her right foot rolling farther in. "His name is Brodie O'Connell. He's a firefighter over at the Wrightsville Beach station. We broke up about a month ago, and he didn't take it well."

"Why don't we sit down, and you can tell me what happened." Noah gestured to her front-room sofa.

"Good plan," Gabby said. "And I'm so sorry, but we have to leave."

"If we don't go now, we'll miss our flight," Finn added.

"Of course." Brooke hugged Gabby. "Thanks for everything." She stepped back and smiled at Finn.

"Of course," he said.

Gabby looked at Noah. "My brother will take excellent care of you. You call him if you need anything." She shifted her gaze to Brooke, narrowing her eyes. "You promise you will?"

Of course Gabby would make her promise. "Okay, but—"

"I know you think it's not necessary." Gabby waved her comment off. "But it *is*. Right, Noah?"

"Gabby is right." He looked at his sister. "Don't let that go to your head, Miss I'm Always Right. But this one time you are."

He looked to Brooke. "Don't worry. We'll sort this out and make sure you're safe."

Gabby hesitated at the door.

"Love," Finn said, tapping his watch, "I hate to leave, too, but she's in the best possible hands."

After Finn finally coaxed Gabby out of the house, Noah again gestured to Brooke's couch. "Shall we?"

They sat—one on either end of the sofa—and shifted to face each other. "You were telling me about Brodie."

She exhaled. Here went the most embarrassing conversation she'd ever had. Noah was such a good man. His reputation was stellar on base, in his career, and in his personal life. Though, outside of friends and family, he didn't seem to have much of a personal life. No rumors about him dating ever swirled around base. She wondered why. He was about to learn everything about her life for the past few months. It'd be nice to learn at least a little bit about the handsome man sitting across from her.

She relayed the details as quickly she could, then sat back, her cheeks burning with embarrassment as she awaited Noah's response.

"Thanks for explaining. I'm sure it wasn't comfortable, but it'll be helpful when I talk with Brodie. Do you know if he's working right now?"

"I have no idea."

"Okay, I'll track him down."

She narrowed her eyes. "Now?" she asked. *At 0310?*

"It's always best to talk with a suspect as close to the crime as possible. If they're guilty, they're usually jumpy."

"Oh."

"I'll call over to the fire station and ask." Noah pulled out his phone. "But could I get his address from you in case he's off shift?"

She read off Brodie's address, and into Noah's phone it went.

He looked up at her. His brown eyes had flecks of gold she'd never noticed before. "You have an alarm system?" he asked.

"Yes, but I haven't used it yet."

"Use it from now on. When you leave and when you're home."

"Okay." She nodded, sleep tugging at her adrenaline-riddled body.

He stood, tucking the phone in his pocket. "I'll make sure you're locked up tight before I leave. You have your service weapon?"

"Of course."

"Keep it on you at all times."

"You don't think . . ." It wasn't that serious, was it?

Darkness surrounded Noah as he headed for the Wrightsville Beach fire station. He tapped the steering wheel of his Jeep while he waited for a light. Brooke had looked so embarrassed every time Brodie's name was mentioned. It was clear in her voice, in her word choices, that she was beating herself up over what happened. But there was no need. Brodie was the jerk. There was no proof that he broke into Brooke's home, but his past actions definitely made him a suspect.

Learn from bad choices, or choices that turned bad on you, and move on. Brooke was a smart, brave woman. She deserved to be treated with love and respect, not Brodie's rage-infused tantrums.

Noah's limbs heated, his muscles growing taut. He despised men who preyed on others with fear and intimidation. Despised bullies, period. Inhaling the crisp night air, he released it in a stream. He needed to keep a cool head when he talked to Brodie, despite the anger boiling inside.

TWENTY-ONE

Noah entered the fire station through the open bay doors. The engine in front of him was being restocked, as if it'd recently been out on a call. A man in fire pants, black T-shirt, and yellow suspenders rounded the corner. He greeted Noah as he put the metal first-aid kit into a cubby on the engine. "Can I help you?"

"I'm looking for Brodie."

The man inclined his head to the door at the rear of the fire truck. "We just got back from a call, so they're all in the mess hall. He has curly blond hair. You can't miss him."

"Thanks."

The guy nodded and went back to work.

Noah moved toward the rear of the engine and for the door. Since his earliest memory of his dad putting his black firefighter's helmet on his three-year-old head, he'd been in awe of firefighters like his pop.

He'd seriously considered becoming one, but his love for the sea had led him to join the Guard and then CGIS to pursue justice for a living. He loved what he did, but he still admired the firefighting heroes who risked their lives to save others.

Entering through the doorway, he heard voices down the hall. He followed the chatter to the second door on the left.

Poking his head in the mess hall, he spotted Brodie O'Connell's blond curly hair across the table. All guys at the table looked up as he entered.

"Hi, I'm Noah Rowley." His gaze fixed on Brooke's ex. "Brodie, could we chat a minute?"

Brodie raised a brow. "What's this about?"

"Brooke Kesler."

Brodie sat back. "We aren't together anymore."

"I know, but I have a few questions for you."

Brodie's shoulders squared as he set his fork down. "Who are you again?"

"Noah Rowley." He pulled his badge. "I'm with the Coast Guard Investigative Service."

Worry creased Brodie's brow. "Is Brooke okay?"

"A little shaken, but otherwise all right."

"Shaken?" He frowned. "What happened?"

"Could we talk in private?"

"All right." Brodie stood and strode toward him. "Follow me." Leading the way to an empty utility room, he flipped on the lights.

Noah stepped in, closing the door behind him.

Brodie's brow furrowed, and he crossed his thick arms. The guy definitely could bench-press some serious weight. "What happened with Brooke?"

"Someone broke into her house."

Brodie's jaw tightened. "Did you catch the guy?"

"Not yet, but I'm investigating it."

Brodie's blue eyes narrowed. "Which brings you here, why?" There was an edge to his tone that hadn't been there a moment ago.

"What time did you come on shift?"

Brodie released a huff. "You can't seriously think I had anything to do with that?"

"I'm just being thorough, so if you could answer the question."

Brodie shook his head. "You've got to be kidding." He took two strides toward Noah. "Did she send you here?"

"Word is that you weren't happy with the breakup, that you've been harassing her."

Brodie's hands curled into fists at his side. "Trying to win my girl back isn't harassing."

His girl? That's not at all how Brooke or Gabby had painted it.

"What time did you come on shift?" He repeated the question with a tad more edge to his tone.

Brodie whistled, taking a step back. "Well, don't this beat all. She seriously thinks I'd break into her place?" He raked a hand through his hair. "I'm not some lunatic."

"Then answer the question."

"I came on shift at 1900."

Noah arched a brow. "And before that?"

"I was asleep until 1700. Ate dinner. Got ready and came in."

"Anyone to vouch for you at home?"

"Other than my dog, Duncan, no. Look, I hope you find whoever did this, and I'm glad Brooke's okay, but we're done here."

"I have a few more questions."

"Dude." Brodie stepped backward to the door, his hand wrapping around the handle. "I'm done."

Noah kept his voice even, though he felt anything but. "Refusing to answer a few simple questions doesn't look good."

"I didn't do anything, man. Unless you can prove otherwise, we're done here."

Noah's jaw shifted. Unfortunately, he had no grounds to bring Brodie in for questioning. No grounds, *yet.*

Brodie smiled. "I thought so."

Noah stepped for the door, pausing in front of Brooke's ex. "I'll be seeing you."

It'd taken hours and a slew of other crew member interviews in the interim, but Peter finally sobered up enough to answer Rissi and Mason's questions. They didn't learn much that they didn't already know, with the exception of how freaked out

Peter was by the curse. He'd drunk himself into a stupor because he feared he'd be its next victim. Ironically, with his fall overboard, he nearly *had* become the next victim, but because of his own foolishness—not some ridiculous curse.

"That was interesting," Rissi said after Peter had left the interview room they'd been given.

Mason exhaled, stretching out his legs. "That's one way to put it. This curse nonsense is growing with each incident."

"Of which, there are too many 'coincidences' for my liking."

He nodded. "Especially given the short time frame."

"Knock, knock," Ed said from the doorway. He held two cups. The scent of sweet maple syrup, sizzling bacon, and yeasty batter wafted in behind him. "Figured you could both use a cup of joe."

"Thanks." Mason relieved Ed of the cups and handed one to Rissi. She inhaled the roasted smell of coffee swirling out of the plastic lid's opening.

"Breakfast is on," Ed offered. "I'm sure you're hungry."

"Thanks," Rissi said, looking at Mason. "I am pretty hungry."

"Then it's time to eat." Mason followed her to the door and paused in the corridor. "Do you want me to take care of the last interview while you eat?" She'd clearly been putting it off, pushing it to the end, but time was running out.

"No, it's best that we both are in on it. Let's eat quickly, and then we can grab Lucas," she said.

"Okay." He was the new guy on the team—it was her call. And honestly, he understood her reluctance. It had to be awkward interviewing your teammate's family. Not to mention Caleb's romantic interest in Rissi was clear. The big question dancing in Mason's mind was what level of feelings she held for Caleb.

TWENTY-TWO

After a hearty breakfast, Mason followed Rissi back to the interview room, which consisted of a table and chairs, two desks along the aft wall, and maps and charts plastered from ceiling to floor on the stern. Two small windows lined the starboard side of the platform but other than yellow pipes, not much could be seen. Mason supposed a view of anything was better than a windowless room.

"Hey, Lucas," Rissi said as a five-eleven, early-twenties guy trudged into the room.

With tousled blond surfer-style hair, he had a different vibe than straight-laced Caleb, but his brown eyes and features were the same.

"Hey," Lucas said, giving Rissi a loose-armed hug. "I heard two CGIS agents were on board and one was hot . . ." He cleared his throat. "I mean . . . good-looking . . . but didn't realize it was you."

"It's me." She shrugged, turning to Mason. "This is my colleague Mason Rogers."

Lucas lifted his chin. "What's up?"

"How ya doing?" Mason said.

"Ready for bed." Lucas yawned as he lounged back in one of the chairs, his legs splayed out in front of him, his orange jumpsuit partially unzipped. "My shift just ended, so as soon

109

as we're done, I'll grab some grub and crash until it starts all over at 1900."

"I'm assuming you heard about Greg Barnes," Mason said, not a fan of Lucas's casual attitude when a man was dead, but at his age most thought death couldn't touch them.

"Yeah." Lucas straightened, hunching over and clutching his hands. "Dude, it's awful." A depth of maturity Mason hadn't expected settled in Lucas's eyes. "I can't believe that happened. Can't believe he's gone."

"Did you know him well?" Rissi asked, pulling up a chair and sinking into it.

"Greg? Nah. He worked first shift. I'm on second. Other than being on the same transport copter a time or two, I rarely saw the guy."

"What were you doing when the fire alarm went off?"

"Working below in the storage facility. They were having trouble with one of the motors."

"Then what happened?"

His brow furrowed. "The fire alarm went off, and I followed protocol. Went up on deck to the port side above the lifeboats."

"Can you tell us what you saw, heard?"

"There was a lot of commotion. None of us were sure what was going on. We figured just a drill, but then I saw Garrett and Jayce heading back to the tower with ash on their faces. Their expressions were . . ." Color drained from Lucas's tan skin.

Maybe he wasn't as flippant as Mason first thought. Maybe he was just putting on a tough-guy front. "Did you talk to Garrett and Jayce?"

"Me?" He shook his head. "Nah."

"Did anyone?"

"Yeah. A couple guys asked them what was going on. I couldn't hear what they answered, but the guys started murmuring there'd been an accident."

"Did you know who was in the accident?"

"I think . . . maybe someone said Greg's name, but Adam cleared the deck right away, sent us back to our stations—except the separator guys."

"Why them?"

Lucas shrugged. "How would I know?"

"No one talked about what happened with the fire?" Mason asked.

"Nah."

Mason took a chair, flipped it around, and straddled it. "What'd you do at that point?" He rested his hands across the back.

"I went back to work." Lucas shifted his gaze to Rissi. "Why's he riding me?"

"He's just being thorough," she said.

"Whatever." Lucas rolled his eyes. "Can I go eat now?" He started to stand.

"We're not quite done yet," Mason said.

Lucas huffed as he flopped back down.

"What happened between when you went back to work and when you walked in here?" Rissi asked.

"I did my job." An edge cut into his voice.

"We're just trying to place everyone, see where everyone was at the time of the fire," Rissi said, her voice tighter than it had been.

Lucas's sandy blond brows furrowed. "Why?"

"It's our job. We need to get the full picture."

"Whatever." He drummed his fingers along his knees. "What else do you want to know?"

"How long have you been working here?" she asked. "Last I heard you were starting your senior year at UNCW. Marine biology, right?"

"Yeah." He looked to the door, then back at Rissi. "I needed a break. I was making good money here over the summer so I stayed on. Wanted to try out something else for a while, figure out what I really want to do." He sat forward, his voice drop-ping a register. "Don't tell Caleb. He'll freak."

"I can't lie to your uncle," Rissi said.

"It's not lying. It's just . . . retaining information."

"A lie is a lie," Rissi said.

"Seriously?" Lucas shook his head. "I should have known you wouldn't be cool."

"Cool?" Rissi's shoulders grew taut. "Your uncle cares about you, paid for your tuition."

"Here we go," Lucas said.

"You can call and tell him." Rissi stood, gathering her note-book. "Or I will."

"What a—"

Mason stood as Lucas got to his feet. "I'd think very care-fully before finishing that sentiment."

"Or what?" Lucas scoffed with a hair flip, his bangs swoosh-ing out of his eyes.

Mason's jaw tensed. "I guess we'll find out."

Lucas backed down as Mason anticipated he would. Lucas was rash and impulsive—qualities he'd possessed before com-ing to Christ himself. It didn't necessarily indicate Lucas was being as cagey as he appeared, but he was hiding something. Mason could feel it. The question was what.

After squeezing in a catnap, Noah stopped at Belle's Diner on the way into work. Two hours' sleep wasn't much, but he'd have a good meal, work his shift, and then go home and crash.

He took his usual seat, and Belle brought him coffee and cranberry juice without him even having to ask.

"Thanks, Belle." He took a sip of the juice and then set the small glass down.

"You look tired."

"Long night," he said, switching to the much-needed coffee.

"Your usual?" she asked.

"Yes, please."

"You got it, honey." Belle headed to the counter separating the dining bar from the kitchen. "Noah's usual."

Billy, the best short-order cook in a hundred-mile radius, poked his head through the opening. "Hey, Noah."

He waved. "Hey, Billy."

"Your order will be right up."

"Thanks." He was famished.

A bell jangled, and Noah's gaze tracked to the front door.

Brooke entered in civilian clothes—a dark pair of jeans, brown boots, and an emerald blouse.

Belle greeted her. "Hey, hon."

Brooke headed for a table and stopped short at the sight of Noah.

"Hi, again," he said.

"Hi." She smiled. "I was just coming in for a bite."

"You chose a good place."

"Yeah. I come in pretty much daily." She leaned in and lowered her voice. "I'm addicted to Billy's chocolate chip pancakes, but don't tell him. It'll just go to his head."

"Oh, really," Billy said, behind her.

She straightened and turned. "Good morning, Billy."

"Miss Kesler."

"How many times do I have to tell you to call me Brooke?"

"Always at least once more."

"Fine, but if you insist on calling me by my last name, then Medic Kesler is more accurate."

"Medic Kesler. Hopefully it doesn't go to your head." He winked.

Noah chuckled.

Billy set Noah's biscuits and gravy in front of him.

"Looks amazing, as always," Noah said.

"Anything else I can get you?" Billy asked.

"I'm good, but thanks."

"Chocolate chip pancakes for you?" Billy asked Brooke with a smirk.

"See this?" She pointed at Billy's smug face. "I told you it'd go to his head."

Noah laughed. "Looks like it."

"Don't mess with the person who makes your food," Billy said. "Didn't you ever learn that?"

Brooke tilted her head, clearly not buying the threat. "We both know you take too much pride in your work to make it less than perfect."

"Oh." Billy smiled. "So my work is perfect?"

Brooke rolled her eyes. "What have I done?"

As Billy strutted to his kitchen, Noah chuckled again and then looked at Brooke. "Would you like to join me?"

"Oh, I don't want to put you out any more."

"Please." He gestured to the bench across from him.

"Okay." She scooted in. "Thanks."

"And you didn't put me out."

She smiled, then shifted her gaze to his plate. "That looks . . . curious."

"It's delicious."

"Just never had it."

"Never?"

"Nope."

"Well, then we must rectify that." He grabbed his spoon and scooped out a bite for her.

She hesitated.

A smile cracked on his lips. "It's good, I promise."

"Okay." The hesitancy on her face didn't fade, but she took the spoon from his hand and slid it into her mouth. She looked up with wide eyes. "Mmm. That is really good."

He chuckled. "Don't sound so surprised."

"Sorry." She lifted a napkin and swiped it across her mouth. "I suppose it's like don't judge a book by its cover. Don't judge a dish by its appearance."

He arched a brow. "I'm not sure if that was a compliment or an insult."

She smiled. "I meant it as a compliment."

Noah laid his napkin across his lap. "I'm going to thank God for my food. Would you like to pray with me?"

"Sure."

Maybe she was a Christian. He didn't know, though. He'd seen her at his church a time or two over the last few months, but he had no idea where she was in her walk. Had she come out of curiosity or as a strong Christian looking for a new church home? Only time would tell.

She reached out her hands to hold his.

He typically put his hands together when he prayed, but if she preferred to hold hands, as many folks did, he'd oblige.

Her hands were soft and warm.

Clearing his throat, he bowed his head.

"Father, thank you for this meal. Thank you that you spared Rissi and Mason. Thank you that Brooke wasn't harmed by her intruder, that she wasn't home at the time. Please let the talk I had with Brodie keep him away. I pray Gabby and Finn's flight is going well, and that you'll keep us all under your provisional care. In Jesus' name, I pray. Amen."

Brooke looked up at him, her expression soft . . . kind. "Thanks for praying for me. I appreciate it."

"Of course." He prayed for every case he worked, for every person who was in danger. It'd take some time to know if his talk with Brodie made a difference, or if Brooke was still in danger, but he prayed the former. He didn't know Brooke well, but he certainly didn't want anything to happen to her. Oddly, he felt more connected to her than he'd anticipated. It was nice but . . . unsettling.

TWENTY-THREE

Within an hour of Lucas's interview, the Coast Guard helicopter that would transport them and Greg Barnes's body back to land was on approach.

Rissi waited with Mason and Ed behind the red safety line of the helipad. It'd been a long night, and she was happy to be headed back to land—just not excited about their mode of transportation. But it looked like Maddie Price was at the controls, and Rissi knew she couldn't ask for a better pilot.

After loading Greg Barnes's body into the copter, Rissi and Mason climbed in, carefully avoiding the body bag situated between them and the front seats.

Ed leaned into the copter's open bay. "I appreciate you both coming out. I'll get Joel's report to you as soon as it's done."

"Thanks," Rissi said.

"And definitely let us know what your guys find when they are done taking the compressor and gas line apart," Mason said.

"Absolutely. Will do."

Maddie flipped the switches, bringing the bird to life.

"Take care," Ed said as the blades began to whir. He stepped back to the edge of the helipad, the wind from the blades whipping everything within its reach.

Rissi leaned forward to greet Maddie. "Maddie Price, this is Mason Rogers, the newest member of our team. Mason, Maddie."

"Nice to meet you," Maddie said, glancing over her shoulder.

Mason smiled. "You too."

"You guys ready?" Maddie took another look at Mason.

Mason gave a thumbs-up, and Rissi nodded, but apprehension warred heavy in her gut. She did not want to be on this bird. On any bird. Not so soon.

Her pulse quickened as they rose up and out over the sea.

"Don't worry," Maddie said. "I'll get you safely home."

Rissi prayed Maddie was right. She'd never been afraid to fly, and she wasn't going to start now, but her queasy stomach refused to agree.

The whoosh of the blades thwacked through her already-ringing ears.

Mason rested his hand over her balled-up fist. He didn't say a word, just reassured her with his presence. She inhaled the strength and calmness his small gesture filled her with.

This was soooo embarrassing. She never freaked out in the air. *Never*. But now she was, and worse still, it was in front of Mason. Though he never showed it, he must have thought her so weak when she used to cower in front of Hank.

She'd grown up since those days, boxed every morning now. No one would ever hurt her like Hank had. She was tough, or so she'd thought as her heart rate sped up, pattering in her chest. *Pitty-pat. Pitty-pat.*

She took a soothing breath and controlled her focus.

Please, Father, help me to know you are in control—always. That I don't have to worry about what is happening under your watchful eye.

Slowly her spiked pulse eased, the tension riddling her limbs loosened. She looked out the window at the sun climbing in the sky. Focused her attention on its orange hue dancing along the seafoam green ocean waves and her pulse settled more . . . then she spotted them.

"Look," she said, resting her hand on the window. "That must be the NTSB investigators down there."

Mason leaned toward her to look out the window. How did he smell so good after a helicopter crash, two plunges into the ocean, and hours aboard an oil production platform? But smell good he did.

She once again harnessed her attention and cast it down to the boats. The largest vessel had a crane anchored northeast of a large area cordoned off by buoys. The red-and-white markers bobbed in the wake of a second boat with a long, flat back that reminded her of an enormous barge.

"They must have found the copter," Mason said.

Had they also found poor Max's body? And what had gone wrong?

"So, Mason," Maddie said after the boats passed out of sight. "Where'd you transfer from?"

"Kodiak, Alaska."

"Wow. We've definitely got nicer weather than Kodiak. Moving here must have really been a culture shock."

"I'm from Boston, so I'm used to different areas."

"If you need someone to show you around, I'm happy to." When Mason didn't respond, she continued. "Let me give you my number. You can put it in your phone."

"Thanks, but my phone is at the bottom of the ocean."

"Right. That must have been terrifying for you both." Maddie shifted her gaze off Mason and onto Rissi. "You doing okay?"

"Yep."

"So . . ." Maddie said, fixing her gaze back on Mason. "Brad and Jason say you are the hero type."

"They exaggerate."

"Risking your life to save others. That's hero stuff, Mason. You're my kind of guy."

Rissi's muscles tightened. *My kind of guy?* Talk about not being subtle.

Flirting wasn't Rissi's thing, but she didn't usually get annoyed by flirty women. Why was it bothering her so much now?

She knew perfectly well why. Because Maddie was flirting with Mason.

But as much as she wanted him to care for her the way she did for him, she had no claims on him. And that realization stole her breath away.

TWENTY-FOUR

Rissi said a prayer of thanks as Maddie set the copter down. She'd survived the flight, but being anxious like that needed to end. She wouldn't let fear stop her.

Stepping to the open bay door, Mason offered his hand.

She took hold, tingles shooting through her at his touch. Because their time together as teens had been forged in trauma, in the intensity of their surroundings and emotions, the bond between them remained. At least she still felt it.

The way he smiled made her think it was a possibility he did, too, but while they shared that past, it had never been romantic. He'd taken care of her when Hank hurt her and held her hand when she was sad. In her sixteen-year-old way, she'd loved him, and part of her heart would always be his, but he'd never verbally expressed feelings beyond friendship.

The thought of having romantic feelings for Mason and him not returning them was painful, but she'd adapt. She always did.

Looking up, she caught sight of Ethan Hadley ambling across the tarmac toward them. Alongside him, Kent, his medical assistant, rolled the stretcher for Greg Barnes's body. A loose wheel on the right wobbled, click-clacking its way across the tarmac.

Maddie climbed out of the copter and strode around to Mason. "Here," she said, handing him a slip of paper. "My number. Give me a call if you'd like that tour of Wilmington."

"Thanks," he said, tucking it in his pocket.

Rissi swallowed. Maybe that was the answer to her wondering.

"Hey, Miss Rissi," Hadley said, tipping the brim of his straw hat. He wore his usual tan Dockers, a light blue button-down shirt, and polished Edward Greens.

"Hi, Hadley, Kent."

Hadley looked at Mason. "I don't believe I've met this young man."

"Oh, right. This is Mason Rogers, our new investigator. Mason," she said, turning to him, "this is Ethan Hadley. The best ME . . . well, anywhere."

Mason extended his hand. "Pleasure to meet you, sir."

"Likewise, young man."

"And this is Kent, his assistant."

"Nice to meet you," Mason said.

After the exchange of pleasantries, Mason helped Kent lift Greg's body onto the stretcher.

Hadley unzipped the bag and glanced inside. "Tsk . . . tsk. Poor man." He zipped it up and with a shake of his head turned his attention to Rissi and Mason. "I'm thankful neither of you came back in a body bag."

Rissi had thought herself immune to the reality of death, but in that moment, her own mortality and the brevity of life hit home with a thwack. She looked at Mason. What would she have done, felt, if he'd died in the crash? She'd just gotten him back in her life. She couldn't picture losing him again. But he could easily transfer stations again, could start dating Maddie . . . So many thoughts and scenarios crashed through her mind, dizzying her.

She'd been in a state of disbelief and elation at his being back, and she hadn't stopped long enough to think beyond the joy of seeing him again.

She wasn't sixteen anymore, and he wasn't her savior. He

was her teammate, and when she got past the newness of his return maybe her distracted mind would settle.

They still had so much to catch up on. What had he been doing during the last decade? Why had he joined the Coast Guard when he'd planned to join the Marines?

Where had he been stationed, besides Alaska? Had he traveled extensively? At least she knew the most important fact—he was a Christian.

Mason and Kent lifted the stretcher with Greg's body into the back of the ME van.

"I thank you, sir," Hadley said, tipping his hat at Mason.

"Anytime, sir."

It tickled her every time she witnessed Mason's formality, his manners. This from the rough-around-the-edges teen who'd worn combat boots, a black Carhartt jacket over his waffle-knit Henley, and faded jeans. He'd had tousled hair and a five-o'clock shadow. He was always getting in fights with Hank, though she'd never seen him start a fight outside of the home. The few other fights of his she'd witnessed came as a result of him standing up for the little guy when they were being bullied. Mason always put himself in the line of fire for those kids, and they'd adored him—as she did.

As Hadley and Kent drove away, a tall man with dark hair and dark shades strode toward them. "Mason Rogers and Rissi Dawson?" he asked.

"Yes," Mason said. "And you are?"

"Jeremy Brandt, National Transportation Safety Board." He flashed his badge. "I need to ask you both a few questions. Would you be able to talk now?"

Mason looked at Rissi, and she nodded.

"Sure," Mason said, shielding his eyes from the sun with his hand.

"Why don't we talk in the hangar? We've set up temporary operations there as we process evidence from prior to the crash."

Smart. There could be signs of a mechanical problem in the copter's hangar—leaking oil, for instance.

Jeremy led them inside, where a CSI team was working the hangar. He walked over to a small circle of chairs at the edge of the hangar, removed his navy blazer, and draped it across the back of his chair. "Please, take a seat."

Mason held out a chair for Rissi and sat next to her.

"Let's start at the beginning," Jeremy said, pulling out a recorder. "Ready?"

"Sure," Mason said.

"Yep," Rissi added.

Jeremy pressed the Record button and set the slim black device on the empty chair beside him. "Agent Jeremy Brandt, interviewing special agent . . ." He dipped his head toward Rissi.

"CGIS Agent Rissi Dawson."

"And . . . ?" He shifted in Mason's direction.

"CGIS Agent Mason Rogers."

"Thank you," Jeremy said. "Now, to the best of your recollections, what brought you to ride on Textra Oil's helicopter NF871 last night?"

"We received a call," Rissi began. "Actually, the special agent in charge of our regional station, Noah Rowley, received a call that there'd been a fatal event aboard oil platform *Dauntless*."

Mason continued, "Noah then sent Agent Dawson and me to meet several Textra Oil employees here at Textra's helipad at approximately 2100 hours, and we were directed to the helicopter in question."

"Which Textra Oil employees did you meet?"

"Head of *Dauntless* operations, Bob Stanton; commercial diver Chase Calhoun; and safety engineer Joel Waters."

"And the pilot was Max . . ." Rissi looked at Mason. "I don't believe we heard his last name."

"No, we didn't," Mason said.

"Had you ever met any of these men before?"

"No, sir," Rissi said.

"His name was Maxwell Schaffer, just for the record," Jeremy said.

Rissi nodded.

"He seemed like a friendly guy," Mason said.

"So you talked with him?"

"He greeted us when we boarded the copter, told us to buckle in . . . That type of thing," Rissi said.

"Did he appear alert?"

"Yes," Rissi said.

"Not tired or groggy?"

"No."

"Did he appear inebriated in any way?"

"No," Mason said. "He was sober, alert. This was not pilot error."

"Oh?" Jeremy cocked his head. "And you know this how?"

"Because Max did everything right, and when the copter started losing its pitch, he did everything he could to regain control."

"So in your words, pilot Maxwell Schaffer lost control of the aircraft?"

"He was unable to regain control of the collective after it stopped controlling the pitch of the rotor blades."

"And then?" Jeremy asked.

"The engine revved, an alarm went off, and we nose-dived for the sea."

TWENTY-FIVE

"He sure was a hard-liner," Rissi said of Jeremy Brandt as they headed for Mason's Triumph.

"That he was."

"I liked him." She shrugged a shoulder. "I mean, he didn't have the best people skills, but I bet he's a dogged investigator."

"That's what we want on the investigation."

She looked over at him, the morning sun glinting off the blond highlights in his hair. It was so weird seeing him as an adult. He had darker scruff on his face, his features more defined, and his shoulders far broader. She wondered what he thought of the woman she'd become. Had she changed outwardly in his mind? She definitely had inwardly. She was no longer a scared teen, no longer afraid of men like Hank Willis. She could hold her own.

Mason smiled at her. "What's got those wheels spinning?"

"Sorry. Was just . . ." She inhaled, refocusing her thoughts. "What does your gut say happened with the copter?"

He rubbed his chin, his thumb running across his adorable chin dimple. She was sure he wouldn't view anything about himself as adorable, but she sure did.

"I definitely don't think it was pilot error, like Jeremy was poking around about."

"Me neither. So where does that leave us? Mechanical malfunction?"

"Either that or . . ."

She narrowed her eyes. "Foul play?"

"It's a possibility."

"But why?"

"That'll be the question if NTSB determines something was tampered with."

"And if so, who was the intended target?"

Reaching his bike, Mason rested his hand on the seat. "I'm not a big conspiracy theorist, but two separate accidents linked to *Dauntless*, along with two deaths, in a matter of hours . . ." He shook his head with a whistle. "My gut's saying there's more there."

She exhaled. "Mine too. Guess we'll have to wait and see what NTSB finds."

"I'm curious what *we're* going to find."

"So am I." Both in regards to the case and in regard to each other. It was as if they'd fallen asleep one night as teens and woke the next morning as adults—the time apart only a dream. But the true dream was being with Mason again.

He unlocked the saddlebag and retrieved her helmet.

Thankfully, she'd left her purse locked in that saddlebag or she'd have a lot of work ahead of her replacing everything. For now, it was just her badge, phone, and one credit card that needed to be replaced. She didn't like not having any money with her while on a case, but as a rule, she left her purse locked up in her trunk, or in this case the saddlebag.

"Did you have your wallet with you on the helicopter?" she asked.

"Yes." He pulled his folded jeans out of the bag they brought them back in and opened the back zipper. He fished in the pocket and pulled out the camo duct tape wallet she'd made him a decade ago.

Her smile stretched across her face. "You still have that?"

"Of course I do. It was a birthday gift from you."

He'd not only kept it, but actually used the meager gift she'd made him all those years ago. "I can't believe it made it through all your plunges into the water."

He tucked the wallet back in his jean pocket and zipped it up. "It's been through a lot."

They'd been through a lot. There was so much she wanted to know about their time apart. What he'd done, seen. So many questions danced through her mind, but for now, they'd have to wait. The team was no doubt anxiously awaiting their return.

"Woolgathering again?" Mason asked at her silence.

She blinked to find a charming smile curled on his lips. "Wool-gathering? I haven't heard that . . ."

"In years," he said.

"Yeah." Not since he'd last asked her that.

He offered her the helmet. "You ready?"

"Yep, but how about you let me drive this time?"

"You know how to drive a motorcycle?"

"Yep."

His smile tugged deeper. "Really?"

"Really. Finn taught me. He's got a lot of land with dirt trails, which are the perfect place to learn the basics."

"I didn't realize he had a bike too."

"Yeah, he's been working on it for the last couple weeks, so he's been driving his car."

"Cool. I'll have to see if he wants to go riding. He seems like a good guy."

"He is. You two will get along well."

"So he dates the boss's sister? How did that happen?"

"That's a *long* story, but a good one." She chuckled.

"I'll look forward to hearing it."

After Mason gave her a short demo of the Triumph's work-ings, Rissi straddled the hunter-green-and-chrome gas tank. She'd driven Finn's Triumph, but Mason's was a 1979 classic T140V. It deserved a whole 'nother level of respect. She inhaled and turned the ignition.

Help me do a good job, Lord.

Mason climbed on behind her, settling in.

A different kind of nervousness skittered through her—a *very* different kind.

Focus, girl.

She started the engine, took a minute to acclimate herself with the bike, and then drove out of the helipad lot. She turned onto the open road stretching before them. Now it was time to release the tension she'd been carrying all night. Now was the time for fun. She lowered her visor and opened the throttle.

Mason laughed as she sped down the road. He started to wrap his arms around her waist but then shifted them to her hips. No doubt he was worried about her bruised rib, but she was fine. His hands cradling her hips were far more dangerous than a bruised rib.

This was going to be a long ride.

"I'm impressed," Mason said, climbing off the bike. "You did a great job. Finn taught you the mechanics, but you have innate talent."

"Oh?"

"There's an art to riding a bike well. Skills are taught. The art isn't. It's like riding a horse. Anyone can learn, but only a small fraction can ride *with* the horse instead of on it."

She liked that.

The station's front door opened, and Caleb exited the building. "Ris . . ." He strode toward her, his long legs crossing the distance in short order. "You okay?"

"I'm good."

His brows furrowed. He wasn't buying it. "Why didn't you let the rescue team bring you back to Wilmington General?"

"I wasn't hurt."

Caleb looked over his shoulder at Mason, brows arched.

"She has a bruised rib and one cut on her shoulder that needed stitches, but she's been icing the rib and the stitches look good."

She glared at Mason. "Seriously? You outed me?"

He shrugged. "I'm not lying to a teammate."

Caleb dipped his chin, his gaze fixing on hers. "You should see the base doctor."

"Really, I'm fine. Mason sutured my cut. I don't even feel that sore."

The muscle in Caleb's jaw flickered. "*Mason* sutured your cut?"

"He's a paramedic." The words rushed out of her mouth. She didn't want Caleb to . . . what? Did it bother him that Mason took care of her? That he saw her bare back? She bit her bottom lip.

Caleb rocked back on his heels. "That came in handy." A mixture of frustration and disappointment lingered in his baritone voice.

She got it. It had bothered her when Maddie flirted with Mason. She had no cause for being upset, but frustration had coursed through her all the same. "I appreciate your concern for me." She truly did. She cared deeply about Caleb as a friend, and that's what made the conversation they needed to have all the tougher. One of two topics she needed to cover with him.

Mason held the door open. "You coming?"

"In a minute." She reached out and touched Caleb's arm as he gestured her inside. "Can I talk to you for a sec?"

"Sure." Curiosity danced in his deep brown eyes.

"We'll just be a few minutes." She let her gaze linger on Mason an extra moment—silently requesting prayer. The news about Lucas dropping out of school would hurt Caleb, and that's the last thing she wanted to do.

Mason responded with a slight nod and reassuring gaze before heading into the station.

"So how are you, really?" Caleb asked as soon as the glass door swung shut.

"I'm fine," she said. At his silence, she added, "Really."

He dipped his head. "You promise?"

"Promise." The only thing that wasn't okay was telling him Lucas had turned his back on Caleb's generous payment of his tuition and hadn't even had the decency to let him know.

"I can tell something is wrong," he said. "What is it?"

She shuffled her feet. A few of the landscape pebbles had spilled over the shrubbery onto the sidewalk. She toed them back over.

"Ris," he said. "It's me. Just be straightforward."

She looked up at him. His set jaw said he was expecting the worst. Her heart cracked for him. They needed to talk about so much more than Lucas, and they both knew it, but in front of the station with everyone waiting and no doubt watching from inside wasn't the time for that conversation.

"Lucas is working on *Dauntless*." There. She said it. She cringed as color rushed Caleb's face.

"Lucas? No . . ." He laughed. "He's at Wilmington, in his senior year."

She slipped her hands into her sweat-pants pockets, so she wouldn't fidget with them. "That's what I thought, too, but he was on the rig."

Caleb's brows arched. "You talked to him?"

"Yeah." She kicked the last loose pebble back by the hedges. "We questioned everyone on board."

His brow furrowed. "Questioned? You questioned Luc?"

"We spoke with the entire crew."

"What did he say?"

"That he'd made good money over the summer and decided to stay on."

Caleb's eyes widened. "What? He *never* went back?" He rubbed the back of his neck. "I didn't even know he was working out there over the summer, and I paid his fall tuition bill."

"I know. I'm so sorry. Maybe it's not too far into the semester to get a refund."

He sighed. "Yeah."

That wasn't the point, and they both knew it.

"I'm sorry." She rested her hand on his arm.

"I just . . ."

"Keep trying. I know."

He held her gaze a moment, and there was so much more than friendship there.

Logan propped the door open with his foot. "You guys going to join us?"

"Be right there," Caleb said.

Logan lifted his chin at her. "You doing okay, kiddo?" Dressed in his tailored gray-blue dress pants with a pink button-down shirt and a sharp pair of Edward Greens, he looked every inch the male model. No wonder women fawned over him. And he let it go straight to his head.

Thankfully, Emmy kept him grounded, and the fact that she didn't fawn over him clearly drove him crazy. Theirs was a dynamic Rissi adored watching. She only prayed Logan would wake up one day and realize he actually loved the girl before it was too late. But he'd have to find his way to God before Emmy was going to let anything happen between them.

"Yeah. I'm fine," she said.

"We're all hanging out around the case board."

She looked up at Caleb. "You cool going in?"

"Sure," he said, gesturing for her to go first. Disappointment hovered raw in his eyes.

She felt so bad for him. He'd tried so hard with Lucas. With his sister. With his mom. But nothing ever changed. They all returned his love and generosity with ingratitude and even stupider choices.

Logan wrapped Rissi in a one-armed choke hold as she stepped through the doorway. "Glad you're okay, kid."

Kid? Him too? She rolled her eyes. "I'm all of nine months younger than you."

"A lifetime in maturity." He winked.

"Ah, that must be it, man-child," she teased. Leave it to Logan to bring levity to the moment.

"Hey," he said, "I wear that moniker proudly. As my dad always said, 'getting old is mandatory—growing up is not.'"

She laughed. Logan was a mess. Hilarious and possessing a heart of gold, but a most-definite mess.

Releasing his playful hold on her, he grabbed a phone from his desk—his pristinely ordered desk. She'd never been inside his home—most team hangouts happened on Finn's extensive property or at Noah's or his family's—but she imagined Logan's home situated much the same way, pristine and pricey. The dude came from money—from some invention his dad patented, along with his mom's "family money"—and he definitely had an appreciation for the finer things. And yet he drove an antiquated pickup. Go figure.

He gave Rissi the phone with a big smile. "I had to call in a favor to get your replacement phones so quickly, but I figured you'd need them for the case. All the contacts and apps should be the same, but let me know if you have any problems."

"Thanks, Logan. This is awesome." And it really was. She avoided dealing with techie things—they made her head hurt—and it was a definite plus having a team member who was a tech genius.

"I'm just glad to see you two weren't hurt more than you were," Emmy said. "Had to be scary."

"Not something I want to experience again," Mason said, his gaze locking on Rissi. Why did she have the feeling he never wanted *her* to have to go through that again much more so than him?

"Well, I have to say, I'm digging the matching sweat outfits," Logan said, moving past Rissi for the case board.

"Yeah. I'm definitely ready to change clothes." Thankfully she kept an extra outfit or two at the station for occasions such as this. One just never knew in her line of work.

"Why don't you go change. We can wait," Noah said.

"It's okay." She took a seat cross-legged on the couch. At least the sweats were dry, warm, and comfy. "I'm fine changing after."

"You'll have plenty of time," Noah said.

She frowned. "What do you mean?"

"After we debrief, you and Mason are off for the day."

She narrowed her eyes. "What?"

"Told you she'd freak," Logan said with a grin.

"I'm not freaking. We just have a lot of work ahead of us, and the sooner we get to it—"

"This isn't optional," Noah said. "You're both off for the day. Go home, get rested up, and you can jump in headfirst tomorrow morning."

She knew better than to argue. The resolve anchored on her boss's jaw said he'd made up his mind, and when he did, he was as determined as she was.

TWENTY-SIX

"What did you learn?" Noah asked as they all settled on the U-shaped sofa and chairs facing the large white case board.

Mason sat on Rissi's left and Caleb on her right. She struggled to keep her focus off them and the undercurrent of emotions flowing between them.

"It appears they had a gas leak in the compressor," Mason began, tugging her attention back to the case. "Ed has a team tearing it apart to determine what failed. As soon as Joel Waters is discharged from Wilmington General, he'll do a full inspection and report his findings."

"I heard from the hospital this morning," Noah said. "They are hoping to discharge Joel tomorrow." He stood in front of the case board, writing out the main points Mason had conveyed—the dry erase marker squeaking over the white surface.

"Great," Rissi said. "So Joel will head out to *Dauntless* and perform a thorough safety inspection of all the parts and systems to determine—based on the machine and instruments alone—if it was an accident, human error, or foul play."

"Instruments?" Emmy asked. "As in plural?"

"Yeah." Mason draped his arm over the back of the couch. "The gas sensor alarm didn't go off."

"We're assuming that's why Greg Barnes didn't realize the danger," Rissi said. "His roommate confirmed that Greg had gone out to smoke on deck."

"That can't be smart on an oil rig," Logan said.

"Seriously," Rissi agreed. "Hard to believe he was so freaked out about the curse that he needed a smoke to calm his nerves."

"Curse?" Emmy's eyes lit. She always loved a good legend, especially one related to the sea. "Is it the same one Tom mentioned at Dockside last night?"

"I think so. Something about a man named Henry whose ship went down, and he apparently cursed the waters around it. The men weren't keen to even mention it for fear of being cursed themselves."

"Some of them *actually* believe Greg's death was caused by the curse?" Noah asked. If ever there was a no-nonsense guy, it was him. Curses were the last thing a sensible man like Noah would buy into.

"Greg's death, the copter crash, Peter falling overboard and nearly drowning," Mason said. "They've been dealing with a lot."

"Definitely sounds like something out of the ordinary is going on out there," Logan said.

Rissi dipped her head, looking up at Logan. He didn't believe in God—yet, she'd never give up trying, praying—but surely, he didn't believe in curses. "You're not suggesting a curse is at work?"

"Of course not," Logan said, resting his hand on his knee—no more than an inch from Em's blue-and-white-striped maxi skirt that fluttered about her as she sat on the sofa's arm just to Logan's left.

"What we need to determine is whether the platform is just having a freakish pattern of mechanical problems, or if someone is causing the problems," Mason said.

"You know who you should talk to," Em said. "Margaret Gregory at the Maritime Historical Museum. She's the head docent over there. If anyone knows this Henry legend, she does. She's a wealth of information."

"But what's the point? We know curses aren't real," Rissi said, not trying to be rude, but why waste their time investigating something that didn't exist?

"*You* know they aren't real," Em said, "but some of the men on that rig don't. When you're spooked about something or get something in your head, it's hard to let go. It doesn't matter if it actually exists."

"That's a good point," Mason said. "Even if we know the curse isn't real, understanding what we're dealing with in the crew's minds would be helpful."

"That makes sense," Rissi said. "We'll add a trip to the museum to today's list and fit it in with questioning the men of crew one. Thanks, Em."

Em smiled. "Happy to help."

"Nice try," Noah said. "But I'm not budging on the day off."

Rissi sat forward. "But the investigation . . . ?"

He shook his head. "Can wait a day." He set the marker down on the ledge. "Need I remind you that you were just in a serious helicopter crash? You're both off for the day. End of discussion."

"Yes, sir," Rissi said, sitting back. She should have let it go from the start, but she just didn't have it in her. She and Noah were very alike in that way.

"We'll start with crew one and the environmentalist group *tomorrow*, and get to Margaret Gregory as well," Mason said.

"In the meantime, I can start running the financials on the environmentalist group," Logan said.

"And I'll start doing a full background check on everyone involved," Emmy said.

"Great. You might want to start with Gwyneth," Rissi said. "She's the leader. I don't think we got her last name." She looked to Mason.

"No, we didn't, but I'd imagine she won't be too hard to find."

"Em is the best at finding people," Rissi said.

"Thanks, Ris." Emmy smiled.

"Caleb," Noah said. "You're with me. We have a distress call to investigate. Coast Guard Petty Officer Towson said the couple aboard have been very jumpy. They found some blood on deck. The couple claimed it was from a fish they gutted, but there were no signs to support that."

"All right." Caleb stood. "Want me to drive?"

"Sure." As he headed for the door, Noah turned to Mason. "Make sure Rissi gets home."

Mason nodded. "Yes, sir."

She didn't need to see Caleb's face to know he wasn't happy with that order, the tautness of his shoulders as he walked out the door said it all.

"Okay, old lady," Logan said to Em. "Let's see who can find the best dirt on the environmental group."

"You're on, and I'm only two years older than you."

He grinned. "You really think you can keep up?"

"Clearly, you've never gone up against her on a mud-runners' course," Rissi said.

Impressed shock broke on Logan's handsome face. "Seriously?" His gaze fixed on Em. "You?"

She linked her arms across her chest. "I'll take you on any day."

"Oooh. I might just take you up on that offer." His infamous sexy smirk curled on his lips.

Em laughed. "I hope you do."

"And you know I'm just razzing you on the age thing, right?" He stepped around his desk, moving to sit on the corner of hers. "I like older women."

She smirked. "And I like *men*. Not boys."

"See that there," Logan retorted. "Why take all the compliments I get from other women when I can have barbs to the heart from you?"

Rissi strode to Logan's side, leaned in, and whispered in his ear. "Maybe you should think about that." She clapped him on his back.

Logan played it off with his laid-back shtick, but beneath all his charm and slew of one-time dates, there was a man very much in need of the love of a good woman, and Rissi couldn't think of a better one than Emmalyne.

Noah poked his head back in the front door. He looked to Rissi, his brows arching. "What are you still doing here?"

"We were just on our way out," Mason said.

"I'll believe it when I see it." Noah waggled his fingers toward the door. "Let's go."

Mason gestured for her to go first. After a quick round of good-byes, Rissi stepped out into the warm sunshine. It was a beautiful day. It was practically a crime to sleep it away.

"Good luck on the call," she said, waving to Noah and Caleb.

"Get some rest," Caleb said before climbing in his car.

"He's quite protective of you," Mason said, handing her his extra helmet.

"Noah?" She knew better.

"I meant Caleb, but Noah is too."

She shrugged. "Being the youngest on the team has its disadvantages."

"It's nice they care so much."

"True." She was so thankful for the team—they'd become her family. A real family.

He raked a hand through his spiky hair. "So you and Caleb . . . ?"

"Are teammates."

Mason arched a brow. "And?" he asked, his voice far lower than when he'd been a teen. His words vibrated deep off his vocal cords, coming out in a gravelly yet alluring register.

"And friends," she said.

He nodded, then his gaze flashed to the station door.

Rissi glanced back to find Logan and Emmy staring out at them.

Mason chuckled. "Ready?"

"Yeah," she said, climbing up on the bike behind him and once again wrapping her arms around his waist. Warmth and memories shot through her. Would her reaction to him always be so visceral?

He started his bike, the deep growl of the engine rumbling through her chest.

"Ready?" he asked, slipping his visor in place.

Most definitely. "Yep."

She was already becoming attached to having Mason around, and it'd only been a matter of days. She needed to be careful. There was nothing to say he was staying for the long haul and certainly no guarantee he felt anything more than friendship for her.

He had just inquired about her relationship with Caleb, but it certainly didn't mean he was asking because of his own romantic interest. If he was interested in her, why would he have taken Maddie's number?

Speeding down the main road toward the sound side of town and her home, she let her thoughts fall away. She focused on the feel of the wind riffling through her hair and the feel of Mason's muscular torso beneath her arms. She just wanted to stay in this moment and soak it in. What could that hurt?

TWENTY-SEVEN

Mason pulled his Triumph into the third driveway on the left as Rissi had directed him. He cut the ignition and kicked down the side stand. Pulling off his helmet, he perched it on the gas tank and looked at Rissi's home, a yellow bungalow with a wide, covered front porch. Old-fashioned red storm lanterns hung from the roof, lining the porch edge. The front door was a matching red.

Rissi climbed off the bike, and he instantly missed the feel of her behind him and the warmth of her touch.

"Nice house," he said. He'd pictured Rissi so many times over the years. Imagining what she was doing, where she lived. He couldn't have pictured a home that suited her better.

"Thanks." After pulling off her helmet and handing it to him, she ran a hand through her windblown hair. She looked at the house and then back at him. "Would you like to come in? Have a glass of sweet tea before you head home?"

"I'd love to, but aren't you supposed to be getting some sleep?" *Shut up, Mason. You know you're dying to go in.* But he was trying to look out for her.

"I'm nowhere near ready to sleep, but if you are, I totally get it."

"No. I'm good." He practically leapt to her side. *Smooth, Rogers. Real smooth.*

"Great." She smiled and led him up the walk and across the white, plank porch.

He looked at the porch swing with cushions piled high, and flashes of him holding her there at night, trailing kisses along the curve of her neck, nibbling her ear . . .

"Mason?"

He snapped his head in her direction. "Yeah?"

"You coming?" she asked, holding the front door for him. When had she opened it?

He took a fortifying breath and strode for the door. *Get it together, man. She's your teammate now. It's been years. You have no idea where she's at, how she feels.*

He was acting like some lovesick schoolboy, but he wasn't a teen anymore. Neither was Rissi—most definitely not. She was a woman. He was a man. And they were both in very different places of life than when they were teens. Yet their bond still remained. Hadn't it? He felt it coursing through his veins whenever he was near her.

"Go ahead and make yourself at home," she said. "I'll grab us a couple glasses of tea. I brewed a fresh batch yesterday morning."

"That'd be great. Thanks."

Rissi disappeared into what he could only assume was the kitchen, and he turned his attention to the surroundings.

Two hammock-style swinging chairs hung from hook bolts in the rafter above. Across from them sat a low-to-the-ground white sofa with a blue, white, and gray beach blanket draped across the back.

Two teal pottery end tables sat on either side, and a pine coffee table on silver wheels was positioned in the center of the sitting area.

"Here you go," she said, returning with two mason jars filled with iced tea.

"Thanks." He lifted the glass to his mouth as she watched, anticipation fluttering in her eyes.

The sweet liquid rolled over his tongue and down his throat. "It's good," he said, after finishing the first swallow.

"Thanks. Living in the South now, you better get used to it as a daily staple."

"Good to know." He took another sip.

She smiled but shuffled back and forth, a nervous bounce to her step.

He wanted her to feel at ease in his presence. Though, truth be told, he was antsy in her presence, too, but not in a bad way. It was more like dancing again for the first time in years—learning how to move in sync, to let go and allow the music to lead you.

It could take awhile for her to once again feel comfortable in his presence, but he prayed they got there, even if it was just as friends. If he was honest with himself, he wanted so much more. But it was complicated. She clearly had a dynamic with Caleb that went beyond colleagues. What that dynamic was he still hadn't fully figured out.

"Wanna sit?" she said, gesturing to the sitting area beside him.

"Yeah, thanks. I'm dying to try out one of these hammock swings. What a neat idea."

"Thanks." She climbed in one and, kicking her shoes off, stretched her bare feet out in front of her, swaying with the natural momentum of the swing.

"Really cool living space." Whenever he'd thought of her over the years, he'd hoped she'd found a place where she was happy, safe, and thriving—even if he never got to be a part of it. But God had most definitely smiled on him. He'd reunited them, and Mason had to believe it was the answer to a decade of prayers.

"You changed your last name." He asked the question most pressing on his mind. "Dawson?"

She set her glass down on the closest end table, swiping a drop of tea from her full, pink lips. "Yeah. Watson wasn't my

name anymore. Hadn't been since I got put in the system. Since
. . ." She pulled her knees to her chest.

He reached his hand across the distance separating them,
and with a soft smile, she grabbed hold.

He'd missed this. Holding her hand, feeling her skin next to
his. Just being there to comfort her.

"I decided when I left Hank's that I needed to stay under
the radar." She sent him a sad smile. "When you were checking my back, I could tell you noticed scars you hadn't seen
before."

He nodded, encouraging her to continue but hating to hear
what Hank had done.

"One day after you left, Hank went ballistic, beat me so
bad I could barely walk after he finished. I made my way to
the attic and then blacked out. When I woke up, I heard him
yelling for me, threatening me, so I hid out until everyone was
asleep, shoved my things in a garbage bag, and left."

"Ris, I'm so sorry. I should have protected you."

"How? You had no place there after you turned eighteen.
And in a way, you did help me."

His brow furrowed.

Glancing down at her feet, then braving a glance in his direction, she said, "Your strength encouraged me to leave, even
though I had no idea where I was going."

She took a deep breath. "I didn't want Hank or anyone from
child services finding me, so I switched my name first to Sand-
ers when I introduced myself." She swallowed. "The woman
who ran the shelter I ended up at, who provided the first safe
haven for me, her last name was Dawson. I thought it was a
good change, so I went by Dawson."

"I'm sure she appreciated it."

"I never told her. I just stayed a short time there and then
moved on—shelter to shelter, city to city. Figured it was best
to keep moving. I changed it legally when I turned eighteen."

He reached out, brushed the hair off her forehead, and cupped her face. "I like it."

Looking down, almost leaning into his handhold, she smiled.

Now it made sense why it had been so hard to locate her. He'd tried so many times and nearly given up hope of ever seeing her again until he walked into his Wilmington station and saw her standing there. He still couldn't fully wrap his head around it. Reluctantly, he lowered his hand back into his lap, his thoughts racing through the painful years apart and how he prayed that was never the case again.

"Now who's woolgathering?" She nudged the toe of his boot with her foot.

"Sorry." He smiled. "Just . . ."

"I get it."

He cocked his head. "You do?"

"It's kind of surreal, right?"

He couldn't have put it better. "Yeah." He rubbed his thighs, trying to keep his hands busy. To distract him from assuming . . . from thinking that she could love him as he did her?

"So you were telling me about Caleb," he said. "He and Lucas don't appear to be much alike?"

"No. Lucas definitely doesn't take after his uncle. Caleb is self-disciplined, a hard worker, a dependable guy, and a great agent."

"Sounds like you really admire him."

"I do. He's a great teammate, but Lucas . . ." She shook her head. "He's a mess."

"It looked like Caleb took the news pretty hard." He lifted his glass for another sip.

"Yeah, Caleb's really been more like a dad to Lucas than an uncle."

"Lucas's dad's not in the picture?" he asked.

"No. I don't think he ever really was. I know he never married Susie. But his stepdad—well, latest ex-stepdad—is a roughneck

144

who's out on rigs most of the time, but he does try with Lucas
. . . when he's around."

"Sounds like a complicated family situation."

She shrugged. "Most are."

"True." He looked down, fingering the raised lettering on
the mason jar. "It's nice Caleb's trying to be a solid influence
for him."

"Yeah." She nodded. "It is." She swung back and forth slowly,
rhythmically. "Can I ask you a question?"

"Sure."

"When you left Hank's, you said you were going to join the
Marines. How did that shift to the Coast Guard?"

"I was headed for the Marine recruiter, and on the way, I
walked by the Coast Guard station. I saw all the boats lined up
and something hit me—the freedom a boat brings. Traveling.
Being away from it all. Being out at sea. So I went in to talk to
the Coast Guard recruiter instead."

"That's cool. You seem to really be at home in the water.
Even if you gave me two heart attacks last night."

His lips curled into a smile. "Sorry. I just couldn't—"

"Sit back and do nothing while someone was drowning. I
totally get it."

"What about you? How'd you end up at CGIS?"

"I wanted to work in a job where justice was done, where
evil people were caught and paid for their crimes. I wanted to
see them off the streets and behind bars before they could hurt
anyone else." She spun the swing partway around, so she was
facing the side of his swing, and he swung to meet her face-to-
face. "I worked my way through college as quickly as I could,
and then applied to the FBI academy. I had an aptitude for
profiling, so that's where they put me. After a while, I wanted
a change. I vacationed down here and fell in love with the place.
So when I saw a CGIS job open up, I jumped on it."

"How long have you been on the team?"

"Two years."

"Very cool. Where did you go to school?"

"University of Mary Washington. They offered me a great financial aid package and a job on campus. And it's really close to the FBI academy so I figured I might as well get used to the area."

Thirty minutes later, Mason realized the time. And as painful as it was to pry himself from Rissi's presence, he managed to do so. He could have stayed with her . . . well, *always*, but Noah was right. She needed her rest, so he thanked her for the tea, saw himself out, and drove home.

TWENTY-EIGHT

Noah tapped the steering wheel as he and Caleb headed back to the station. The distress call had been nothing more than a stupid prank, and everyone involved would be paying a hefty fine.

Noah spotted an open parking spot in front of Hunga Bunga Java. "I'm going to grab a coffee. You want one?"

"Sure," Caleb said, his right leg still bouncing. It hadn't stopped since he'd seen Mason and Rissi heading out together.

Noah pulled into the angled spot, cut the ignition, and they headed inside.

Several of the women's heads turned at their entrance. Many of them eyed Caleb with big smiles, but he never looked back—hadn't looked at anyone but Rissi in a couple of months.

Thus far they'd been able to maintain a solid work environment in spite of Caleb's obvious feelings, but since Mason's arrival on the team, that fine line was getting thinner. Noah had seen it stretching, felt the undercurrent rippling through the station, and it'd only been a handful of days. Noah needed to make sure whatever was going on, or wasn't going on, happened outside the workplace.

"Hey, boys," Lindy said, greeting them at the counter. "Red or black today?"

It'd been a long twenty-four hours, without much sleep. "Black-eye for me," Noah said.

"I'll take a red-eye," Caleb said.

"You got it." Lindy grabbed two insulated cups and hit the espresso machine.

Five minutes later, they headed back to the Jeep with their own coffee-espresso combos in hand plus drinks for Emmy and Logan.

Noah waited until they were back on the road before broaching the subject that had been heavy on his mind the last forty-eight hours. "There's something I want to discuss with you."

Caleb swallowed the sip of coffee he had in his mouth and set the cup down. "Okay."

"It's clear Mason's arrival has created a new level of tension for you."

Caleb's jaw tightened. "I . . ."

"No need to respond," Noah said, before he went any further. "I just want to remind you, Rissi, and Mason that we're a team. All of us. And we need to keep the team strong and focused while on the job."

Caleb gave a hard nod. "Understood."

"Great." Caleb was an excellent agent and always would be, but when love came into the picture, it had a habit of affecting everyone and everything around it. He'd learned that the hard way and had seen "love" destroy more than one good man. Which was why he avoided it. He had a family to look out for—his mom, sisters, niece, and nephew—had a job he loved, a team to run, and a life of his own. No need to shift his focus from what he already had.

Now that he'd cleared the air with Caleb, he needed to have the same talk with Rissi and Mason, but he'd give them their day of rest first.

TWENTY-NINE

Rissi lay down, her head hitting the pillow with a poof—down feathers spreading to cradle her head. How was she ever going to sleep with thoughts of Mason invading her mind? He'd been in her heart and mind since he'd first walked through the children's home door all those years ago. Or more accurately, when he'd swaggered in, setting a tone from the start. One that led to dark places on Hank's part. But Mason had never lost his nerve or his fight—always ready to battle his way through Hank's "punishments." He'd been her hero.

Walking into the station all these years later, the same feelings came rushing back, swelling to the surface, but with a new level of maturity.

She rolled on her side, staring out her half-drawn shade at the sun's rays gliding across the water. Knowing sleep would continue to elude her, she got to her feet and lifted her phone. If Noah was going to insist she and Mason take the day off, she might as well make the most of it.

Her thumb hovered over the phone screen. *Just do it. You know you want to spend the day with him. What's the worst that can happen?*

He could say no.

Before she could chicken out, she dialed his number. Taking soothing breaths—or the closest she could manage to them—she waited as his phone rang.

"Hey, Rissi," Mason answered. "What's up?"

So he'd already programmed in her name. Her lips twitched into a smile. "There's no way I'm going to be able to sleep today. I'm heading out for a little adventure. Wanna join me?" She was about to backtrack and insist no pressure, but he answered before the words could slip from her mouth.

"Absolutely. What are we in for?"

"You'll see. Just dress for some hot conditions."

"Oookay." With temps in the low eighties, he was probably wondering what she was getting him into.

Rissi knocked on Mason's door. Since he was so new in town she'd expected to find him living in a temporary apartment while he looked for a place to settle in.

Mason settling in. She liked the idea.

Instead of an apartment, he'd gone with a cool seventies-style beach cottage on the sound side of Wrightsville Beach. Tall marshes dotted the waterways on her left. The sound of seagulls squawking contrasted with the beautiful silence of the white-and-gray egret standing regally at the marsh's edge.

She stepped up on the porch of the blue clapboard cottage with white storm shutters.

The front door was open, and through the screen, she heard a whirring and crunching sound. She knocked.

The sound continued. She knocked a bit louder. "Hello?" She didn't feel right just walking in.

The crunching stopped, and Mason appeared from around the corner. "Hey, sorry. Was grinding some coffee beans for tomorrow morning." He strode barefoot to the door. "Come on in."

She opened the door, and a cat swiped across her path.

"Oh." She smiled. She hadn't pictured Mason as a cat person.

"Hey, Socks. There you are." He bent to pick up the black cat with white paws. "Little guy just showed up on my doorstep looking for food. I've asked around, but no one knows who he belongs to. Until I find his home or figure out he doesn't have one, which I'm starting to think is the case, he's welcome to stay here. I'm normally a dog person, but I have to admit, he's a pretty chill cat." He nuzzled the purring cat behind the ear.

"Can I hold him?" she asked.

"Sure." He handed her Socks. The little guy was soft, warm, and active. He climbed up and across her shoulders, lying on the back of her neck, his paws draped over each shoulder.

Mason laughed. "He likes you."

"Looks that way."

"So where are we off to today?"

"Nags Head."

A smile lit his face as he arched a brow. "Outer Banks?"

"Yep. We should arrive just as the day starts cooling off."

"I'm guessing I should grab swim trunks?"

"You can, but you won't need them."

His charming smile widened, his chin dimple deepening. "Now I'm even more curious."

Mason glanced over at Rissi lounging in the passenger seat of his Impala. She'd asked if they could take his car as she'd never ridden in an Impala, and with the windows rolled down, sun spilling across her hair, and her bare feet propped up on the open sill, he had to say it suited her well. *Guardians of the Galaxy: Awesome Mix Vol. 1* played over the speakers. He inhaled, soaking it all in—the soft floral scent wafting from Rissi's hair every time the wind shifted toward him, the completeness he felt when she was near, and the peace. Somehow, she anchored his soul.

Thank you, Lord.

He couldn't envision a more perfect day.

Rissi sighed and closed her eyes, soaking up the sun.

Mason smiled. She always had loved the light. Especially when it shone through the square rafter window in her crawl-space. He'd watched as she looked out over the neighborhood roofs, staring across the bridge that separated the good part of town from the bad—both of them wishing they were on the other side, wishing they were out from under Hank's grasp.

But that was in the past, and this was the present. He longed to reach over and hold her hand, but he needed a better under-standing of her relationship with Caleb. She'd said they were just friends, and Rissi was always truthful. But the feelings be-tween them were deep, even if they were only that of friendship.

So many questions swirled in his mind, but the last thing he wanted to do was make her uncomfortable, so he kept his hand locked on the steering wheel and his eyes on the road ahead. Or, at least, he tried to.

THIRTY

The ride Mason never wanted to end did. But the Outer Banks were spectacular. High sloping dunes, rough surf, blue skies stretching as far as the eye could see.

"Okay, ace," he said, looking over at her with a smile. "Where to now?"

"First stop, Morning View Coffee, and then Jockey's Ridge." She had a definite twinkle in her eye when she said the latter.

"And Jockey's Ridge is . . . ?"

"A state park in Nags Head."

"Where we're going to do . . . ?"

"Sand surfing."

He laughed. "What?"

"You use a board like you would a snowboard, but you ride down the large sand dunes in the park."

"No way!" He'd never heard of such a thing. How cool.

"Yep. It's awesome."

He tapped the wheel. "I can't wait." He loved seeing Rissi like this. So free, with her adventurous streak finally set loose. He couldn't wait to see her fly down the dunes.

She directed him to Morning View Coffee, and he followed her inside. The first thing he saw upon entering was the huge bronze coffee roasting machine enclosed by glass except for a side entrance from behind the counter. "They roast their own beans?" he asked as they moved across the space.

"Yep." Rissi turned her attention to the woman behind the counter. "Hey, Ashley."

"Hey, Rissi. Off to sandboard?"

"Yep." She turned to Mason. "This is Mason Rogers."

"Hiya, Mason. Nice to meet you." She leaned over the counter and shook his extended hand.

"You too."

"Your usual?" Ashley asked Rissi, grabbing a large iced cup.

"Definitely."

Ashley wrote on the cup in black Sharpie and set it to the side. "Mason, what can I get you?"

He looked up at the chalkboard menu. Everything looked great, and the espresso Ashley pulled from the machine smelled amazing. "I think I'll do a double espresso con panna."

"You got it. Anything else?"

"A couple muffins to go," Rissi said. "Just surprise us."

Ashley smiled. "On it."

Rissi gestured to the purple sofa lining the back wall. "Want to sit while she makes our drinks?"

"Sure."

"Hey, Mags," Rissi said, bending to pet a golden retriever lying next to the turquoise-and-white surfboard serving as a coffee table.

"Hey there," Mason said, bending to pet the dog before following Rissi to the sofa. More surfboards hung on the walls above photographs of the sand and surf, and unique artwork.

"They're all done by local artists," she said, bending her left leg and angling it so her foot draped over her right knee as she sat.

"Cool place," he said, glancing at the TV playing surfing videos mounted over the coffee bar.

"I love it." She smiled. "I never pegged you for a whipped-cream-on-your-espresso kind of man."

"I like whipped cream, and I'm proud of it."

She laughed.

He scooted closer, unable to help himself. "What kind of man did you peg me as?"

She shrugged. "I don't know."

He scooted closer still. "Come on. You're the profiling expert."

She hesitated.

He propped his elbow on the couch and rested his head on his hand. "I'd really like to know."

"All right." She shifted to face him better, her blue eyes sparkling in the sun streaming through the large window behind the counter. "As a teen, I viewed you as the strong, tough guy, who could also be gentle and very kind. Someone who pushed the limits, thrived off danger, and needed no one."

His brow arched. "Needed no one?"

"I don't mean that in a bad way. I just mean you never had to depend on anyone. You were the strong one and always held your own." Her lips twisted as she cast her gaze down. "I was the weak, vulnerable one."

"Order's up," Ashley called before he could respond.

They stood, each grabbing their cup. "Thanks," they said in unison.

Ashley smiled. "You two have fun."

Once back in the car, Mason shifted sideways to face Rissi better.

"What's up?" she asked, her voice tentative.

He cleared his throat, fighting the urge to reach out and cup her face. "You got two pivotal points wrong in your assessment of me."

Her brows arched. "Oh?"

"First"—he hated being vulnerable, but she was worth it— "I did depend on someone back then, very much."

She frowned.

He reached for her hand, unable to stop himself. She didn't

pull away as he threaded his fingers through hers. "I depended on you."

Her face tightened, her beautiful blue eyes narrowing. "Are you messing with me?"

"No. I would never joke about something like that." He scooted closer until their knees were touching, her hand still in his. "I needed you back then." He swallowed. "And I still do."

"I don't understand. . . ."

"You think you were the weak one, but you're wrong. You never let Hank break you. You never gave him the satisfaction of pleading with him or crying in front of him. You were so strong. And you kept your sweetness through it all. You didn't let it change who you were. That takes a tremendous amount of strength."

Tears rimmed her eyes.

He continued before he lost his nerve. "I needed you to help me remain me. Before I got to Hank's, I was so angry. So bitter. So over-the-edge. But then I met you. I saw strength in many forms. You didn't view me as an outcast. You looked at me with love."

She looked down. "So you knew about that?"

His heartbeat drummed in his chest. "About . . . ?"

She looked him in the eye and after a sharp inhale and short exhale, she said, "About my feelings for you."

"As a friend?" His voice cracked.

She hesitated, and hope nipped at him. Did she feel the same way?

"Or more?" he asked, aching to know.

She tilted her head to the right as her shoulder came up to meet it in a soft shrug.

His heart beat faster. "Is that a yes?"

"Yes," she said slightly above a whisper.

His mouth went dry. "And now?"

She nibbled her bottom lip.

"Ris?" He searched her face, her beautiful, wonderful face.

"And still," she said, looking him directly in the eyes, her voice steadfast.

Warmth rushed through him. "Why didn't you tell me?"

"Back then our friendship meant everything to me, and I was afraid if you didn't feel the same way, we'd lose our friendship."

"And now?" he asked again, his voice a throaty whisper.

"And now . . . I didn't want to make you uncomfortable if you didn't feel the same. I mean, it's been years, and I didn't want to freak you out saying I still have feelings for you, which I probably just did. . . ."

He cupped her face, cradling it in his hold. "You didn't freak me out."

She blinked. "I didn't?"

Instead of telling her, he'd show her. Leaning in, he hovered his lips over hers. To his bliss, she leaned in to meet him.

He pressed his lips to hers, the kiss soft and slow.

He'd dreamt of this moment more times than he could count and now that it was here, he didn't want to rush a thing. After a decade, he was finally kissing the woman he loved.

Tenderly, he deepened the kiss, losing all sense of time and reason.

"Hey, boss," Logan said as Noah entered the station, Caleb behind him.

"Hey, guys. I brought sustenance," Noah said. He handed Logan a cup. "Your vanilla almond-milk latte."

"Thank you."

Caleb tilted his head. "You know that's a girly drink?"

"I'm perfectly comfortable with my masculinity, thank you very much." Logan took a sip. "Ah, that's the stuff."

Caleb shook his head with a chuckle.

"Emmalyne," Noah said, "one iced pumpkin spice latte." He set it on her desk.

"Thanks." She smiled, took off the lid, and lifted the cup to take a sip. "Delicious."

Logan smiled at Emmy.

She frowned. "What?"

"You got a little something . . . " Logan said. He stepped toward her and pulled out his silk handkerchief. "Allow me."

She leaned back. "Really, I'm okay." She swiped at her mouth.

"Suit yourself," Logan said, sliding the handkerchief back into his jacket pocket with two perfect points. "But you missed a spot."

Emmy swiped again.

"You got it," Noah said. "It was just whipped cream."

She smiled. "Thanks. The dangers of pumpkin spice lattes, I suppose."

"So where are we at with the environmentalists?" Noah asked, sitting on the corner of his desk across from Emmy's and Logan's.

"Talk about interesting," Logan said.

Noah arched a brow. "Oh?"

"You go first, Em."

"All right." She lifted a yellow legal pad sparsely filled with notes.

Caleb frowned. "That doesn't look like much."

"That's because it's not," Emmy said.

"Not much to find?" Noah asked, surprised. Emmy was the master at digging stuff up. If she couldn't find much, none of them would.

"Actually," Emmy said, crossing her legs. "Such a small amount of information being somewhat readily available means there's a lot more being suppressed."

Noah cocked his head. "As in hidden?"

Emmy swiveled her chair around. "I believe so."

"To what end?" Caleb asked.

"That's where the fun comes in," Logan said, rubbing his palms together. "We dig beneath the surface. Unearth what's hidden."

"Don't take this the wrong way," Emmy said with a smirk at Logan. "But he's right."

"Yes!" Logan said. "Eyewitnesses." He pointed at Noah and Caleb. "You heard it. She said it. I'm right."

Emmy rolled her eyes. "I knew the words should have never left my mouth."

Noah needed to maintain a certain level of authority over playful antics on CGIS time, but watching Logan and Emmy was hilarious. He never got involved in their banter, because as much fun as it would be, it wasn't the professional level of leadership he needed to exude. He loved being a team leader, watching out for his teammates and running the unit, but sometimes he wished he could metaphorically kick off his shoes and just cut up with them.

"Did you find anything we can look into?" Caleb asked, stoic as always. Speaking of letting loose, Caleb desperately needed to decompress and enjoy life more, but Noah doubted that would happen any time soon. Especially after Mason's arrival.

"The organization's registered name is the Freedom Group. Here's the headquarters' location," Em said, ripping off a page of legal paper and handing it to Caleb.

"It's up in Holly Ridge," Caleb said, showing Noah the address.

"Then I guess we're going to Holly Ridge. Anything else we should know?"

"They are claiming to be a nonprofit," Logan said.

Noah arched a brow. "'Claiming'?"

"I need to dig a lot deeper to find their real finances, but what they are making publicly available isn't adding up," Logan said. "There's more there."

"Okay, we'll let you get back to it while we head up to Holly Ridge," Noah said.

"Yes, sir." Logan turned and headed back to his desk.

"Other than finding the basic information on the Freedom Group's website and a few online articles on events benefiting the organization, I'll have to dig deeper too," Emmy said.

"And Gwyneth?" Noah asked.

"Gwyneth Lansing is nowhere to be found on their website," Logan said.

"That's odd." Noah frowned. "But you found her last name. That's a good start."

"Logan only found her full name by tracking down the Freedom Group's corporate tax returns," Emmy said.

Noah narrowed his eyes. "So how is she connected to the group?"

Emmy sat back in her chair. "She's the executive director."

"Well, that raises some questions we're going to need answers to," Noah said.

"And . . ." Emmy sighed. "I think we're just scratching the surface. There's definitely a lot more going on than meets the eye."

THIRTY-ONE

A thought occurred to Mason as they pulled into Jockey's Ridge after grabbing rental boards across the street. He'd been so excited about spending the day with Rissi, he hadn't thought about her rib. "Are you sure this is the smartest thing to be doing with a bruised rib?"

"Eh." She shrugged. "I can barely feel it."

"But if you fall on it . . ."

"Don't worry," she said as he opened the passenger-side door for her. "I don't plan on falling."

He smiled. He liked the confidence she'd grown into. Could the woman be any more alluring?

Noah approached the one-story glass-and-metal structure before him. *Freedom Group* was scrolled in bright blue letters with the *p* shifting up into a wave over the doors leading into their office.

The walls of the building were all glass, but one-way, so everyone inside could see out, but no one on the outside could see in.

Noah pulled the door handle, and it remained in place.

Caleb arched a brow. "Locked?"

Noah nodded. "I'm beginning to think everything about this organization is off."

A beep sounded to their right. Noah cast his gaze to the speaker as a woman's voice came over it. "May I help you?"

"Yes. We're here to speak with one of your group members." That sounded the least confrontational.

"Do you have an appointment?"

"No, we do not."

"Then I'm afraid I'm unable to help you."

Noah pulled out his badge and held it up to the tiny camera mounted above the speaker. "I believe you are."

All pleasantness faded from her voice. "Just a minute."

Five minutes and a very impatient Noah later, the door buzzed open.

Noah kicked off the wall he'd been perched against and followed Caleb inside.

A woman in a gray pencil skirt, tall black heels, and a white-and-black silk blouse greeted them. "How may I help you?"

"Special Agent Rowley and Special Agent Eason," he said as they held up their badges. "And you are?"

"Jane Dudish. I'm the PR liaison for the Freedom Group. I understand you have some interest in our organization?"

"Yes, we do," Caleb said.

Jane was quite attractive and exuded a pleasant air. Not a bad play on the Freedom Group's part. He suspected Jane was able to give just enough information to make a visitor feel welcomed and informed, so they left happy but without any real knowledge about the group.

"How can I help?" she asked.

"What can you tell us about the Freedom Group?" Noah asked, starting with the long list of questions they'd amassed on the way over.

"I'll be happy to share our history, our vision, and our work, but may I ask what interest the CGIS has with us?"

"More curiosity than anything else," Noah said. No need to

make her uneasy. The more they kept things pleasant, perhaps the more they'd learn. Though his gut said otherwise.

"I see." She clutched her clipboard against her chest. "And how did you hear about us?"

Caleb looked to Noah, and Noah nodded for him to proceed.

"Members of your group rescued members of our team last night after their copter crashed in the ocean."

"Oh." Jane nodded as if it'd just clicked in her head. "Of course."

"We owe your organization a great amount of gratitude and thanks," Noah said.

Jane smiled, her countenance brightening. "If you gentlemen will follow me, I'll show you around and tell you more about the Freedom Group."

Noah smiled at Caleb as they filed in behind her.

Jane led them to a portrait of a man probably in his early fifties, with brown hair and weathered skin. He wore a navy blue polo shirt with a red Ralph Lauren emblem on his chest.

"This," Jane said, "is our founder, Skip Malone."

"Is Skip a nickname?"

Jane smiled. "Yes. His given name was Malcolm Malone the third."

"Meaning he was related to Malcolm Malone, the inventor of the glass hull in the sixties?"

"Yes. That would be Skip's grandfather. He created resin infusion and vacuum bagging. Vacuum bagging has a wet laminate cured under vacuum, which pulls out the excess resin, creating a light yet strong laminate. Resin infusion is a variation of vacuum bagging in which the resin is infused into the dry laminate after the vacuum is created. Both methods produce clean and light fiberglass parts."

So the family was loaded.

"We'd like to speak with Skip," Noah said. "Could you arrange a meeting for us with him?"

Jane pushed the brim of her red-framed glasses up her slender nose. "I wish I could, but . . ."

What excuse was she going to provide?

"He died two years ago in a sailing accident."

"I'm sorry for your loss," Noah said.

"Thank you. As you can imagine, we all took it extremely hard. But," she said, straightening her shoulders, "we've continued his legacy, fighting for the protection of sea life. Growing up on the water and scuba diving, Skip saw lots of marine life and was in awe of their beauty. But he also saw the damage being done to their homes by illegal dumping of chemical waste, trash carelessly tossed in the water, oil spills . . . The list goes on. Instead of watching the destruction of the animals and the ocean he loved, he decided to do something about it. In 2005 Skip founded the Freedom Group."

"Which does what, exactly?" Caleb asked.

Jane gestured down the hall on their left. "Follow me and I'll show you."

Her heels clicked along the black tile floor into a room with glass-enclosed displays and numerous wall hangings with detailed plaques beside each picture.

"This is our history, gentlemen."

An hour and a half later, they'd learned all the wonderful things the Freedom Group had accomplished, but there was no mention of Gwyneth Lansing.

"The CGIS agents rescued last night mentioned a Gwyneth was especially kind. How does she fit into the organization?"

"Gwyneth prefers to remain behind the scenes."

"Meaning?" Noah prompted.

"She prefers her work highlight all Skip did for the organization and not bring attention to herself."

Noah followed a nagging gut. "Were Gwyneth and Skip close?"

Jane's gaze darted about the room, fixing on a gentleman standing in the shadows by a side door.

She cleared her throat. "I hope you found this time helpful. We greatly appreciate your interest in our critical work and hope you'll consider partnering with us so we can continue to protect our seas and the marine life." She handed them each a brochure. "This has information on the next steps you can take."

"Do you mind if I ask who that is?" Noah said.

She blinked. "Who?"

"The man over . . ." Noah looked back, but the man was gone. "There was a man standing there a moment ago."

"It could have been anyone. We all visit this room often to remind ourselves why we do what we do. Now, if you'll excuse me, I have a meeting to attend. You can leave through that door." She indicated a side door with an Exit sign illuminated in red above it.

"We'd love to chat with more of your employees."

"Volunteers," she corrected.

Caleb's brows furrowed. "Everyone here is a volunteer?"

"Ninety-five percent."

"And the other five?" Caleb asked.

"Are paid positions. As with any organization, you need several full-time people to keep things running smoothly."

"We'd like the names of the five percent," Noah said.

"I'm afraid that's not public knowledge." Jane clutched her clipboard tighter. "Now, I'll see you out."

They had no search warrant to demand records, an employee list, or even to speak with anyone else without their consent, so their work here was done.

Once they stepped outside, Jane waved and shut the door behind them, clicking it into place.

Caleb slipped his hands into his Dockers pockets. "Well, that was . . ."

"Interesting?" Noah said.

"Exactly." Caleb slid on his aviator sunglasses. "So now what?"

"We call and see what Emmy and Logan have found and give them a lot more to look into."

THIRTY-TWO

Mason looked at Rissi standing atop her teal-striped board. She'd described sand surfing well.

He was going to like living in North Carolina. Not that he hadn't enjoyed Alaska while stationed at Kodiak. He'd made some good friends there—in particular the adventure-loving McKenna clan. But sandboarding in the warmth with the ocean in view could definitely hold its own with snowboarding. But wherever Rissi was is where his heart would be.

He watched the breeze ruffle her hair, fluttering strands about her face. She pulled the hairband off her wrist and knotted her hair up into a loose bun, tucking back the flyaway strands.

She smiled. "Ready?"

He smiled in return. "Let's do this."

"Come on," she called, jetting over the edge of the dune.

Adrenaline pumping through his veins, he followed, sand kicking up in his wake. Thoughts of Hank returned as he watched Rissi carving the sand in front of him. He'd been so careful to keep a distance from her whenever Hank was watching, knowing the monster would take sick pleasure in trying to rip their friendship apart. He squeezed his eyes shut at the memories, but now they were free of such constraints. And it felt amazing.

Hearing she cared for him . . . he didn't think he could ever be happier than he was in this moment.

Rissi dug the edge of her board into the sand, rocking to a sideways stop.

He stopped beside her.

"Not bad." She smiled.

The breeze fluttered an unruly strand of hair about her face. He took hold of the silky strand and tucked it behind her ear.

She gestured to his board. "You like?"

"Love it."

Picking up her board, she shook off a layer of sand. "Ready for another run?"

"Always."

"Race you." Rissi gestured up the dune, a twinkle in her eye.

A smile tugged at his lips. "You're on."

Her laughter filled his ears as his feet sank in the hot sand. He'd never heard a more beautiful sound.

"Hey, Em," Caleb said, calling while Noah drove.

"Noah and I found some more crumbs for you to follow. The founder of the Freedom Group—"

"Skip Malone," she said before he could finish.

"Yes," Caleb said. "So you learned about him?"

"Yes, but you start. What did you find out?"

"Very little, other than his name, the money his family had due to his grandfather's fiberglass invention, and his love for the sea and its animals."

"Well, I've got something much juicier," Emmy said.

He wasn't sure if he should be excited or a bit terrified. Things usually were a little twisted when it came to what Emmy found intriguing.

"Skip died in a sailing accident," she said.

"We were told that too."

"But were you told that there was an investigation into his death?"

"No," he said, looking over at Noah. "We most definitely were not told about an investigation."

Noah's brows hiked up.

"Skip's death," Caleb explained quickly to Noah.

Noah's eyes widened.

"The Coast Guard found Skip's boat afloat at sea. A fishing trawler radioed it in. They found Skip dead. He had a large wound on his head—looked like he got nailed with a baseball bat, according to Petty Officer Second Class Valverde, who was on the response team."

"Impressive, Em. How did you find all that?"

"I have my ways." He could practically hear her smile.

"It's odd. . . . I don't recall that case." He usually remembered each and every one they worked. And a death at sea would have fallen under CGIS jurisdiction.

"It wasn't our station's patrol area. Skip was sailing off Oak Island's coast."

"So that CGIS station took the case."

"Yes, but the ME on the case, Dr. O'Connor, determined the cause of death to be the impact of the boom hitting his head."

That happened, especially with green sailors. They'd forget the boom swung with force when coming about, but surely a man who grew up on the water would have known better.

"And CGIS signed off on it?" he asked.

"Yes. But the family wasn't satisfied. It didn't make sense to them. Sailing was like breathing to Skip. They insisted he wouldn't make such a newbie mistake. They hired their own investigator."

"Do you know the investigator's name?" Caleb asked as Noah swerved around a large pothole.

"Austin Kelly of Kelly Investigations Limited."

"You got an address?" Caleb asked while fishing through Noah's glove box for a pen.

Noah flipped down his visor and pulled one out of the black storage pouch, along with a flip pocket notebook.

"Thanks," Caleb said.

Noah nodded. "Hang on again." He swerved around another pothole.

They really needed to repave Sawyer Road.

"The investigator's office is here in Wilmington. 1303 Thistlewood Lane."

"Got it. Thanks, Em."

"You're welcome. We'll keep digging."

"Keep us posted." Caleb hung up and summarized the information for Noah as he punched the address into the GPS.

Noah swung a wide U-turn, and they headed for Austin Kelly's office.

Caleb found the few private investigators he'd met over the years to be very determined. Sometimes in a productive way and at others, obnoxiously so. He wondered which way this Austin Kelly guy would be.

THIRTY-THREE

Caleb tapped the doorframe as they approached Austin Kelly's building. He'd tried calling the man. Twice. All he'd gotten was an automated message to leave a voicemail. Hopefully he was back in the office now that they were here, or it would be a wasted trip—enjoyable as it'd been with the Jeep top down on such a nice day.

Kelly Investigations Limited resided on the second floor of a two-story colonial-style brick building that resembled a court-house or old bank with the cream columns in front.

Caleb moved to open the building's front door but found it locked. Turning to the silver metal frame with names lining it in columns and black buttons beside each name, he buzzed Kelly's office.

"Yes?" a woman answered.

"Hi. We're here to speak with Austin Kelly."

"Do you have an appointment?"

"No. I'm afraid not, but it's important we speak with him."

"What's this in regard to?"

"Skip Malone's death."

The door buzzed, and Noah pulled it open.

They climbed the stairs to the second floor, exiting into a carpeted hall with large potted palms—the fronds hitting Caleb midchest.

A blond woman dressed in a knee-length, navy knit dress,

heeled sandals, and a gold, sun-shaped necklace stood at the office door to greet them. She was strikingly beautiful in a natural way. Long blond hair, green eyes, and subtle makeup. "Come in, gentlemen," she said, gesturing them inside.

The bright yellow office was small. One room. He'd anticipated at least two. One for the detective and one for this woman. He was guessing she was an assistant as Emmy didn't mention Kelly having a partner. A cherrywood desk sat in the center of the room with a high-back brown leather chair facing them from the opposite side.

"Please, have a seat," she said, sitting down behind the desk.

"We need to speak with Mr. Kelly," Caleb said, disappointed he wasn't present. "Can you arrange for a meeting with him?"

She steepled her fingers, her nails painted a light pink. "That might prove difficult."

Caleb cocked his head. "Why's that?"

She leaned forward. "Because I'm not a *him*."

After a moment of stunned silence, Noah said, "I'm so sorry, Ms. Kelly. We were under the impression that Austin . . . that you . . ."

"Were a man," Caleb blurted.

"Well, clearly you were wrong, and I have to say a little sexist."

Sexist? Their assumption had been reasonable, given her first name, and he didn't appreciate her questioning his integrity. "Would it be sexist if my name was Sally, and you assumed I was a woman?"

"Perhaps, but Austin can be either male or female whereas Sally is predominately a female name."

"Where I grew up, Austin was predominately male," Caleb countered. "Actually, every Austin I knew was a male, and—"

"We're hoping you can help us," Noah said, cutting in.

Her piercing gaze shifted from Caleb to Noah. "Help you, how?" She twirled her gold pen in her slender fingers.

"We're investigating the Freedom Group."

"About time someone did. Are you with the Holly Ridge Police Department?"

"No. CGIS," Noah said.

"So the ones who mucked it up in the first place."

Caleb tucked his chin in. "Excuse me?" Now she was insulting his brotherhood?

"I'm sorry, did I speak too fast for you?"

Noah smothered a laugh with a cough.

"I don't know what happened with the Oak Island CGIS on this case specifically," Caleb said, "but I know the service. We're very good at what we do."

She shrugged a nearly bare shoulder, her dress strap merely an inch wide. "Perhaps you are. Sometimes," she added. "But not on my case."

Caleb scooted forward. "*Your* case?"

"Yes." She rested her arms on the cherry desk.

He planted his hands on it—his fingertips inches from hers.

"CGIS wrote it off as an accident," she said. "I discovered the truth."

"Well." Caleb sat back. "Please, enlighten us."

"Skip Malone was dating a woman in the organization," she began. "Rumor goes, they fell madly in love. Since they worked together, they tried to keep their relationship a secret. Never being romantic in public. Coming and going separately."

"If that's the case, then how do you know they were together, that it wasn't just rumor?" Caleb asked, not doubting that she knew, but curious how she'd figured it out.

"I found a source who'd been with the organization from the start and saw them together several times when they thought no one was around."

"And your source's name?" Caleb asked, betting she wouldn't divulge a source, but it never hurt to try.

She didn't answer, at least not verbally. She simply dipped her chin and lifted her brows.

"So your source saw them together," Noah said, "but I'm assuming there's an 'and then'?"

"You're right." She smiled at Noah. "The source once heard them arguing because he said she was—and I quote—'too intense.'"

Noah frowned. "Meaning relationship-wise?"

"No." Austin folded her hands together over the leather desk mat. "She pushed the limits when it came to her love for the environment."

Caleb had not seen that coming.

"Apparently, she was willing to break the law to 'protect the endangered,'" Austin said with air quotes.

"To what extent?" Noah asked.

"My source didn't know. She just heard him tell Gwyneth that he couldn't believe she'd done it, that he wasn't covering for her. Then she disappeared. She only showed back up after Skip's death. Now she basically runs the group."

"Wait," Caleb said. "Are you talking about Gwyneth Lansing?"

Austin sat back, linking her arms across her chest. "The very one."

"You think she had something to do with Skip's death?" he asked, rather stunned at the turn of events.

Austin cocked her head. "I think she killed him."

THIRTY-FOUR

Noah held the door for the women entering the family restaurant he and Caleb had just grabbed dinner in. It was in the building next to Austin's, and the fresh scent of tomatoes and basil had beckoned as they'd walked toward the Jeep. The recipes of the Rossi family from Urbino, Italy, passed down from generation to generation, were beyond scrumptious.

Noah stretched his back. He'd be full for days, but that fresh-from-the-oven bread, the garden-fresh herbs and tomatoes, the handmade pasta . . . He'd be returning again.

"Well, this was a worthwhile visit," he said as they strode across the parking lot.

"Yes. Worthwhile," Caleb said. "But she was so . . . so . . ."

"So?" Noah smirked, knowing it pricked at Caleb's irritation.

"So annoying," he finally said.

"Better than a self-righteous prig," said a female voice.

Noah and Caleb spun around to find Austin standing less than five feet away.

"Prig?" Caleb's voice hitched.

Noah bit back a laugh. He loved Caleb like a brother, loved his entire team. But he had to admit she'd nailed him.

"Oh, I'm sorry," she said. "It means—"

"I know what it means." Caleb's jaw tightened, a muscle twitching.

Man, she'd really gotten under his skin. "Was there something you wanted?" Noah asked.

She dragged her gaze away from Caleb, pursing her lips before nodding back toward the restaurant. "I saw you stop in for dinner, so I decided to make you a copy of my file on Skip. He was a good guy from everything I've gathered on him. His family really loved him." She handed it to Noah.

"Thanks," he said, grateful for her generosity in sharing information. "Family, as in wife?"

"No." She shook her head. "Siblings."

"I didn't realize Skip had any family." Noah tapped the folder in his hand. "I'm surprised none of them took over the Freedom Group."

"None of them were passionate about the environment the way Skip was." She looked at the brown folder. "I hope you'll see something in there that I missed."

Noah flashed a glance at Caleb to keep him from saying something rude.

He held quiet, but his flickering jaw said it was killing him.

Noah smiled. He'd never seen a woman get a rise like this out of Caleb.

"Do me a favor?" Austin asked.

"Sure," Noah said.

"Keep me in the loop. That case still itches at me. I know the evidence is hiding in there somewhere."

"We definitely will," Noah said as he opened the driver's side door.

Caleb was quiet for a couple of minutes after they pulled out onto the main road. Then he slipped on his sunglasses and leaned back against the headrest. "Okay, so she's not *completely* annoying."

Noah chuckled.

"So, what did you think?" Rissi asked Mason on the way out of the park. The warmth of the sun still soaked in her skin, and with Mason beside her, it was the perfect end to a perfect day.

He looked over with a smile that stole her breath away. "I had the best time."

"Good. I'm glad. Now there's one more stop before we leave OBX."

He arched a brow. "Oh?"

"Yep. Make a left up there where that red car is turning out."

"Okay." He flipped on his blinker and made the turn.

"One more left and : . . there you go."

He looked at her, a smile tickling his handsome face. "Sonic?"

"Yep. It's tradition. Hit the drive-thru."

"And what am I ordering?"

"Two large tater tots and two Route 66 cherry limeades."

Mason pulled through the drive-thru and insisted on paying. The guy working the register handed him their drinks, which he passed on to Rissi for the moment and set the bag down between them.

"Those tots smell delicious," he said as they pulled away.

She smiled. "Wait until you taste them at the beach."

He chuckled. "What?"

"It's weird, but I'm telling you, they taste better at the beach," she said, popping one in her mouth. "Make a left down that next street."

He did and followed her directions to the sound-access parking lot, which at this time of evening was empty.

She kicked off her shoes, grabbed the bag of tots and one limeade, and hopped out. "Grab your drink."

He followed suit, and they walked down the ramp to a nearly empty park on the sound side.

"Let's grab a seat." She led the way toward the water, looking both ways. To their right, a couple with two black labs frolicked in the water. To their left, two people who looked rather like dots walked in the distance. *Perfect.*

She sat cross-legged on the sand and pulled out the first bag of tots, handing them to Mason and then grabbing the last one for herself. "Taste one."

He did. "Mmm. You can really taste the saltiness."

She smiled. "It's the sea air. It brings out the salt in the tots. Now," she said, stretching her legs out in front of her and crossing one ankle over the other, "for the view." She stared at the magnificent orange sunset. "Pretty spectacular, right?"

"Extremely," he said, his gaze fixed on her.

They stayed to watch the sun slip fully beneath the horizon before heading for his car. Twilight faded into night—the sky black and star-filled.

Mason glanced over at Rissi looking content and surprisingly refreshed considering the lack of sleep they'd had. Turning his gaze back to the long stretch of road before them, he prayed she'd sleep well after the day full of adventure. He always did after a day spent outdoors. He loved that she sandboarded and, according to Finn, surfed. He wondered what else she enjoyed, and prayed he got to experience many more adventures with her.

Unable to help himself, he glanced over at her one more time. She was breathtaking. It didn't matter that her hair was all cattywampus in an askew ponytail with an adorable flowered knit headband wrapped about her head. Or that she had no makeup on, her skin tinged pink across her nose and cheeks from the sun and wind. Her sandy bare feet were up on the seat as she sat cross-legged, her arm outstretched, letting the wind stream through her fingers. *Breathtaking.*

He wished he could pull the car over and kiss her senseless, whispering words of love that had gripped his heart since the first day he walked in the home and saw her. Those blue eyes tinged with hope, the defiant set of her jaw, the tenderness of her smile at him. No one had looked at him like that since his parents died. Looked at him with caring. And then with love.

He glanced in the rearview mirror, and the headlights that had been a fair distance behind drew closer. They were on Route 12, which ran the length of the Outer Banks. Turning left, Mason crossed the bridge, taking them off the barrier islands and onto Route 64. The car followed, the only one behind them. Several cars passed from the other direction, but traffic was sparse.

"I love off-season," Rissi said as the cooling night air fluttered inside. "So much less traffic and congestion."

"Summers bring in a lot of visitors?"

"*A lot* is an understatement. You'll see."

The thought of eight more months at Rissi's side until summer hit warmed him, but the idea of crowds did not. Being an introvert, he preferred open spaces. It was part of why he'd loved Kodiak so much. But Kodiak didn't have Rissi.

He made the sharp right turn onto S. Andrews Street into Jamesville, following the GPS for the fastest time back so Rissi could get some much-needed sleep.

He instinctually glanced back. The SUV swung wide into the turn at the last minute, its tires squealing. He stiffened, looking once again in his rearview mirror as the square-shaped headlights swiped across it.

Rissi shifted, glancing over her shoulder, a frown on her face. "What was that all about?" she asked.

"Looks like he . . ." Mason squinted as they passed the lone street light. It illuminated the inside of the car and the silhouettes of at least three men—based on build. "Actually, *they* nearly missed the turn."

She studied his profile. "What's wrong?"

"Probably nothing," he said, his gut disagreeing. He tapped the steering wheel. "That SUV has been behind us since we left Nags Head."

Rissi's nose scrunched. "Really?"

"Could just be a coincidence," he said, not wanting to worry her if he was overthinking the situation. "They may be headed the same way as us, but . . ." He needed to know. "I think we should find out."

"Absolutely," she agreed.

Mason depressed the gas pedal, the Impala emitting a deep engine roar. He loved that sound. Continuing to accelerate, he pulled a handful of car lengths ahead. The SUV hung back.

He should relax, but something still wasn't sitting right. "Any good side roads around here?" he asked. "Just two lanes?"

Rissi looked around, clearly trying to place exactly where they were—trees and night surrounding them. "Yeah," she said. "About a mile up, you have your choice. Batters Road is on your right and on the left is Stephens Road. It's got a sharp-angled turn from this direction."

"Is it a dead end? Or does it feed out somewhere?"

"It feeds out on a number of side roads that branch off of it. But, I should warn you, it gets really narrow in the tight turns, and there's a one lane bridge."

"Great." Gripping the steering wheel with one hand, he flipped the right blinker on with the other. The green arrow flashed on the dash. *Click-click-click.*

He slowed, drawing the SUV in closer, and allowing the cars coming in the opposite direction to draw closer until they were nearly upon them. A semitrailer led the pack. *Perfect.*

The SUV slowed, pulling back a few car lengths. Mason held until the semi was nearly upon them, then gunned it, banking hard left onto Stephens Road.

Rissi swung around, watching the series of cars as they flew by. "Did it turn right?"

"No." She shook her head. "It's trying to find a break in between the passing cars to turn left."

"All right. Time to find a good side road or secluded driveway."

"Good idea," she said.

The Impala bumped over the gravel road, bouncing over a pothole.

"There," Rissi said, pointing to the small driveway barely visible. Surrounded by trees, an arched trellis covered in thick ivy marked the opening to the dirt road leading up to a house in the distance.

Pulling in far enough not to be spotted from the road, he killed the lights and engine. "Let's get their license plate." He wished North Carolina required front plates as Alaska had. If so he'd already have it.

"Ready?" he asked, opening his door.

Without question, Rissi pulled out her gun and stepped from the car.

She was right in tune with him. Just as she'd always been.

Closing the doors as silently as possible, they hurried along the inner edge of the tree line for where the property met the road. Dropping on their haunches behind bushes, guns drawn, they held very still as the SUV's headlights came into view. Driving far slower than it had been, it rounded the curve, its headlights flashing over the lawn. They ducked down lower. The SUV passed by and continued on.

"Got it," Rissi whispered.

"Let's call it in."

"I'll give the plate number to Em," she said as they stood and moved quietly back to the car, just in case the SUV backtracked.

Mason turned his vehicle around, leaving his headlights off until they were back on 64 heading south with no sign of the SUV behind them.

///////////////////

Brooke came home to a locked door and her lights reassuringly on.

She dropped her keys in the bowl by the door and moved into the kitchen. Her throat parched from hours on the copter inhaling sea air, she strode to the fridge to grab some OJ.

Pouring a glass, she took a sip, leaning back against her kitchen counter. Another long watch. She was ready for some decompression.

She pushed off the counter as an explosion reverberated from her garage.

Her gaze flashed to the door leading to the garage and found it partly ajar.

Her chest tightened, sweat beaded on her skin. *Please let me make it out.*

Forcing in a breath—shallow as it was—she sprinted as fast as she could to the front door. Fumbling with the dead bolt, she glanced behind her. *Come on. Come on.* Finally sliding the thick bar out of the slot, she yanked the door open and bolted across the lawn for Roxy's.

Heavy footfalls sounded behind her fence.

Dear God.

She braved a glance over as the motion-sensor floodlight kicked on. Clad all in black, the person jumped over the rear privacy wall, disappearing into the night.

THIRTY-FIVE

Noah rushed through the quiet streets, his cherry flashing on the dash, red beams rhythmically circling across his Jeep's hood. What was Brodie thinking? That he could continue harassing Brooke and he would just stand by? Had he not made himself clear when they spoke? He was investigating the case, and he would do what was necessary to find the stalker and see him behind bars. More importantly, he'd make sure Brooke was safe and felt secure in her own home.

He pulled in, Roxy's porch light switching on. He was so thankful Brooke had a close neighbor, one she could rely on. Roxy stepped onto the porch, a white lounge outfit on, then Brooke behind her, in a navy blue Coast Guard polo and pair of gray utility pants.

"Stay there while I check things out," he called over as he climbed out of his car.

Only the front room and kitchen lights were on, so he moved through Brooke's home, gun in his right hand, flashlight in his left—his right wrist crossed over the left. Once the main part of the house had been cleared, he opened the door leading off the kitchen to the garage. Maneuvering through the doorway, keeping his back flush with the wall, he scanned the area. Deeming it safe, he flipped the wall switch and stared at the level of destruction with a lead weight in his gut. *Poor Brooke.*

A classic VW bus was riddled with dents—the sort you'd

get from a swift beating with a baseball bat—its windows all shattered. He stiffened at the message scrolled across the side in red spray paint. *You think he can protect you from me? You're mine, and you're going to pay.*

Once Noah had called Emmy and Logan to come run the place again—this time focusing on the garage and backyard—he let Brooke know it was safe to come back over. Roxy joined them.

"I'm so glad you're here for our Brooke," Roxy said.

Color flushed Brooke's cheeks. "He's just helping out his sister. I mean, she asked him to help while she's out of town."

He swallowed. She wasn't wrong about the reasons he'd started with this investigation, but now he was here for her. How that had happened, he had no clue. "I'm happy to be here. I mean, not happy with what Brodie is doing, but I want to help."

"See. He wants to be here," Roxy said, a pink-and-white polka-dot headband thing in her thick red hair.

He narrowed his eyes. Were those streaks of pink?

"You like?" Roxy asked, patting her hair. "My granddaughter said streaks of color are all the rage, so I figured why not." She smiled, and it was contagious. Roxy had the ability to add an air of levity to any situation and he was grateful. Brooke had gone through enough. She needed a spark of joy in the darkness.

And, Roxy was right. He did want to be here, and not just as a favor to his sister. His thoughts had shifted. Brooke lived in them far more than he was prepared for. He knew he needed to stall those feelings in their tracks, but something deep inside said he didn't care if he was ready or not. And that scared him more than anything.

"You okay, handsome?" Roxy asked, peering up at him—her eyelids caked with blue eyeshadow. It suited her.

"Yep. Sorry." He cleared his throat. "Just processing." He turned his attention on Brooke. "Let's start at the beginning. Did you notice anything amiss when you pulled up?"

She paced her living room rug. "Well, I thought I saw a

shadow wisp by the garage window when I got out of the car, but I told myself I was just being paranoid. I figured, or tried to convince myself, it was just a reflection off the windowpane."

"And then?" he asked, surprised at the ache pulsing inside to wrap her in his arms and comfort her.

She ran a shaky hand through her hair. "I came inside, and everything looked normal. I moved into the kitchen to grab a drink, and that's when I heard it. . . ."

"It?" he asked.

She wrapped her arms around herself. "Loud. Explosive. Like glass shattering. I looked to the door leading into the garage." She rubbed her arms. "It was cracked open. I always, *always* lock that door, so I bolted to Roxy's. As I ran by my fence, I heard footsteps. Someone running fast. I looked up and saw a man in black hop over the back wall of my fence."

Noah stilled. "You *saw* someone?"

She nodded.

"You should have told me right away. We need to start a search." Pulling out his phone, he dialed the local police, who had a larger force and could canvas more area. They answered, he identified himself, and then handed the phone to Brooke. He listened intently while she described the flash of black she saw. His muscles tightened at the very thought of someone being so near. Of someone . . . He cut those thoughts off before his heated anger got the best of him.

Brooke ended the call and handed the phone back to Noah. "The officer said they'd send a few patrol cars to canvas the area, but with the lack of description and the time lapsed, it was unlikely they'd be able to find him."

"So it was a *him*?"

She sank down and grabbed a throw pillow, her fingers fidgeting with the cream tassels fringing it. "I don't know." She shook her head, her brow creased. "I'm so sorry. I should have thought to tell you about the intruder. I was just so startled."

He sank down beside her on the couch and wrapped his arm around her shoulders. "It's okay. I'm sure it was very unsettling."

She looked up at him and blinked. The hurt on her face radiated in his chest, his muscles squeezing tight.

"Thank you," she said. "For being here."

He nodded, fearful of what might leave his mouth if he opened it. As soon as Brodie was stopped, he needed to keep his distance from Brooke Kesler. Not because of her. She was wonderful. Rather because of his reaction when he was around her. One he'd vowed never to feel again.

After a deep exhale, Brooke straightened, and he pulled his arm back to his side, an electric sensation pulsing through it. He cleared his throat, somehow managing to get back on task. "Have you been in the garage yet?"

She swiped at the tears on her cheeks. "No."

"I know this isn't easy, but—"

"I'll be fine," she said, standing.

He followed her to the garage, and Roxy bounded after them.

"Not the VW!" Brooke shrieked, lunging off the lone concrete step.

"Whoa!" Noah hooked her around the waist before her feet hit the floor and yanked her back. She fell into his hold, the top of her head cresting the bottom of his chin. He startled at how good she felt.

"There's broken glass all over the floor," he said on a clarifying exhale. "We can't touch anything until Emmy runs it."

A quiver of a sob racked through her, but she nodded.

He let go, and she stepped from his embrace. An empty hollowness clung to his arms.

Dude, get your head in the game. This isn't you. Not anymore.

"I'm so sorry, love," Roxy said, hugging Brooke in her slender

185

arms, her hot pink athletic top a stark contrast to Brooke's blue shirt. "Let me get you a glass of water."

"Thanks." As Roxy headed toward the kitchen, Brooke wiped her eyes and let her gaze run over the destruction.

Noah wondered why the classic VW meant so much to her, but between Roxy's comment and Brooke's reaction, it clearly did. "I will figure out a way to prove Brodie did this." His jaw tensed. He wouldn't stop until he did. "And I promise I'll keep you safe until he's behind bars."

"Thanks." She sniffed. "But it's not that. That's not why . . ." She gestured to her tear-filled eyes.

Confusion riddled through him. If she wasn't upset about Brodie's break-in . . . "Then, what?"

"That was my grandparents' VW bus," she said, her voice cracking. "We spent summers in it road-tripping." A bittersweet smile crossed her face. "We had the best adventures in it." Her shoulders dipped. "I was planning to restore it."

"You still can," he said, his voice more of a hushed whisper than he'd intended.

"Yeah." She exhaled. "I just can't believe Brodie would go this far. He knew how much the bus meant to me. Even promised to help me fix it up before we broke up." She raked a hand through her hair. "What's wrong with him?"

"Some men get angry, even violent, when they don't get things their way. He wants you, and he's blistering mad you don't want him back."

"Why would I? He's controlling, loses his temper, and—" She stopped short.

Noah's jaw clenched. Had Brodie touched her? His muscles tightened. The very thought of a man laying a hand on a woman burned his blood. If that was the case, his next meeting with Brodie would be far from polite. He didn't want to Hulk-out on her, but that's how he felt—ready to throttle the man who'd hurt her. He worked to keep his voice even, his temper in check.

"Is that why you have the restraining order against him? Because of his . . . temper?" he asked, refusing to force her to share something she wasn't ready to.

Her right foot rolled in and her jaw shifted in that way his sister Kenzie's did when she was trying not to cry. "Yes." Her voice was barely audible, but he'd heard it, and thoughts of throttling Brodie flashed in his brain.

He crooked his finger ever-so-gently under her chin and angled her head up.

Shame wallowed in her eyes as her gaze locked on his.

"*You* are a very strong woman." He admired her a great deal.

Confusion misted in her eyes, spreading across her pinched face. "What?"

"You broke it off with Brodie. You got a restraining order on him. You're the brave one. Brodie is a pig."

She looked down, then back up at him. "Just so you know . . . it wasn't like that. . . ." She cleared her throat, rolling her right foot in again. It was the cutest nervous tell he'd ever seen.

"I mean," she continued, and he just listened, giving her the time and space she deserved. "It could have been." She released a shaky exhale. "Brodie touched me once, and I ended it."

A mix of emotions tracked through him—rage for what Brodie did, compassion for the amazingly brave woman standing before him. "Thank you for trusting me enough to share that with me."

"You're one of the most trustworthy men I know."

"Me?" he couldn't help asking.

"Your reputation around base aside, the faith and trust your sisters have in you says it all."

Warmth spread through him that after all she'd been through she trusted him with something very personal and painful.

She exhaled. "I just wish . . ."

"Wish?" he prompted.

"Wish I'd never dated Brodie in the first place."

He leaned against the doorframe, slipping his hands into his tactical-pants pockets. "It's easy to regret the past or choices we've made. Believe me, I understand." Those bad memories liked to resurface, never quite leaving him. "But," he said, pushing off the doorframe and stepping back to her side, "living in the past only gives people who've hurt you more power over you. It's best to forget them and move forward, never looking back." Now, if only he could practice what he preached.

A question dangled on the edge of her tongue. He could read it in her fidgeting hands and more so in her softly narrowed eyes. "You understand?" she finally asked.

He usually bypassed answering by changing the subject, but she'd trusted him enough to share what fully happened between her and Brodie.

He brushed a hand over his buzzed-cut hair—some active-duty habits died hard. "Understand about bad choices?"

She nodded.

"Yeah. I'm sorry to say I do." He gestured to the VW. "But I'll be happy to help you restore it."

Her eyebrows lifted. "You will?"

"Sure. I restored my '87 Jeep Sahara."

"That would be awesome. Thanks."

"Absolutely, but for now, my first priority is keeping you safe."

"I'll lock up good and set the alarm." She tilted her head. "What is it?"

"I set the alarm when I left."

"Did it go off when you got home?"

"No." Her face pinched. "How could he . . . ?"

"Did you have the alarm while you and Brodie were dating?"

"No." She shook her head. "I put it in after we broke up and he started harassing me."

Not good. "When Em gets here to process the place, I'll make sure she runs prints and diagnostics on the alarm. Is your code something familiar like your birthday or—" He stopped short as she grimaced. "Your birthday?"

She gave a full-tooth oops smile. "I wanted to make it easy to remember."

"I get it, but unfortunately that makes it easier for other people to figure out." Which meant the intruder most likely knew her well enough to know her birthday. "Brodie knows your birthday?"

She nodded.

His and Brodie's next talk definitely wouldn't be as cordial as the last.

Brooke rolled over in bed, stretching out. She'd lit a lavender and eucalyptus candle on her dresser and sprayed a relaxation mist she'd picked up last week. Anything that could help the drumming of her heart settle.

Emmy and Logan had come out and processed the house, alarm system, and garage. They found numerous prints, some belonging to Brodie in the garage, but as he'd spent time there while they were dating, that couldn't prove anything. But they didn't have to let him know that, according to Noah, who was going to pay him another visit in the morning.

But tonight, Noah was on her couch. He'd insisted on staying, not liking the escalation of the threat. Not only had Brodie been in her home, he'd caused a lot of damage, and his intrusion was a clear sign that he wanted her to doubt that she was truly safe in Noah's care. But it hadn't worked—at least not the latter. Noah was the first man she felt secure with in longer than she could remember. He was as stable as they came. A good agent and a good man.

Brooke blinked at the flame's shadow dancing along the ceiling. Rumor around base was that Noah wasn't much for dating. Sort of a self-proclaimed bachelor. She'd met a few in her day, but they were rare. She'd just assumed he was committed to his job or not the relationship type, but tonight when he'd talked about understanding making bad choices when it came to relationships, his face had an edge of hurt to it. Perhaps Mr. Handsome had more reasons for remaining single than she knew.

Fluffing the pillow and resituating, she looked to the window. She always kept it cracked, but not tonight. Noah recommended everything be locked up tight, and considering someone had hacked her alarm system, she couldn't agree more.

She stared at the drawn shade, wondering if Brodie was out there watching, planning his next point of attack. Her jaw clenched, heat burning through her. She was done allowing him to scare, hurt, or intimidate her. He knew how much she loved that VW, all the memories of adventures and fun it held for her. He'd hit her where it hurt, but contrary to what he'd tried to accomplish, he'd only ticked her off. Lifting her pillow, she looked at her service weapon and smiled. Next time he came, she'd be ready. If Noah didn't kill him first.

The branch scraped his forearm as he shifted, sweeping leaves to the side for a better view. The main light in Brooke's bedroom shut off a while ago, but something flickered through the drawn shade. He'd gotten to her. *Good.*

He smiled. "Sleep well, Brooke," he whispered, his exhale warm in the cool night air. "You're going to need it for tomorrow."

Extricating himself from his camouflaged position, he moved down the silent street, a near whistle dancing across his tongue.

At first, he'd floundered, but now he had purpose.

Make Brooke suffer like he had.

THIRTY-SIX

Mason hopped out of his Impala and walked around to Rissi's side of the car.

"Other than the follow," he said as she climbed out and shut the door behind her, "I had a great time today. Thanks for introducing me to sand surfing."

"I'm glad you had fun, and that was some impressive driving, losing the follow like that."

"I just hope Emmy can find who the car belongs to."

"Me too."

But for the brief moment they had left together, he didn't want to think about that. Didn't want to think about anything but her. "And you?" he asked, stepping less than a foot from her.

"Me?"

He dipped his chin. "Did you have fun?"

She smiled. "Of course I did."

"I'm glad." He took a step closer until nothing separated them but the air. "It's good to see you happy. To see you free."

"Same," she said, her eyes locked on his.

The day had been perfect, but he wasn't ready for it to end. Not yet. She needed sleep. They both did, but after a decade apart, saying good-bye, even for just the night, was painful. "I'm still pumped up from the day," he said, knowing it was the fact he'd spent the day with her that had him amped. "You wanna come up for a cup of coffee? I'm pretty sure I have some decaf." He'd completely understand if she passed.

"Okay," she said, "but I'll take regular."

"Living on the edge, huh?" he said at her caffeine-fueled choice so late at night.

"Actually, caffeine doesn't keep me awake at night. No clue why."

"Interesting. Yet one more thing I learned about you today."

"Is that right?" she asked, following him up his front steps. "And what else did you learn?"

He unlocked the door and pushed it open for her. "Animals like you, and you have a really gentle nature with them. Both Socks and . . . Mags, was it?"

"Yep," she said, ducking under his arm to enter. "Maggie is such a cool dog. She goes surfing on the front of Ashley's board."

"Seriously?" He followed her inside and shut the door behind them.

"You'll have to see it sometime," she said, leaning back against his front table.

"I'd like that." He reached around her for the table lamp.

She didn't move, just stood there as his arm wrapped around her. He clicked on the lamp, and it emitted a soft glow. The rest of the cottage remained shadowed in darkness. He knew he should move, but he couldn't. Not when he was this close to her. "Maybe next time we go sand surfing?" He stood directly in front of her, his knees brushing hers.

"Next time?" She smiled. Her gaze fluttered to the ground, then lifted and locked back on his. "I didn't scare you away?"

"Not at all." He rested his left hand on the table, both arms now encircling her. He moved ever so slightly closer and swallowed, his throat parched. "And . . . I'm not scaring you away?"

Her mouth was so close, he could feel her breath tickling his chin.

She shook her head.

He reached up and cupped the back of her neck, his fingers spreading through her hair, then leaned in close, whispering against her ear. "*This* doesn't scare you?"

"No." She inched closer to him. "Should it?"

It scared him. Not the fact that he loved her, but the depth and intensity of his love was like nothing he'd ever experienced.

He shifted to face her, his gaze dropping to her lips. He hovered over them, their noses touching, and pressed his forehead to hers. He didn't want to push too hard, too fast.

"Do you want me to move?" he asked, praying with everything in him she said no, but he had to be sure she wanted this as badly as him.

"Yes," she murmured against his lips.

His stomach dropped, but he shifted to step back.

She grabbed ahold of his shirttail, halting him. "Wrong way."

Adrenaline coursed through his veins. "Rissi," he whispered, as his lips melded with hers.

Years of longing, wanting, loving . . . flooded into the single, earth-shattering kiss.

Mason held Rissi's hand as they walked up her porch. Their remaining time together ticked down to seconds.

She rested her shoulder against the doorframe, keys jingling in her hands. She looked up at him with a sweet smile. Man, she took his breath away.

"It was sweet of you, but you really didn't have to drive home with me."

"Of course I didn't have to," he said, stepping closer. The jangling wind chimes competed with his pulse whooshing through his ears. He brushed a strand of silky hair behind her ear and dipped his head as he said, "You are the strongest, bravest, most capable woman I know, but . . ." He paused with a shake of his head. "Nah, it's getting too late. I better go."

"But what?"

"It can wait."

"What can?"

"I was going to tell you a story, but"—he looked at his watch—"it's late, and we have to be at the station in a handful of hours."

"And you have to meet Jason and Brad in less than that for your swim."

His brows hiked up. "How'd you know about that?"

"They told me while you were giving me a heart attack searching for Max."

"I had to try."

"I know. So did Jason. He said your exploits in Kodiak were legendary."

A smile cracked on his lips. "Oh, he did, did he?"

She ran her hand along the edge of his jacket. "Mmm-hmm."

He swept a hand through his hair. "He needs to get some new stories."

"Not until he tells me some of those. And speaking of stories, I want to hear yours."

"Okay, but the quick version and then you get some shut-eye. Deal?"

"Only if you will too."

He chuckled. "Yes, ma'am." He looked around. "Why don't we sit on the swing." He gestured to the porch swing with oversized mandala-patterned pillows on it.

He waited until she sat and then took the seat beside her, his knee touching hers—the only illumination was the glow from her porch light and the full moon overhead.

She propped her elbow on the back of the swing and rested her head on her hand. "Story time, mister."

He rubbed his thighs. "Okay, so the reason I asked if I could see you home was because of something that happened in boot camp."

She waited for him to continue.

"So, I was a lowly recruit. It was my first week in, and we were all marching to chow. We stopped outside the mess hall to wait for our turn to enter, and I saw Senior Chief Harding."

He shifted sideways to better face her. "Picture a grizzled Lou Gossett Jr. from *An Officer and a Gentleman*. He never cracked a smile. Never relaxed his . . . well, anything. So the base XO was heading for the chow hall. As she neared the senior chief, he ripped the most perfect, crisp salute I'd ever seen. She returned it, and then he dashed to the door to hold it open as she entered.

"Time passed," he continued, "and in week six, I was interviewing for recruit company commander because our current one got rolled back. During the interview, Senior Chief was talking about military bearing. He asked if I had any questions, and I couldn't help myself. I asked about his salute and then breaking ranks as he hurried to open the door for the XO."

The breeze riffled through Rissi's hair, and the scent of pineapple wafted on the wind. His mind snagged. *Pineapple?* Must be her lotion or shampoo. Whatever it was, he'd never imagined it could smell so good.

Refocusing on the story so he could finish up and she could get some shut-eye, he jumped back in. "That was the first and only time I saw Senior Chief smile. He went on to explain that there's military bearing and gentlemanly bearing and that the two aren't mutually exclusive. That talk anchored in my brain."

She cupped his face. "I love that." Her gaze dropped to his lips, and closing the distance between them, she kissed him tenderly, then stood and headed for her door. "'Night, Mason. Sleep well."

He'd try, but after that kiss . . . not likely. Maybe the brisk night air slapping his face on his walk home would shake him out of his stupor.

He waited until Rissi was inside and he heard the dead bolt click in place before he turned for the sidewalk. He shrugged his hands into his pockets and released an exhale, an edge of concern clinging to him. There was no need for worry. Rissi could most certainly take care of herself, but things were shifting. Someone had been following them. The question was who and, more importantly, why?

THIRTY-SEVEN

Despite being short on sleep, Rissi woke early. She jabbed the punching bag in her guest room, trying to work out the energy still pulsing through her from their kiss . . . kisses. She hit the bag with an uppercut, once, twice, a third time. Her limbs warmed, sweat beading on her brow. She still couldn't believe they'd admitted their feelings for each other, let alone kissed.

She took a deep inhale and released it. Pulling off her gloves, she grabbed her terry cloth towel and swiped it across her forehead. Her water bottle rested on the bedroom window ledge. She grabbed it, managed to drop it on the floor with a clang, then retrieved it. She shook out her hands. Maybe she'd been going too long. She looked at the maize bag and decided to work on her hooks tomorrow morning instead. She glanced at the analog clock on the wall. She was cutting it close. She'd just had so much energy buzzing through her when she woke. She closed her eyes, feeling Mason's lips on hers again. Her teenage dream had come true, but as an adult, it was even sweeter—deeper and far more powerful. Things like this didn't just happen.

Thank you, Jesus. This was all you. How can I thank you for all you've done?

She shifted her head side to side while shaking out her heated arms.

Her doorbell rang, and she looked once again at the clock—

0630. A little early for visitors. Grabbing her Glock off the side table, she moved for the door. Not one to be paranoid, it felt odd having her guard up at home, but after last night's follow, it was better to be packing than sorry.

Gun in hand, she stood to the side of the door. "Who is it?"

"Caleb."

She lowered the gun, slipped it into the back of her workout capris, and opened the door.

Caleb stood on her porch with two iced coffees and a ribboned bakery box. "I thought we could share breakfast."

"Sure. Just let me get cleaned up."

"What's with the extra security?" he said, gesturing to her Glock. "And you never ask who it is, though I repeatedly ask you to."

Mason had also asked. She wasn't sharing that with Caleb. He'd been asking her for years, and now Mason asks, and she decides it's a good idea. But given the circumstances . . . "We were followed last night."

"What happened?" he asked, setting the bakery box and her coffee down on the turquoise runner atop the buffet table.

"We were leaving the Outer Banks."

He frowned. "I thought you were supposed to be resting."

"I couldn't sleep, so we went sandboarding."

He arched a brow. "We?" A mixture of wariness and hope hung on his handsome face.

She bit her bottom lip. This was going to hurt him, and that's the last thing she wanted to do. "Me and Mason."

"I see." His expression and voice held even. "Why don't you get cleaned up before the cinnamon buns get cold."

"Samantha's Bakery?"

"Your favorite." He smiled, but it lacked his usual joy when it was just the two of them.

"I'll be down in ten," she said, hurrying up the stairs.

After a quick shower, she pulled on black knit shorts and her

Sharks T-shirt she'd gotten at the last game. Running a brush through her hair, she left it to air dry.

She found Caleb enjoying his coffee on the front porch. He handed her the iced drink, which looked suspiciously like the Hawaiian High she often ordered.

"How did you . . . ?"

"Lindy told me it's your favorite."

"She's such a sweetheart." Rissi took a seat in the rocker beside him and swallowed an indulgent first sip.

Caleb arched a brow. "Good?"

"Mmm-hmmm."

"Try one of these." He offered her one of the gooey cinnamon buns on a paper plate that had been in a slit in the side of the box. "Be careful," he said, handing it over. "It's warm."

The scent of vanilla, cinnamon, and sugary glaze swirled beneath her nose. She shifted the plate from her lap to her hands. Caleb was right, they were warm. Warm enough to make the bottom of the plate resting atop her bare legs a bit too hot.

So he'd gone to Hunga Bunga Java's and Samantha's. Was today going to be the day she'd been dreading? It was past time, but her heart still ached over the thought of hurting him. He was her friend.

She swiped a dollop of icing from the corner of her mouth before it plopped on her top. "Thanks for breakfast."

"No problem." He took a sip and set his cup on the porch floor. "I want to talk to you about something."

Her heart sank. She knew it.

Caleb inhaled. "I know you don't feel the same way I do."

"Caleb, I—" She set her plate on the edge of the planter table beside her.

"Please," he said. "Let me get this out."

She nodded.

He cleared his throat. "I should have said something when these feelings started, but I didn't want you to feel any pressure.

Then I was nervous about your answer, and then . . . time slipped away. Now it's too late." He looked at her. "It is too late, isn't it?"

It wasn't that it was too late. It was simply that she didn't share those feelings for him, but there was no need to go there. It would only hurt him. So she nodded instead.

Caleb took a stiff inhale. "I thought so."

"Caleb, I hope you know how much you mean to me. As a friend. As a teammate."

"I know."

"I'm sorry."

He cupped his hand over hers. "There's nothing to be sorry about. You either care for someone romantically or you don't. Your heart belongs somewhere else. I knew it the first time I saw you and Mason together."

Words tumbled in her mind, but the right ones wouldn't come.

He squeezed her hand, then pulled it back and stood.

"Please, stay and have breakfast," she said.

"Actually, I think I'll get in a short run before work."

"You sure?"

"Yeah." A soft smile creased his lips. "I'll see you at the station."

"Okay. Thanks for the roll and coffee."

"You're welcome." He paused at the edge of her porch and looked back at her. "I'm happy for you. You know that, right?"

Tears beaded in her eyes. He was such a good man. A good friend. She nodded.

He turned and strode to his car.

She watched him pull away, praying God would bring him the woman created for him.

Rissi ran in to Hunga Bunga Java. She'd volunteered to grab coffee for the team on her way into work. It allowed her to pick one of the drinks of the day each morning without making someone else call her with the specials.

She decided to order another Hawaiian High—espresso, almond milk, chocolate, coconut, and banana. Even after downing one less than an hour earlier, she savored the first sip.

"You must really like those," Lindy said.

"It's amazing." Best espresso drink. Ever.

"Excellent." Lindy, being the manager of Hunga Bunga Java, handled all the drink creations. She also picked up shifts at Dockside. Rissi admired her. It couldn't be easy holding down two jobs and raising one adorable son all on her own. But when her husband up and left, he'd given Lindy no choice.

"Want the usual for the rest of the gang?" she asked.

"Yep. Plus, one . . ." Rissi studied the specialty drink list, wondering which Mason would like. *Mason* . . . How was she going to walk into work and act like nothing had happened between them?

"One?" Lindy asked.

"Oh. Sorry. Brain hasn't kicked in today." It hadn't kicked back in since Mason's lips first touched hers.

She exhaled. It was going to be a long day. "Let's try the Italian Slammer."

"You got it, darling."

Her hands full of carrying trays and a bag of bakery items, Rissi maneuvered her way into the car and settled everything in place for the remainder of the ride into work. Her heart thumped in her chest, her pulse hammering in her ears.

Please, Father, help me focus. Help me to be professional and guide me and Mason through it all. Amen.

Reversing out of the drive, she pulled onto the main road leading back to the station. When she hit play on her iPod, Chris LeDoux started singing "Riding for a Fall" in that gravelly voice she loved.

As she arrived at the office parking lot, she found Mason leaning against the grill of his Impala.

Had he been waiting for her?

Tingles shot through her. *Calm down, girl.*

He strode to her and, draping his arm along the roof, leaned in the opened window. "Can I help you carry anything?"

"Yeah. Thanks. That'd be great." She collected the first drink carrier and handed it through the window to Mason.

"One more," she said, handing him the second one.

She grabbed the bakery items and her purse, then realized she still had bare feet. She felt around the floorboard with her right foot. Finally touching one of her flats, she slipped her foot inside.

"Need help in there?" Mason asked, setting the drink trays on the hood of her Fiat.

"No. I'm okay," she said, completely stretched out across the passenger-side floorboard.

He came around to the passenger door, opened it, and bent down. A moment later, he held up her shoe. "Allow me," he said, slipping his fingers around her ankle. He lifted her foot toward him, pausing for the briefest of moments, then he trailed his finger along the arch of her foot.

She swallowed, her mouth parched.

He slipped her foot in the flat and stood.

"Thanks," she managed to mutter.

He retrieved the drink carriers from the hood of her car and gestured with a lift of his head for her to enter first.

Now, if only she could walk straight.

THIRTY-EIGHT

"All right. Everyone is here," Noah said. "Grab your coffees, and let's hit the case board. We've got some major updates."

Mason sat on Rissi's right, but this time Caleb sat on the far end of the couch. Emmy sank down beside her and whispered, "Hey, lady."

She smiled. "Hi, Em."

"We need to talk after this."

"Okay. Good talk or bad?"

"Depends who you are," she whispered.

Noah stood at the case board, staring at the new dry erase markers lined up on the silver tray.

He lifted one. Neon pink.

Rissi tried to stifle a laugh, but her amusement squeaked out.

Noah dipped his head, his brows arching as he pinned his gaze on Emmy. "Neon now? And pink of all colors?"

Emmy crossed one leg over the other. Rissi didn't remember ever seeing her in dress pants. Usually it was a skirt or dress, but she looked adorable as always with the navy slacks and a white blouse with blue polka dots and frilled fabric at the edge of her shoulders. "Neon is back in," she said.

Noah just shook his head. Rissi was tempted to remind him it was his own fault. When Em volunteered to be in charge of purchasing office supplies, he'd jumped on the offer. But Em had warned him that she'd find a way to bring light into the darkness they often encountered at work.

Eighties-colored markers were definitely a hit in Rissi's book.

"You said you had some big updates," she said, trying to shift the heat off Emmy.

"Yes," Noah said. "Let's start with Caleb."

"Right." Caleb explained how he and Noah had spent yesterday afternoon and what they'd learned thus far. "We plan on sitting down today and combing through the file Austin Kelly provided."

"We knew there wasn't something quite right about Gwyneth," Mason said, leaning forward, resting his forearms on his thighs, shifting ever so slightly closer to Rissi in the movement.

Rissi bit back a smile. She loved him so near, but she retargeted her focus on the casework ahead. "Let us know what you find."

"Of course." Noah nodded. "Now, let's dig into the excitement you two had yesterday." His astute gaze shifted between her and Mason. Warmth flooded her cheeks. He was talking about the follow, wasn't he? She inhaled. Noah was an excellent investigator. Surely, he saw the shift between her and Mason. She had to do her best to keep their relationship out of the workplace, at least until she and Mason knew where things would go, but she was jumping the gun.

"I ran the plates," Emmy said, saving her from having to open her mouth. Noah wanted to know about the tail, but when it came to yesterday's excitement her thoughts went in a very different direction—straight to her right.

"The car was reported stolen from an airport garage two days ago," Emmy continued.

"Great." Mason sighed.

"Oddly enough," Emmy said, a curious smile dancing on her lips, "it was returned to the same slot in the middle of the night."

"What?" Rissi turned toward Emmy, frowning. That was a first.

"I've tracked down a lot of stolen cars, but I've never seen one returned." Emmy passed a series of photographs to Rissi.

Taking hold, she thumbed through them. A black SUV parked on level three near the far end of the garage. She passed the first photograph to Mason. His finger brushed hers for the barest of seconds but tingles still shot through her. Taking a fortifying breath, she moved on to the second photograph. It was time-stamped the next day and showed an empty spot where the SUV had been. The final photo time-stamped from this morning showed the vehicle returned to the same spot. Rissi shook her head, passing the last photograph on. It had to be the most bizarre theft she'd witnessed, and she'd seen her fair share.

"Clearly there are cameras there," Caleb said, passing the pictures on to Logan. "Did they capture who took the car and subsequently returned it?"

"Airport security is running through the footage now," Emmy said.

"I'm heading over there when we're done here to take a look," Logan said.

"Good." Noah nodded.

"Who does the car actually belong to?" Rissi asked.

"A Rick Carson." Emmy handed Rissi a small stack of printed-out pages. She took one, passed the rest on, and stared down in surprise. "He has a record?"

"Yep," Emmy said.

Rissi could hear the smile in her voice. "Not every day a criminal reports something of his own stolen." It was almost comical. Returning her attention to the printout, her gaze scanned down the page. *Assault. Breaking and entering.* "Grand theft auto?" she asked, nearly in sync with Mason.

"So the guy who got his car stolen has stolen cars on at

least . . ." Mason eyes skimmed to the bottom of the sheet. "Five counts?"

"Yep," Emmy said, shifting to cross her ankles rather than her legs.

"Our Em always finds the dirt," Logan said, squeezing Emmy's shoulders.

"I'm betting we find Rick Carson stole his own car," Rissi said.

"Wouldn't that be a twist." Logan chuckled.

"Okay," Noah said. "Let's move on to Greg Barnes's death. I got a couple calls on my way in this morning. First, Joel Waters is being discharged this afternoon and is scheduled to head back out to *Dauntless* this evening."

"Wow. Not a lot of rest there," Em said.

"No, but it sure sounds like he's needed on the rig. The second call I received was from Ed."

Rissi scooted forward, anxious to hear what Ed had to say.

"The mechanics finished taking the compressor apart. They discovered what they believe to be the cause of the problem. They need to wait for Joel to make the final determination, but right now it looks like the gas leak was the result of a failed flange gasket. The weird thing is one of the bolts in the flange was missing."

"So it fell out or was defective?" Caleb asked.

"Ed said no to both."

Rissi frowned. "I don't understand."

Noah exhaled. "Neither do the guys on the platform. They took the entire compressor apart, and the bolt is gone."

"Gone?" Mason said.

"Gone. As in nowhere in the compressor. Since it's an enclosed piece of machinery, if the flange bolt had fallen out of place, they would have found it within the machine itself. They even did a sweep of the entire surrounding area and nothing."

"And it couldn't be defective because . . . ?" Logan asked.

Em patted his face. "You're so pretty," she teased.

"You say that like it's not a compliment," he teased back.

Rissi rolled her eyes. Those two.

"According to the records," Noah said, "Greg Barnes performed the safety inspection less than a month ago, and he noted that all parts were intact and in proper working order."

"Okay, so what happened to the bolt?" Rissi asked, her mind racing through the possibilities, but she kept coming back to one.

"Someone took it out on purpose," Mason said, sitting back and crossing an ankle over his knee.

"That's how it looks," Noah agreed.

"Which would make the gas leak foul play," Rissi said, "but was Greg Barnes's death intentional?"

"It's hard to imagine someone would know Greg Barnes would need a smoke and that he'd take it there," Logan said.

"But what if it was his daily habit?" Mason said.

"Or what if this curse stuff was used to really freak him out, knowing he'd smoke," Rissi said. "But it's still thin."

"Maybe it had nothing to do with killing Greg Barnes and everything to do with halting production," Mason said, shifting, resting his arm on the back edge of the couch. "Ed mentioned the environmentalists taking some nasty tactics."

"Any hard evidence to support that?" Noah asked.

"Not yet," Mason said.

"Caleb and I were told there are rumors surrounding Gwyneth and her willingness to break the law if it meant supporting her cause," Noah said. "Which coordinates with what Ed Scott told you."

"I'll run with that," Emmy said, noting it down on her legal pad. "I'll see what I can dig up now that I have a direction to go. If Gwyneth has broken the law at some point, there may be charges filed against her, a mug shot . . ."

"If she was ever caught," Rissi said.

Noah took a stiff inhale, then exhaled. "It does appear she's really good at covering her tracks."

"I found the same thing in my preliminary searches," Emmy said. "But if I dig deep enough, I'll find her."

Rissi smiled. Em was the master of finding anyone or anything. Last summer, she'd found a petty officer first class who'd gone AWOL eight years earlier, and he ended up serving his time.

"Okay, Em," Noah said. "You concentrate on finding what you can on Gwyneth. Logan, how are things coming with the Freedom Group's finances?"

"They take a lot of large anonymous donations. Donations I can't find anyone writing off on their taxes."

"Interesting." Noah noted it on the board, and Rissi smothered a smile as the neon pink writing filled the white space.

"They work almost exclusively off donations, not grants," Logan continued. "However, most marine biologists, which the crew of the *Freedom* predominantly are, work off grants. It's an odd combination. Em and I are still trying to compile a complete list of the team on board. Everything surrounding the organization and its namesake ship are murky. But I'll dig deeper as soon as I get back from the airport."

"Okay." Noah directed his attention at Mason and Rissi. "What's your plan for today?"

"We're going to start interviewing crew one. They were the crew on rotation between when the safety inspection was performed, and the day that Greg Barnes died."

"Crew one rotated out the morning of Greg Barnes's death," Mason added.

Noah tapped the marker against his palm. "Definitely convenient timing."

"Agreed," Mason said.

"All right, one more thing before we go," Noah said. "Coast Guard Medic Brooke Kesler's home was broken into the last two nights."

"What?" Concern flipped Rissi's gut. "Is she all right?" Brooke was a sweet lady and a fantastic flight medic, and they'd been spending more time together because of their mutual friendship with Gabby.

"She's fine," Noah said, an ounce of concern clinging to his usually steady voice.

Rissi quirked a brow. Not like her boss at all. He was always confident, steadfast in their ability to work a case or protect someone. But . . . she studied his set jaw. He was worried about Brooke?

"Finn did a full run-through after the first break-in before he and Gabby headed to the airport," Noah said. "They called me in to keep an eye on Brooke and to work the case. Em's been working the evidence samples Finn collected, along with the samples she and Logan collected last night."

"Any suspects?" Caleb asked.

"She has an ex, Brodie O'Connell, who has been harassing her for ending things. The perpetrator left a message in lipstick on her mirror basically saying 'You hurt me. Now I hurt you.' Finn took a sample of the lipstick."

Em nodded.

"If that doesn't sound like an angry, unstable ex, I don't know what does," Rissi said.

"One more thing," Noah said, once again addressing Rissi and Mason. "The NTSB liaison, Jeremy Brandt, called just before you two walked in. They salvaged the wreckage, and it's being systematically combed through. They'll figure out what happened and will continue to keep us in the loop."

"Great," Rissi said, anxious to know what had gone so wrong.

THIRTY-NINE

"Okay," Noah said. "Logan, get a mug shot and anything you can find on Rick Carson, our car owner and possible thief." Noah shook his head. "Never thought I'd say that sentence in my lifetime."

He shifted his gaze back to Logan. "Take any photos you find online that might help you identify him, then head on over to view the airport surveillance footage."

"Roger that," Logan said, striding for his desk.

"Caleb, head over to the address that Em has on Carson. Interview him, see if you can shake anything loose."

"On it," he said, getting to his feet.

"Ris and Mason, you already know what you're working on." Rissi nodded.

Noah set down the pink marker. "I'm going to have a chat with Brodie O'Connell."

"Keep us posted," Rissi said.

"Will do," Noah said, heading for the station door, followed by Caleb. He turned and looked at Rissi. "Good luck today."

"Thanks." She smiled.

"I'm going to grab a drink for the road," Mason said, heading for the kitchen. "Can I get either of you ladies one?"

"A gentleman," Emmy said. "I'd love a LaCroix."

"You got it." He looked to Rissi. The way he looked at her was unlike the way he looked at anyone else—like she was the only one in the room. "And you?"

"I'll take the same as Emmy. Thanks."

He nodded and disappeared into the kitchen.

Emmy leaned over as the door shut behind him.

"So what did you want to talk about?" Rissi asked.

"We need to keep this between us," Em said.

It wasn't like Emmy to keep things on the down low. Emmy never slandered anyone or repeated a rumor that might be hurtful, but she definitely kept up on the lives of those around her, and of those they investigated. Which made Rissi wonder how much Emmy knew about her and Mason. If this was an attempt to get juicy details, she was going to throttle Em.

Logan came and joined them. "News time?" he asked.

"Yeah." There was definite hesitancy in Em's voice. What was she about to tell them?

Emmy's gaze shifted to Mason exiting the kitchen with three coconut LaCroixs in hand. "Sorry, man," he said to Logan. "Want me to grab you something?" he asked as he passed out the cold sparkling waters.

"I'm good, but thanks," Logan said. "Sit down and join us. Em has some news."

"What's going on?" Rissi asked, wondering why she hadn't shared during case-board time.

"I got a line on Gwyneth Lansing," Em began. "Gwyneth spent last academic year teaching marine biology at University of North Carolina Wilmington."

"Okay." Lucas attended UNC Wilmington, but so did a ton of other students. Rissi wasn't ready to jump to any conclusions, but it was intriguing both had been on the same campus.

"We looked at her class rosters," Logan said, "to see if any names lined up from the *Dauntless*. It was a long shot, but it panned out."

Rissi shifted, concerned with the direction this was going. "What did you find?"

"Caleb's nephew, Lucas, took two of Gwyneth's classes before he dropped out and went to work on *Dauntless*," Em said, straight to the point albeit with compassion.

Rissi's stomach plummeted. "Are you sure?"

"We checked twice," Logan said. "Even called the registrar to confirm."

Rissi shut her eyes. It didn't prove anything specific, but it did prove a connection between someone on *Dauntless* and someone on the *Freedom*.

"I have the dorm information of Lucas's old roommate, who also was in one of Gwyneth's classes." Emmy handed Rissi a slip of paper with the guy's name, the dorm name, and his room number. "Maybe he can tell you if the two ever interacted beyond normal classroom conversation."

Rissi knew what Em and Logan were getting at, but they were skirting around it. She prayed they weren't right, but they had to make sure Lucas wasn't involved with Gwyneth in any way other than student to teacher. "We'll stop by the campus today."

"If you need us, we can help with interviewing crew one," Emmy said.

"Thanks. We'll talk with"—Rissi looked down at the slip of paper—"Seth, and if we need to follow a lead, we'll call you."

"Sounds good." Logan nodded.

"I can't believe this is happening," Rissi said as she and Mason walked out to his Impala. While her Fiat was adorable, his car was downright awesome.

He held the passenger door open for her before walking around to his side. The scent of rugged spice swirled in the air. Did he always have to smell so alluring? She needed to concentrate on the interview before them, not on how amazing he looked or smelled.

Mason turned the key and the 350-ci V8 engine growled to life.

They pulled out of the lot before Mason asked, "Which part is hard to believe?"

"Lucas taking Gwyneth's class. The fact that there's a connection between them . . ."

"Yeah." He turned right and tapped the wheel. "I gotta say that doesn't look good."

"Not at all."

Noah once again found Brodie at the fire station. This time the firefighter who greeted him in the bay wasn't nearly as affable.

He flashed his badge. "Noah Rowley. CGIS. I'm looking for Brodie O'Connell."

"I know who you are," the dark-haired man said. "And you're barking up the wrong tree. Brodie's a good guy."

Good guys didn't lay a hand on women. "Where is he?"

The guy gestured to the back hall. "Studying for his lieutenant exam." Without another word, the guy turned back to reloading the fire engine's gear.

Noah found Brodie three doors down on the right. He sat at a round table, his back to the wall, his head down and focused on a thick test prep manual.

Noah knocked on the doorframe.

Brodie looked up, and his gaze hardened. "What do you want now?"

"Brooke's house was broken into again, and a lot of damage was done."

Brodie closed the book. A large red badge atop a blue oval covered the center of the manual. "I'm sorry to hear that, but it wasn't me."

"I didn't say that it was, but interesting you should go right to being defensive."

"Dude, come on. If you're here it's because you think I'm the one who did it." He stood and tucked the exam prep book under his arm. "But I didn't."

213

He started for the door.

Noah took a full stance in it, blocking Brodie's way. "We're not finished."

"So this is how we're going to play it?" Brodie asked, his shoulders squaring.

"Looks that way."

"You know I could kick your butt."

Noah cocked his head. "I'd like to see you try."

"And get arrested for hitting a CGIS agent. I don't think so."

"Look. You can answer my questions here, or I can haul you into the station."

"This is ridiculous," Brodie said, his cheeks flaring red. "I didn't do anything."

"Where were you last night between 1930 and 2100?"

"At Riley's." His jaw tightened.

"As in Riley's Pub?"

"Yeah, my rotation ended at 1900, and then me and a few of the guys headed to Riley's."

He had to be lying. *Wasn't he?* An unsettling, disjointed feeling swept through Noah. If Brodie really had an alibi, then who'd been at Brooke's?

Caleb pulled up the right side of the circular driveway, around the edge of the cobalt blue tiled fountain with a Greek-style sculpture of a woman holding a basket of grapes.

He rolled to a stop in front of the two-story, eighties-style home. Off-white with large windows and he'd bet at least five thousand square feet.

Stepping from the vehicle, he caught sight of the four-car garage. And just his luck, one of the bays was open.

Glancing back at the house to make sure no one had noticed

his arrival, he moved for the garage. A silver Aston Martin Vanquish was parked in the open bay.

If he owned a sweet ride like that, he'd never bother with an SUV.

"Hello," he called into the garage.

No answer.

Pulling his Glock, just in case, he stepped in and cleared the area. In the third stall over sat a black SUV that fit the description Rissi and Mason had given. He pulled out his phone and tapped off some pictures, making sure to get the license plate.

A side door opened, and a man matching Rick Carson's mug shot stepped out. "Who the heck are you, and what are you doing in my garage?" He pressed a red button on the wall.

"You didn't need to do that." Caleb lifted his badge from the chain around his neck. "I'm CGIS. I have some questions for you." Carson calling the police was superfluous.

Within moments two exceedingly muscular men appeared behind Rick Carson in the doorway, guns drawn.

Caleb looked behind him. Another two were positioned by the open bay door.

Okay, so not the police. And definitely not the best situation. At least he had a closed door serving as a wall at his back, and he was an excellent shot if things went sideways.

"I just want to talk," he said, his tone even. "That's all. We can talk here, or we can go into the station."

"Talk." Rick looked at his men and laughed. They followed suit. "Come, then." He held out an arm, gesturing him over. "Let's talk."

Caleb followed him through the door and past the two men who looked more like mercenaries than security detail. They entered a walled courtyard separating the main house from the garage.

Finally, he led Caleb out yet another set of doors on the far side of the courtyard. "By the pool is a good place to talk. Good view," Rick said. He wore white linen pants and a Tommy Bahama resort shirt with oversized pineapples on a peach background.

Caleb glanced over Rick's shoulder at the four-lane Olympic-style pool overlooking the Atlantic Ocean.

"Sit," Rick said, gesturing to a glass-and-wrought-iron table and the four chairs around it.

"Thank you." Caleb sank into one, questions pinging inside his head. Why would a man as rich as Rick Carson steal his own car and then chase down Rissi and Mason? Or . . .

Caleb looked back at the men he'd mentally named Brawn and Muscle. Where had the other two gone? He couldn't be certain, but he bet they were going through his car.

Assessing Rick in his element, Caleb decided he needed to alter his approach. "Thank you for taking time to speak with me."

Rick waved a man in a white shirt and black bow tie over. "Eddie, I'll take a rum and Coke, and our guest . . ." He looked to Caleb.

"Just a Coke please."

"Are you sure? It's British Royal Navy Imperial Rum."

That was high dollar. "Thank you, but I'm on duty."

Eddie returned with a glass of Coke with a lime wedge on the rim for Caleb and the rum and Coke for Rick.

"Thank you, Eddie, that will be all." Rick took a sip of his drink while Caleb did the same. "Please, proceed with your questions." He checked his watch. "I have a noon tee time."

"You reported your car stolen from the airport two days ago. Is that correct?"

"Yes."

"And where were you flying to?"

Rick dipped his chin, his brows arching. "Is that pertinent to the theft of my car?"

"It could be."

216

"Dayton, Ohio. I had business there. I spent two days and flew back late last night."

"How late?"

"My flight landed shortly after 11:15 p.m. Or if you prefer military time, 2315."

Conveniently *after* Rissi and Mason were tailed by his SUV.

"And when you returned?"

Rick took another sip, this one longer than the first. He set his perspiring glass down on a coaster. "My driver, Matthew, picked me up. Then I received a call early this morning from airport security telling me that my car had been returned." He laughed and reached for a box. "Cigar?"

"No, thank you."

"Can you imagine that?" Rick laughed, his belly moving beneath his pineapple shirt with the chuckle. "A thief returning a car. I've never heard of such a thing."

"How did you discover your car was stolen if you were out of town?"

"I asked Grigor"—he pointed to the man Caleb had nicknamed Brawn—"to see if I left some important papers in it. He went to the airport, and it was gone. I reported it stolen immediately."

"And?"

"Airport security said they'd run through their surveillance, but I doubt they ever did. I never heard back from them."

"Did you call the police?"

"Yes, I did. They said they'd look into it, but the police and I aren't exactly simpatico, you know."

"I see that." Caleb laid one of Rick's mug shots next to a printed out rap sheet.

"Interesting." He tapped the table. "You checked me out. Why?"

"Your car tailed two of our agents quite aggressively last night."

He took a puff of his cigar and blew out a stream of smoke. "I'm very sorry to hear that. I suppose that explains why it was stolen."

"Then you wouldn't mind if we sent a CSI agent out here to run the vehicle."

"Yes, Mr. Eason. I would."

Interesting. He hadn't given his name. "It's Agent Eason."

"Of course." Rick's jaw tightened, but he still attempted a smile. "Agent Eason, I'm over the theft. I have my car back. I see no need to prolong the issue."

"Okay." Caleb shifted gears. "Then let's talk about your record for stealing cars."

Rick set his glass down. "That was a long time ago."

Caleb exhaled. "Not so long."

"I guess that depends on your perspective."

"I suppose." Caleb looked around at the mansion and expansive grounds surrounding them. "Do you mind me asking why a wealthy man like you would have such a record?"

Rick reclined in his chair. "I wasn't always wealthy."

"No?" He already knew that but wanted to see if Rick would tell the truth. If he lied about something as simple as that, who knew what else he'd lie about.

"No. I was a bum and a thief."

"So what happened? What turned your life around?"

"I found Jesus."

"Jesus?" He hadn't seen that coming. He knew men like Rick Carson could be saved and redeemed, could have Jesus reach in and pull them out of the muck and mire and set their feet on the Rock of Ages. But . . . something in his gut said Rick Carson was feeding him a load of bull.

"And how did finding Jesus equate to all this?" he asked.

"I went straight. Started turning my life around. Went to Narcotics Anonymous, and that's where I met my sweet Bella."

"Bella?"

218

"Yes. My fiancée. I'd introduce you, but I'm afraid she's out shopping. You know women." He chuckled.

Uh-huh. He had the distinct feeling Bella was the loaded one, and Rick was just along for the ride. "What do you do for a living now?"

"I manage the estate."

By hiring staff to do everything, it appeared.

"And I'm Bella's executive advisor."

"Advisor for what?"

"The company her dad left her."

Caleb hated always being right.

"And what company is that?"

"Financial Freedom."

"The dot.com company?" It had revolutionized online banking and investments.

Rick smiled. "That's the one."

"So your fiancée is Bella Armstrong?"

"Yes. My Bella."

Financial Freedom was worth billions. "And Bella runs the company?"

"She manages it."

Meaning she had others run it, and she got rich off her dad's creation.

Rick Carson hadn't changed. Not in Caleb's estimation. He was just running another con. One he feared would end badly for Bella Armstrong.

After thanking Rick for his time and being shown out by the muscle twins, Caleb climbed in his car. He took one last look at the sprawling estate.

Rick stood at the center, second-floor window, smoking his cigar, watching him as he pulled away. He lifted his head at Caleb as he blew out a stream of smoke.

Caleb smiled. *Game on.*

FORTY

Mason parked in UNCW's general parking lot. They'd decided to take a break from interviewing crew one as each interview sounded exactly like the one before . Everything was in fine working order when they'd swapped rotations with crew two, but each one believed in the curse and blamed it for the copter crash and Greg Barnes's death. Rissi couldn't listen to one more retelling, and so they were switching their focus.

Mason stepped around his Impala, the sun's rays bringing an almost sparkling hue to the hood. He opened the passenger-side door for her.

"Thanks," she said, climbing out.

Mason's green-gray eyes narrowed. "You're worried."

She considered arguing, but he knew her like no one else did. Just like when they were teens. "I am."

"For Caleb?" he asked as they stepped onto the sidewalk leading from the parking lot to the main campus.

"If Lucas is in any way tied to what happened to Greg Barnes, he needs to answer for it. I know that." She sighed. "I also know it'll kill Caleb. He tries so hard with his family, and they only let him down time and time again."

"That sucks." Mason glanced at her hands, then slid his into his jacket pockets. She longed to hold hands, too, but it wasn't professional, so she followed Mason's choice, shoving her hands in her white blazer's pockets.

A smile curled on his lips at her action, his gaze locking with hers.

She shrugged with a soft smile. "Whoa!" she said.

He stopped short and looked forward at the old oak tree less than an inch before him. "Thanks," he said. "Guess I better pay better attention to where I'm going."

"Probably a good idea." She tried to smother a laugh, but it was no use.

"You think that's funny, huh?" His best attempt at a serious expression spread on his face, but after a moment, he, too, gave up and broke into laughter.

Finally stemming the lightness of the moment, Rissi led the way around the wildflower preserve toward Seahawk Landing—the farthest student apartment complex on campus.

"You said Lucas's mom was not a great influence?" Mason said, picking up their earlier conversation from the car ride over.

"Susie bounces from husband to husband. Making one bad choice after another."

"That stinks," Mason said.

"Yeah, but I suppose Susie learned it honestly."

"As in her mom?" he asked.

"Yeah. She's really a number," she said as they banked right at the edge of the preserve, passed two halls, and turned left. She glanced at the shiny signs for homecoming hanging along the sorority apartments' balconies and Frat "Row" suites.

She'd always wondered what it would have been like to attend homecoming or prom.

"I guess we missed out on that stuff," Mason said, gesturing to the teal, navy, and gold sign on their right.

"Yeah." She toed the pavement. "I'm sure it's not all it's cracked up to be."

He studied her a moment but let the subject drop. "You sure know your way around here."

"Not my first time questioning someone on campus."

"Gotcha. So . . . Caleb and Susie's mom?"

"Right. Their mom, Darlene, is . . ." She searched for the right adjective. "Well, horrible. Caleb's been the only adult in the family since his parents split years ago."

"I'm sorry to hear that," he said.

Rissi raked a hand through her hair. "It's been a losing battle for Caleb with his family. I'm pretty sure I would have walked away, but not him. He keeps trying. He never gives up on them."

"He's a good guy."

"Yeah, he is. So is Noah." She had hit the lottery with her team family.

"And Logan?" Mason asked with arched brow.

"He's a character, but deep down he's a good guy too. Our team has really been blessed."

"It sure seems so." He lifted his chin. "What's the deal with him and Emmalyne?"

"They're a mess," she said with a smile as they passed the garage that had been too full to park in when they arrived.

"But they clearly care for each other?"

"Yes, but until Logan gets over himself and shows Emmy the man he truly is, it'll always just be a playful friendship."

Mason grinned. "It's definitely an interesting dynamic."

"That it is."

They entered Seahawk Landing, and after showing their badges to the student behind the front desk, they climbed the stairs. Locating apartment 310, Rissi knocked.

A guy in his early twenties with shaggy brown hair answered the door. "Yeah?"

"Seth Andrews?" she asked.

"Yeah."

Mason flashed his badge. "Agents Rogers and Dawson. We're with Coast Guard Investigative Service, and we'd like to ask you about Lucas Eason."

"Lucas doesn't live here anymore."

"We know. We want to ask you some questions about when he was living here."

Seth frowned. "Is Luc in some kind of trouble?"

"No," Rissi said. He wasn't yet. "We're just trying to figure out a few things about him."

Seth braced his hand on the doorframe, his arm stretched out, effectively blocking them from his room.

"We want to know about his classes . . . one of his professors . . ."

That sparked something in Seth's eyes.

"I'm guessing you know which professor we're talking about?" Mason said.

"Yeah. Freaking nut job." He lowered his arm and stepped back. "Come on in."

As dorms went, it was a nice one. The door opened into a living room with a couch, coffee table, and two chairs that looked as if they belonged in a hospital waiting room, but Rissi was guessing they were standard dorm issue. A door on her left revealed a bedroom, as did the open one to the right. Suite style, like she'd lived in at Mary Washington.

"Take a seat, if you want," Seth said, kicking his socked feet up on the coffee table after sinking into the couch.

Mason pulled out a chair for Rissi.

"Thanks," she said, taking a seat.

"So what do you want to know about Professor Lansing?" Seth asked.

"Did you take any of her classes?"

"I took conservation biology last fall."

"And Lucas?"

"Yeah, we both took it. And Luc went nuts for that stuff."

"Nuts, how?" Rissi asked, leaning forward, resting her elbows on her knees.

Seth smiled at her, his gaze lingering. "As in he started going to protests with that enviro group Professor Lansing runs."

"So they knew each other? Gwyneth Lansing and Lucas?" She needed confirmation.

"Oh yeah, they *knew* each other."

Mason's brow arched. "Knew each other as in *knew* each other?"

"Definitely. I mean, they were all secretive about it. Meeting up off campus. But he told me about it . . . about her."

Rissi cringed. *Gross.* "Gwyneth has to be at least a decade older than him."

"Eight years, I think," Seth said. "I mean, she wasn't bad to look at, and she was smart, but she was such a weirdo."

"Weirdo, how?"

"She'd go off on these tangents and rants about oil companies and chemical plants and such. I mean, I get that they aren't enviro friendly, and that sucks, and I'm all for protecting wildlife. I'm a marine biology major like Luc was, but Luc talked me into going with him to one of the protests. We went out on a boat to protest the *Oceanic Nautilus*—the drilling rig they used to lay the subsea wells the *Dauntless* uses to pump and produce oil."

"Wait," Rissi said. "Sorry to interrupt, but did you just say Lucas protested against the oil rig whose platform he now works on?"

Seth ran a hand through his hair. "Yeah, I liked Luc, but he just started disappearing more and more after he met Gwyneth."

"He called her by her first name?" Mason said.

"Not on campus, but on that boat, he sure did. And the crowd on that boat was either talking smack just to sound tough or they were way extreme on protest tactics."

"Such as?" she asked.

"They were talking about setting fires, vandalizing chemical plants, railroad cars that carry chemicals. Ecoterrorism kind of stuff."

"Did Lucas say why he was dropping out of school to join the *Dauntless* and work for an oil company, of all things?"

"His old man—well, his last stepdad—worked rigs. Lucas called him a roughneck, whatever that meant. He was a mechanic, and he taught Luc the trade. Luc spent his last couple summers working with him on the rigs. So when he dropped out of college, he said he could make good money, and he could make a difference."

"Make a difference?" Rissi frowned, not liking where this was going.

"Yeah. I told you the dude got weird."

"Any idea where he lives now when not on the *Dauntless*?"

"Yeah. He moved in with some surfer guys in Topsail. I helped him move. He didn't have a lot of friends here. I think that's part of why he left."

"And the other part?" Mason asked.

"Her."

Noah looked to the door as Caleb entered the office. "Hey, man."

Caleb lifted his chin in greeting. "Hey."

"Good timing." Noah grabbed a notebook from his desk.

"Oh?"

"I just got back from talking with Brodie."

"How'd it go?"

"He had an alibi."

"A strong one?" Emmy asked. She was a wonder woman when it came to poking holes in lies. Logan called her the human polygraph.

"Three of the other firemen on duty while I was there confirmed his alibi. Said they were all out drinking at Riley's Pub."

"His buddies backing him up makes his alibi questionable," Logan said.

"True, which is why I'm heading to Riley's tonight."

"We can go now," Caleb said.

"Thanks for the offer, but I want to wait until later tonight. See if the same staff is working as last night when Brodie and his friends claim they were there. Conveniently while Brooke's house was being broken into and vandalized."

"Did the police have any luck with the man she saw going over her fence?" Emmy asked. "I know they didn't find him last night, but maybe one of the neighbors saw something or heard a car peel away."

"They did a thorough canvas of the neighborhood," Noah said. "Unfortunately, nothing but a dog barking three streets over around the time the man disappeared."

"Did they talk to the dog's owner?" Caleb asked.

Noah looked around the room. This was why he loved his team. They were all in sync. Well, all but Caleb and Mason. That adjustment would take time. "Officer Jenkins spoke with her. He said she swore something was wrong with, and I quote, her 'pumpkin poo.' Apparently, Pumpkin Poo isn't a barker."

Logan chuckled. "Sorry," he said, his laughter continuing.

"No worries," Noah said with a smile. "I cracked up too."

"Did she see or hear anything?" Caleb asked.

"No," Noah said.

Emmy crossed her legs. "We did learn one thing. It seems Brooke's stalker is familiar with her neighborhood. Being able to get out unseen by anyone other than a dog."

"Good point," Noah said.

"Which again points to Brodie," Caleb said, then shifted his attention to Noah. "You want me to come with you to Riley's?"

"That'll be helpful," Noah said. "We can cover more ground, talk to more people that way."

"I'll tell you who'd be more helpful," Logan said. He shifted his attention to Caleb. "No insult meant."

"None taken, but I'm curious where this is going," Caleb said with narrowed eyes.

Logan hopped up on the corner of Emmy's desk.

"Are you going to tell us who you're thinking of?" Noah asked.

"Em."

She looked at him, curiosity dancing in her wide green eyes. "I'm happy to go, but why me?"

"Because you're a woman, of course."

Emmy arched a brow, pinning her intent, viperlike gaze on Logan. "You better be going someplace nonsexist with that comment."

He held up his hands, a little twinge of mock fear in his eyes. Noah tried not to chuckle.

"I am," Logan assured.

Emmy linked her arms across her chest, her polka-dot blouse bunching beneath them. "I can't wait to hear this one." She moved around her desk to face him.

"Just hear me out."

"I'm listening." She tapped the red soles of her Louboutins against the floor.

Noah'd had no clue what they were until his sister Gabby freaked over the red underside of the shoes. Apparently, they were high fashion—which didn't surprise him about Emmy—but also extremely high priced. She had said they were a gift. Actually, that's all she'd say, no matter how much Gabby pressed her about who the giver was.

"Okay. Two guys, such as yourselves," Logan said, looking to Noah and Caleb, "look like cops. You two walk in Riley's, and everyone's defenses go up."

Noah and Caleb looked at each other.

"I think we were just insulted," Noah said.

"I agree," Caleb said, crossing his arms.

"Not at all," Logan said, hopping off Emmy's desk. "But, Em, if you saw these two enter a restaurant . . ."

"Yeah. I get what he's saying."

Logan smirked.

"Don't push it," she said.

Logan's smirk turned into a wide grin. "I know no other way."

Emmy inhaled, then released it slowly. "That's precisely the problem."

Logan frowned, but she continued. "You two definitely give off the cop vibe."

"I'd ask what that is," Noah said, "but I'm not sure I want to know."

"All I'm saying," Logan said, standing between Noah and Emmy, "is that if you walk in with Emmy on your arm, where are all the guys going to look?"

Logan had a point after all.

"All right," Noah said. "Emmy, you and I will head to Riley's tonight."

"Sure. What time are you thinking?"

"2100. I'll pick you up."

"The time works, but I'll meet you at your house. I'm having dinner with a friend not far from your neighborhood."

"Great. It's settled," Noah said.

"A friend?" Logan said. "Male or female friend?"

She walked back around her desk and retook her seat. "None of your business."

Logan exhaled. "Fair enough, but tonight, for Riley's wear something . . ."

She arched a brow. "Something?"

"Something less professional and more date-like."

She stared at him like he had to be kidding.

"You do go on dates, don't you?" Logan asked, his tone casual, but there was something in his gaze. . . .

Noah studied him. Was he hoping she'd say no?

"Of course I go on dates," Emmy said.

"What did you wear on your last one?"

"A white short-sleeve blouse, navy pencil skirt, and white sling backs."

"Nice." Logan smiled. "Wear that."

"Okay, now that we're done discussing my wardrobe, what happened with Rick Carson?" she asked Caleb, curiosity alight in her eyes.

Caleb shared what he'd learned.

Noah sat back. "Rich?" He shook his head. "I hadn't seen that coming."

"Believe me, neither did I."

"And you think he's conning this woman? That he lied to you about changing his ways?" he asked Caleb, but he already knew they'd agree on the answer.

"I do." Caleb nodded.

"I can spot a con a mile away," Logan said, folding a piece of spearmint gum into his mouth, then offering everybody one.

"You want to head over and take a crack at him?" Noah asked Logan.

"Actually," he said, straightening his pink shirt collar. Only Logan could get away with pink. Despite his protesting it was salmon, the shirt was pink. "I want to take a crack at the fiancée."

Em rolled her eyes. "Of course you do."

"It's not like that," he said.

"Uh-huh."

"Give me more credit," he said. "I highly doubt Rick Carson is going to give us the information needed. His fiancée might."

"Fine," Noah said. It wasn't a half-bad idea. "See if you can talk to the fiancée without Carson around."

"And warn her about Carson," Caleb said.

"Will do." Logan nodded.

"Before you go," Noah said, "what happened with the airport surveillance footage?"

"Right." Logan strode to his desk and grabbed a manila file folder, which he handed to Noah. "Here you go."

Noah flipped through the screenshots he'd pulled from the

footage. "Could any of these be Rick Carson?" he asked Caleb as he handed each to him.

"No, but I'm pretty sure I know who that is."

Noah arched a brow.

"He's one of Carson's . . . henchmen, for lack of a better word. He has that build."

"Which is quite distinctive," Emmy said.

"So . . ." Logan slipped his hands into his gray dress pants. "That's your type. World Wrestling Federation guys?"

"Maybe." She shrugged a shoulder, her gaze on an open file on her desk and not at him.

"Carson said he sent Grigor to fetch some papers out of the vehicle."

"Last name?" Emmy asked, ready to type the name in and start searching.

"Sorry. Didn't get one. But Carson said the SUV was gone when Grigor got there."

"Apparently not." Noah held up the photo of Grigor climbing in the SUV. "And . . ." He held up the next picture of Grigor driving it out of the garage.

"Fast-forward to the middle of the night that Rissi and Mason were followed, and Grigor returns the SUV to where he took it from, " Caleb said.

"Do you think Rick was in Dayton?" Noah asked.

Caleb shook his head. "Not even a little chance. The flight manifest has his name on it, but once past airport security, he could have bribed anyone who looked remotely like him to take his place on his flight."

"You think Carson was in that car following Rissi and Mason?" Noah asked, getting to the heart of the matter.

"I do." Caleb gave a nod of agreement.

FORTY-ONE

When Logan left to meet Bella Armstrong at a coffee shop and Emmy was engrossed in searching for answers on Rick Carson, Noah grabbed the folder Austin Kelly had given them and tucked it under his arm. "Let's head into one of the interrogation rooms, Caleb. It'll be quieter, and we can dig into the file there."

"Sounds good," Caleb replied.

Once settled in their seats, Noah flipped the file open. "Let's see what we have here." He took the first half of the file and gave the remainder to Caleb.

A couple of hours and a pot of coffee later, Noah flipped over the last page in his pile. Austin Kelly had done her work well, but he was curious about Caleb's insight.

When Caleb finished, he stacked his papers, photographs, and newspaper clippings back into a neat pile and tapped it upright on the desk to straighten it further.

"Well?" Noah said.

"She did an impressively thorough job."

"Why, thank you."

Noah and Caleb both turned to see Austin at the door with a wide grin on her face.

"Sorry," Logan said, standing in the open doorway beside her. "She asked to see you. Actually, insisted on it."

"It's okay," Noah said.

Logan nodded. "You guys need anything else?"

Noah was anxious to learn what Logan had found out from Bella, but that could wait. "Another pot of coffee would be great," he said. Rissi often brought in the morning espresso drinks, but when it came to ground office coffee, Logan made the best. He supplied them with his favorite Kona coffee blend.

"I prefer tea," Austin said. "Green kombucha with a little honey. I have some with me." She pulled a packet out of her backpack and handed it to Logan. "Thank you."

Logan smiled. "My pleasure."

"I didn't realize you were staying," Caleb said.

"I'm sure you gentlemen could use my . . . What was it you called it? Oh right, my impressively thorough job insights." She set her backpack on the table and pulled out a chair.

Noah smothered a smile. He liked Austin. She was bold and sassy. And after spending the last couple of hours reviewing her meticulous work, it was clear she was a brilliant investigator. Plus, he liked that her backpack, white linen pants with blue stripes, and a short-sleeve navy top that hit the high waist of the pants sent a definite beach boho vibe—as his sister Gabby would describe it. He didn't quite understand what *boho* meant, but thanks to Gabby endlessly pointing out styles to him, he could at least recognize it when he saw it.

Caleb looked to Noah. "She's joining us?"

"Yes." Noah smiled. "I believe she is." If for nothing else, to watch her and Caleb go at it. But in all honesty, he truly believed she would be a great asset to their investigation.

"Where are you boys at?" she asked, making herself comfortable.

Caleb's brows arched. "'Boys'?"

"I'm sorry. Do you prefer *guys*? *Dudes*? *Men*?"

"The latter will be fine." The muscle in Caleb's jaw flickered.

"We've finished reading through your file," Noah said. "I took the first half and Caleb the second, and we were just about to discuss."

"Wonderful. Then it looks as if I've arrived at the perfect time."

"Debatable," Caleb murmured under his breath.

Noah took the fresh cup of coffee Logan brought in and sat back with a smile. *This is going to be fun.*

FORTY-TWO

The address Seth provided led Mason and Rissi to a U-shaped complex that looked more like a motel with monthly rental units than an apartment building.

Mason glanced around. It looked sketchy. "Is this the right place?"

"I'll double-check." She looked at her phone. "Yep, this is it."

Longboards lined the front porches while surfboards and skimboards rested against the exterior wall.

Rissi removed her blazer, pulled her hair up in a ponytail, and stepped from the car.

Mason arched a brow.

"Trust me. They'll view us . . ." She looked him up and down. "Well, *me* less intimidating this way."

A smile tugged at his lips. "Are you implying I'm always intimidating?"

"Not always." She smiled. "At least not with me." She winked and headed for the front corner unit marked Office.

"Interesting choice of location," he said, looking around as he moved in step with her. Looked like yet another bad choice by Caleb's nephew.

He opened the white storm door for her and then followed her into a dim ten-by-ten room. The whir of fan blades hummed from the bar-height front desk.

A fly buzzed by Rissi's head before zinging past his. He swatted it away and moved to ring the reception-desk bell.

It twanged. A moment later a fifty-something man stepped through the beaded strings separating the back room from the front office.

"Yeah?" His brown bowling shirt embroidered with *Harvey's Howlers* was buttoned askew. His white undershirt was gray around the collar.

"We're with CGIS," Rissi said, flashing her badge. "We need to speak with Lucas Eason's roommates."

He scratched his belly. "Who?"

Mason pulled the copy he'd printed of Lucas's driver's license. He held it out to the man he assumed was the manager of the place. "Him."

"Oh, that kid. He and his buddies are renting unit eleven."

"Great." Rissi slid her badge into her back pocket.

"Thank you," Mason said, and the man nodded.

They walked along the cracked parking lot, toward the unit at the far end of the *U*.

The breeze whipping off the ocean swirled sea air around them. He loved the smell of the sea. It was the same no matter where he went. One of God's great constants. The sun peeking through fast-moving clouds cast their shadows on the pavement before them.

A guy with long curly hair hanging a couple of inches below his shoulders exited unit eleven. He kicked the longboard up into his outstretched hand with a flick of his foot, making the wheels clink.

He glanced up, his inquisitive gaze flickering over Mason before settling on Rissi.

He smiled and adjusted his board shorts with his free hand.

"Hi," Rissi said, approaching him.

His smile grew. "Hi, yourself."

"I'm Agent Dawson, and this is Agent Rogers."

"Agents?" the guy said. "Cool."

"With Coast Guard Investigative Service. We're hoping we can ask you a few questions about your roommate Lucas."

The guy's brown eyes narrowed. "Why? Is he in some kind of trouble?"

"No, we're just interviewing everyone who works on the *Dauntless* and those closest to them."

"Why?"

"Because there was a death on board, and we're trying to figure out what happened."

"Somebody died. No way!"

"I'm afraid so," Rissi said.

"So can we ask you a few questions?" Mason asked.

The guy looked at Rissi. "*She* can."

Mason took a step back and let Rissi go for it.

Two more guys around Lucas's age approached on long-boards. "Who you talking to, Beckham?"

"They're agents with Coast Guard . . ."

"Investigative Service," Rissi finished. She stepped toward the guys who had just walked up. "I'm Rissi."

They introduced themselves as Ollie and Chauncy.

Ollie looked at Beckham. "Why you talking to cops, man?"

"They aren't technically cops, and someone died on Lucas's platform."

Chauncy looked at them, his dark eyes settling on Mason. "If they are asking about Lucas, that means they think he had something to do with the death."

"As far as we know, the death was an accident," Mason said.

Chauncy's gaze narrowed. "Then why the questions?"

Mason slid his sunglasses down his nose, looking at the cocky kid over them. "Protocol."

"Uh-huh." Chauncy wasn't buying it.

"Nice trucks," Rissi said, looking at his board. "Paris?"

Chauncy cocked his head. "Yeah. How'd you know?"

"Same trucks I have."

"You longboard?"

"Yep. I like how your trucks are mounted. Let me guess, hard wheels?"

"Yeah." Chauncy's eyes narrowed again as if he still wasn't buying it. "What kind of deck do you have?"

"Dervish."

"Sweet," Beckham said.

Chauncy sized her up and down, and Mason's muscles tensed. He didn't like the way Chauncy was looking at her and was about to put him in his place when Rissi asked, "Mind if I give it a try?"

"Sure," he said, handing her the board.

She inspected it. "Mine are a lot softer, and I keep my trucks loose to make it easier for me to turn."

"Most boards are made for guys, so for your weight I bet that works best."

"Yeah." She smiled. "Mind if I give it a try? I'm always curious how other boards ride."

Chauncy shrugged. "Sure."

"Thanks." Standing on the board, she got up to a decent speed before leaning back and curving hard. She shifted her shoulders ninety degrees, then pushed with her back foot into a slide, making a one-eighty.

"Dang." Chauncy whistled, shaking his hand like he was dropping a hot coal. "You just did a slide."

"Yep," she said, flipping the board up into her hand.

"Not many chicks can slide." Chauncy's smile widened.

"Nice custom," she said of the wood-burned pirate design underneath. "I've got a sea turtle and Hawaiian tribal design."

"Cool," Beckham said, sharing his stickered bottom. "All the states I've longboarded in."

"Awesome," she said.

A half hour later, all their questions answered, Mason held the car door open for Rissi. He smiled as he shut it and moved around to the driver's side. Clearly, there was more than one way to garner information.

"You did great back there," he said, turning the ignition.

"Thanks, I—" Her reply was interrupted by a hand to the Impala hood, as the guys rushed up to his car.

"Cool ride, dude," Beckham said through the open window. "Can we look under the hood?"

Twenty minutes later, Mason and Rissi finally pulled out onto the frontage road. The sand dunes and blue water were gorgeous. He really could get used to living in North Carolina, but wherever Rissi was, was home.

"When'd you learn to longboard?" he asked.

"When I was eighteen—my freshman year at college. My roommate rode. She let me hang out with her and her friends, and they all took turns letting me ride. Then all of them pitched in and got me my own board for Christmas."

"They sound like great people."

"Yeah, they were. I really wasn't sure what to expect after leaving the home. I kept to myself at the shelters and moved often, but for college I needed to stay put with my scholarship."

"You took a leap of faith."

"Yeah. I suppose I did. That's when I came to know Him."

Mason looked over at her, his brows peaked.

"Jesus," she said. "My roommate was a Christian, and we talked a lot. Then one night I went with her to Cru, and Jesus saved me."

He smiled as joy for her swelled inside. It was good to hear her salvation story.

"Okay," she said, shifting so her knee was bent under her. "What about you?"

"Two of the guys I bunked with in basic training were Christians. They kept inviting me to their Bible study, but I wasn't ready for it, at least I didn't think I was. But my drill instructor was watching me do my hundred push-ups one night—"

"Dare I ask why?"

"Nah. Better to let that one go."

She shook her head. "Continue."

"So there we are out in the rain, my hands splayed in the sinking mud, my face right up on it every time I lowered. He stood right there next to me and sang 'Upon the Water,' one of our five drill songs, but then he broke into a song I'd never heard before. It was just the two of us, so maybe that's why he did it. Maybe he knew my soul needed help—that I needed help. He sang 'Amazing Grace'—the version where Chris Tomlin added the 'my chains are gone' lyrics. That night changed everything."

"He led you to Christ?"

"The Holy Spirit invaded my life that night. Opened my eyes to Jesus, and I've never looked back."

"Did you ever tell your drill instructor?"

"Not outright, but I showed up to his Bible study the next night."

Mason reached over and clasped Rissi's hand. "God never ceases to amaze me." He'd taken two broken kids and made them whole in Him. And then, as if that wasn't enough, He'd given them meaning and purpose in the same vocation. And, on top of that, blessed them with each other. "He's given me so much. And now He's brought me back to you."

She smiled, and it warmed his entire being.

He spotted a scenic pull-off a couple hundred feet ahead and pulled into it.

"What are we doing?"

He shifted it into Park. "Ris, I don't want to rush you or for you to feel uncomfortable, so if you don't . . ." He exhaled. If she didn't feel the same . . .

"Mason." She reached up and cupped his cheek. He leaned into her hold. "What is it?" she asked.

He lifted her free hand to his lips and brushed a featherlight kiss across her knuckles.

Please, Jesus. Let her feel the same. I love her so much. I feel like I was created to love her.

Then tell her, God's Spirit whispered in his soul.

She blinked, studying him. "What is it?" She asked again.

He exhaled. "I don't want to freak you out, but . . . "

"But?" Worry filled her gaze.

"I love you, Ris. I always have. Always will."

Her smile lifted to her cheeks. "I love you too."

Joy gushed through him. "You do?"

She nodded. "Always have. Always will."

"You have no idea how long I've waited to say that, to hear that." Every nerve ending in him sparked to life. He rushed forward in thought. "Obviously now is not the right time with everything going on and things being so new . . . well, not new, but finally acknowledged . . ."

Rissi's eyes narrowed. "Wait . . . Are you saying it isn't the right time for us?"

He stroked the back of her hand. "No. Just . . . if this is . . . if *we* are forever, then we'll have to figure out our work situation."

"Oh." She looked down.

He'd said too much. "I jumped too far ahead, didn't I." He'd waited so long to be back at her side, and now that he was, he never wanted to part.

"You didn't," she said, shifting to sit sideways, and he did the same, their knees knocking.

His pulse quickened. "Then what is it?" What was going on in that beautiful, brilliant brain of hers?

"You said *forever.*"

"And that freaked you out. I'm sorry. I'll slow down." He was pushing her to be where he was—a man desperately in love.

She shook her head. "No. The only thing that freaked me out was the part before it."

His brow bunched. "What part?"

"*If* this is forever." She glanced down at their intertwined hands. "You said *if*." Her fingers shifted in his hold. "I know we just found each other again and that all of this is so new in some ways, but the thought of not being with you again . . ."

He clutched her hand tighter, gazing into her eyes. "I'm not going anywhere. I promise."

The bright sunlight illuminated her already captivating eyes.

"Are you sure I'm not freaking you out, that *I'm* not thinking too fast?" she asked.

He rested his hand on her bent knee. "There is no too fast when it comes to us."

"There isn't?" she asked, searching his eyes for confirmation.

He cupped her face. "I don't know about you, but to me, *this* was ten years in the making. I always believed we'd find each other one day, that God would put us together." His thumb brushed across her soft cheek, his chest warm and tight. He was laying it all on the table. "You're it, Rissi. You've always been the one."

She smiled. "And you can't imagine how long I've waited to hear that."

He lowered his mouth, hovering over her lips, brushing his along hers. He moved to her neck, nuzzling up along the curve of it, pressing a tender kiss at the nape.

She sighed, and he couldn't hold back any longer. He took her mouth in his, pouring the love of a decade into that exquisitely blissful kiss.

"I think we should grab a late lunch," Noah said after they'd gone through the entire case Austin had assembled and shared in detail with them. Far more than was in the file. She was a brilliant investigator, and this case meant so much to her. All the information stored in her head, the way she stiffened whenever

Gwyneth's name was mentioned. After what she'd shared, he didn't blame her anger one bit. From what he'd just learned, Gwyneth was despicable. Numerous questions were still brewing, but before tackling them came the need for sustenance.

Austin reclined in her chair. "Where do you want to go?"

"What sounds good?" Noah asked.

"A salad," Caleb said.

"That's a given," Noah said. The man ate like a squirrel. "And you, Austin?"

"I could go for a burger."

Caleb's brows quirked. Apparently not what he pictured her ordering.

"Rye and Brown's delivers," Noah said. "They have fantastic burgers and thick-cut fries. They even add apple cider vinegar as a favor to me."

Austin's nose scrunched. "Apple cider vinegar?"

"He's from Maryland," Caleb said. "It's a thing there."

"I'll go see what Emmy and Logan want." Noah strode for the door, then paused and looked back at Caleb and Austin warily eyeing each other.

"You kids behave now." With a smile tugging at his lips, he exited the room, shutting the door behind them.

Emmy had that scheming gleam in her eye as Noah approached her desk. "So what's the scoop in there?"

"Always wanting to play matchmaker." Noah chuckled.

"Is she single?" Logan asked.

Em shook her head with a sigh. "There he goes, looking for his next conquest." Hurt lingered in her eyes, but she played it off by keeping her tone ambivalent.

"Not for me," Logan protested. "What about Noah?"

"Oh, please." Emmy shook her head. "He's perpetually single, and he likes it that way."

He did. Or had. Something had started niggling at him. It was probably because he was enjoying Brooke's company so much, but Em was right, he was content with his single, focused life . . . wasn't he?

"You're not seriously thinking Caleb, are you?" Logan laughed.

"Why not?" Em said.

"Rissi," Logan said.

"If you haven't noticed, there's something called Rissi and Mason. Or as I like to call them, Massi."

Both stared blankly at her.

"Like Macy."

Neither batted an eye.

She grunted in a rather feminine way. "You two are hopeless."

FORTY-THREE

Caleb watched as petite Austin Kelly decimated the giant burger and fries in front of her. Where did she put it?

Austin wiped her mouth and tossed her trash in the can along the far wall. "You were right," she said to Noah. "That was amazing."

"You liked the fries too?" he asked.

"They were stellar."

Stellar? Caleb chuckled. Who said *stellar?* The lady was brilliant when it came to casework, but she was also . . . Well, he didn't really know how to define her, which was new.

"I'm going to check in with Em and Logan real quick," Noah said. "Be right back."

Austin looked at Caleb's nearly finished salad. "How was your rabbit food?"

"Vegetables are healthy for you."

"And so tasty." She rolled her eyes.

"Actually—" he shoved a forkful of spinach into his mouth, then swallowed it—"they are." He grabbed the last forkful and finished it off.

"I suppose it's a good thing you enjoy rabbit food, if that's what you choose to eat."

His gaze narrowed. "Just to be clear, you're giving me a hard time for eating my vegetables?"

"No. Just find it funny that a guy like you prefers salad to a burger."

He arched a brow. "A guy like me?"

"You know, six-four, broad shoulders, intense scowl . . . " Her eyes narrowed. "On second thought, I suppose the rabbit food fits you."

"And why's that?"

"You're very regimented."

Regimented? The way she said it certainly didn't sound like a compliment, but how could discipline ever be considered a bad thing?

Noah reentered the room. "Ris and Mason just pulled up. I say we take this party to the case board."

"Sure," Caleb said, standing. He lifted his chin at Austin. "Your input today was helpful."

Her eyes widened. "Was that a compliment?"

He tilted his head. "It was a thank-you."

A quick flash of surprise, of something he didn't fully recognize, flitted across her face, but as fast as it'd come, it was gone.

"I'd like Austin to join us," Noah said.

Caleb hitched to a stop.

Noah stepped past him with a smile. "There's a lot of information to convey about Gwyneth, and I'm sure Rissi and Mason will find it helpful for their case."

Taking seats on the couches facing the case board, Caleb picked the seat as far away from Austin as possible. Saying she was frustrating was an understatement, and yet . . .

"Ris and Mason," Noah said, thankfully saving Caleb from continuing with the insane thought about to track through his mind. What was wrong with him? The woman was totally annoying.

"Apologies for not doing this sooner," Noah said, gesturing to Austin. "I'd like to introduce our guest. This is Austin Kelly. She's a private investigator. Skip Malone's family hired her to investigate his death."

"Nice to meet you," Rissi said. "I'd love to hear what you found."

"I've asked her to join us for that very reason," Noah said.

"Wonderful." Rissi smiled.

Mason dipped his chin from the other side of Rissi. "Nice to meet you."

"And you," Austin said.

"Mason," Rissi said, "we left the drinks in the back seat."

"Right. I'll be back in two shakes."

"I'll come help." She rose and headed for the front door he'd just gone out.

Something had shifted between them. Their visible connection appeared even deeper. Instead of contemplating the possibilities—none of which he wanted to consider—Caleb chose to keep his focus on the board. *Just keep looking at the board.* Seeing Mason and Rissi together was hard, but he understood. Having Miss Sass involved in the case, even remotely, kept him off-kilter. And he was a man who craved stability.

///////////////////////////

Mason retrieved the drink carriers they'd left in the car. It was a good thing Rissi had thought to bring another round of espresso for the team. With all they'd learned, they could be in for a long afternoon.

Rissi waited at the door and opened it with a smile as he entered. He so badly wanted to kiss her, but reined his thoughts in. *Work. We are at work.*

When this case was done, they were going to have to address the working together situation. He'd served in the same unit as a husband and wife pair, but they weren't allowed to be partnered together. Which meant, if he and Rissi stayed at this station, they wouldn't be allowed to be on calls or cases together. But that was for another day. Right now, they had to give everything they had to figure out what was going on with the *Dauntless* and if any foul play had been involved in Greg Barnes's death. Accidents happened at a rather alarming rate on oil rigs and platforms, making it one of the most dangerous jobs in the world, but something rattled in his gut that there was more beneath the surface, and it was their job to find it.

As Mason and Rissi handed out the drinks, he smiled at her. It was a smile she could get lost in forever. She took a seat on the couch beside Austin, whom she was quite curious about.

Mason sank down on Rissi's right, his arm a breath from hers. She wanted so badly to feel his warmth and hold him close. She took one of those supposed cleansing breaths, hoping to settle the sensation of bees buzzing through her.

Logan took a sip of his drink. "Thanks," he said to Rissi. "They made it good today."

"So, honey lavender latte, huh?" Emmy said.

"Yep." He took a long sip.

Laughter bubbled out of Emmy.

Logan wiped his mouth. "You shouldn't make fun of it until you've at least tried it." He handed Emmy his cup, and she took a sip.

"Well?" he said with his charming smirk. It was no wonder ladies went gaga over him, Rissi thought. He had Southern charm down. Add in his ripped physique, tailored clothes, the amazing house he'd recently bought with his bountiful trust fund, and the fact he was in law enforcement, he appeared to be the total package. Deep down Rissi believed he would be perfect for the right woman, but he, unfortunately, seemed content to swim in the shallow end.

Emmy handed the cup back. "Okay, I'll admit it's good."

"Good?" Logan's lips twitched. "You can do better than that."

"Okay, fine," she said, handing a file to Rissi. "It's delicious."

"Thank you," he said, a cocky smile fixing on his handsome face.

Rissi rolled her eyes. She opened the folder, and Mason scooted closer still, looking over her shoulder as she read, or attempted to read, the contents.

Focus! So maybe the kisses weren't the smartest move, but she could pull it together and do her job.

She started at the top again, read the page, and then flipped to a stack of printed online newspaper articles.

"Whatcha got?" Noah asked.

"Thanks to Emmy's—"

Logan cleared his throat.

Rissi smiled. "And *Logan's* investigative genius, they found an interesting background on Gwyneth Lansing. Although it looks like she went by a different name for a while."

"Gwyneth Hill," Caleb said.

"Yeah," Rissi said. "How'd you know?"

"It was in the file Austin put together." Caleb went on to explain Skip's relationship with Gwyneth and the questions surrounding his death.

"Wow. So you think Gwyneth was on his boat the night he died?"

"I do," Austin said. "The dockmaster said he saw a woman get on the boat with him."

"Could he identify her?"

"No. She had a wide-brim hat, her hair pulled up, and large sunglasses."

"Sounds like whoever it was didn't want to be recognized," Rissi said.

"But didn't your source say Gwyneth disappeared after being

confronted by Skip about her questionable tactics? Why would he take her out on his boat?" Caleb asked.

"She said Gwyneth can get just about anyone to do just about anything. The few people who would talk to me all said she is brilliant but manipulative."

"Can we talk to your source?" Mason asked.

Austin shook her head. "I doubt she'll talk to you. I doubt she'll talk to me again."

"Why is that?" Mason asked.

"When we talked, she was so skittish. Even though she clearly wanted the truth to come out, it was as if she was terrified of Gwyneth."

"Why?" Logan asked.

"If she's capable of all you say she is and all we found"—Emmy indicated herself and Logan—"I'd be scared too."

"What else did you two find?" Noah asked.

Emmy crossed her legs. "In her early twenties, she went by Gwyneth Hill. Under that name she was charged with harassment, trespassing, and vandalism. The group she worked with then—Activists for Animal Rights—was caught tossing stink bombs on whaling boats, cutting their lines, breaking into factories that dump chemical waste, even monkeywrenching."

"Monkeywrenching?" Mason asked.

"Sabotaging equipment that they believe is environmentally damaging," Em said.

Rissi flipped through the articles Emmy had handed her. "Looks like they were accused of starting a fire at a series of sporting goods shops after they were closed for the night."

"Sporting goods?" Mason said. "Seriously?"

"Apparently, they believed the shops encouraged unethical treatment of animals by selling hunting and fishing gear."

"Okay," Noah said. "So we're dealing with extremists. Everyone be on your guard."

Everyone nodded in reply.

Noah exhaled. "Today's been quite the busy day." He went on to share about Brooke's second break-in along with the vandalism. Whoever was stalking her, his threats were definitely escalating and that was never a good sign.

Rissi was thankful Noah was on it. Brooke couldn't ask for a better investigator. He went on to explain Brodie's supposed alibi and the plan for him and Emmy to hit Riley's Pub tonight to see if anyone besides Brodie's buddies could account for his whereabouts.

Rissi silenced her thoughts and focused on her Father. *Please, Lord, be with Brooke. Put a hedge of protection around her and everyone looking out for her, especially Noah. Please guide him to find whoever is responsible and help him bring them to justice. The battle is yours, Lord. In Jesus' name, I pray. Amen.*

Next Caleb shared about his interview with Rick Carson and Logan about the airport footage. Noah wasn't exaggerating. It'd been a busy day for the team. One after which they usually decompressed with a bonfire dinner on the beach at Finn's, but tonight she just wanted to be with Mason. Just the two of them picking up where they'd left off.

"I also had a talk with Rick Carson's fiancée earlier today," Logan said.

"Oh?" Rissi asked.

"Yep. Bella Armstrong."

Rissi's brows hiked. "As in financial guru's daughter, Bella Armstrong?"

"One and the same," Logan said. "Apparently, she met Carson at a thousand-dollar-a-plate garden party back in May."

"I'm sorry," Rissi said, almost choking on the iced latte Mason had just handed her. "Did you just say the Carson fellow from the mug shot was at a garden party?"

"Bella said Rick was dressed in an impeccably tailored suit and was nothing but charming."

"Charming?" Caleb guffawed. "Carson? You've got to be kidding."

"I know." Logan stood up and smoothed his shirt. "Not everyone can be as charming as me."

"Or as arrogant," Emmy said with a playful smile.

"I prefer to think of myself as confident." He winked at her.

"Let's continue," Noah said, nudging the two back on pace.

"Rick lied to me," Caleb said.

"Color me shocked." Rissi sighed. She hated men like that. Ones that used and hurt and lied.

"What did he lie about?" Noah asked Caleb.

"He told me he met Bella at a Narcotics Anonymous meeting after Jesus saved him and he turned his life around."

"Uh-huh . . . " Logan said.

"How'd it go with Bella?" Caleb asked.

"Well, clearly another lie," Logan said, "but Bella said Rick introduced himself as a yacht enthusiast who dabbled in hedge funds." He shook his head. "I'd delved into Carson's financials, and knew it was a bald-faced lie."

"Did you tell her?" Rissi asked, outraged at anyone who was being taken advantage of or preyed upon by cons like Rick Carson.

"Of course I did," Logan said, taking a seat on the sofa arm by Emmy's side. "Not only that, but I showed her Carson's rap sheet."

"And?" Emmy asked, looking up at him.

"She thanked me and left the coffee shop."

"That's it?" Emmy frowned.

"Surely she'll confront Carson, if she hasn't already," Rissi said. Every self-respecting woman would. "But I worry how he might respond. He's a dangerous man."

"I caught her at the car and expressed my concern. She said not to worry. The men Carson has waiting on him hand and foot are employed by her. And the head of the pack—a Samuel Barton—

has been with her family for years. She said he'd never let anything happen to her. That he was good at taking out the trash."

"Interesting comment," Rissi said. "Almost makes it sound like she's endured men like Carson before."

Emmy rubbed her arms. "I hope not. No woman should be treated like that."

Caleb leaned forward. "What I want to know is how Carson pulled off the rich vibe long enough to convince her to marry him. That had to take some money upfront for clothes, a car—things she'd expect to see with a man of substance."

"I know how he set up the illusion of being a rich hedge fund manager," Emmy said with a twinkle in her eye.

"How?" Caleb asked.

"He came into ten thousand dollars the week prior to the garden party."

"How did that happen?" Rissi asked. "Rich relative?" She was joking, but seriously, how had someone like Rick Carson come into so much money?

Emmy smiled like she had a secret to tell.

"Spill it, girl," Rissi said, anxious to know how Rick had acquired the funds.

"They came from the Freedom Group."

Rissi's jaw slackened. "What . . . how?"

"The Freedom Group paid ten thousand dollars via PayPal to a corporation called Satterley Investments."

"Okay?" Rissi edged near the end of the seat cushion.

"Logan?" Emmy prompted, nudging him beside her on the couch arm.

"Emmy told me about the large cash transfer," he began, "so I did some financial digging, and there is no Satterley Investments. The company doesn't exist beyond an email address where the money went via PayPal. An email address that no longer exists."

"Then where did the money go?" Caleb asked.

"Here comes the interesting part," Logan said. "The same day the Freedom Group sent the money, Rick Carson deposited ten thousand dollars into his bank account."

"So you think Gwyneth was funneling him money?"

"Maybe laundering it or just paying off a man she had ties with. Who knows," Emmy said. "Perhaps she and Rick were in it together for him to con Bella Armstrong out of her fortune. You put a shark and a con together and no good is going to come from it."

Rissi looked at Mason. "Ed said if any foul play was involved in Greg Barnes's death, we should be looking at Gwyneth and her crew." Rissi pulled her blazer about her shoulders, the station temperature a little cool even for her.

"You cold?" Mason didn't wait for her to answer, just pulled off his navy fleece and handed it to her.

She slid it on over her head and slipped her arms in the sleeves. It was soft, warm, and smelled of him. She looked up, and everyone was watching them. "So how does it all fit together?" she asked, more in an attempt to shift their attention off her and Mason than seriously thinking anyone had the full answer yet, but together they were getting there.

"I'm not sure yet," Emmy said, "but I'll . . ." She glanced up at Logan. "*We'll* keep searching until we put all the pieces together."

"You guys make quite the pair," Mason said.

Pink rushed Emmy's cheeks, and Logan cleared his throat, though a longing for something lingered there.

"I meant as an investigative team," Mason said.

"Right." Emmy released a nervous laugh. "Of course. What else would you be talking about?"

"I'm going to have another talk with Carson," Caleb said, redirecting the conversation.

"Good plan." Noah nodded. "All right, folks, you all have your assignments. Let's get moving."

As soon as the meeting wrapped, Rissi caught up with Noah

a few feet from his desk. "Hey, can I talk to you for a minute?" This was one conversation she wasn't looking forward to, but Noah needed to know about Lucas.

"Sure," he said. "What's up?"

She glanced around. Caleb was watching. "Can we talk in private?"

FORTY-FOUR

"Is everything okay?" Caleb asked Noah as he returned from speaking privately with Rissi.

"She was filling me in on what they learned today." Noah clamped a hand on Caleb's shoulder. "We need to talk."

Caleb's brows arched.

Noah hated the conversation he was about to have. He'd asked Rissi to remain in the conference room, so she could be there when Caleb got the news. He understood things were strained with Mason in the picture, but he still felt Rissi could be of help. Besides, Caleb would have questions Noah probably couldn't answer.

Caleb followed him into the room, and Noah shut the door behind them.

"What's going on, Ris?" Caleb asked.

She stood at the edge of the table. Swallowing, she began, "Emmy discovered that Gwyneth was a visiting professor of marine biology at the University of North Carolina Wilmington last year. Lucas took two of her classes."

"And so did a hundred other kids," Caleb said.

"Yes, but Lucas's roommate said that he and Gwyneth spent time together alone off campus."

Caleb's jaw tightened. "What are you saying?"

Rissi exhaled. "I don't know any other way to put this. Lucas and Gwyneth had or are still having a romantic relationship."

"What?" Caleb stepped back. "No. For one, she's like a decade older than him."

"Eight years, apparently," Rissi said.

"You can't really believe . . . ?"

Rissi rested her hand on Caleb's arm. "I'm sorry to tell you all this, but after Lucas dropped out of school, he moved in with some guys in Topsail."

Caleb narrowed his eyes. "What else?"

"Logan found that Lucas withdrew the funds for his tuition from his student account. It took a while to trace it, but Lucas donated it to the Freedom Group."

Caleb sank into a chair, and Rissi pulled up one beside him. "I'm so sorry."

He raked a hand through his hair. "So what does this mean?"

"It means we have to assume Lucas took a job on *Dauntless* to, at the very least, be a spy for Gwyneth," Noah said.

"And Greg Barnes's death?" Caleb paled. "Please tell me he had nothing to do with that?"

"We have no idea if Greg Barnes's death was anything other than an accident at this point, but we need to look into all the things that have gone wrong on *Dauntless*." Rissi took a breath and released it. "We need to make sure Lucas played no part in any of it."

Caleb sank back. "I can't believe this is happening."

Here came the part Noah hated most. "Given the circumstances . . . "

"Yes?" Caleb said at his pause.

Noah exhaled a thick stream of air. "We can't have you working this case."

Caleb didn't argue, but pain streaked across his creased brow.

Caleb strode out to his car, anger and disappointment tensing his muscles until his arms felt rigid. The air held the heaviness of rain, dark clouds brewing overhead.

"Hey, Caleb," Logan said, striding out of the station toward him.

Caleb lifted his chin. "What's up?"

"Why don't we grab a burger."

"I appreciate it, but . . ." He dealt with blows better alone. Or maybe it was just that he'd always chosen to go it alone.

"Come on," Logan said. "I'm buying."

Rain plopped on Caleb's head. First a drop, then another and another. He had to eat, and Donna's Burger Shack was legendary for its burgers. "All right. I'm guessing Donna's?"

Logan shrugged. "Where else?" He pulled out his key fob and clicked his locks open. The truck beeped in response, its headlights flashing. "I'll meet you over there."

The winds picked up as the sky let loose, the rain pelting as Caleb hopped in his car. They'd had a series of storms earlier in the month, but now forecasters were saying a bigger swell was heading inland over the next couple of days. The restless weather echoed the restlessness of his soul.

He still couldn't . . . well, *wouldn't*, wrap his mind around the thought that Lucas had . . .

He rubbed the back of his neck.

Please, Lord, don't let this be true.

Brooke headed for her car. It'd been a productive day off. She'd accomplished so much around the house—the most satisfying project being repainting the spare bedroom. She'd gone with a sky blue. Now she just had to decide what to do with the room. She already had a guest room, two seemed superfluous. Perhaps a home office? She really had no need. The best use might be turning it into a cozy reading room.

Maybe after grabbing a spicy chicken sandwich, fries, and a

Coke from Chick-fil-A, she'd pay a visit to Tim's Woodworks and see what kind of bookshelves he'd made lately.

Approaching her car, she fished her keys from the bottom of her purse and clicked the fob button to open her door. Rain sputtered from the sky, soft drops sprinkling her face.

She opened the door, tossed her purse on the passenger seat, and was about to climb in when something skittered across the tan leather seat. She followed the movement to the floorboard, where a mass of black scurried.

Spiders.

She jolted back, her gaze fixing on the one dangling from the rearview mirror on a thin silk strand. It spun. A distinct red hourglass marked its underside. She staggered back, her hands breaking her fall as she collided with the pavement.

Black widows.

She kicked her car door shut and scrambling to her feet, bolted for the house. Keys jangling in her trembling hands, she finally got the door open. She burst in and locked it behind her. Brodie had gone too far.

Noah pressed the gas pedal flush with the floorboard, his chest tight. No need to panic. Brooke was locked safely in her home. He'd intended to be there earlier, but he paid Brodie a quick visit. He'd been ready to throttle him, but once again, Brodie had an alibi. He'd been on shift, but his worry over telling Brooke that Brodie had an alibi for the night the garage was vandalized was superseded by the fact someone had put poisonous spiders in her car, and it couldn't have been Brodie. He'd confirm the bar story as that was possibly a group lie among Brodie and his friends, but him being on shift was a solid alibi.

If somehow Brodie was involved, he'd crossed the line to attempted murder. On the other hand, if Brodie's alibis held tight and he hadn't put the black widows in Brooke's car, then who were they dealing with? Maybe one of Brodie's friends? Regardless, an UNSUB scared him far more than someone they could keep an eye on.

Noah slammed the brakes. *Another red light.* Was he bound to hit every single one?

Drumming his fingers on the steering wheel, he attempted a deep breath but only managed a jagged inhale, his chest squeezing in response.

The light finally turned green, and he exhaled, brief as it was, and floored it. The engine roared, and a gaggle of elderly ladies gathered along the row of high-end storefronts shook their snow-white heads as he sped past.

He plopped the emergency cherry on the dash and switched it on. Brooke's call had rattled him.

Two more turns, and he slowed as he entered Brooke's neighborhood. Too many little ones to speed.

Another left and two rights, and he coasted to a stop in Brooke's hedge-lined drive.

Brooke ran out her door and crossed the lawn before he climbed out of the car.

She rushed to his side. He wrapped her in his arms, fighting the urge to press a reassuring kiss to her forehead. *Where did that come from?* He loosened his hold and took a step back.

"Thanks for coming," she said, her words throaty and breathless.

"Of course. I told you anytime, and I meant it."

She wrapped her arms around herself. "Thank you."

"You said they were black widows?"

Brooke nodded, tears in her eyes.

"Okay, I have animal control on the way as well as an exterminator. Wasn't sure which was best in this case."

An hour later, with every last spider wrangled up by the animal control officer and exterminator working together, Noah was nothing but thankful to see them drive away with the spiders in a safety tub. What happened to them now, he didn't ponder. He was just relieved Brooke wasn't in danger—at least not from black widows. If she hadn't been so observant, if she'd climbed into the car by rote memory as he had so many times, she could have died.

No way he was leaving her alone. Not now. Not until Brodie or whoever was after her was behind bars.

"I'm headed to my sister Kenzie's for dinner with the family. I'd really like you to join us."

Surprise crossed her face. "Oh?"

"I just have a bad feeling about leaving you alone." He glanced around the neighborhood, the rain a fine mist on the quiet street. "What do you say?"

"Okay." She nodded. "Thanks for the invite."

"Hey, Kenz," Noah said, opening his sister's front door and holding it for Brooke to enter before him.

Brooke smiled, but there was a hint of apprehension in her eyes. Gabby had brought her to a family dinner a couple of weekends ago, but, come to think of it, she'd seemed rather quiet then as well.

Curious. Was she nervous being around their boisterous family? Or perhaps she just took a while to warm up around people she didn't know well.

"Brooke," Kenzie greeted her, rounding the hall with Owen clinging like a monkey to her side. "So glad you could join us." She hugged Brooke, and Owen attempted to tickle her.

"Thanks for having me." Brooke hugged her back and laughed for Owen's benefit.

"Sorry about this little monkey," Kenzie said, swinging him around into both her arms. "He's in a tickling phase." She tickled him in her arms, and he belly laughed.

"Raspberries," Noah said, zurberting his tummy.

Owen laughed harder, flopping about in Kenzie's arms. Brooke smiled.

"Come on in," Kenzie said, gesturing with her head toward the noise. "Wings are just about ready."

"Kenz makes the best wings," Noah said, placing his hand on Brooke's lower back to guide her into the family room. "Watch your step." He smiled. "It's usually a maze around here."

"Uncle Noah!" Fiona jumped up from watching *Animal Mechanicals*. She wore her favorite pink tutu over her leggings. A gift from Aunt Gabby.

Fiona bolted for Noah, hugging his legs with such force he almost wobbled back. He reached down and swooped her up into his arms. "How's my favorite princess?"

Her bottom lip puckered out. "Owen keeps stealing my tiara."

"Well, we can't have that, can we?"

"No. Every princess needs a crown." She looked at Brooke and brightened. "You're a princess too. You need a crown."

She wiggled in Noah's hold, and he set her down. She clasped Brooke's hand. "Come with me."

Brooke smiled, the expression lighting her face and easing the trauma of what had occurred earlier. That'd been his greatest hope. She had a pressure-filled job and now couldn't even feel safe in her own home. Despite being one of the bravest women he knew, she was still human. Every human had some level of vulnerability, and it seemed the stalker had nipped at hers.

Brooke and Fiona disappeared around the corner.

"There's my boy," Nana Jo said, looking up from stirring her famous shrimp pasta on the counter separating the kitchen from the family room. "Get over here and give your momma a kiss."

"Yes, ma'am." He kissed her on the cheek as he snuck a spoonful of Old Bay shrimp from the pasta bowl.

"Don't think I didn't see that, Noah James."

"Yes, ma'am." He smirked.

"So you brought a lady to dinner?" Her eyes and attention were a little too focused on the pasta salad.

"Someone has been breaking into Brooke's house and vandalizing her property."

Nana Jo stopped stirring. "The poor dear."

"Gabby asked me to make sure she stays safe while she and Finn are away." And, truth be told, he liked the time he spent with Brooke. She was independent, focused on her work, and proud to serve her country. They had a lot in common, and when it came down to it, he enjoyed her company.

Noah looked over to find her and Fiona standing at the edge of the hall—both wearing tiaras and holding sparkling silver wands.

A smile curled on Noah's face. "Well, don't you two look like princesses." He knelt down so he was eye level with his niece as she entered the room. "You're beautiful."

"Thanks, Uncle Noah."

"You're welcome, kiddo." He tapped her button nose.

"And you"—he stood, dipping his head to look into Brooke's warm brown eyes—"are beautiful as well." She was beautiful, but he hadn't expected the thought to leave his mouth.

Brooke smiled. "It's the tiara," she said, righting it.

His smile widened. "It does look quite fetching on you."

She laughed. "Maybe I need to purchase one of my own."

"Supper's ready," Kenzie called, pulling the most amazing-smelling wings from the oven with a kitchen towel.

"Kenzie," Nana Jo said with a side of scolding.

"What?" Kenzie asked, setting the hot pan on the trivets.

"Pot holders were invented for a reason." Nana Jo sighed. "Hopeless." She shook her head. "Both my children are hopeless."

"Um, you have three children," Noah pointed out.

"I meant the two present, but Gabby's the observant one of you three."

"Hey!" Kenzie swatted her mom with the towel still clutched in her hand.

Nana Jo tilted her head. "What can I say, darling. You and your brother are oblivious at times." She stepped back from the island and wiped her hands on the red *Nana Jo Cooks Best* apron Noah had given her last Christmas.

"I take offense too," Noah said, snagging another shrimp while his mom wasn't looking. "Being observant is kind of a requirement for my job."

His mom came around the island, sidling up against him as Brooke and Fiona followed Kenzie to the table. "If only you had a fraction of that skill when it came to women."

"What?" He shrugged. "I happen to like my single life." He had focus, purpose. What more could he need?

Nana Jo shook her head. "Case in point." Rolling her large blue eyes, she sighed and headed for the seat beside Brooke.

Noah swallowed. *Please, God, let Momma behave.*

Miracles could happen, right? He took a deep breath as he sank into the chair opposite the table from Brooke.

Because that's what would need to happen for his mom to not say something he'd regret.

FORTY-FIVE

"Thanks for joining us for dinner," Noah said as he stepped inside Brooke's house later that night.

She smiled. "Thanks for having me. I enjoy spending time with your family."

He rubbed the back of his neck. "Sorry about my mom. She tends to talk without a normal human filter."

Brooke laughed. "It's okay." Seeing Noah's face turn cherry red when Nana Jo had asked when he was going to start dating again had been pretty funny. But then she suggested asking Brooke out, and Brooke's cheeks had flushed with heat. Probably turning about the same shade as Noah's.

"Basically, she's crazy," he said, still mortified.

"It's really okay. I had a lot of fun." His deer-in-the-headlights expression had been priceless, but it made her wonder why Nana Jo had specified the word *again*. Had something happened with his last relationship? He'd mentioned understanding bad choices. Had the steadfast Noah Rowley chosen the wrong girl? Was that why he was a self-proclaimed bachelor?

"I'm glad you had fun," he said, as she set her key in the bowl by the door and hung her purse on the hook.

He leaned against the back of the couch, his hands braced on either side of him. His black casual button-up shirt and dark-washed jeans looked good on him. He was such a handsome man. He looked up at her, his expression soft, his gaze much deeper. He'd never looked at her quite like that. "You looked adorable in the tiara," he said.

"Thanks." She stepped back to her purse and grabbed the pink-and-silver tiara out. "Fiona sent it home with me."

He chuckled.

She tried it on, playfully checking out the look in the full-length hall mirror before realizing that Noah now stood a few feet behind her. "Perfect," he said, his voice a register lower than she'd heard it before.

She turned, and their gazes locked.

He took a step closer. "I—"

A knock interrupted him.

No! What was he about to say? It had—he had—looked like it was something meaningful.

Noah pulled his gun from his waist holster and opened the door a crack.

"Don't shoot. It's just me," Logan said.

"Hey, man." Noah opened the door wider, allowing him to step in.

Logan? She liked Logan. He was affable, funny, and charming, but what was he doing at her house?

"Just wanted to let you know I was here."

Noah clapped him on the shoulder. "Thanks."

"What's going on?" she asked.

"Emmy and I have to go check out Brodie's supposed alibi for when the garage was vandalized," Noah said.

Her brows perked up. "He has an alibi?"

"Not a good one," he said. "But Em and I are headed to Riley's Pub to check it out."

Brodie hung there a lot. "But if his alibi proves to be true?" she asked, her thoughts tumbling forward. "Then who . . . ?" Who had been in her home? Who was stalking her?

Noah rested a gentle hand on her shoulder. "I'm on this. You don't have to worry."

She nodded. She believed him. Trusted him. It was a new sensation. With guys she was always waiting for the other shoe to drop. Granted this wasn't a romantic situation, but still, trusting a man outside of the rescue swimmers she would bank her life on was new. But she needed to remind herself that he was there to protect her. Not because he wanted to date her or even wanted a friendship. The first made her sad, the latter even more so. What would she do when her stalker was behind bars, and Noah was no longer around?

"Knock, knock," Emmy said, strolling in through the open doorway.

Brooke had never actually seen it happen—it'd always been more a turn of phrase—but Logan's jaw literally dropped.

"Wow," he said.

"You like the dress?" Emmy said, turning around as the dress twirled about her knees. Red with short sleeves, cut just above the knees with gorgeous yellow hibiscus patterned on it. Her hair was down, flowing to the middle of her back. Brooke didn't think she'd ever seen it down.

"You look . . ." Logan fumbled for words.

Emmy arched a brow.

"Amazing," he finally said, still not taking his gaze off of her.

"Thanks." She looked to Noah. "You ready to go?"

"Yep, let's do this."

Logan finally dragged his stunned gaze off Emmy and looked to Brooke. "I'll be right out front in my car. If you need anything, anything at all, text me," he said. "Let's put my number in your phone so it's a quick dial."

"Not necessary."

Logan and Noah both frowned.

"I'm not going to have you sitting out in your car. You can hang in here," she said.

"I don't want to disturb you."

"You won't be. I was just going to make some popcorn and watch a movie."

Emmy smiled. "I'd say poor Logan if it's a chick flick you're planning on watching, but he's the one man I know who enjoys them."

"What can I say?" Logan said with that charming smile of his. "I'm a romantic at heart."

Emmy burst out laughing.

"Okay," Noah said. "We're leaving. You two have fun." He shifted his gaze to Brooke. "I'll be back soon."

She nodded, thankful for his reassurance, but she and Logan would be just fine. Both armed and watching a chick flick. It was a new combination.

Brooke lay in bed, staring at the ceiling fan twirling rhythmically around, wondering how much longer until Noah would be back. She glanced at the clock—0100. She hadn't anticipated him and Emmy being gone so long. She'd wanted to wait up and see if Brodie's alibi had been confirmed or dismantled.

Who was she kidding? She wanted to see Noah.

She rolled over. She'd felt funny bailing on Logan to come to bed, but it was getting late, and she had an early watch. Not like she'd be able to sleep though. Her heart hammered in her throat as her mind tracked back through all that had happened over the last few days.

Her eyelids heavy, she was just about to finally doze off when she heard the front door creak open and voices emanating from downstairs.

Noah was back.

She hopped out of bed, pulled her robe over her knit shorts and tank top, and headed downstairs.

Noah looked up as she bounced down to join the group. He smiled. "Hey."

"Hey." She smiled back.

"You should be sleeping."

"I'm fine." She took the last step into the foyer, her hand resting on the curled, cherrywood rail. "How'd it go?"

"Well, I don't think Emmy will ever be dateless again," Noah said, chuckling.

Logan visibly bristled.

"She got more numbers than a phone book," Noah said.

"That's an exaggeration," Emmy said.

"Please, come sit," Brooke said, gesturing to her front room. "Can I grab anyone a drink? I've got apple cider from Hagman's Farm in the fridge," she offered.

"Yes, please," Emmy said, glancing at Noah and Logan holding up their hands. She laughed. "Looks like we'll all take a glass."

"Warm or cold?" Brooke asked.

"Warm, please," Logan said, followed by Emmy and Noah.

"Four warm ciders coming up."

"Let me help you," Noah said, following her into the kitchen.

"It's sweet of you to offer, but I've got this." She grabbed the gallon of cider from the fridge.

Noah ducked his head back in the front room and then scooted back to Brooke's side. "I wanted to leave those two alone for a few minutes."

Brooke arched a brow as she grabbed cinnamon, nutmeg, and cloves. "Are you trying to play matchmaker?" Interesting for a boss and his team, let alone a guy period.

"No," he said, leaning against the counter next to the stove as she set a silver pot on the front burner. She clicked it on, the gas flame dancing to life.

"I want to give them time to do their thing," he said.

She poured the cider into the warming pot. "Their thing?" she asked, curiosity tickling her.

"They have this way they work in tandem." He leaned over, glancing in the front room, then shifted back with a smile.

"I'm guessing they're doing it now?" Brooke asked, slowly stirring in the cinnamon and nutmeg.

"Yep." He watched as she slipped the cloves into a white mesh bag and dropped it in.

"There," she said. "Fifteen minutes and we're good to go on cider." She set the spoon on the holding tray. "Should we head back in?"

Noah leaned over to look in the other room, then leaned back by her side. "Not yet. They're working their magic."

She arched her brows. "Their magic?"

"They just have this way where they start off with quips, then argue to see who can figure out whatever piece of the puzzle needs solving, and they both come back with something valuable. Sometimes the same thing as each other, but often two different leads. I've never seen anything like it." Noah arched his shoulders, stretching them out.

"You sore?"

"Just been a long few days."

"I have something that'll help that."

"Oh?"

"It's called Deep Blue. It's this essential oil cream a friend of mine gave me, and it really works." She grabbed her extra tube from a nearby drawer of miscellaneous items. "Just rub it on the sore area, and it'll loosen it right up."

"Cool. Thanks."

"I can help you if you want." Her voice squeaked. She cleared her throat. "Not sure where that came from. Here," she said, taking the tube back. "Just lean your head forward."

He did so, and she rubbed the aromatic cream on his neck.

"Wow. That does feel good," he said within seconds.

"Works fast, right?"

"Yeah. That's good stuff."

"You want me to get your shoulders?"

"You're a medic. I'm sure you know what you are doing." He smiled over his shoulder.

She warmed. She loved seeing the relaxed, playful side of him. "Okay, if you could unbutton the top two buttons of your shirt, I can slip the fabric off of your shoulders."

He did so, and her heart halted. *Whoa!* She knew he was fit. She'd seen him running on base every morning, but the man was sculpted.

"All good?" he asked over his shoulder, his gaze locking with hers once again.

"Yep." She squirted the cream into her hand. Far more than she needed. Hopefully he didn't notice her fumbling.

Taking her right fingers, she swiped a dollop from the puddle in her left palm and started at the base of his neck, moving out across his left shoulder. His muscles were taut, but she wasn't sure if that was from the stress from overworking or if he was just that sculpted. She kneaded the cream into his muscles, and he took a sharp inhale.

"You okay?" she asked.

"Yep. All good." The words sounded fine, but his voice sounded tight. She was about to ask again, just to make sure she wasn't hurting him or anything, when Logan and Emmy rounded the corner.

"Well, I can see we're interrupting," Logan said, with a snarky grin.

"Don't be ridiculous," Noah said, straightening.

"All done," Brooke said, stepping back and moving to the sink to wash her hands. She'd just rub the extra into her hands, but she'd learned the hard way that any touch to your face or inadvertent rubbing of the eyes with Deep Blue on your hands was a very bad idea.

Noah rebuttoned his shirt and, with a tug on the bottom,

straightened it out. "What did you two knuckleheads come up with?"

"We have some good ideas for where else to start digging on Gwyneth and her probable connection with Rick Carson," Emmy said.

"Great. You can get started in the morning."

"Actually"—Emmy shrugged—"we're both pretty wide awake, so we're going to grab a couple of milkshakes from Red's and head on into the office for an hour or so."

Brooke loved Red's. The 24/7 diner worked great for a chocolate malt no matter when she got off watch.

"I'd say don't work too late, but we all know neither of you will listen." Noah shook his head.

"Here," Brooke said, grabbing two to-go cups. "Take some cider with you."

"That's so sweet of you." Emmy smiled. "Thanks."

She ladled the sweet, clove-scented drink into the tumblers.

Logan took a sip. "That's delicious. Thanks, B."

Noah's brows hiked up. "B?"

"Just something we came up with. Right, Logan?" Brooke said.

"Yes, ma'am." He strode over and gave her a kiss on the cheek. "Sleep well."

Noah's and Emmy's gazes both landed on her, questions clearly racing through their minds.

"Thanks." She turned to Emmy. "'Night, Emmy. Thanks for your help tonight."

"No problem. Anytime."

She and Noah saw them out, and for a moment it was like they were a couple seeing friends off for the night. It felt . . . surreal. Like a lost dream she'd given up on years ago.

She locked up while Noah set the alarm. "So you never said what happened with Brodie's alibi."

He gestured to the couch, and she sat, pulling her legs up to her chest and tossing a Hurricanes hockey team blanket across her bent knees. She wasn't sure she was ready to hear this, but she certainly wasn't ready to go to bed without knowing.

Noah draped his arm along the back of the couch. "Brodie was at Riley's Pub with his crewmates, like they all said."

Fear clamped hold, her pulse spiking. "Then who—"

"But," Noah interrupted, giving her hope it was still Brodie. Not that she wanted anyone stalking her, but an unknown stalker scared her more than Brodie being a vengeful moron. "It doesn't sound like he was there all night. Everyone remembers him coming in with his crewmates, ordering a beer or two, then no one remembers him being around until he started a game of pool around 0100."

"So he could have ducked out."

"It's definitely possible."

"What now?"

"Now you go to bed. You need your rest."

"So do you."

"Agreed."

Twenty minutes later, she lay back in bed, calmer than she'd been the last time around. Knowing Noah was sleeping down the hall in her guest room gave her peace. He was strong, resolute, and an excellent agent, but that's not what was tugging at her heart. It was his kindness, his strong yet gentle manner. His love for his family. His playful side she'd come to see. He really was the sweetest man. She rolled over, staring at the shut blinds. Why couldn't a guy like him fall for a girl like her?

He stood outside, using the old oak tree in her lawn for cover this time. Her silhouette passed in front of her bedroom window before moving out of sight.

So she thought the agents helping her would dissuade him. On the contrary, he was more committed than ever.

The fear on her face when she spotted him in her backyard had filled him with bliss. Bliss because he'd accomplished the first part of his mission—filling her with fear. Raw, gnawing fear.

Her bedroom light switched off, and he smiled, the tree's knotty surface bumpy beneath his gloved hands. He was just getting started.

FORTY-SIX

Fresh morning coffee in hand, Rissi and Mason strolled down the Riverwalk and she, once again, fought the urge to hold his hand. Still feeling horrible for breaking the news to Caleb about Lucas, she'd tried calling him last night, but it'd just gone to voicemail. She'd tried again this morning, but he'd probably been on his daily run.

Since she and Mason had their investigative plan for the day and weren't heading into the office for the morning meeting, Noah had called to update them about all that was happening with Brooke. *Black widows?* Rissi shivered. Things were quickly getting out of control, and in an effort to make sure she stayed safe, Noah had decided to stay in Brooke's guest room until either they were able to prove it was Brodie and put him behind bars, or Gabby and Finn returned, and they could take turns with Brooke. From her boss's voice, it sure didn't sound like he minded handling guard duty in the meantime.

Curious.

She and Mason decided to take Em's advice and visit Margaret Gregory as soon as the Wilmington Maritime Historical Museum opened. If Lucas was using the curse as a cover to sabotage things on *Dauntless*—or even if he wasn't behind all that was going on, so many of the crew were buying into the curse that it was clearly affecting rig operation. It was time they learned exactly what they were dealing with.

The museum was located along a flat-stone street at the end of the Riverwalk. Mason held the door open for her, and they stepped inside. White wainscoting covered the bottom half of soft blue walls. Glass cases stood all around the front room, with portraits and informational plaques artfully lining the walls.

A refined woman greeted them. "Hello, how may I help you?"

"Hi. I'm Rissi Dawson, and this is . . ."

"Mason Rogers," he said, extending his hand. "Pleasure, ma'am."

"'Ma'am'?" She laughed. "I appreciate the politeness, but I hate *ma'am*. Makes me sound like an old dowdy."

"That surely was not my intention."

"I know, young man, but you may call me Margaret."

"Margaret," he said with a smile.

Rissi smiled. Their day was starting off well, apparently being greeted by the very woman they hoped to see.

Margaret shifted her warm gaze to Rissi. "How may I assist you today? Are you here to tour the museum?"

"I'd love to look around." She loved all things related to the sea. "But first, we'd like to talk to you about a local curse." She felt funny even saying the word.

"Ah, the one that has all the sailors spooked?"

"Yes, ma—" Mason stopped as Margaret looked at him over the rim of her glasses. "Margaret," he said.

"Captain Josiah Henry's curse," Margaret said with a pleased smile.

"That's the one," Rissi said. "It's got the *Dauntless* crew all worked up."

Margaret shook her head. "Based on the murmurings around town, I can say they have good reason to be worked up."

"You *believe* in the curse?"

Margaret waggled her finger in the air. "Of course not." She headed toward the hallway and indicated for them to follow.

"But I can imagine how, when they are out at sea for three weeks at a time and things keep going wrong, it is normal to start looking for explanations. And men at sea seem more susceptible, shall we say, to legends."

"But it's not real."

"I assume not, but"—she shrugged her petite shoulders, her pearl necklace swishing across her blouse—"you never know." She winked.

"Can you tell us about it?" Mason asked. "About Henry."

"Surely," she said, leading them to a portrait on the wall of a handsome man in a dashing suit with dark hair and green eyes.

Margaret leaned in, lowering her voice as if she were about to impart a take-it-to-the-grave secret. "Have you heard of the *Apparition*?"

"No."

"Well, Josiah Henry was captain of the *Apparition*."

"Excuse me," Rissi said, not trying to be rude, "but this plaque says he captained the *Providence*."

"You're right, my dear. *Apparition* became the nickname of the *Providence* because it was said she moved like a shadow through the British blockades off our coast during the Revolutionary War. Captain Henry's first mate was a man by the name of Wells Blackwood the Fourth. Rather a fitting name for a traitor, don't you think?"

She headed for the back hall and bid them to come with her. "Let's chat over a cup of tea, shall we?"

"Thank you," Rissi said.

"That's very kind of you," Mason added.

Once Rissi and Mason were settled at a round table in the center of a large office space, Margaret set out tea. Rissi guessed the room probably used to be the dining room of the old house—the large, ornate fireplace being the key factor in her determination.

Rissi wanted to ask Margaret about the house's history, but

they needed to stay on task. It certainly would be fun to come back and spend another day learning from Margaret though. She was a delightful lady.

Margaret poured the Earl Grey and offered the traditional cream and sugar cubes. Once seated, she continued, "It is believed that Wells sold out the ship and all hundred and forty souls on board to the British Captain Bartholomew Norrington.

"Blackwood was a loyalist to the king posing as a patriot aboard the *Providence*. The scoundrel passed a message to Bartholomew and when the *Providence* appeared on the horizon, moonlight glinting off the otherwise dark ship, Norrington and his men ambushed it. They spared Blackwood, seized the cargo, and sank the ship with everyone else on board, except a lowly deckhand who managed to escape."

Margaret leaned in closer, delicate spider lines creasing the corners of her narrowed blue eyes. "Before the ship went down, Captain Henry vowed revenge on Blackwood for his treachery and on all British warships in the area." She straightened and lifted her rose-patterned teacup. "And he upheld his promise." She took a proper sip.

"How?" Mason asked, setting his cup on his saucer with a repercussive *ting*. The cutest expression of a kid who'd just broke Mom's vase crossed his handsome face.

But Margaret simply smiled. "That is why tea is a woman's sport." She laughed. "The cups are not made for stalwart hands."

"True." Mason shrugged.

"I like you, my dear." She smiled at Rissi. "Both of you. I hope what I share is helpful to you both."

"Very much so," Rissi said.

"Good. Now, where was I? Oh yes, every British warship to enter the area throughout the remainder of the war sank nearly on top of the spot where the *Apparition* went down. At that point no one called it the *Providence* anymore. She had lived up to her nickname and was a haunting ghost looking for ships to devour. The deckhand who escaped told the story and it spread. And, as most legends do, it grew deeper and darker with time."

She took another delicate sip before proceeding. "Many a sailor has claimed to see the *Apparition* moving like a shadow through the night."

"Why do people think *Dauntless* is being affected?"

"Because it's tied in less than a nautical mile from where the *Apparition* went down. When the drilling crew came in and set up the subsea part of the well, the men disturbed not only the ecosystem, but Henry and his crew's resting spot."

She placed her teacup in the saucer and smoothed her sophisticated bob cut. "*If* you believe in the curse, then it would seem that Captain Henry is angry that Textra Oil paid no respect to the *Apparition*. Rumor has it that the commercial diver working for Textra also dove the wreck of *Apparition*, which has never been done before. Add in the men working in submersibles on the line sweeping over the wreck as if it were some carnival attraction, and hauling and placing all that equipment, pumping oil so nearby . . ." She inhaled, then released it. "It's no wonder the men are spooked."

"So you think the men were spooked because of the location before any of the problems started?" Mason asked.

"Yes," Margaret said. "I think that's precisely correct."

"So if a person wanted to sabotage the *Dauntless* and delay or even stop production . . ." Mason said.

"They'd start playing into the crew's fears," Rissi said.

"Exactly." Mason smiled, his green eyes lighting with the motion.

Margaret's gaze swished slowly between the two of them, and her graceful smile widened.

Rissi's phone vibrated in her pocket. "I'm so sorry. Can you excuse me? It's my boss."

"Of course, dear."

"I'll be right back," she said, then stepped outside. The air was heavy with the threat of rain. It had drizzled last night, but it was coming in stronger today. "Hi, boss," she said. "Mason and I are interviewing the docent from the historical museum."

"I hope you've learned some helpful information, but you guys need to come back in."

"Sure. We'll head right over. What's going on?"

"Jeremy Brandt of NTSB called."

"And?"

"The copter was rigged to crash."

FORTY-SEVEN

"The copter was sabotaged?" Mason asked as they entered the station. He had hoped it would be deemed an accident. Sabotage added so many facets to the investigation, but the highest priority was determining who the target had been.

"I'm afraid so," Noah said.

"Someone was trying to kill us or someone else on the copter," Rissi said. "How could they even know any of us would be on that helicopter?"

"There was a death aboard *Dauntless*. They might have known we'd send out investigators, but it's more likely they intended to harm Textra Oil."

"You're thinking the Freedom Group?" Rissi said as she paced. "And to think I credited them as our rescuers."

"Some of the group might be legit," Noah said.

"I highly doubt Gwyneth is." Rissi shook her head.

"It was awfully convenient that they were on their run back out to the *Freedom* when we went down," Mason said.

"And it puts Gwyneth on land when the copter might have been sabotaged." Rissi looked to Noah. "Do we know when it was sabotaged?"

"The mechanic they determined compromised the helo's collective is named Randy Patterson. He's being questioned by NTSB now. Brandt extended the courtesy for me to come over and get briefed by him after the interrogation."

"That was thoughtful of him," Rissi said.

"Yeah." Noah nodded.

Mason had seen that taut look on Noah's face a few times since his arrival on the team, and it never lined up with anything but bad news.

"Seems like this is our day for bad news," Noah began, confirming Mason's intuition. "Ed Scott called right before you guys got here, and two things have recently happened on *Dauntless*."

Noah took a sharp inhale, and Rissi glanced between him and Mason as he continued. "First, Chase Calhoun is dead."

"The diver? Dead?" Rissi sputtered.

"I'm afraid so. According to Ed, he was impaled by a stingray."

She covered her mouth with her hand. "Oh my goodness."

"Migration season. There are so many. Apparently, Chase had gone down for a preliminary assessment and . . ." Noah ran a hand across his chin. "Actually, I'll let Ed and the crew present at the time tell you the rest. I wouldn't want to relay any inaccurate information."

"Tell us?" Mason asked. "You want us to head back out?"

"Yes, but this time pack a bag. I have a feeling you two might be there awhile."

"Yes, sir," Mason said.

"But the storm's coming in," Emmy said.

"It's not supposed to hit bad until tomorrow," Mason said. "We should be fine."

"It might take longer than a day," Noah said.

"Oil platforms weather storms all the time. We'll be fine," Rissi said.

"You said there were two things that happened." Mason wasn't sure whether he really wanted to know, but he and Rissi needed an idea of what they were walking into.

"Right. Second thing is that they found the missing flange bolt."

"Great. Then that rules out foul play," Rissi said.

"I'm afraid not. It was found in one of the crew washing machines."

Why did Mason have the feeling he knew whose stuff it had been found with?

"Adam Jones said he was waiting to do his laundry and heard a clanging noise start up in one of the machines. When the cycle ended and they took out the clothes, they found the bolt lying in the empty machine."

"Whose wash was it?"

"Lucas's."

───

"Hey, Mason," Maddie said, shifting to look back at them as they climbed into the Coast Guard helicopter. "Rissi. Good to see you both again, but I'm guessing if you're heading back to *Dauntless*, it's not for the best reasons."

"No, unfortunately not," Rissi said, storing her duffel in the back rack beside Mason's.

"We've got one more passenger joining us," Maddie said.

"Oh?" Rissi asked.

"Bob Stanton," Maddie said. "Apparently some bigwig with Textra Oil. Noah insisted you guys fly out on one of our copters until all of Textra Oil's are checked and deemed safe by the NTSB. Bob needed a ride out, so Noah offered to let him tag along."

"We've met Bob," Mason said, glancing over to see Bob making his way over to the bird with a black boot on his left foot.

"Hi, guys," Bob said as Mason helped him up into the copter. "Thanks," he said as he settled in his seat.

"I didn't know you'd be joining us," Rissi said.

"My platform is out of control. I'm going to ensure we are back on schedule ASAP."

"Back on schedule?" Rissi said, her voice heightening.

"Yes." Bob dabbed the rain off his face with his white handkerchief. "We've been behind since the first incident."

"And by *incident* you mean Greg Barnes's death?" Mason said.

"Yes," Bob said without compunction.

"All right, good-looking," Maddie said to Mason, as he was the only one not seated. "Buckle up, we're ready to go."

Mason sank into the seat beside Rissi.

Rissi leaned over and whispered as the blades purred to life, "Looks like you have a fan."

Maddie seemed nice but was not for him. The only woman for him was sitting on his left, and it took all the restraint he had not to reach out and hold her hand.

"And we're off," Maddie said over the comm as they settled their headsets over their ears, positioning the microphone in front of their mouths.

The blades thwacked as they flew out over the ocean.

Mason's sat phone rang. He pulled it out of the interior pocket of his windbreaker.

Sliding his headset off, he answered. "Rogers," he hollered over the deep *whoosh* of the blades reverberating in his chest.

"This is Jeremy Brandt. NTSB. We spoke previously."

"Yes. I remember. Have you learned anything?" He purposely asked without being specific. Being on a copter headed to *Dauntless* wasn't really the best time to learn what had gone wrong the first time around.

"Your boss gave me this number. He said you'd want to know."

Mason covered his right ear as he held the phone to his left. "Know what?"

"He told you the copter was sabotaged?"

"Yes."

"Someone sheared the pitch control rod, so when you flew

far enough, the collective stopped being able to control the pitch, and you went down."

"Noah said you got the guy."

"Yes. Randy Patterson. He's one of the mechanics for Textra's copters, and he approved the preflight inspection."

"Disgruntled employee?"

"No. This is the part your boss said you'd want to know. Randy confessed to doing it but says he did it for the woman he loves."

Mason's jaw tightened. "Let me guess . . . Gwyneth Lansing."

"You got it."

FORTY-EIGHT

Mason hung up and replaced his headset, staring blindly at the rain pinging off the windshield and snaking sideways in rivulets along the panels closest to them.

"What was that about?" Rissi asked.

He looked at Bob and then to her. "I'll tell you when we land."

"I'm head of operations. Anything you tell her, you can tell me," Bob said.

"I'd like to speak with my partner first." *Partner.* He loved the sound of that. And it thrilled him to think of it on another level than just work.

"Very well, but I want a full update when you two are finished talking."

Mason nodded. "I'll share what we can."

Bob exhaled heartily and stared out the window.

Rissi studied Mason a moment. She raised her microphone and slid her headset off one ear and then leaned close, waiting for him to do the same. "You okay?" she asked.

It was clear to Mason that a piece had just been added to the puzzle, but he continued to wonder what exactly he and Rissi were walking into at this heightened state of the investigation. With a second death on *Dauntless*—even if they had a preliminary cause—and a sabotaged helicopter, they were looking at someone very willing to kill.

Rissi bumped his shoulder with hers. "What's got you concerned?"

"I like knowing what I'm heading into." Especially when the woman he loved was at his side. Not that she couldn't hold her own—far from it, but she was still the woman he loved, and he had an innate longing to protect her.

"Really?" she asked.

He frowned. "You don't?"

"I kinda like the hunt. Having to deduce what's going on as it unfolds."

"So you like the danger of an unknown situation?" She never ceased to surprise him. It's what would make life with her so exciting. Life with Rissi. He couldn't imagine a better future. He prayed with everything inside that dream would become their reality.

Rissi exhaled. "*Danger* is probably the wrong word."

He shifted, draping his left arm across the back of the seat, to face her better. "What word would you use?"

"Thrill," she whispered against his ear. "I like the thrill of the hunt."

As he leaned back against his seat, he couldn't help but smile. The quiet yet fierce girl he'd known as a teen was fiercer still.

Moments later, the piercing glare of *Dauntless*'s lights illuminated its vast presence.

"Hold on to your hats," Maddie said as she lowered the copter toward the helipad. A man in an orange jumpsuit with reflector strips stood below, directing Maddie where to land with two orange sticks that reminded Mason of Star Wars lightsabers. A movie series he'd only gotten to see as an adult. He'd missed so much of a "normal" childhood, but he was catching up.

The man below guided the copter down until it rocked to a full stop on the helipad.

The door opened from the outside as the blades stilled. "Be safe," Maddie said as Rissi stepped out first.

"Thanks," Mason said as he followed.

Ed met them at the edge of the helipad with Adam beside him. "I'd say it's nice seeing you two again, but the circumstances are far from good. Let's head inside."

They followed Ed down the metal stairs, into the tower, and then up to his office just off the main control center.

Rissi leaned into Mason. "So what was the phone call all about?"

He looked at Ed and Adam walking ahead of him, and Bob pulling up the rear. "Jeremy Brandt from NTSB called," he said under his breath. "Turns out Randy Patterson sabotaged the copter at Gwyneth's request."

"Why am I not surprised Gwyneth was involved."

"We can brief Ed, Adam, and Bob. Since it was Textra's copter, they're going to know soon enough. But I'd like to start with our questions first."

"Agreed."

He glanced back. "You need any help, Bob?"

"Nope." Bob looked down at the black boot fixed around his fractured leg. "This boot is pretty indestructible."

"Okay," Mason said. "Let me know if you change your mind."

"Thanks."

Once the five of them were in the office, Ed closed the door.

"Tell us about Lucas and Chase. Go step-by-step," Mason said, not wasting any time.

Ed sighed. "There's a lot to tell."

"Just start with what happened first," Rissi said, taking a seat. Everyone followed suit.

"Okay . . ." Ed exhaled. "That would be Adam finding the flange bolt in the washer Lucas had just used."

"How do you know it wasn't there before Lucas put his load in?" Rissi asked.

"Henry Smith did the load before Lucas," Ed said. "Henry confirmed there was no clanging sound when his cycle ended. The bolt must have been in a piece of Lucas's clothing because it was quiet until the last few minutes of the cycle, then it clanged loudly." He slipped his hat off, clutching it in his oil-stained hands. He looked to Adam, who nodded.

"I was there," Adam said, "waiting for the machine. I heard when the clanging started. Once the cycle ended, Lucas and I looked to see what was making all the ruckus. Lucas pulled his clothes out, and I looked in with my pocket flashlight. And there it was. That missing bolt for the flange. At least that's what it looked like. I pulled it out, and Lucas's face paled. I told Henry, who was still waiting on the dryer, to keep an eye on him while I ran to find Ed."

Before Adam could continue, the door opened, and Joel Waters stepped in. He looked good for recently being discharged from the hospital.

"Perfect timing," Ed said.

"Hey, Joel," Mason greeted him.

He gave a chin lift to him and Rissi.

"What can you tell us about the equipment?" Ed asked.

Joel's safety glasses hung around his neck. "I inspected both the compressor and gas sensor, and it's my final determination that the fire occurred when a gas leak on a failed flange gasket was ignited by the flame of Greg Barnes's lighter. The missing bolt had been located on a two-inch line from the compressor starter exhaust line to the vent system. The gas source was either a leaking valve upstream of the starter or gas migration from the vent system."

"And the bolt Adam found in the washer?"

"I matched it up. It was the missing bolt."

"What I don't get," Rissi sid, "is if Lucas is guilty, why not pitch the bolt overboard?"

"Maybe someone came in as he was finishing up, so he slipped it in his pocket," Adam offered.

"Rookie mistake," Mason sid, "but it does happen."

Rissi took a stiffening breath. "Where is Lucas now?"

"We have him in his bunk room. Garrett and Jayce are taking turns sitting outside his door."

With no law enforcement on board, firefighters guarding the kid made the most sense.

"I want him off my platform and in custody," Bob said. "And Textra will be suing him for the delay in the schedule and the vandalism to our property."

Of course they would. With Bob it all came down to time and money. Did he even care that three men who worked for him and his company were dead? "We're going to need to talk with him first," Mason said.

"Can't you talk to him back on land with him behind bars?" Bob said, his face reddening, the small vein along his right temple throbbing purple.

"We know how to do our job, Mr. Stanton," Rissi said. "So we're going to need you to give us the space and time to do it."

Bob sat down with a sigh. "Very well."

"As I said, we need to talk with Lucas," Mason said to Ed. Ed nodded. "Of course."

"But first we want to know what happened with Chase, and we need to examine his body."

"Examine his body?" Adam frowned. "He was killed by a stingray. Why on earth would you need to look at his body?"

"It's protocol," Rissi said.

"Okay." Adam held up his hands. "I don't understand your reasoning, but you gotta do what you gotta do."

"What happened with Chase?" Rissi asked.

"I can tell you what I know, but I wasn't one of the men who pulled him up," Ed said.

"Neither was I," Adam added.

"We'll talk to the men who were there, but an overview from you would be helpful."

"Sure," Ed said. "Chase went down on an assessment dive to see what work would be needed on one of the risers that's been giving us trouble. Apparently, topside heard a huge grunt from him over the comm. They asked if he was all right. And when they got no response, they retracted the line, pulling him up. They said when he reached the dive deck, he had white foam around his mouth and a puncture wound near his heart. Karl was called, but it was too late."

Rissi looked at Mason. "We're going to need to see the body and talk to Karl."

FORTY-NINE

Sadly, Mason and Rissi knew the way to the medical bay. Entering, they found Karl, and beyond him lay a body bag on one of the exam tables.

"Why isn't he in the freezer?" Mason asked.

"It's been a busy morning."

"As soon as we examine him, we'll need to move him to the freezer," Rissi said.

"Why is it so urgent?" Karl's brow furrowed.

"Because stingrays insert venom into the victim. To definitively prove it was a stingray that killed Chase, the ME will need a sample of that poison. The longer you leave him out at room temperature, the faster the poison dissipates. Cooling the body slows the dissipation," Rissi explained.

"That makes sense," Karl said. "I'm sorry. I didn't know."

"May we?" Mason asked, indicating the body bag.

"Of course."

"Could you close the door?" Rissi asked.

"No problem." Karl moved and shut it, then rejoined them.

"Can you tell us what happened?" Mason asked before unzipping the body bag.

"I was in here, bandaging up a cut Jayce had gotten on his hand while sharpening his knife. I was just about finished when the call came through that Chase had been hurt and to bring my bag." He cleared his throat. "I rushed out onto the diving deck where Chase lay. He had white foam inside his dive mask. We removed it to see if I could perform CPR, but it was clearly too late, and then I saw the wound."

"What kind of wound?" Rissi asked.

"It looked like a stingray wound to the heart. We removed his tanks, put him in the body bag, and transported him here."

Mason folded his arms across his chest. "You removed his tanks?"

"Yes."

"And where did you put them?" Rissi asked.

"I think Adam took care of that. You'll have to ask him."

"Did anyone check them before he went down or when he came up?" Mason asked.

"You'd have to look at the maintenance log, to see who had the last rotation, but everyone knows to check their own equipment before going down."

"Where do they store the equipment?" Rissi asked.

"In the dive room."

She looked at Mason, and he made a mental note to check that next. They'd need to bag Chase's tanks and bring them back for Emmy to inspect in Finn's absence. Man, he'd picked a crazy week to head out of town.

"Let's take a look at the body," Mason said, unzipping the bag.

Chase lay pale, still in his regular dive suit, which explained how the stingray barb had punctured it. If he'd been welding rather than assessing what work needed to be done, the thick welding attire would probably have saved his life.

The puncture was centered almost perfectly over his heart. One inch by perhaps another. It was round, but not perfectly cylindrical. "Did you find a barb in the wound?" Mason asked.

"One wasn't visible," Karl said.

It could easily be deeper in the wound. Mason looked at Rissi. "We should take photographs. I'd like to open his suit to take a better look at the injury, but we better leave things intact for Hadley."

"Agreed." She nodded.

After finishing the preliminary photographs and seeing Chase's body into the secondary freezer. Mason and Rissi headed for Ed's office.

They needed to have another chat, and then it was time to talk with Lucas.

FIFTY

Before leaving the medical bay, Mason requested that Karl retrieve Chase's tanks and a copy of the maintenance log and secure them with the body until they could be taken back to Emmy. Then he radioed the *Freedom* to let them know he and Rissi would be taking a raft over to talk some more with Gwyneth. But according to her team, she'd returned to land. Taking another trip back to shore so soon after arriving on the *Freedom* seemed suspicious at best.

Rissi called Emmy to let her know Gwyneth was back on land and to expect the tanks. When she and Mason headed for Ed's office, they found him, Adam, and Bob Stanton arguing about delays in production.

Bob really was a piece of work. Three men were dead, and all he was concerned about was money.

Ed greeted them as they entered. "How did things go with Chase?" He shook his head. "I can't believe we lost another one."

"Things went fine," Rissi said. "Losing Max, Greg, and Chase in a matter of days has to be . . . staggering."

"Unfortunately, you work rigs as long as I have, you see loss."

There was a reason the profession was listed as one of America's most dangerous jobs. She imagined it was woven in the fabric of the workers' lives to lose crewmates, but nearly back-to-back like this . . . Apprehension coursed through her. In two of the three deaths, foul play had been confirmed. The question was, how involved was Lucas?

"I know now is not the best time, but we need a few things from you before we speak with Lucas," she said, her chest tightening. She couldn't believe she was about to question Caleb's nephew about a possible murder, or at least negligent manslaughter. It seemed surreal, and never in a million years would she have thought she'd be here. But the old sin nature had a way of hooking in a person's veins. Lucas probably figured what he did was for a worthy cause—as if that somehow justified it.

"Okay?" Ed said after her prolonged silence.

"Sorry." Rissi shook her head. "I was just collecting my thoughts. We"—she pointed between herself and Mason—"believe you should fully shut down operations until we sort this out."

Bob stood. "That's not an option."

"Two men have died *on* this rig in a matter of days, and the remainder of the crew appears to be—"

"I understand," Ed said, cutting in. "Believe me, I'm responsible for this crew. It's my job to keep these men safe, and I failed two of them."

"You can't control whether or not equipment is sabotaged," Mason said.

Bob squinted. "You aren't suggesting that's what happened with Chase too? He was stung by a stingray. What does that have to do with equipment?"

Clearly the big boss preferred things cut-and-dry. As soon as they could get the investigation over with, the sooner things went back to normal, though Rissi doubted that would be the case. There was an uneasiness coursing through *Dauntless*, one she doubted would be instantly restored with their leaving.

"We won't know until his breathing apparatus is checked," Mason said, "but it's possible his mixture was off, and he had a seizure because of it. It might not be what he died from, but we can't write off such a failure as at least a part of the equation until our crime-scene investigator processes the equipment."

"So all you have is conjecture," Bob said, crossing his arms.

"With Chase, yes," Mason said. "With Greg, no."

"As I've said, you've got two dead crewmen," Rissi reiterated. "Until we figure out the full circumstances surrounding both deaths, we strongly recommend putting a halt to operations." In a realm where time equaled massive money, Rissi knew it was never going to happen, but she had to advise them all the same. The body count was rising. Not to mention Max, who'd been on a Textra copter sabotaged to go down. A chill raced up her spine. She still wanted to know who the intended target or targets had been.

She looked at Mason as a thought flashed through her mind. Chase had been in the copter rigged to go down, and now he was dead. Maybe they would find something off with his equipment.

Mason shifted his gaze in her direction. An understanding they'd chat when in private passed wordlessly between them.

"I understand your concerns," Bob said. "And I share them, but we're even further behind schedule than we were a couple days ago."

Ed quirked his head, something clearly catching hold of him.

"What is it?" she asked.

Ed rubbed the back of his neck. "Just wondering if the crew of the *Freedom*, particularly Gwyneth, finally did what they threatened to do."

Mason looked at Rissi, and she gave a slight nod for him to run with it.

He shifted his attention on Ed. "What did she or they threaten to do?"

"I would have said more your first trip out, but I assumed the explosion was an unfortunate accident." He took a stiffening breath. "But Gwyneth vowed to destroy our platform from the inside out."

Rissi's brows arched. "From the inside out?"

Ed nodded.

"We should have her arrested," Bob said, his round face nearly tinging purple.

"Our team is on it," Rissi said, knowing Emmy and Logan wouldn't stop until they tracked Gwyneth down.

"They better be." A thick vein swelled along Bob's left temple, throbbing.

"We need to speak with Lucas," Mason said.

Joel poked his head in the door. "Sorry to interrupt, but Erik and Jayce are at it again."

"Jayce?" Rissi shifted. "Isn't he supposed to be watching Lucas's door?"

"It's probably Garrett's turn," Adam said.

Ed pushed off the counter he'd been leaning against. "Sorry, folks, I've got to handle this. The rig hotheads are at it again."

Ed and Joel rushed out of the office.

Rissi looked at Mason, and they followed, running down the tower stairs.

What in the world was going on?

Down more steps and along the narrow passageway, they followed Ed toward the galley. Twenty yards away, loud voices and . . . cheers, of all things, emanated along the corridor.

Ed paused with his arm blocking the doorway, gripping the frame on the other side. "You might want to wait out here," he said to Rissi.

She rose on tiptoes to peer in over Ed's arm. Two men were brawling across the galley floor as a cheering group hollered. "Nail him!" "Watch your jaw!" "You've got this!"

Blood dripped down Jayce's face.

"I'll be fine, but thanks," she said.

"All right," Ed said, lowering his arm to his side. "Your call."

Mason stayed by her side, his shoulders squared. She'd seen that protective stance before.

"That's enough!" Ed roared, not wasting any time in moving into the thick of the melee and pushing the two sweaty, bloody men apart.

Both lunged at the other again.

"Enough!" Ed planted his palm in the center of Jayce's burly chest and physically pushed him back.

Joel helped haul back the man Rissi assumed was Erik.

"Let go of me," Erik roared.

"Settle down." Joel gripped Erik's arms, his knuckles whitening from the strain.

Adam stepped to his side to lend a hand, if necessary. Erik was a big boy—definitely the body-builder type.

"Whatever." Erik ripped out of Joel's hold and stormed toward the galley door. "I'm out of here."

"We need you to stay," Mason said, stepping between him and the door.

Erik paused, his chest heaving. "What for?"

"We've got questions for you."

FIFTY-ONE

Rissi sat beside Mason on one side of the galley-style table, Erik, Ed, and Jayce on the other—in that order.

Forearms resting on the table, she began, "What were you fighting about?"

"The fact that he's an—" The expletive left Erik's mouth with a hiss.

"Not appropriate," Ed said. "There's a lady present."

"And?" Erik spat.

"And," Ed said, his voice crisp, his words punctuated, "you use that kind of language in front of her again, and you're fired."

Erik scoffed. "What is she, some hoity-toity princess?"

Mason straightened, his shoulders squaring.

Erik lifted his chin with a laugh. "And what are you, her protector?"

Mason smiled. "Oh, she doesn't need a protector. She can hold her own."

Erik eyed her up. "Is that right?"

Rissi leaned forward, only too happy to practice her boxing moves. "Try me." She smiled.

"Stay put, Erik," Ed said through gritted teeth, "or you're fired. Not that I wouldn't love to see this lady kick your butt."

The veins in Erik's tightly gripped fists bulged, but he stayed put.

Mason gave Rissi a quick wink, then shifted his attention on Erik. "Let's start at the top."

Erik's tongue rubbed the inside of his cheek, making it bulge out like a sulking kid. "Which means?"

"What were you and Jayce arguing about?"

Erik remained silent, so Mason shifted his attention to Jayce.

Jayce shrugged. "I was just calling it like I see it."

"Which is?" Rissi asked.

"Word is Chase's tanks were dry when he surfaced. No way he used that much air during the short time he was down there."

That was news. "We heard Chase was dead by stingray barb when he was pulled up by the topside line."

"Yeah, but maybe he would have survived if he'd had enough air for the ride up." Jayce pinned his narrow gaze on Erik.

"Are you saying you think Erik had something to do with the dry tanks?" Rissi asked, needing Jayce to be absolutely clear with his statement.

"He was the last one to do maintenance on the equipment," Jayce said, casting his attention back on her. "I mean, I suppose it's possible there was an equipment malfunction, but it seems really unlikely given everything else going on around here. And I heard him and Chase arguing less than an hour before Chase went down to check the riser."

"So you think . . ." Mason prompted.

"I think someone messed with Chase's equipment," Jayce's voice held steadfast, his gaze shifting to Erik, "and since Erik was the last one to check it . . ."

"*Seriously?*" Erik scoffed. "Dude, when I checked Chase's tanks, everything was full. What happened between me checking them and him putting them on, I can't say. Besides, the dude was killed by a stingray. What does that have to do with his tanks?"

"Uh-huh." Jayce studied Erik a moment, then shook his head. "Seems like the easy way out to me, dude."

Erik strained forward, trying to lean across Ed to Jayce, but Ed held him at bay. "Everyone knows Chase and I didn't get along, but you seriously think I'd kill the guy?"

"Loathed each other is more like it," Jayce said. "You two spent more time fighting with each other than working."

Erik's teeth ground loud enough for Rissi to hear. "That's an exaggeration."

Jayce arched a brow. "Is it?"

Erik stood, and Jayce followed suit.

"You wanna go?" Jayce asked.

Mason rounded the table as Ed grabbed Jayce, and Mason clamped his hands on Erik's bulky arms, pulling him back.

"I said *enough*!" Ed's holler echoed off the galley walls with a thunderous clap.

Jayce settled, but Erik wrestled against Mason's hold.

"You best let go, boy," Erik said, who looked all of a handful of years older than Mason.

Mason's jaw set. "I suggest you listen to your boss and take a seat."

"Or what?" Erik scoffed.

Mason opened his mouth to reply, but Ed got in Erik's face before the words left his mouth. "I said take a seat, or you're out of here." He held Erik's brooding gaze.

It took a moment, but Erik finally flopped into his seat with a thump.

Mason shook out his hands but remained standing.

"Why did you and Chase loathe each other, to use Jayce's words?" Rissi asked.

"Chase was a—" Another expletive started to fly, and Ed took a step forward.

Erik cut off the nasty word and rephrased. "He was a jerk."

She was starting to wonder if the same couldn't be said of Erik. "Why do you say that?"

"Because he was always going for other guys' girls, always

301

talking smack, pretending to be a 'charming' guy but he was a—" He stopped short, catching himself this time.

The air quotes on *charming* looked personal. Had a girl chosen Chase over Erik?

"I'm going to need a list of names of the guys with girlfriends you think Chase messed with."

Erik snorted. "You better have a long piece of paper."

"Did he hit on any girls you were interested in or dating?" Mason asked.

Erik shrugged. "Not any worth mentioning."

"*Please*. Who are you trying to fool?" Jayce said.

"Shut up, Jayce." Erik pounded the table, and the napkin pile in the center bounced. "This is none of your business."

Jayce looked at Rissi. "Chase was running around with Erik's girl, Charlene."

"Is that true?" Rissi asked, turning her full attention on Erik.

He swiped a hand over his head. "She wasn't *my* girl. We just fooled around now and again."

"And Chase and Charlene . . . ?" Rissi began.

Erik shrugged. The tiny muscle along his rugged jaw twitched. "Hooked up," he said. "But what do I care? I got what I wanted from her first."

Rissi winced at his derogatory statement. Erik was a pig, and it sounded like Chase was even worse.

"If you didn't care," Mason said, pushing off the wall and coming to sit beside Rissi, "why the argument with Chase?"

At his silence, Mason repeated, "Why the argument, Erik?"

"Chase was always talking smack," Erik said.

Jayce shook his head with an exhale. "That's true. Seems like that's all Chase did. Talk about what girl he'd hooked up with last, or who he was going after. Didn't matter who they were with."

"How many guys on the rig did he do this to?" Rissi asked, but she was met with stony silence.

"How many of the crew's girlfriends did he hook up with?" Mason asked, his words straight to the point.

Erik sniffed, then rubbed his nose. "I don't know." He shrugged. "Maybe a handful."

Which equaled a handful of suspects *if* Chase's death wasn't the result of the stingray puncture to his heart. What if he had run out of air, causing a seizure, and he was stabbed by a stingray's tail as topside pulled him up through the migrating swarm?

Rissi pushed a notepad and pen across the table. "We're going to need names."

FIFTY-TWO

Garrett sat reading in the passageway outside of Lucas's bunk when Mason and Rissi approached.

"Hey, Garrett," Rissi said.

"Hey, you guys. You ready to talk to Lucas?"

"Yep." Then they had a new round of suspects who may or may not be related to Chase's death. They'd be interviewing them all. She'd been taught to turn over every stone, even the smallest pebble, as that's where the truth often lay.

Garrett stood. "All right. I'm going to run for a relief break, grab some coffee, and I'll be back."

"Thanks." Taking a stiffening breath, Rissi prayed, *Please, Lord, let the truth come to light. Please be with us all.*

She opened the door to find Lucas laid out on his bed, his laptop propped on his thighs, watching a movie with a lot of gunfire retorting.

"It's about time." He shut his MacBook, flipped his legs over the side of his bunk, and sat up, his head cresting the base of the upper bunk. He leaned forward. "What do you want now?"

"Now, I'm going to read you your rights," Mason said.

Lucas gaped at Rissi. "Is he kidding?"

"I'm afraid not."

His eyes, the same shape and color as Caleb's, widened. "You're arresting me?"

This was going to be even harder than she'd expected. "We

have you tied to Gwyneth Lansing and her protests, Lucas. We've traced the tuition money you stole from your uncle and donated to the Freedom Group, and now we have the missing flange bolt tied to you. That's more than enough evidence to bring you in for questioning. But we'll start here, for now." They'd take him into the station when they headed back to shore.

Mason finished reading him his rights, and Rissi pulled up a chair, sitting facing him.

Mason remained standing, giving her space to work.

"Tell me about your relationship with Gwyneth Lansing," she began.

Lucas's gaze shot to the side, his jaw shifting. "I don't know what you're talking about."

"Really? Because we've been told you were in a relationship with her."

Color flared in his cheeks. "That's a lie!"

"So you're claiming you don't know Gwyneth Lansing?" She kept her voice calm. Lucas was getting stirred up enough for the both of them.

"All I know is what the guys on the platform say about her and her team."

"You're lying." Rissi's jaw held firm.

"No," he said, looking directly at her, "I'm not."

He'd literally just lied to her face. Heat swelled inside, but she continued to keep her voice even. "School records indicate you were in two of her classes. Your roommate, Seth, said you told him about your relationship with her."

Lucas swallowed, the red hue slipping from his cheeks.

She crossed her legs. "Why don't you tell us what happened?"

He remained silent.

Time to play hardball. "You know, you weren't the only one she formed a relationship with to get what she wanted."

His brows pinched together. "What are you talking about?"

305

"She manipulated a guy named Randy Patterson who does maintenance on Textra Oil's helicopters. He admitted to shearing the pitch control rod, which caused the helicopter we were on to crash into the ocean and kill the pilot. Randy's facing murder charges, and you might very well be too."

Lucas's hands gripped the edge of his bed, bunching the blue blanket between his fingers. "I didn't kill anyone."

She leaned forward. "Greg Barnes died because of what you did. That's at least manslaughter. Your only chance for a lighter sentence is if you talk to us. If you cooperate, we'll put in a good word for you with the DA."

Lucas's eyes glazed over.

Reality was sinking in.

"We know you are Gwyneth's mole aboard *Dauntless*," Mason said, striding forward and sitting on his haunches beside Lucas's bunk. "But let me guess, since Greg's death you haven't heard from her."

Lucas pressed his lips together, his gaze cast sideways.

"She's in the wind," Mason said.

Lucas's gaze tracked back to him, his body stiff.

"Two of our agents are tracking her down as we speak," Mason continued. "And I guarantee she'll throw you under the bus."

"You have no idea what you're talking about," Lucas said. "I'm done talking until I get a lawyer."

"That's your right," Rissi said.

"And you . . ." Lucas sneered at her. "Caleb is going to hate you for this."

She knew that wasn't true. Caleb knew she couldn't ignore the evidence. Lucas was guilty. It was only a matter of whether Greg's death was an accident or premeditated. One way or another, they'd get it out of Lucas. But for now, they'd leave Garrett guarding him while they interviewed crew members who had a bone to pick with Chase.

306

FIFTY-THREE

Mason paced the galley, waiting for the last suspect to arrive.

He arched his back, rolling his shoulders. It had been a long day. He hoped they wrapped up before Tropical Storm Edward, which had been brewing all day, was due to nail them.

"I'm gonna grab another cup of joe," he said, casting his tired gaze at Rissi. She sat at the long galley table, her legs kicked over the bench, feet swaying back and forth. "Would you like one?"

"Yes, please. I could definitely use the caffeine. If only they had an espresso machine."

He smiled as she stretched her arms out, stood, and moved about, stretching her back, shaking out her hands. "Yeah, not quite seeing these roughnecks with a Starbucks setup."

She chuckled.

"Two coffees coming up." He moved to the coffeemaker on the counter, poured two mugs full, and handed her one.

"Thanks." She smiled over the blue ceramic edge as she gulped a sip and put the mug down. "That's not half-bad."

He took a swig, then another, the warm liquid jerking his senses.

"So who's left?" she asked, rising up on the balls of her feet. With her upright posture, she looked like . . .

"What?" she asked at his smile.

"You look like a ballerina." He'd wondered if she'd dreamed

of dancing as a teen. Oh, she'd never told him outright, but he'd seen her practicing moves when she thought she was alone. He'd watched for just a moment, awed by her beauty and grace, but then let her enjoy the peaceful reprieve.

She lowered her arched feet level with the floor, a sheepish smile on her lips. "I sometimes do it without thinking."

"Sorry. I didn't mean to make you uncomfortable."

"No. It's fine. I guess I use it as a relaxation technique."

"Is that why Emmy says you perform 'random acts of ballet'?"

Her jaw slackened, her gorgeous blue eyes widening. "She said that to you?"

"One morning, while you were on your morning coffee run, I was working through the papers on my desk, and I heard Emmy comment to Logan about how she hadn't seen you perform 'random acts of ballet' since my arrival."

A shy smile tugged at her lips. "It's just a way to stretch after a long day."

"Well," he said, stepping closer to her, "you look good doing it."

A blush crept across her cheeks as she attempted to smother the smile gracing her lips.

"In here?" a male voice echoed in the hall.

"Yeah," Ed's voice responded from a farther distance away. "In the galley, Brian."

Brian Denton, their last Chase-messing-with-his-girlfriend suspect on board, entered with a less-than-amused expression on his face. "Boss said you wanted to see me."

"Yes," Mason said, moving for the table. "Take a seat."

"What's all this about?" Brian rubbed his eyes. "One minute I'm sleeping. Next thing I know I'm being shaken and told I have to answer some questions."

"Please take a seat"—Rissi gestured to the opposite side of the table from her and Mason—"and we'll explain."

308

"Whatever," Brian mumbled. It took some maneuvering for him to shift his lanky legs over the bench seat, but he did, then gazed at the mug in Rissi's hand.

"Can I get you some coffee?" Mason asked.

"That'd be great." He raked a hand through his brown, tousled hair.

Mason moved to grab him one.

"So what's this all about?"

Rissi explained the situation before Mason made it back to the table and handed Brian a mug.

"Yeah, I'm sorry the guy's dead, but I doubt any of us are really going to mourn his loss." Brian dumped a long pour of sugar from the glass jar on the table into his cup, then swirled it around. Brown liquid sloshed over the side, and he caught it with his thumb before it could drip on the table. Licking his thumb, he said, "Just right," before smacking his lips.

"Can you tell us what happened between you and Chase?"

"Not a lot to tell." He gulped down a few swigs, then swiped his mouth with the back of his hand. "I'd started seeing this gal, Jen. It was new, and we were just seeing where things headed. As usual Chase showed up at the Stormy Gull—"

"The old bar out by the piers on the south end of town?" Rissi asked.

Brian tapped his nose. "You got it."

"Thanks." She noted it down. "Please continue."

"Everybody knew that me and Jen were sort of together, but I was on shift on *Dauntless*. My crew-one buddies said one night Chase took one look at Jen and went straight for her. Laid on the charming crap he uses on all the girls." He shifted his jaw, his fingers drumming the table in a fast trill. "Next shift change, my buddy tells me Chase and Jen left together."

"Did you confront Chase?"

"When he arrived on the rig to fix the risers, and things settled down a bit after Greg's death, I talked to him."

"And?" Mason asked.

"And . . ." His fingers drummed louder. "He gave his usual spiel about he can't help if the women prefer him." Brian curled his fingers into a fist. "It's like the guy took pleasure in jabbing at the rest of the crew. The single girls he didn't much care for. Always the ones already taken."

"It was the conquest for him," Mason said. He knew jerks like that. Arrogant . . . egotistical . . .

"Yeah." Brian linked his arms across his chest. "He's one of *those* guys."

FIFTY-FOUR

Mason studied Rissi as she leaned against the port side rail. The fierce wind swirling over the frothing sea whipped her hair about her face. Lifting her hands, she pulled her hair into two clumps and fashioned them into a loose bun-style thing. A few wavy wisps caressed her neck.

He longed more than anything to stride up behind her and press a kiss to the beautiful nape of her neck, but he restrained himself. He'd just gotten off the phone from updating Noah. The temps on land were rising, but the storm at sea was headed straight for *Dauntless*.

"Thought you could use this," he said over her shoulder. The sweet scent of pineapple drifted on the wind ruffling her hair.

"Thanks." She smiled, taking the mug he offered. Her fingers brushed his for the faintest of moments, sending a surge of energy up his arms.

She took a sip as he shook out his hands.

"It's good," she said, inhaling the scent swirling up in the steam rising in a faint fog from the blue-and-white speckled mug.

He gripped the rail separating them from an eighty-foot drop into the raging sea.

"Storm's moving in swiftly," she said, turning to face him, her back resting against the rail.

He studied the clouds, the wind tracking them like leaping

frogs across the sky. "Looks like we're going to have to wait out the storm before they send a copter out."

Rissi exhaled. "That sucks."

Mason shrugged his hands into his pockets. "I agree, but at least chow's on. I say we take a break and eat."

"Sounds good."

———

Ten minutes later, Rissi sat next to Mason in the galley, devouring the sloppy joe the rig chef, Leroy, had served her with chips. She'd waited far too long to eat, and her hypoglycemia had kicked in with a fury. Thankfully, her bottoming-out corresponded with the second shift's dinner break.

The volume of a constant high-pitched murmur buzzed around as the men talked. No doubt all curious about the investigation.

Greg's death had been the result of sabotage. And now that they knew Gwyneth had coerced Randy Patterson into tampering with the Textra copter, so was Max's.

Chase's cause of death, on the other hand, at first seemed cut-and-dry—accidental stingray barb to the heart. But, with his reputation of hooking up with other guys' girls and the anger they'd witnessed in a good number of crew members toward him . . . something wasn't sitting right with her or Mason. Unable to return to land until the storm passed, they'd keep digging, starting with searching Chase's room.

Rissi gazed around the bustling galley, studying the men's faces, wondering if she was staring into the eyes of a killer.

Mason's hand rested in the center of her back, fingers splayed. "You okay?" he whispered in her ear, his breath tickling her neck.

She nodded, thankful to have him here with her. She finished her meal, and as she stood to renew their investigation, her stomach suddenly flipped, hard. She covered her mouth.

Mason's gaze fixed on her. "You okay?"

Queasiness rumbled through her gut, followed by a loud gurgle. "Ris?"

Her stomach flipped again—fierce and swift.

She bolted from the table, racing for the bathroom she'd spotted on their way into the galley.

She'd barely slammed the door behind her and dropped to her knees before her meal left her.

Sinking back on her heels, she grabbed a tissue and wiped her mouth, flushing the toilet, thankful one of the few single bathrooms aboard had been by the galley.

A knock sounded at the door. "Ris?"

She hung her damp head, a cold sweat clinging to her. Talk about embarrassing. "Come in."

Mason opened the door and knelt beside her, his hand on her back.

"Do you feel better now?"

Did she? She started to stand when another wave hit.

A half hour and three disgusting bouts later, she was finally able to leave the bathroom.

Sweaty and shaky, she hardly felt well, but there was apparently nothing left to come out of her.

Mason held her arm, steadying her as she pressed the cool, damp cloth he'd given her to her forehead.

"I found you a place to rest."

She shook her head. "We've got more investigating to do."

"Darling, you need to rest. Besides that, half the crew aren't in any shape for questioning."

She frowned, the slight movement ricocheting pain through her skull. "What?" she managed to eke out, thankful she could open her mouth now without getting sick.

"You aren't the only one sick." He steered her toward the back corridor. "When I went to grab your washcloth, Joel told me he thinks it's a case of food poisoning. The rest of the men think it's the curse."

"Seriously?"

"I'm afraid so."

"But you're not sick?"

"I had a grilled cheese, remember? They suspect the sloppy joes." He steered her into a bedroom at the end of the hall and over to the bed.

"Where are we?"

"Ed's quarters. He's on shift, and said you could rest here. I'm sure it won't be a problem for the night."

"For the night?" She stumbled to her feet. "We have an investigation to continue."

He gently settled her back onto the bed. "You're in no shape to investigate, and everyone is stuck on this rig for the duration of the storm. No one is going anywhere, especially with half of the crew sick."

Her head swirled, her body swaying.

"Lie back," he said, helping her.

A soft pillow cradled her head.

"Do you want covers?" he asked.

She shook her head and regretted the motion, her world spinning. "No." The dampening sweat wasn't enough to cool her heated skin. "Food poisoning doesn't usually come on that fast."

"Not normally, but who knows what caused it. It might have been something fast acting."

"Wait . . . do you think someone intentionally poisoned the food?"

"Most of the men are blaming the curse, but I think it's another sabotage attempt."

"To what end?"

"To shut down the platform or stall our investigation."

"You think the killer is worried we're getting too close?"

"If so, I'd say our prime suspect, based on what we know, is Erik."

"Was he part of the shift eating?" she asked, her voice weak.

What had been in that meat? Her belly churned. *Please don't let me get sick again.* She'd add *not in front of Mason*, but he'd seen her at her worst.

"No," Mason said, "Erik was on the first shift to eat."

"Convenient." She sank deeper into the pillow, sweat beading on her brow.

"Even more so that Jayce was on the second shift."

"So he's sick too?"

"Word is it didn't hit him nearly as hard as the rest."

"Strong constitution?" Clearly better than hers.

"Or maybe he just ate less."

"All right. So what's our next step?"

"You rest." He placed a container by the bed. "Just in case you can't get to Ed's bathroom in time."

"I'll be right here," he said, pulling up a chair beside the bed.

"But the investigation?" Her voice was growing weaker still.

"Any crew members left to question are probably sick. And with a killer on the loose, I'm not leaving your side."

She nodded, hating being in need but loving his presence.

A shiver shot through her body, her legs cramping. She reached for them. Charley horses.

"You're dehydrated. Here, drink this." He handed her a Gatorade.

"Thanks." She held the cool bottle against her cheek.

He stood and leaned over the end of the bed. His hands wrapped around her calves, and he massaged them until the excruciating pain ceased.

"Thanks," she whispered.

She shivered again, her body trembling.

"I've got you," he said, smoothing the damp hair from her face as she drifted into a hazy sleep.

Noah picked Brooke up from work and brought her home. After sharing a take-out dinner, they started cleaning up the vandalized garage. Knowing how much the VW meant to her, he didn't want to wait any longer now that Emmy had released the scene.

"So tell me about some of your adventures in the VW. You said it belonged to your grandparents?" he asked, helping Brooke sweep the large pieces of glass off the ground in front of its grill.

"Yeah, we used to take road trips in it." She dumped another dustpan full of shards into the double-walled cardboard box Noah had fashioned to help safely dispose of the glass. "Pop-Pop and Nanna took me to baseball games up and down the Eastern Seaboard. That was our thing."

"That's a nice memory to carry." He got to his feet and emptied his own dustpan into the box, the pieces clinking against the others.

"It is." She quickly shifted her attention back to clean-up duty.

She sniffed, and he stilled. Was she trying not to cry?

She slipped her hair over her shoulder, revealing misty eyes and a pink nose. She had been crying.

He felt like a heel for bringing up the subject. Clearly, he'd hit a memory she held dear. One he was betting Brodie knew about.

She bit her bottom lip, then released it, standing up with the last of the glass contained. "After Pop-Pop and Nanna passed, my parents inherited it. We'd take off traveling up and down the coast, surfing our way from Maine to Florida."

"I didn't know you surfed." He was coming to learn a lot about her, and he liked what he learned. She was bright, strong, and sweet. It was a captivating combination that kept him wanting more and more time with her.

"Yep," she said. "You know, you're about the only person I've told about trips on this bus besides Brodie. He knows how much it means to me, and he just used it against me, took what

316

I told him and did this . . ." She gestured at all the damage. "He did this to hurt me. And he did a good job of it." She wrapped her arms about her waist.

"I'll talk with Brodie again. And I'll find the evidence we need to charge him. I promise."

She sighed. "I've heard a lot of promises over the years."

"I keep mine," he said.

She smiled softly. "Thank you."

He held her gaze, an emotion he hadn't felt in years stirring inside.

Her cell rang, breaking their deep gaze, and she answered it. "Kesler."

After a brief silence, she said, "I'll be right over." She hung up.

"Everything okay?"

"Yeah. I just need to get to the airfield. There's a capsized boat, and with the storm blowing in, they need all hands on deck. I've got to hurry."

"I'll take you there," he said. "With my emergency light, I can get you there quicker."

"Thanks."

He didn't like the idea of her or anyone else being out in the burgeoning storm, but it was what she did, and he found her dedicated service exceedingly appealing.

FIFTY-FIVE

A shrill, piercing sound jolted Rissi awake. A fuzzy hum filled her ears, her mouth dry.

What is happening?

Her head swam, the space around her disorienting.

She wasn't home. Where was she? And whose bed was she in?

"You got sick, remember?" Mason said from nearby.

Now she remembered. "Right." She'd been sick. "We're on *Dauntless*," she muttered. Her pasty tongue rested against the parched roof of her mouth.

"Here," he said, pressing the rim of a water bottle against her lips.

She tipped it back, swallowing. The tepid water rolling down her throat felt blissful. She blinked. "Why is it so dark?"

"The power went out. Auxiliary generators came on but went back out right away."

"The noise?" she said, praying it didn't bring her splitting headache back.

"An alarm, but I don't know what for. I wasn't leaving you."

"We need a flashlight," she said, fumbling for her phone in her pocket. "Where's my phone?" She patted her pockets down.

"I laid it on the desk, but it must have fallen. I'll take a look."

A blinding light streamed in her eyes.

She lifted her hand, shielding her face as Mason jetted to his feet, gun in hand.

"It's just me," Ed said, hands up, palms facing them as he stood in the now open doorway. He gripped a large square flashlight in his right hand. "Just checking to make sure you two are all right."

"Yeah. We're okay," Mason said. "Her fever broke, thankfully. What's going on out there?"

"Power outage."

"And the generators?" Like he'd said, they'd flickered for a moment.

"You're not going to believe this, but someone cut two of the main wires."

"Please tell me the crew aren't blaming this on the curse too?" Rissi said, sitting up and shifting her legs over the side of the bed.

"Whoa," Mason said. "Don't sit up too fast."

She nodded and moved slowly.

"I think everyone finally realizes we have a saboteur," Ed said. "I just wanted to let you know about the generators being tampered with before we start fixing them."

"I need to see it and take pictures before anything gets touched," Mason said.

"I figured, but we need the power back ASAP. Here." He handed them another flashlight. "I'm going to head back. Can you get there on your own?"

Mason nodded, the beam's light casting his shadow on the wall behind her.

———

Mason turned to Rissi, still not happy with the lack of color in her cheeks. He hated to leave her alone, but this could be critical to the investigation. "Will you be okay while I check it out?"

She planted her feet on the floor. "I'm coming with you."

"You need to stay and rest. You're in no condition to be up and about."

"This isn't a negotiation," she said, standing but looking a little shaky. "I either go with you or on my own."

"Seriously?" Mason sighed. "Why do you have to be so dog-gone stubborn?"

"Pleeeease." She drew out the word. "Don't tell me that if the situation were reversed, you'd stay in bed—because we both know better."

He opened his mouth to argue, then shut it again. "Fine, but sit down while I look for your phone." He knelt down and slid his hand along the floor. It took several seconds, but he finally found it under the bed. "Found it," he said, standing.

She got to her feet, steadier this time, and took the phone from him. "Great. Thanks."

"Ris," he said.

"I'm going to the generators." She walked to the door. "You coming?"

He sighed. "You know I am."

He kept a steadying hand on Rissi's lower back, ready to catch her if she swayed at all. The woman was making him as nervous as a momma on the first day of kindergarten.

She looked back at him a time or two as they worked their way through the maze of dark corridors—the only light coming from the flashlight Ed had provided.

Faces shown now and again as they passed random crew members in the passageways and wove around equipment, but they finally reached the generators.

"About time," Erik said. "We'd like our lights back on, not to mention needing the equipment."

"We just need to examine and photograph the damage to the generator before anyone touches it," Mason replied.

"Yeah, yeah." Erik wiped the sweat from his grimy, grease-smeared brow and flung the drops off to the side.

Rissi gagged beside him. Covering her mouth, she turned her head to the side.

"Oh, please don't hurl, lady, or we'll have a chain reaction," Erik said. "I just got done heaving my guts out, and I have no desire to do it again."

"Deep breaths in and out through your mouth," Mason said, rubbing her back.

"I'm okay," she said after a few solid breaths. "Thanks." She offered a soft smile, and he smiled back as she brushed away a rogue hair sticking to her forehead.

"Great." Erik rubbed his hands together. "Now, do what you need to do so we can get this baby started?"

Figuring out who sabotaged it was far more important to Mason than getting it running. Between the storm howling outside and the darkness inside, things felt primed for danger.

FIFTY-SIX

Noah gazed up at the heavens, and a fierce green tint to the darkening sky hit a chord of instinct within him.

He'd only seen that particular shade of green once—right before a tornado had touched down about a mile from his childhood home. The outer bands had rumbled over his house like a freight train.

Pressing the gas pedal to the floorboard, he sped toward the office, hoping the team had already started storm preparations.

He hated the thought of Mason and Rissi out on the *Dauntless*, but by now it was too late to head in. They were trapped until the storm passed.

Wind battered the soft top of his Jeep, yanking it up as far as the straps would allow it to go, then releasing it with a puckering suction until it pulled it up again.

He wished he'd insisted Rissi and Mason return before the storm hit. From the point of view of the investigation, they'd made the right call to stay, and he'd agreed, but he didn't like it.

Sideways rain streaked across his windshield. He flipped on his wipers, turning them on high as the rain pummeled down. Shrill pings shot off his window as golf ball–sized hail fell.

Please, Lord, get me to the office safely. Put a hedge of protection around my team and Brooke's as they head out in this mess. Let them rescue the people in need.

"Erik!"

Mason looked up from his examination of the generator to see Jayce striding straight for Erik.

"You're so full of it!" Jayce roared, his face contorted in angry lines. "You're a liar."

Erik stepped forward, only a handful of inches separating the two. "You're calling me a liar?"

Jayce's hands curled into fists at his side. "You bet I am."

"You—" Whatever Erik was going to say was cut short as Jayce's right uppercut collided with his jaw, the force jarring his head back.

Erik rebounded and swung, nailing Jayce in his right rib cage.

"Come on, guys," Ed said, rushing forward. The other men present—Brian and Adam—rushed forward to help. Brian grabbed Erik in a bear hug from behind, while Adam grabbed the still-swinging Jayce.

"Cut it out!" Ed yelled. "What's wrong with you two?"

"He went after Lisha," Jayce said.

Erik laughed.

Jayce swiped his nose, bouncing back and forth on the balls of his feet in Adam's grasp.

Erik smirked, "So?"

"So you—"

"Enough!" Ed hollered. "Unless you two knuckleheads want to be fired, I suggest you stop now."

Jayce struggled against Adam's hold. "I don't care if I get fired. He slept with my fiancée."

Ed's jaw slackened, and his gaze flashed to Erik.

He chuckled. "*She* slept with *me* is more accurate."

Jayce lunged forward "You're gonna play that game?"

Adam scrambled to restrain him.

"What can I say?" Erik shrugged. "She was all over me."

Jayce flung his head backward, colliding with Adam's face.

A crack resounded, and Adam let go, clutching his nose. Blood spewed through his fingers.

Jayce rushed Erik, tackling him to the ground and whaling on him.

It took a moment, but Ed finally managed to pull Jayce off a bloody Erik.

"You're just as bad as Chase." Jayce spit blood from his mouth, his busted lip the only sign that he'd been involved in the fight. "You hated Chase for sleeping with Charlene, but then you go and do the same thing with Lisha. You better hope you don't end up like Chase."

Erik's eyes narrowed. "Meaning?"

"Meaning dead."

FIFTY-SEVEN

Hail struck the copter, pinging off the windshield as Brooke and her team soared above the frothy sea raging below.

An SOS had come from a sightseeing vessel six miles off the North Carolina coast. Any captain foolish enough to head out with an impending storm warning in effect was beyond stupid. That the storm was moving in far swifter than anticipated was no excuse. One thing Brooke had learned in her eight years as a Coast Guard medic was you didn't mess with Mother Nature.

Gabby maintained God still controlled the wind and the waves, but if that was so, Brooke wasn't sure she wanted to believe in a God who allowed such destruction.

She had believed when she was a kid in Sunday school, but life had a way of slowly eroding it out of her.

"Two minutes out," Dean, the pilot, said over the headset.

Jason and Brad, the two rescue swimmers, readied to jump. Prepared to risk their lives if necessary to save a crew that should have known better than to be out in the elements.

Brooke double-checked her equipment, ready to treat any injuries the crew or guests had sustained.

The wave-thrashed vessel came into view, a white dot in the throes of a heightening and churning sea.

"You've got ten minutes," Dean said. "Any longer and the winds are going to get too fierce for this bird."

Jason gave a thumbs-up as he perched on the copter door's edge, his flippers dangling thirty feet above the sea below.

"Clear," Dean hollered over the intensifying winds.

Jason jumped as the copter shook, an unnerving rattle creaking through its hollow cavity.

"Hang on," Dean instructed as he fought the throttle to counteract the amassing wind surge.

"Jumper two. You're a go."

"Roger that," Brad said before jumping into the turmoil waiting below.

Please let them be safe.

Not really expecting anyone to be listening or to answer, Brooke prayed all the same. Apparently, some childhood habits died hard.

Once the fight was over and Jayce left, Mason grabbed his flashlight off the metal shelf and bent to examine the generator. Someone had indeed cut pivotal wires. It certainly wasn't elegant, but it was effective.

But to what purpose?

Rissi handed Mason the camera, and he stooped, taking shot after shot, hating that they were going to have to compromise evidence, but they needed the power back on.

"How soon can it be repaired?" Adam asked, entering the room with white bandage strips across his nose. No doubt he'd have two black eyes in the morning.

"It would probably only be an hour's job, but the replacement wires have gone missing," Joel said. "Our only chance to get power soon is to fix the back-up generator."

"What's wrong with that?" Mason asked.

"Someone threw a wrench in it, and it's wedged in the gear shaft. That ain't coming out easily."

"Seriously?" Adam said, gently smoothing the bandage's edge on his right cheek.

"But you'll be able to fix it, won't you?" Mason asked.

"I think so." Joel exhaled. "It just depends what got damaged, but if I do get it running, there'll only be enough power to keep the critical systems running."

"Critical as in . . . ?" Rissi asked.

Joel wiped the sweat from his brow. "Any system considered necessary for the crew's safety."

"The freezers?" Mason asked.

"Not essential. This storm will pass by morning, and any supplies we need to replenish, we can."

Mason turned to Rissi, and the tightness in her jaw told him she had the same concern. "Chase's body," he said.

She nodded.

Mason grabbed her hand, and they headed for the auxiliary freezer. He kept his pace moderate, not wanting to exacerbate any of her symptoms.

"What's the big deal?" Erik called after them. "Chase is already dead."

Adrenaline shot through Mason's limbs. If the poison inside of Chase dissipated, they would never be able to confirm whether or not the stingray had caused his death.

Opening the freezer door, Mason used his flashlight to look at the thermometer. Just as he feared—the temperature was rising. Pulling out his sat phone, he called Hadley and explained the situation.

"You need to move him to the medical bay. Everything you'll need will be stored there. First thing, take a blood sample and bring it back to the freezer. Bury it in a pile of things still frozen. It should keep it cold enough until the storm passes and you can get it back to the lab."

They rushed the stretcher through the pitch-black passageway, but the lights flickered on as Mason rolled it into the medical bay. Rissi searched the cabinets for a syringe and blood sample tube.

Mason did as Hadley instructed, taking the blood from Chase's exposed neck, and Rissi ran it back to the freezer while he continued following Hadley's instructions.

"Next, you want to take pictures of the wound. I assume one of you has a camera or a phone handy?"

"I do," Mason said.

"Take photos of the wound from the outside of the suit before you open it."

"All right." Mason took the pictures, nodding to Rissi as she returned from the freezer.

Hadley continued. "Is the suit's zipper in the front or back?"

"Back," Mason said.

"Okay, you'll need a scalpel to cut the suit to take close-up pictures of the wound."

Rissi nodded and searched the supply cabinet. She let out a stream of breath as she slid the scalpel through Chase's dive suit.

Footsteps echoed in the hall, and Ed rounded the doorway. "Everything okay back here?" he asked.

"Yes. We're just performing an exterior autopsy."

Ed's brow furrowed. "What?"

Rissi explained the situation while Mason took the requested pictures of the wound.

"All right." Ed tapped the doorframe, his ring clanging against the metal. "I'll leave you to it."

Mason turned his attention back to Hadley on the phone. "Pictures done, Hadley."

"I'd like a swab of his mouth. In the pictures you sent upon your arrival, I noticed a white crusting there."

"The men said he was foaming at the mouth when they hauled him onto the platform," Rissi said.

"Interesting," Hadley murmured.

It took a few drawers, but Rissi finally found the Q-tips and a makeshift evidence baggie.

She offered the Q-tip to Mason.

He lifted his chin. "You go for it."

She leaned over the body as Mason separated Chase's lips.

The fire alarm shrilled, and Rissi jerked, but she managed to get a sample in the bag.

"Are you kidding me?" Mason said.

A few seconds later, Adam stopped at the door. "Let's go, folks."

"We need to finish this," Mason said.

"Fire alarm protocol has been enacted. Head to the port side of the platform above the lifeboats in case it's necessary to abandon ship."

"Seriously?" Mason said.

"Dead serious," Adam replied. "Let's go."

Mason and Rissi followed Adam down the steps out onto the platform and moved with the crew to the port side.

Garrett and Jayce—sporting a busted lip—rushed past them, heading for the living quarters.

"What's going on?" Mason asked. Was there really a fire?

"They need to clear the building," Adam said. "To make sure no one is inside and determine whether there is a fire or if some knucklehead triggered the alarm."

Mason prayed the latter, but his gut said it was the former.

FIFTY-EIGHT

Reaching the station, Noah hopped out of the Jeep and raced for the front door. Hail bounced off his hands as he covered his head.

The windows had been boarded and the building secured. He had the best team.

Logan waited for him at the front door, pushing it open as he reached it.

He ducked inside, and Logan pulled the door shut behind him.

"Thanks," he said, flicking the rain off his hands.

"No problem," Logan said.

"Where are we at?"

"Prepped and ready," Logan said.

"And the team?" He glanced around at the empty desks. During storms like this, it was protocol for the team to be available at the office.

Finn was still in Cali with Gabby, introducing her to his mom. Rissi and Mason were on *Dauntless*, which still ate at him, but where were Emmy and Caleb?

His thought stopped short at the sight of Caleb cutting a swath across the station directly for him.

"Have you heard from Rissi and Mason?" Caleb asked, his leg twitching beneath his tight stance. "Are they okay?"

"I'm having trouble patching through, but I'm sure they are fine." They had to be.

"Where's Em?"

"In the ladies' room," Logan said, putting a storm grill in the box window. "She should be back any minute."

"Here I am," she said, rounding the corner.

"Thanks for getting everything stormproofed."

"Our pleasure," Logan said.

"How's Brooke?" Emmy asked. "Shouldn't you be with her or her with you?"

"She's on watch."

"In this storm?" Emmy asked.

"We're talking about the Coast Guard. When everyone else heads home, we go out."

"I'll say a prayer for her," Emmy said, closing her eyes straightaway and praying silently.

"Any other news I should be aware of?" he asked the group after Emmy finished praying.

"I just got done talking to Bella Armstrong," Logan said. "Wanted to see if she'd confronted Rick and, if so, had he conned her more?"

"And?" Noah asked, his thoughts warring to be present and to be thinking of Brooke. Praying for her. As soon as he was done hearing Logan's update, he'd take to one of the interrogation rooms and hit his knees. Praying for them all.

"She kicked him out."

"Good for her," Emmy said.

"Any idea where he is now?" Noah asked.

"I'm afraid not," Logan said. "I think Emmy and I are going to have to work our magic." He rolled his chair beside Emmy's at her desk.

"One thing I did find," Emmy said, "is an online article about a protest outside a chemical company. It got rowdy. Police were called in. Arrests were made."

"Let me guess," Caleb said. "Gwyneth was one of them?"

"Yup." Em smiled her I've-got-something smile. She pulled

331

a paper out of the printer. "Here's a picture of Gwyneth at the protest."

"Thanks," Noah said, examining it and wondering what leads that information would open up. He didn't doubt Emmy's skills, so something had to be there, but what? His eyes scanned the other faces, and he stopped short on the man to Gwyneth's left. "Rick Carson?"

"Yep," Emmy said. "I found three more like it."

"How far back?" he asked.

"At least five years."

"So they are far more intertwined than we realized," Logan said.

Emmy nodded.

"Caleb, keep searching for Rick and maybe you'll find Gwyneth too."

A half hour after the alarm sounded, Garrett and Jayce appeared, their faces covered with ash and soot.

"There was a fire?" Rissi asked.

"Yeah," Jayce said, "but it's out now."

"Where was it?" Mason asked.

"In the medical bay."

"What?" The pitch of her voice rose at least an octave. "But we were in there when the alarm went off, and there was no fire."

"It was an electrical fire, originating in the ceiling light and spreading out from there," Garrett explained.

Rissi blinked, already knowing the answer in her gut, but praying she was wrong. "Chase's body. Was it damaged during the fire?"

"I'm afraid so." Jayce sighed. "His body is pretty badly burnt. Thankfully Ed and Adam joined us and helped put the fire out before it moved beyond the medical bay."

Rissi looked at Mason. Their eyes met, and she knew he was thinking exactly the same thing as her. What were the chances of a fire starting directly over Chase's body? At least they'd gotten the blood samples, and no one else knew. They'd keep it that way, because too much was going wrong for it all to be accidental. What was someone covering up? Was Chase's death another incident of ecoterrorism—trying to prevent him from fixing the riser? Or maybe he'd seen something else down there.

Lucas was clearly not responsible for all that had been going on, since he'd been confined to his quarters, guarded by either Jayce or Garrett—except for during the fire, when he'd been under the watch of several crewmen, according to Jayce. Which meant either Lucas hadn't been involved with the food poisoning or the sabotaging of the generators . . . or he had an accomplice on board.

Rissi sat across from a fidgeting Jayce.

"When did you find out about your fiancée and Erik?" she asked, hoping he, and Erik in the adjacent room with Mason, would provide helpful insight into their investigation.

At his silence, she continued. "Was it here on the rig?"

Jayce flopped back, a scowl curling on his face. "I'd rather not say."

She narrowed her gaze, trying to apply a little pressure without him feeling threatened, though his expression was already one of defiance.

Rissi leaned forward, resting her arms on the table. "You can bet Erik's talking in the next room with my partner. You want his to be the only voice we hear?"

Jayce swiped his finger across his nose.

Rissi held back a smile. It was working. She was getting to him.

"All right. We'll take Erik's word for it." She grabbed her

legal pad and got to her feet. "Hopefully he doesn't throw you under the bus."

She'd barely made it to the door when he cleared his throat. "Wait."

Pausing with her hand on the knob, she turned.

Jayce straightened. "Sit back down."

She arched a brow.

He raked a hand through his blond hair. "Please."

Retaking her seat, she set her legal pad in front of her once again and pulled a pen from her pocket.

Jayce released a stream of air. "I just learned what happened, and when I did, I FaceTimed Lisha, hoping it was just a nasty rumor." He shook his head, looking down at his boots, then back at Rissi. "The truth was clear in her eyes."

His hands balled into fists at his side. "I guess I should be thankful my laptop had enough juice to keep running after the lights went out, or I still wouldn't know." His jaw tightened. "But I got the truth straight from the whore's mouth. She didn't even try to deny it. Just started crying, saying she was sorry." He pushed the soles of his shoes against the floor, shoving his chair back with a grating screech. "Pathetic."

"You said you just learned what happened."

Jayce's brow furrowed. "Yeah?"

"Which means someone on board told you. Who was it?" And why had he waited until now?

"Someone on the crew." He shrugged.

"And the name of this *someone*?" she pressed.

He rubbed the back of his neck. "That's between me and him."

She pulled her badge from her pocket and flipped it open. "I'm a CGIS agent, and I am asking you a direct question."

Jayce stood. "I know my rights and I don't have to answer."

"You're right, but why the secrecy?"

"Because he asked me to keep it between us, and I gave him my word I would. And unlike Lisha, *I* keep my word."

334

Why *had* the mystery man waited until just before the lights went out to tell Jayce about Erik and Lisha? It appeared strategic, but what was the play? To draw attention to Erik? They needed to figure out who this mystery man was. Because she had a sinking feeling someone on board was playing a very dangerous game, and they were all pawns in it.

As Mason exited the room next door, Erik trailing behind, Rissi whispered, "Any luck?"

Erik paused as they passed, giving Rissi a once-over and smirking at Mason.

Mason's fists curled. If he weren't a CGIS agent, he'd knock that smug smile right off Erik's face.

He waited until Erik was out of earshot. "Not much," he said beneath his breath. "How about you?"

"Jayce only said 'someone' on the crew told him about his fiancée and Erik."

Mason paused midstep. "As in he wouldn't say who it was?"

"No," she said, crossing her arms. "Said he'd given the man his word."

"Interesting."

"Agreed. And so is the timing. Sounds like he was told only a matter of minutes before the power crashed."

"So whoever told Jayce could very easily be the one who cut the power."

"But to what end? To freak people out about the curse or something more sinister?"

"I'm thinking the latter."

She sighed. "Unfortunately, so am I."

FIFTY-NINE

After returning from the distress-call run, Brooke finished fastening her storm shutters in place, filled jugs of water, and placed flashlights throughout her home.

Dripping wet, she trudged upstairs. She'd be sopping up the floors after changing, but dry clothes definitely took priority.

She hung her wet clothes over the shower rod, grabbed a towel off the rack, and wrapped it snugly about her.

Drops of water from her clothing plopped off the tile floor in a rhythmic cascade. She placed a towel along the outer edge of the stall. The thick fabric absorbed the drops, but the plopping sound, now somewhat muffled, still echoed as she strode into her bedroom and changed into her favorite comfy jeans—stonewashed, smattered with well-worn holes, and frayed at the ankles. She pulled on an equally soft tee from the Garth Brooks concert she'd been elated to attend last summer in Florida.

She bounced down the steps to the main floor, the wooden boards creaking beneath her. She was anxious for Noah to return. He'd called to say he was just a few minutes out, and she'd been looking forward to seeing him ever since they'd parted.

As she reached the foyer, another creak sounded.

She frowned. Her foyer floorboards had never creaked before. She climbed back to the first step and down onto the foyer. Nothing.

Hmm. Must have been a fluke.

She headed for the kitchen, ready for something to eat and hoping to make it before the electricity most likely dropped.

She put a pot full of water on the burner and moved to grab the ingredients for pasta. Tomatoes and mozzarella cheese from the fridge, olive oil from the counter, basil from the small container on her windowsill, and lastly, she headed for the pantry to get garlic, onion, and angel hair pasta.

She opened the door to a man dressed in black.

Her throat constricted, choking her cry for help.

She bolted for the front door, dropping the ingredients along the way.

Rounding the edge of the couch, he clamped his hand on her hair.

Yanking backward, he pulled her onto the couch.

She kicked out, her bare foot colliding with his chin.

A grunted expletive flew from his mouth as she scrambled over the back of the couch and grasped the door handle.

Heavy footfalls sounded away from her as she swung the door open and screamed.

SIXTY

"Whoa!" Noah said as Brooke flailed back at his presence. "What's wrong?"

"He . . ." She spun around and froze.

Noah pulled his gun and stepped in front of her.

"Where?" he asked, shielding her with his body, his gaze darting about until it landed on the open back door, rain spewing in, slickening the floor.

Brooke's gaze shifted to the back door. "He must have . . ."

Noah rushed into the kitchen. Grabbing a flashlight off the counter, he shone it across her backyard.

No one.

"Whoever it was, he's gone."

Brooke's shoulders dropped, her tense stance softening.

He called the local police to canvas the area again as he shut and locked the back door, then moved to do the same with the front one. He took time to clear her home just in case and made sure it was locked up tight before he sat with her on the couch.

"Can you tell me what happened?"

Adrenaline burned through his taut limbs as she relayed the events up to his arrival.

"Was he wearing gloves?"

Her face scrunched. "I . . . don't know. Sorry."

He rested a hand on her arm, trying to reassure her she was safe. "I'll have Emmy come out and run the place in case he didn't."

She nodded as he placed the call.

"Hey, Em, could you and Logan come over to Brooke's house? She just walked in on an intruder." One who was still on the loose.

Rissi and Mason stood on the deck as the sun peeked through the clouds. The storm had thankfully shifted course, passing quickly over them and around Wilmington and Wrightsville Beach. Word was only the outer bands hit home, and the damage to their town was minimal. Rissi and Mason made their way up to the control room and found Ed, Adam, and Bob talking over coffee.

Thankfully, the food poisoning had passed just as quickly as the storm, but they'd saved a sealed container of the food in the fridge for Emmy to test upon their return to shore.

According to Bob, all Textra's helicopters had been deemed safe by the NTSB and were en route. After all that crew two had endured, they were swapping rotations—with extra pay for any crew one members willing to return early.

Mason was more than ready to be off the platform, and surely Rissi felt the same.

After all she'd been through, she deserved some rest.

"What?" she said, narrowing her eyes as she caught him staring.

"Just thinking." *How much I love you.*

"Just thinking?" she said.

He smiled. "Yep."

The whoosh of copter blades whooshed through the air, cutting off their short moment in time.

Mason indicated for Rissi to go ahead. With Lucas, Jayce, and Erik in custody, they loaded up the suspects along with Chase's body.

All the remaining men were anxious to get off the "tin can," as several put it, but two more birds were on the way. For now, Mason had never heard a sweeter sound than the whirring of blades as they lifted up above the helipad and out over the open sea.

He looked back one last time as *Dauntless* faded into the distance. Wilmington had only been home for little more than a week now, but he'd never felt happier to be home as he did when they touched down at Textra Oil's helicopter airport.

He couldn't wait to continue interrogating Erik, Jayce, and Lucas, but this time at the station. Being in its interrogation room always seemed to prompt previously reluctant suspects to talk.

When finished, he longed for nothing more but to take Rissi home and tell her how deeply he loved her. Over and over again.

Mason escorted Jayce off the copter as Rissi escorted Erik. Hadley met them to take Chase's body, his dive gear, and the vial of his blood. Noah and Logan were there to drive them back to the station. To keep office tensions as settled as they could be, given the circumstance with Lucas, Noah would be handling that part of the investigation going forward.

Mason had just reached the car and was about to settle Jayce into the back seat when a woman about Rissi's height of five-seven, but far curvier, rushed forward. Her bright pink dress flapped about her legs as she headed straight for Jayce.

Jayce stiffened. "What are you doing here, Lisha?"

"I came to make sure you were okay. I saw on the news that there had been two deaths on *Dauntless*, and they were rotating you off the rig early. I was so worried about you." She rested her hand on his arm, hot-pink painted nails gleaming in the sun. "Are you okay?"

His jaw tightened. "I will be when you leave."

"Snookums." Tears welled in her eyes.

"I told you we're done. You slept with Erik. What'd you expect? I'd just take you back?"

"Erik was a mistake."

"You got that right." Jayce climbed in the back seat and indicated with a lift of his chin for Mason to close the door. They pulled out of the lot, leaving a crying Lisha standing there.

SIXTY-ONE

The team waited to begin interrogations until Emmy tested the food they'd brought back and discovered it was laced with arsenic. Thankfully not enough to kill anyone. Now the pivotal question was who had done it. They had suspected Erik retaliated for Jayce spreading the word about Erik's extreme dislike for Chase, but something had shifted when Rissi had spoken with Jayce. Something niggled at her to the point she was betting Jayce had been the one to poison the food. He'd gotten sick from it, but as Mason said, not even close to the extent of everyone else. Why would he poison himself? Perhaps he'd taken a few bites as a way to cover his tracks. Maybe it was a brilliant move on his part, setting Erik up for something he did.

Emmy continued to process evidence while Rissi entered the interrogation room where Jayce sat nursing a Coke.

Mason was interrogating Erik, and Noah headed in with Lucas. Thankfully, Caleb was out on a call—for now, at least.

She could handle herself with jerks like Erik, but Rissi was thankful Mason had chosen to question him. The guy rubbed her the wrong way.

Jayce looked up at her, impatience furrowed on his brow. "Are we really going to keep dragging this out? I don't know who killed Chase."

She pulled out the chair with a squeak as the metal legs scraped the floor. She sat and laid the yellow legal pad on the

table, dropping the pen on top of it. *Come on, gut, be right.*
Let's see what kind of reaction I get. She looked Jayce dead in
the eye. "Let's talk arsenic."

His face slackened.

Bingo. She'd been right. "Why'd you do it?" she asked, getting straight to the point, hoping the sound of utter confidence
in her voice would get him to confess.

Jayce shrugged. "Erik deserved it."

"So you contaminated the sloppy joes to get back at Erik
for . . ."

"Sleeping with my fiancée."

His story wasn't fitting together. He'd said he'd heard about
his fiancée and Erik just before the lights went off, but the food
poisoning had occurred hours prior. She decided to hold off on
pointing that out for the moment.

"And you were going to let him take the fall?" she said.

"Again, he deserved it." The tension in his voice heightened.

"What about the rest of the crew who ate it and got sick?"
She inadvertently rubbed her still-sore stomach.

Jayce shrugged. "Collateral damage."

"You'll be charged."

"Charged?" Panic broke on his face.

"Yep. It'll be up to the DA to decide on the severity of your
crime."

"Crime? It just made a few people sick."

"More than a few, and poisoning food could easily be construed as attempted murder."

He rocked back in his seat. "Murder?" All color drained
from his face. "I didn't kill anyone."

"But you know who did?" She kept pressing, her gut telling
her she was on the right trail.

"It was just a little arsenic. Not enough to do anything like
that."

"Like I said, that'll be up to the DA to decide."

"Whoa." He shook his hands out. "This is getting way out of hand."

She leaned forward, her arms resting on the table. "I can put in a good word for you. . . ."

He swallowed, his chest rapidly rising and falling.

"Jayce, look at me." She needed to rein his focus back in.

His darting gaze settled on her.

"If you knew Erik slept with Lisha when you poisoned the food, why the big show like you just found out in the generator room?"

Jayce stiffened.

Now they were getting somewhere.

"I . . . uh . . ."

She leaned forward, propping her weight on her elbows. "You help me, I help you."

Jayce's leg bounced. "He said I had to keep it between us."

"Who?"

He shook his head.

"So he knew about the food poisoning?" She'd keep it general for now. Discover what this "he" did.

Jayce nodded. "Yeah, he gave me the stuff."

"Why would he do that?"

"He said Erik needed to pay."

Which was most likely a cover to distract her and Mason from doing their jobs, but thankfully Mason hadn't eaten the poisoned hamburger, and it had saved him hours of being sick.

"Why confront Erik in the generator room, as if you'd just found out?"

"He told me to."

Another distraction, but to what purpose? She took a sharp inhale as the pieces started to fit into place. He needed the cover of darkness to try to dispose of evidence. He no doubt slipped out during the blackout and rigged the wiring in the medical bay to catch fire when the electricity came back on. She started sifting through the faces in her mind. "Did this man tell you why he needed the blackout, why he started the fire?"

"No . . ." Jayce stared at his feet.

"You're lying."

Jayce's tongue pushed up under his top lip, bulging it out.

"Jayce. Another man is dead."

"Not a good one."

"That doesn't make it okay to kill him." Surely if this mystery man needed to dispose of evidence, there was more to Chase's death than a stingray accident.

"I didn't kill him."

"Then, who did?"

He swallowed.

"If you don't talk, you're our top suspect."

Perspiration rolled down the sides of Jayce's cheeks. "It was Ed."

Her jaw slackened. "Ed?"

He nodded.

"Ed killed Chase?" Disbelief rattled through her.

Jayce shrugged. "I don't know for sure that he killed Chase, but he's the one who had me poison the food and cause the distraction."

"Why would Ed want to kill Chase?" Ed had been nothing but helpful. Surely Chase hadn't gone after Ed's wife.

Jayce's fingers clutched his Coke can. "Chase was dating someone Ed cared about."

"Who?" She anxiously awaited the answer, her mind racing, trying to put what Jayce said together into something that made sense.

"I don't want to get anyone in trouble," Jayce said, his gaze darting about the room.

"A man's dead," she said again, not bothering to keep the frustration from her tone. "If you aren't going to help me . . ." She grabbed her legal pad and pen and stood. "I'll go call the DA."

"No. Don't. Please," Jayce said.

She retook her seat.

He exhaled, rubbing his hands along his thighs. "Chase was dating Ed's daughter behind her dad's back."

She hadn't even known Ed had a daughter. She'd only seen a picture of him and his wife in his bunk room. No one, not even Ed, mentioned a daughter while they were on *Dauntless*.

Was Jayce just trying to cover his butt? Was he throwing Ed under the bus? "Who else knew about Chase and Ed's daughter?"

"No one that I know of. I'm guessing they were very secretive because Chase knew Ed would kill him if he found out. Kasey was just out of high school."

Eww. Chase was pushing twenty-seven.

"How do you know, then?"

"I saw them."

"When was this?"

He rubbed the back of his neck. "About three months back. Lisha and I were up in New Bern for the weekend, and I spotted Chase and Kasey walking down by the river. They were holding hands, then Chase leaned over and gave her a kiss."

"Did you tell Ed?"

"I should have, but I knew it'd break his heart to find out she was dating him. Everybody knows Chase is only after one thing."

"Then how did Ed find out?"

Jayce shook his head. "I don't know."

"I don't know" was the remainder of Jayce's answers, and in this case, she truly believed he didn't know.

She waited in the hall until Mason exited the interrogation room Erik was being held in. Frustration blanketed his face, irritation sparking in his eyes.

She linked her arms across her chest. "That good, huh?"

Noah exited the interrogation room he'd been in with Lucas.

"How'd it go, boss?"

"He gave up Gwyneth and admitted to removing the bolt, but he swears he had no idea Greg would be out there and that he had nothing to do with Chase's death."

"We need to go speak with Ed Scott right away," Rissi said.

Mason looked to Rissi. "Ed?" He tucked his chin in. "Why?" His eyes narrowed. "What did Jayce say?"

"You're not going to believe this."

SIXTY-TWO

Rissi brought Mason up to speed in the car as they headed to the Scott residence. They didn't have any hard evidence—nothing but Jayce's confession—so unless they got a similar confession out of Ed, they weren't much closer to determining the cause of Chase's death.

Hadley called, his timing nearly perfect.

"Hey, Hadley," Rissi said. "You're on speaker. Please tell us you found something."

"I have, indeed. There wasn't stingray venom in Chase Calhoun's blood, and with the time since death and the fact the vial of blood was cooled for a sufficient amount of time, I can say with almost one hundred percent certainty that a stingray was not the cause of death."

"Is that finding sufficient proof?" Mason asked, praying it'd hold up in court.

"I'd say so, but there's more," Hadley continued. "I did find poison in his system, which is probably where the white foam around his mouth in his mask came from."

Mason frowned. But he'd just said—

"But it wasn't stingray venom. It was arsenic."

"Arsenic?" Rissi said.

"Afraid so, and though his body was badly burned, I still managed to recover a piece of metal that was lodged in Chase's rib—the tip close to his heart. It looked almost like a barb."

Stingray tails were most definitely not made of metal, so what had he been stabbed with? "So you're saying . . . ?" Mason asked.

"Chase Calhoun was stabbed in the heart with a metal weapon that I'm betting had arsenic in the tip."

"Wouldn't the arsenic paralyze him?"

"Most definitely."

So Ed, if it was Ed, dove down and stabbed Chase with a poison-laced barb, rendering him paralyzed. "Sounds like he wanted to be up close and personal when he took his life, but he needed Chase to be unable to communicate topside."

"The topside crew reported hearing him grunt," Rissi said. "That must have been when he was stabbed. Do you have anything else for us?"

"No, that's it for now."

"Thanks, Hadley," Mason said. "Call when you learn more."

"Will do."

Mason followed Rissi along Ed Scott's landscaped stone path leading to his front door. Such attention to detail, every pebble in place and not a single weed.

Rissi knocked, and a woman answered—about Ed's age with soft auburn hair cut short and behind her ears. The woman from the picture in Ed's bunk. "Yes?"

"I'm Rissi Dawson, and this is Mason Rogers. We're with CGIS. We'd like to ask you some questions about your husband and your daughter."

She hung her head. "Come in. I've been expecting you."

Rissi looked at Mason before entering.

"Please take a seat," Mrs. Scott said, gesturing into the living room. Rissi and Mason sat on the floral sofa, and she sank into the first living room chair she reached. "When he didn't come home, I knew he did it."

Rissi looked at Mason, then back to Mrs. Scott. "Did what?"

"Killed that monster for what he did to Kasey."

Mason looked to the picture on the mantel of the girl. She looked like a younger version of Mrs. Scott. "Kasey is your daughter?"

"Yes." She burst into tears.

"Here you go," Mason said, handing her a handkerchief from his back pocket.

"Thank you." Mrs. Scott sniffed.

"Can you tell us what happened?" he asked in a gentle voice.

She nodded, tears streaming down her face. She lifted the handkerchief, dabbing her eyes with it.

"I'm sorry," Mason said. "I know this is difficult . . . but a man's dead."

"Who deserves to be." Her entire frame shook.

Mason looked back at Rissi, his surprise echoed in her eyes.

"Why does he deserve to be?" Mason asked. Chase dating their daughter must have been upsetting, but enough to murder the man?

She sniffed in puffs of air. "Because he . . ." Another sob racked her body. "He . . . raped our baby."

Bile burned Mason's throat.

As Noah entered Brooke's house with coffee and croissants for all, Emmy held up an evidence bag with a long blond hair in it. "We found this caught in the top hinge of the pantry door."

"Brodie doesn't have long hair," Brooke said, coming down the stairs.

Noah's gut clenched. Someone else was definitely stalking her.

"We also found a black glove in the woods behind your house," Logan said. "We flipped it inside out, and Em found a match."

"That quick?"

Em smiled. "The fingerprint scanners are mobile nowadays."

An hour later, Noah entered the interrogation room with a folder and a cup of coffee.

Tony Krenshaw was six-foot-two, two hundred pounds, with blond hair that fell below his shoulders.

Noah set his coffee on the table separating them and pulled back a chair with a squeak as it tracked across the floor.

"Can I get you anything, Mr. Krenshaw? Water? A soda?" He didn't want to offer anything hot that he could chuck at Noah. Sadly, other suspects had helped institute that rule.

Krenshaw's gaze remained locked on the video camera mounted in the upper righthand corner of the room.

"Mr. Krenshaw?" he asked again at the man's distracted silence.

No answer.

Noah narrowed his eyes. Something was off with the man. He shifted his gaze to Krenshaw's fidgeting hands and zeroed in on the torn skin surrounding his nails, the deep scratches along his forearms.

"Mr. Krenshaw," he said again, his tone more pointed.

Finally, Krenshaw pulled his bleary gaze from the camera and fixed his bloodshot eyes on Noah.

"Mr. Krenshaw. I'm going to ask you a series of questions. I need you to do your best to answer them. Okay?"

He nodded, scratching his misshapen nails along the skin from his wrist to his elbow.

Noah turned to the two-way window and signaled Caleb to the door.

Caleb opened the door, and Noah indicated for him to wait there.

"Please excuse me one moment," Noah said, standing.

Krenshaw's empty gaze rested on his fingers as they dug into his skin.

As Noah strode toward the door, Caleb stared past him at Krenshaw. "Everything okay?"

Noah shook his head.

Caleb handed Noah a printout. "Logan dug up some helpful information. Krenshaw's wife died after a Coast Guard team was called to an accident at sea." He exhaled. "Brooke was the medic."

Noah scanned the report and turned his attention back to Caleb. "We're going to need a psych eval on Mr. Krenshaw. See if Margo's on call. She's the best."

"Will do," Caleb said with a nod.

"See if you can get her here fast. I'm worried this guy's going to hurt himself. We'll need someone watching him at all times."

Caleb studied the man over Noah's shoulder, his brows hiking up. "Agreed." He took a sharp inhale. "I'm just glad we got him when we did. He clearly needs help."

Noah knew exactly what Caleb was thinking, and he agreed. A mentally unstable man had been in Brooke's house while she was there alone.

He deeply feared what could have happened, what would have happened if he hadn't shown up when he did.

A wave of queasiness sloshed through his gut at the possibility.

He closed his eyes to utter a prayer of thanks that God had led him there just in time, and that Brooke was safe in the station.

SIXTY-THREE

Thankfully, Margo was on call and at the station in under an hour.

Given Mr. Krenshaw's state, Noah had followed protocol and waited to continue speaking with him until after his full psych eval.

Unable to listen in because of doctor-patient confidentiality, Noah met Margo as she stepped from the room.

She handed him her assessment.

"What do you think?"

"You were right. He's mentally unstable. I'll need more time with him, but my initial assessment is that his grief over his wife's loss intensified his depression that he's had since he was a teen. As can happen when we get older, his age, grief, and time decreased his meds' effectiveness, and he stopped taking it because he didn't believe it was making any difference. Unfortunately, left untreated his condition worsened, and he's entered a state of psychosis. He needs to be hospitalized and treated in a psych ward."

"Of course," Noah said, his heart aching for the man and his situation.

"His hair is a match," Logan said, coming up behind him.

"So there is no doubt he was the intruder in Brooke's home." Noah turned to Margo. "He'll be charged with breaking and entering, harassment—the list goes on."

"I understand," Margo said. "Charge him, and when he's arraigned, I'll recommend in-patient treatment."

Given the man's loss and mental state, Noah took no pleasure in reading the man his rights as he made a formal arrest, but he was relieved Brooke's tormentor would be securely behind bars.

Krenshaw waived his right to a lawyer, so Noah began his official questioning.

"Why were you in Brooke Kesler's home last night?"

"To punish her," Krenshaw said.

Noah swallowed as fear over what could have happened tracked through him. "Punish her for what?"

"Killing my Sally."

"I'm very sorry for your loss, but Medic Kesler didn't kill your wife," he said, not sure how much was actually getting through to the man. "She was the medic who tried to save her."

Krenshaw slammed his fisted hands on the table, shaking the cup of water Margo had left behind. "She failed, and Sally is dead."

"But it wasn't Medic Kesler's fault. She did everything she could to save your wife."

"Wrong! If she'd done everything, Sally would still be alive. She killed my wife, so she deserved to be punished."

"That's why you left her threatening messages?" Which now made sense in light of the accident report. Krenshaw believed Brooke had killed his wife, and he planned to do the same to her.

"Yes," he seethed.

"And left the black widows in her car?"

"Yes, but she eluded their venom. So I had to go back."

"Last night?"

"Yes." His legs bounced in an agitated beat.

"And what did you plan to do?"

"End her life like she ended Sally's."

The thought of Krenshaw succeeding squeezed the breath from Noah's lungs.

After taking down his full confession, Noah led a cuffed Krenshaw from the room.

Caleb met him in the hall. "I'll take him to a holding cell while you put in for his arraignment."

Noah nodded, watching Caleb lead Krenshaw away.

Thank you, Lord, for protecting Brooke.

"What's wrong?" Brooke asked as he entered the break room.

"His charges just got upped to include attempted murder."

Brooke's face slackened. "What? He was going to *kill* me?"

"Come here." Noah tugged her into an embrace.

"Did he say he was there to kill me?" she said against his chest.

"Hey," he said, tipping her chin up. "Look at me."

Her gaze locked on his, her eyes trusting.

"Krenshaw is going away for a long time. You're safe now."

She shifted. "I remember his wife. I saw the newspaper article about her death." She looked down at the ground. "I tried to save her . . . But what if . . ."

"Hey." She stepped back from his embrace, and his arms suddenly felt empty. "Don't play that game. Everyone knows you're one of the Guard's best medics. You have the reputation of giving one hundred and ten percent all the time. You're gifted, and don't let anyone tell you otherwise."

"Thanks," she said, shuffling her shoe along the floor. "I can't tell you how much I appreciate everything you've done."

"I was happy to."

"I think I'll go home. Take a hot bath, watch a good movie."

"Sounds like a good plan."

Rising on her tiptoes, she placed a kiss on his cheek before waving good-bye.

He remained rooted in place—his entire being transfixed on that kiss. What was happening to him and his self-proclaimed bachelorhood?

Rissi sat silently beside Mason as they drove upstate to Ed Scott's fishing cabin.

Ed had told his wife before he'd set anything in motion that one day they'd come for him, and to avoid embarrassing her by being hauled out of their home of twenty years in front of their neighbors, he'd head upstate. Somewhere private. Somewhere peaceful.

As soon as they had Ed in custody, they'd have to find and talk to Kasey, whose whereabouts Lena Scott hesitated to share. Perhaps Ed would be more helpful in that endeavor. In the meantime, Caleb was tracking down Kasey's location, but given the circumstances, Noah had asked that Emmy be the one to question her. It was a good call. She was the right team member for the job.

Mason reached out and took hold of Rissi's hand.

She shifted, looking out the window. Mason rubbed her hand with the pad of his thumb.

He took a deep inhale and released it slowly.

I know you are in control, Father. You have a plan. You can take something as ugly as what this evil man did to Kasey and bring restoration. That's what I pray for, Lord—renewal and restoration for Kasey and this family.

Ed's cobalt F-150 sat parked in front of the log cabin, the lake spread out in front of it.

Ed sat on a pier, a fishing rod in one hand, a beer in the other.

"Took you long enough," he said as they crunched their way through the fallen autumn leaves.

Mason exhaled. How could he arrest the man when, had Mason been in the same place, he would have been tempted to do the same thing? If anyone ever laid another hand on Rissi . . .

Adrenaline burned through his veins. He wouldn't do it. Judgment was the Lord's. But he'd be tempted. This wasn't going to be an easy arrest.

Rissi's hand landed on his back. She didn't have to say anything. She knew.

He nodded and headed down the pier.

The weathered boards creaked beneath his footfalls.

"I'm afraid we're going to have to arrest you for the murder of Chase Calhoun," he said.

Ed held up his beer bottle. "Mind if I finish this first?"

Mason looked back at Rissi, and she nodded her agreement.

"Sure," Mason said.

"Want one?" He indicated the blue cooler by his Adirondack chair.

"On duty, but thanks."

"You can at least take a seat."

"All right." Mason waited until Rissi joined them and was settled in an Adirondack chair before taking a seat.

"It's a beautiful sunset," Ed said, as he cast his line over the rippling water.

Mason looked at the orange and purple streaks across the sky. "It sure is."

"Outside of Lena and Kasey, I think that's what I'll miss most. Not getting to see the sunset from my cell."

"Why didn't you go to the police when it happened?" Mason asked. No report had ever been filed. He'd checked.

"Kasey was mortified. She refused." He washed down a swig of beer. "That monster turned my beautiful girl into a shell of herself. If killing him is what it took to make her feel safe again, I have no regrets."

SIXTY-FOUR

Mason escorted Ed through the station door. He'd seen no need for cuffs. The man had been the most compliant prisoner ever—had waived his right to a lawyer and written out his confession in the back seat of Mason's car.

He'd done what he believed was right and understood the consequences.

Mason could sympathize with Ed's thinking, but he still had to believe, or at least pray, if something like that—God forbid—ever happened to someone in his life, he would remember he answered to a much higher authority.

The admonition from Romans 12:19, saying that the Lord alone has the right to take revenge, resonated in his mind.

"Daddy!" A young woman Mason recognized from the graduation picture on the Scotts' mantel ran to Ed.

He engulfed her tiny five-two, maybe one-hundred-and-ten-pound frame in a bear hug.

"I'm so scared for you, Daddy." Tears streamed down her freckled face. "I should have gone to the police."

He brushed her strawberry blond hair from her eyes. "He's gone now. You don't ever have to be afraid again."

Sobbing, much as her mother had earlier that day, Kasey Scott fell into her father's embrace and nestled there.

He rested his head atop her head. "It's okay, darling. You're safe now. That evil man is gone."

357

"We got a lead on Gwyneth," Caleb said, rushing over to Noah's desk.

"Let's go get her."

Noah followed Caleb out to his car. "Where is she at?" he asked.

"Logan tracked her credit card under the name Gwyneth Hill to a new apartment rental out in Oak Island."

"Near where Skip Malone died," Noah said.

As they reached Caleb's car, Austin pulled into the parking lot and strode toward them.

"What's going on?" she said.

Noah grinned. "I think you're going to want to come along for this."

"You and I can handle this, can't we?" Caleb asked.

Austin linked her arms across her chest. "I don't think that's your decision. Is it?" She shifted her gaze to Noah.

"You're welcome to come," Noah said.

Caleb's jaw tensed, but he opened the car door for her and walked over to the driver's side door. The lady irked him to no end, but his mom had raised a gentleman.

Close to an hour later, they approached the property. Noah took the front staircase, while Caleb covered the rear patio door.

Austin, unarmed, waited in the car per Noah's instructions.

Seconds later, Gwyneth flew out the patio door, followed by Rick Carson. They both froze at the sight of Caleb's gun aimed at Gwyneth's center mass. "Got 'em," he said into his radio.

Noah joined him around back.

He took tremendous pleasure in handcuffing Gwyneth and escorting her around the house to the car while Noah did the same with Carson.

Austin stepped out of the car door, her attention pinned on Gwyneth alone.

"You again?" Gwyneth hissed.

"Told you I wouldn't go away until you were behind bars."

Austin stepped to the side while Caleb put Gwyneth in the back seat, shutting the door with a satisfied smile. Noah did the same with Carson, putting him in on the other side. Gwyneth and Rick were knitted together in crime, now they'd be knitted together in jail. Emmy and Logan were uncovering even more crimes the two had committed, the cons they played on innocent men and women. The charges against them were piling up.

Caleb shifted his attention to Austin. "Feels good, doesn't it," he said, his arm draped along the roof of the car as Gwyneth and Rick argued inside.

"Justice always does." Shielding her eyes from the sun with a cupped hand, she looked up the handful of inches separating them. "That was good work you did today."

He shifted, linking his arms across his chest, trying not to smile. "Is that a compliment?"

She looked back at Gwyneth in cuffs, then to him. "It's a thank-you."

Epilogue

TWO WEEKS LATER

Rissi entered her house, dropping her purse and keys on the front table. She'd barely taken a step toward the kitchen when a knock sounded on her door.

She opened it to find Mason in a tux, holding a vibrant orange lily corsage in one hand and a dress bag in the other.

"You look incredible," she said, never having seen him dressed up.

"Thanks."

"Off to a party?"

"In a manner of speaking."

He smiled, a mischievous twinge to it. What was he up to?

"This," he said, extending the dress bag to her, "is for you."

She narrowed her eyes. "I don't understand."

"You will."

She unzipped the bag. A gorgeous cobalt blue gown rested inside. Satin, spaghetti straps, a gentle V neck, and straight lines the rest of the way down. A solitary diamond necklace hung over the handle of the hanger, resting in the open neckline. "What's this all about?"

He liked surprises, she knew that, but this had to be one of the most intriguing.

"Do you trust me?" he asked.

"Of course." He was the first person she had truly trusted—and still did.

"Would you try it on?" he asked.

"Okay." But not knowing what was going on was eating her up.

She climbed the stairs and quickly slid on the gorgeous gown. She pulled her hair out of the side braid, running a brush through the gentle waves. She added blush to her cheeks, mascara to her lashes, and finished with a soft rose lipstick. Not knowing where they were headed made it difficult to know what style of makeup to wear, but this would have to work. She slipped on a nice pair of open-toe heels and headed downstairs.

Mason waited at the bottom. His eyes landed on her and widened.

Her heart rate picked up. Was something wrong?

"You look amazing," he said, not taking his stare off of her.

She held it, making her way down the steps.

"This is for you." He offered her the corsage. "May I?" he asked, holding up a stick pin.

She nodded and held still as he fastened it to the upper right side of her gown.

"Can you help me with this?" she asked, holding up the necklace.

"Of course."

She turned around and lifted her hair. He clasped it and then pressed a warm kiss to the nape of her neck.

Heat and love rushed through her. "Will you tell me where we're going now?"

"No," he said with an impish grin. "But I'll show you."

She frowned. What was he up to?

"Cover your eyes."

"What?" She laughed.

He didn't.

"You're not joking."

"Nope."

She inhaled and covered her eyes as he asked.

"No peeking," he whispered in her ear, his breath tickling her skin. He placed his hands gently on her upper arms, directing her toward the back of her house.

She heard the whir of the sliding door being opened.

"Watch your step," he said.

She lifted her feet, stepping over the door's metal track.

"Ready?" he asked.

She nodded, curiosity bubbling over.

"Okay." He slid his hands over hers and pulled them away from her eyes.

Strings of white lights hung across the patio, attached to the trellises on either side. Luminarias outlined the twenty-by-twenty brick square.

"Find My Way Back" by Eric Arjes played in the cool night air.

She gazed around in wonder. "You did this for me?"

"I'd do anything for you. You must know that." His expression held such gentle admiration that her eyes misted with tears. "But I can't take all the credit. Emmy and Logan helped."

She smiled at Emmy's touches. Vases of flowers positioned on the long table lined with beautiful silver trays filled with finger food and a large punch bowl. "Is this . . . ?" *He didn't.* . . . She held her hand to her mouth.

"Your prom," he said.

More tears welled in her eyes. Only Mason would do this—restore one of her dreams that she thought had been lost.

He held out his hand. "May I have this dance?"

"Yes." She couldn't help but smile amidst the tears.

"Do you like it?" he asked, his voice low and incredibly sexy.

362

"I love it," she managed to say despite the wealth of emotions churning through her.

He brushed his lips over hers. "And I love you." Cupping the back of her neck, he pressed his lips to hers, deepening the kiss. After a moment, he pressed his forehead to hers, gazing into her eyes. "You literally steal the breath from me. All you have to do is walk into a room."

"All you have to do is say you love me, and I melt," she whispered back.

"Then prepare to melt a lot because a day won't go by without me telling you how much I love you."

She leaned into his warmth. "And I love you."

"Forever?" he asked.

"Forever," she promised.

Acknowledgments

My Lord and Savior: Thank you for carrying me every day. Thank you for knowing the number of hairs on my head, for collecting my tears in your bottle, and for blessing me with a love for telling stories.

Mike: For your constant support, always showing me how much you love me, and for making me belly laugh nearly every day. I couldn't have asked for a better life or a deeper love.

Kay: My sweet and sassy girl. Thanks so much for all you do, for your compassionate heart, your hilarious quips, and for raising the bear.

Ty: My brilliant, caring, sarcastic girl. Thanks for being my go-to medical research expert, being such a good mom to the boys who fill my heart with joy, and for always inadvertently wearing the same outfit. You've got great taste!

Joy: Thank you for daily check-ins, encouraging memes, and coffee quotes. You know me so well. Thank you for your surprise gifts that are always exactly what I need at that moment.

Crissy: Thank you for being my go-to reader, for our all-over-the-place FaceTime chats, and for your constant prayers.

Amy: Thank you for your generosity, our morning coffee chats, and your constant encouragement.

Dave: Thank you for always believing in me as an author, for caring about me and my family, for reining me in when I go off on one crazy story tangent after another, and for letting me stretch my story wings. It's a privilege to work with you.

Kate: I feel so incredibly blessed to be working with you. Thank you for all your hard work, for your great eye, your support, your kindness, and for doing such an amazing job.

Karen: Thank you for all the hours you spend working to make my stories the best they can be, for your encouragement throughout this crazy writing journey, and most importantly for your friendship.

Janet: As you know, succinctness is not my forte, but I'm going to give it a try so I don't ramble on for an entire page. I am so incredibly blessed by your friendship. Thank you for your prayers, for lifting me up when I'm sinking, and for knowing just the right thing to share when I need it most. You have a particular gift for that. You're my anchor in the writing world with its ups and downs, calm seas and swift storms. Thank you for taking this journey with me. And, more often than not, guiding the way.

Katie: For your prayers, your check-in calls when I need them most, for our überfun getaways, and, of course, for loving llama pj's as much as I do.

Dani's Darlings: To the most wonderful, caring, creative, and hilarious group of ladies I get the privilege of spending time with every spring.

Praised by *New York Times* bestselling author Dee Henderson as "a name to look for in romantic suspense," **Dani Pettrey** has sold more than half a million copies of her novels to readers eagerly awaiting the next release. Dani combines the page-turning adrenaline of a thriller with the chemistry and happy-ever-after of a romance. Her novels stand out for their "wicked pace, snappy dialogue, and likable characters" (*Publishers Weekly*), "gripping storyline[s]," (*RT Book Reviews*), and "sizzling undercurrent[s] of romance" (*USA Today*). Her ALASKAN COURAGE series and CHESAPEAKE VALOR series have received praise from readers and critics alike and spent multiple months topping the CBA bestseller lists.

From her early years eagerly reading Nancy Drew mysteries, Dani has always enjoyed mystery and suspense. She considers herself blessed to be able to write the kind of stories she loves—full of plot twists and peril, love, and longing for hope and redemption. Her greatest joy as an author is sharing the stories God lays on her heart. She researches murder and mayhem from her home in Maryland, where she lives with her husband. Their two daughters, a son-in-law, and two adorable grandsons also reside in Maryland. For more information about her novels, visit www.danipettrey.com.

Sign Up for Dani's Newsletter!

Keep up to date with Dani's news on book releases and events by signing up for her email list at danipettrey.com.

More from Dani Pettrey

In college, Griffin and his three best friends, Luke, Declan, and Parker, planned to live out their futures side by side in law enforcement. But then Luke vanished before graduation and their world—and friendships—crumbled. Now years later, their lives become entwined once again as they reunite to solve mysteries, encounter dangerous criminals, and find love.

CHESAPEAKE VALOR: *Cold Shot, Still Life, Blind Spot, Dead Drift*

BETHANYHOUSE

Stay up to date on your favorite books and authors with our free e-newsletters. Sign up today at bethanyhouse.com.

f facebook.com/bethanyhousepublishers   @bethanyhousefiction

OB Free exclusive resources for your book group at bethanyhouseopenbook.com

You May Also Like . . .

When multiple corpses are found, their remains point to a serial killer with a familiar MO but who's been in prison for over twenty years—Special Agent Kaely Quinn's father. In order to prevent more deaths, she must come face-to-face with the man she's hated for years. In a race against time, will this case cost Kaely her identity and perhaps even her life?

Dead End by Nancy Mehl
KAELY QUINN PROFILER #3
nancymehl.com

On a mission to recover the Book of the Wars, Leif and his team are diverted by a foretelling of formidable warriors who will decimate the enemies of the ArC, while Iskra uses her connections to hunt down the book. As they try to stop the warriors, failure becomes familiar, and the threats creep closer to home, with implications that could tear them apart.

Kings Falling by Ronie Kendig
THE BOOK OF THE WARS #2
roniekendig.com

When elite members of the military are murdered on the streets of Washington, D.C., FBI Special Agent Bailey Ryan and NCIS Special Agent Marco Agostini must work together to bring the perpetrator to justice. As the stakes rise in a twisted conspiracy and allies turn to enemies, the biggest secret yet to be uncovered could be the end of them all.

End Game by Rachel Dylan
CAPITAL INTRIGUE #1
racheldylan.com

◈ BETHANYHOUSE